FOREVER,
NEVER,
AFTER

NICOLA JANE

Forever, Never, After

Cover Designer: Wingfield Designs

Editor: Rebecca Vazquez, Dark Syde Books

Formatting: Nicola Miller

Spelling Note

Please note, this author resides in the United Kingdom and is using British English. Therefore, some words may be viewed as incorrect or spelled incorrectly, however, they are not.

TO MY READERS

This story has been in my head for many years. It was only now that I found the strength to write it.
It's the only story I've written that has made me cry many times over, and trust me when I say it takes a lot for me to part with my tears.
I hope you love the story as much as I do.

PLAYLIST:

Eyes Closed – Ed Sheeran
Wish You The Best – Lewis Capaldi
Happier Than Ever – Billie Eilish
Leave Me Slowly – Lewis Capaldi
Picking Up the Pieces – Paloma Faith
Helium - Sia
River – Eminem ft. Ed Sheeran
Before He Cheats – Carrie Underwood
Send My Love (To Your New Lover) - Adele
Rumour Has It - Adele
Fuck You – Lily Allen
Don't Cha – The Pussy Cat Dolls ft. Busta Rhymes
Used To Be Young – Miley Cyrus
Are We a Thing – Leidi
I Like Me Better – Lauv
Never Ever Love a Liar – Bea and her Business
Always – Bon Jovi
Love the Hell Out of You – Lewis Capaldi

DAN

I follow the sound of laughter. It's pretty much what I'm met with every day when I arrive home, and I always have the same thought. I'm one lucky son of a bitch.

Isabella stomps her chubby little legs across the grass towards me, her arms already reaching out. She's giggling so much, she can't quite get the words out, but as I sweep her into my arms, she manages a warning. "Mummy," she pants, "run away."

I clock my wife, Megan, holding up a water balloon and I dive back inside, slamming the door closed before she can get us. She presses her nose to the glass, causing another round of giggles from Izzy. "Let me in," she says in a growling voice.

"No," Izzy screeches, shaking her head and causing her brown curls to bounce.

"Then send out Daddy," she demands.

Izzy looks at me, her brown eyes wide. "Don't go out there," she whispers.

"I'm not afraid," I say, placing her on the ground and puffing out my chest. "I'll save us both," I add, using my best superhero voice.

I open the door, holding my hands up in submission, which delights Izzy some more. "I'm coming out. Put the

I stand abruptly, stuffing my used tissue in Lauren's hand. "I am," I say a little too eagerly.

He gives a small smile, heads over to the desk at the front of the room, and opens a laptop. "Name?"

I straighten my shirt, making sure I show a little cleavage, and head over to where he is. "Ashley Daulton."

I inhale the scent of his woody aftershave and my stomach does a flip. He's hot. Seriously hot. The way his shirt sleeve is folded halfway up his arm, showing just enough tanned skin and a few tattoos, piques my interest. I take my time to study his strong jaw and neatly trimmed beard. When he looks up at me, I gasp. His bright blue eyes are electric, made brighter by his tan. "Well, Ashely Daulton, you're three weeks late. My lectures began at the start of October."

"I was having a crisis," I tell him, knotting my fingers together.

"A crisis involving a family death?" he asks, standing straighter until I'm the one looking up at him. His hands rest on his hips, and I know under that white shirt are more tattoos and a definite six-pack, maybe even an eight.

"Not exactly."

He arches a brow. "Then maybe a crisis involving a family member who got into a serious, life changing accident?"

I shake my head. "No, not that either."

"She got dumped," says Luis, and I glance back over my shoulder to glare at him.

"Shouldn't you be gone?" I ask.

"Can you be dumped by a married man?" asks Molly, and the other two snigger.

"I'll call you later," I say, my tone clipped. I wait until they file from the room. "Sorry about them."

"So, you had a relationship breakup?"

I nod. "I was pretty cut-up." His eyes soften slightly.

"Were you together long?"

"Almost a year," I whisper, feeling the threat of tears again.

"Sorry to hear that," he tells me, gently patting my shoulder. I inhale sharply as his touch sends heat right through my body. "Breakups can be hard, but don't let it define you. You've got three weeks' worth of star-crossed lovers to catch up on."

"Maybe you can go over what I've missed sometime. I'm free most evenings." I bite my lower lip for effect.

He stares at me for a few seconds. "Ms. Daulton, it's not my job to offer free tuition to students who cannot make my lectures on time. If you want to pass my course, you'll need to catch up on your own time and work extra hard."

"Will you be impressed if I do?"

He narrows his eyes. "It takes a lot to impress me." His mobile rings out and he pulls it from his pocket. He glances at me before he says, "Excuse me, I have to take this. It's my *wife*." And I don't miss the way he emphasises the word 'wife'.

MEG

"Sorry, I know you're probably busy," I begin.

"Don't be ridiculous. I've always got time for you," Dan replies, and I find myself smiling. Even after eleven years, he still makes me giddy.

"I'm meeting the girls for lunch and I forgot to ask if you want to go to Zoe's party on Saturday?"

"What are we celebrating?"

"Does Zoe need a reason?" I ask, getting Izzy in a head-lock to wipe her butter-splattered face. *How can toast make so much mess?* "But it's to celebrate her new job."

"Do people have parties for that sort of thing?"

I smile again. He hates socialising. "They do when they

land a contract for a very well-known actress. I'll hardly see her. But I can go alone. I know how you hate these things."

"Baby, I'm going wherever you are."

I hand Izzy her juice, and she immediately drops it, splashing purple liquid everywhere. "Damn it," I mutter, lifting her and moving her to the couch. "Remind me why we chose a cream carpet?"

"Because you said it looks like we have our shit together if we have expensive décor."

I grin. "Well, that was before our little whirlwind came along. Now, I think we need black throughout the house. So, shall I tell her yes?"

"Yes. On one condition . . . I don't have to wear a suit."

———

My friend, Sofia, rocks her one-month-old gently, and I hand Izzy my mobile phone, so she can watch her favourite cartoon. Zoe eyes us both with annoyance. "Don't you have people who can watch these while we have lunch?"

I grin at Sofia, who rolls her eyes. "We're not all loaded like you," she retorts.

"I'm not having children without a nanny present at all times," says Zoe firmly.

"This is my nanny," I tell her, pointing to the mobile phone clutched in Izzy's sticky fingers. I know other mums judge me whenever I hand that mobile over to my three-year-old just to keep her quiet, but she'd cause a riot in here if I didn't. Honestly, I'd be insane without it.

We order lunch, and Zoe wastes no time telling us all about Saturday night. "Do not be late. Nine o' clock sharp, and everyone must wear something pink."

"Pink?" I repeat, grimacing.

"Have you even read the invite?" she snaps.

"I haven't," admits Sofia. "In case you didn't realise, my life's pretty hectic right now. I'm not sure I'll even make it."

"You have to make it," Zoe gasps, her eyes wide in panic. "You two are my best friends. You absolutely have to be there."

"Can I bring Harry?"

Zoe screws her nose up. "It's not really a baby kind of event," she says. "I'll pay for a sitter."

"He's eight weeks old. I don't want to leave him with a sitter."

"Bring him to mine," I suggest. "You know my babysitter, and she won't mind an extra one. She loves babies."

Sofia reluctantly nods. "Fine. But I'll only stay for an hour and I'm not wearing pink."

———

I'm dishing up dinner just as Dan arrives home. He fusses over Izzy before heading my way. Wrapping his arms around my waist, he kisses my neck in the way I love. I lean into him and smile when I feel him poking in my lower back. "I missed you," he murmurs against my hair.

"So it seems."

"I thought I could bath Satan tonight and get her to bed early."

"Wow, you really did miss me." I turn in his arms. "And as lovely as it sounds, I promised her three stories after her bath."

He groans, pulling out my shirt to peek down at my braless breasts. "Can you read them really quick?"

"I can try."

He grins, pulling me closer for a kiss. "I love you."

"I love you too." I hand him the salad bowl, and he carries it over to the table. "You'll be pleased to know you're not required to wear a suit for the party."

"Good news."

"However," I pause while he groans, "there is a pink theme."

"Which we don't have to adhere to, right?"

"It'll make my life easier if you do," I say hopefully.

"What's it worth?" he asks, quirking a brow suggestively.

It's my turn to groan. "Fine. But you warn me when you're about to . . . yah know. I'm not having that stuff in my mouth."

He grins wide. "If you swallow, I'll even wear matching pink underwear. Fuck, I'll even put pink bows in my hair."

I laugh. "Daddy, you said a bad word," Izzy tells him, appearing in the kitchen doorway.

"You're right, princess, I'm so sorry," he apologises, kissing her swiftly on the head. "I was trying to make a deal with Mummy, but she's playing hardball." He looks my way and laughs. "How does she hear every bad word from my mouth, but when I ask her to tidy her toys, she's suddenly deaf?"

I carry our plates to the table as Dan fastens Izzy into her highchair. She's getting too big for it now, but she's so clumsy, I hate the idea of her sitting at the table and spreading the mess. "A pink shirt will be fine. No need to upstage Zoe by adding extras."

He laughs. "Extras are what I love best."

Two

DAN

I take the papers as the students pass my desk. "Thanks," I occasionally mutter. My students hate that I ask them to print their essays rather than email them over, but I prefer to read them like this.

I notice Ashley lingering at the back. It's not the first time she's waited behind to speak to me this week, and although she seems like a lovely girl, my head is warning me to be careful. She puts me on edge.

Today, she licks her glossed lower lip as she hands me her paper. "I think you'll be surprised," she tells me confidently, and I resist the urge to scoff. So far, she's not participated in any of the lessons when I've fired questions. She sits front row but shrinks down in her seat whenever I ask anything. I doubt she's even bothered to catch up on the last few weeks. I glance over the paper. "It's handwritten," I state. Most students print it from their computer.

"I like the old-fashioned way," she says, shrugging.

"Me too," I mutter, reading the first paragraph. I scowl and hand it back to her. "If you're going to copy your words from the internet, at least change them slightly."

"I . . . well, I . . ."

"You copied someone else's work, Ms. Daulton."

"How the hell can you tell?" she asks, sounding exasperated.

"I know every trick in the book. I was once a student too. Look, I don't ask for much. Turn up to my lectures, make notes, write your own essays. If you want to pass this year, try harder."

"I do," she says firmly. And I really believe she does, but so far, she's failing. "I do. I'll try harder."

I give a tight smile and take my seat, readying myself for the mammoth task of making a start on marking. She lingers before clearing her throat to get my attention again. "Can I work in here?"

I glance at the empty room. "Wouldn't you prefer the library?"

"I like complete silence," she insists, and I smirk.

"And that isn't happening in the library?"

"Please, I'll be as quiet as a mouse. I swear, I won't disturb you." I give a nod, and she grins. "Thanks." She takes a seat in her usual spot at the front and opens her laptop. I pick up the first essay and do my best to ignore her.

———

I glance up at the sound of Ashely gathering her things and check my watch. It's almost seven and my stomach growls in hunger, like it's just realising I've missed dinner. "Crap," I mutter, pulling my mobile from my bag. There are three missed calls from Meg and a text.

Meg: I bet you've lost yourself in marking and forgot about us. Good job. I love you but dinner is ruined, so grab yourself something on your way home. I have a migraine coming so I'm going to grab an early night. Xxx.

The message was sent half an hour ago, so I decide not to reply in case I wake her. "I'm starving," Ashley announces. "Fancy grabbing something to eat?"

I shake my head. "I should keep going with these," I reply, pointing to the papers.

"Doesn't your wife mind you staying late?"

"How are you getting on?" I ask, changing the subject.

"Good. I think you'll like this one much better." She looks pleased with herself.

"Enjoy dinner."

"I'm literally grabbing something on campus. Come on, you must be hungry? And I could really do with picking your brain on some of Shakespeare's language."

My stomach grumbles again, and we both laugh. Maybe she's not so bad, and she wouldn't be the first student unable to understand Shakespeare. "I guess I could eat a burger." I throw my pen down. If Meg's in bed, that means Izzy is too. I could grab a takeout burger and finish off a few more papers.

She smiles triumphantly and waits for me to grab my jacket before leading the way.

The campus is lively, and we weave our way through the students and head for a nearby burger place. Inside, it's empty. "That can't be a good sign," I mutter, and Ashley laughs.

"I've eaten here loads. It's fine."

I approach the counter. "Can I get a cheeseburger and fries to go?" I ask.

"The patty machine is broken. We're waiting on the engineer," the server replies in a bored tone.

"Why are you open?" I ask.

He shrugs. "Drinks."

"Actually, I know somewhere much better," says Ashley, grabbing my arm. "It's a quick walk and the food is to die for." She's already leading me from the place before I have a chance to argue.

She takes us off campus and around the corner to a small restaurant. I hesitate, glancing around. "This looks . . . intimate," I say, frowning.

Ashley rolls her eyes. "Don't be weird," she says, laughing. "We're both hungry, we both love English lit, we can grab food, and I can pick your brain for this essay." She pushes the door and steps inside, pausing to look back at me. I sigh. I don't want to make it weird by insinuating she's wanting some kind of romantic meal. She's at least ten years younger than me and extremely attractive. I'm the last guy she'd be looking at in that way. I nod, following her inside.

A maître d' greets us. "Table for two?" he asks, grabbing a couple menus.

"Actually—" I begin, suddenly having doubts, but Ashley cuts me off.

"Yes, please."

He takes us to a nearby table where a candle flickers in the middle. I immediately blow it out and sit down, shrugging from my jacket. "Wine?" he asks.

"Just water for me," I reply.

"A bottle of red," Ashley tells him, also taking a seat.

Once he's gone, I shift uncomfortably. "I was quite happy to skip dinner."

"If it's money, I can pay," she says innocently.

I smirk. "It's not about the money, Ashley. This is a little weird, don't you think?"

"Only if you make it weird." She scans the menu.

"If someone should see us together, we'd have a job explaining it."

She sighs, placing the menu down again. "If you're not comfortable, leave. I just want dinner, and it's even weirder coming to this sort of place and eating alone. But, hey, if you want to abandon me while I'm hungry, go ahead. I don't want to make you uncomfortable."

I relax slightly and smile. "You're right, I'm overthinking."

She returns the smile and picks up the menu again. "Have you made many friends here?"

I frown. "Why do you ask?"

"You're new, and all the other lecturers seem a lot older," she says, shrugging. "Apart from the History department—they're mainly young."

"How about you?" I ask, steering the conversation away from me. "This is your second year, how are you finding uni life?"

The waiter places a jug of water in front of me and opens a bottle of red. He pours a small amount in the glass and looks at me to try it. I do it just so he'll leave, nodding to approve it. He fills two glasses before walking away. "You take mine," I tell her, sliding it towards her.

She slides it back. "One won't hurt. And yes, I love this life. I have a great group of friends. It took me a while to settle, especially because I came to uni later than everyone else."

"What made you join later?"

"I wanted to take a gap year and see the world. I didn't get very far." She smiles shyly. "Have you always worked in universities?"

I shake my head. "Nope. Secondary school English teacher." She winces, and I laugh. "Exactly. It was tough."

"What made you change?"

I pick up the wine and take a sip. "The money, the freedom. It's a little less full-on than secondary school, but I find this is more my thing. I get to talk about what I love rather than teaching a curriculum set up by people who know nothing about teaching. Plus, most of my students here want to learn, and that wasn't the case in school."

"I want to go into teaching," she confesses.

"It's not all bad," I say, grinning, "but you won't get away with copying your lesson plans off the internet."

She blushes. "Things got messed up for a while, but I'm

all good now. I've realised that men are not worth giving up your dreams for. No offence."

"None taken. Is that why you didn't travel?"

She nods. "I always seem to pick the wrong guys. The last one wouldn't commit, and the one before that, well, he wasn't a nice guy."

"You know what they say—you have to kiss a few frogs to find your prince."

The waiter clears his throat. "Ready to order?"

Ashley scrambles to look at the menu again. "Sorry, we haven't even looked."

"Do you like seafood?" I ask her, and she nods. "Do you trust me to order?" She smiles, nodding again. "Great. We'll take two mussels in white wine sauce."

"Would you like the wine to accompany that?" he asks, and without thinking, I agree. It's something I'd do when out with Meg, and for a second, I panic, but it's too late now and cancelling will make me look a fool. Besides, it's just food with a struggling student. *Christ, a student.* I don't quite know what the rules are now I'm at a university, but I'm pretty sure I'm breaking them, even if it is innocent.

"See, that's exactly how I want a man to treat me," she continues, only deepening my panic. "I want him to order my food, to take care of me and make me feel special. I want him to know what I need before I do." She must feel my awkwardness because she shakes her head. "God, I'm sorry. I'm talking shit."

I laugh at her dismissive attitude. "It's fine. My wife will tell you it takes a good few years and a whole lot of arguments to get a well-trained man."

ASHLEY

I take a sip of wine and smile seductively. His wife is right, which is why I always go for the ones who're ready trained.

"One day, I'll find him. In the meantime, I'll probably continue to kiss frogs."

"I'm sure there are enough guys in this place to entertain you."

I scoff. "Yeah, if I want to pick up an STD."

The food arrives along with a bottle of white wine. The waiter pours two more glasses, and I watch the way Dan's throat bobs as he finishes off his glass of red. *God, I want to kiss his throat.* "How long have you been married?" I ask, tearing some bread and dipping it into the sauce. I close my eyes in delight as my taste buds go into overdrive. I groan, and when I open my eyes again, Dan is staring in wonder. I bite my lower lip and give him my best shy smile. "Sorry, it just tastes so good."

He clears his throat, tearing his eyes away. "Ten years," he says proudly.

Christ, ten years is a long one. And his eyes light up when he thinks about her. But I force a smile like I'm actually interested and ask, "How did you meet?"

"We worked in the same school. She was a teaching assistant, and I was in my second year of teaching. We hit it off straight away."

Great. They worked together, so they were probably friends first. It's always harder to come between a friendship. "Does she still work in the same place?"

"She left to have our daughter, Isabella. We decided it would be best if she stayed home until Izzy started full-time school."

I want to groan. Even worse, they have a kid. He doesn't look the type. "Wow. She gave up her job to raise your child? That's amazing," I say, all the while wanting to vomit. Another reason I won't be having children. "Does she enjoy it?"

He thinks over my question. "There are days when she misses work, but most the time, she's happy. Izzy is really bright, and I think that's down to Meg being home with her. We can start her in school at four rather than putting her into nursery at three because she's not got to rush to work. And it's not forever. One day, she'll go back."

"To be a teaching assistant?"

"Maybe. We haven't talked about it."

"I can't imagine having children and settling down."

He smiles. "It just sort of happens. One day, you're winging uni and partying every night, then you're married with a child."

I shudder, and he laughs. "Don't you miss partying?"

"I'm thirty-five. My partying days are over."

"Don't be ridiculous," I say, topping up his red wine glass. "And you definitely don't look thirty-five."

We finish dinner, and Dan calls over the waiter to ask for the bill. I pull out my purse, but he insists on paying. Outside, we stand awkwardly. "I should get back to the papers," he says.

"I'm going to head into town to meet some friends."

He looks concerned for a minute, but he hides it well. "Argh, more partying," he says, smiling. "Well, enjoy your night."

"Thanks for dinner," I say, and before I can talk myself out of it, I reach up and kiss him on the cheek, letting my lips linger a second longer than is comfortable. He doesn't immediately pull back, and I smile to myself as I slide my hand over his shoulder and then step back.

He takes a bigger step back. "What the fuck was that?" he snaps, looking around nervously.

"Oh my god, I'm so sorry," I say quickly. "I just meant it as a thank you."

"Yeah, well, don't do that again." He turns on his heel and stalks away. I smile to myself. I can't wait to kiss him properly.

"Oh please, don't tell me you're going after your teacher," groans Lauren when I tell her where I've been.

"You saw him, right?" I ask. "He's fucking hot."

"You have to give her that," says Molly. "Mr. Headford is gorgeous."

"Jesus, Molly, we're in university. No one calls the lecturers by their surname," Jared says impatiently. "Isn't he old enough to be your dad?"

"He's thirty-five," I snap.

"Still, twelve years between you," he points out.

"And very married," adds Lauren.

"How do you know?" I ask.

"I saw his wedding band, and he had a photograph on his desk."

"Did he?" I ask. "I hadn't noticed."

She arches a brow. "The ring or the picture?"

I smirk. "He's a gentleman. He even ordered my food."

"Controlling," singsongs Molly.

"I bet he knows how to treat a woman in bed," I say dreamily.

"I'm sure his wife taught him everything he knows," Lauren mutters.

"The way I see it, you can't tempt a man who's happy," Lindsay adds in, and we high-five. "If he's so smitten with his wife, he won't look Ashley's way."

"Does he have kids?" asks Molly.

I shrug. If I tell them the truth, they'll be against this completely, and I'm not ready to give up on him.

MEG

Saturday has come all too quick, and although I usually love lazy weekends, we're celebrating Zoe tonight, and that's tiring all in itself.

I check my face in the mirror one last time. I don't often wear makeup these days, and I certainly have no idea how to do all the stuff younger women do, like contouring. But at least I look a little less tired now my eye bags are hidden under a tonne of concealer.

Izzy holds up a red lipstick. "My turn?" she asks.

I laugh, taking it from her. "Ladies of the night wear red," I say then laugh again, "or at least, that's what my mother used to say." I place it in my makeup drawer and reach for a clear lip gloss instead. *Nice and simple.*

Dan comes in, stopping when he sees I'm still not dressed. He checks his watch. "Half an hour until the babysitter arrives."

"I know, I know, I'm going as fast as I can with a toddler under my feet." I glare, hoping he takes the hint.

He sweeps Izzy up in his arms, and she giggles as he pretends to bite her tummy. "Which is why I'm here to remove said toddler and put her to bed."

"Noooo," Izzy wails.

He sticks her bottle in her mouth—the bottle I've been trying to wean her off for the last six months. My mother keeps pointing out she's too old to have her milk from a bottle, yet it's the only way she seems to fall to sleep at night. I keep reasoning that she'll eventually give it up. She isn't going to be drinking from it when she's eighteen . . . at least not a baby's bottle.

Once they're gone, I open the banking app on my phone. I've got to transfer money into savings for a holiday I plan to surprise Dan with. He's been working so hard lately, he deserves it. We all do.

I frown at the top expenditure. Eighty pounds for dinner at a restaurant. I close the app and search it up. It's a place near the university where Dan works. I frown. It's weird that he never mentioned it, and it's a lot for one person. I give my head a shake. What exactly am I thinking, that he had dinner with another woman? I laugh to myself. Dan is the most trustworthy guy I know, and I did tell him to grab some food on his way home.

I take my dress from the cupboard and hold it against myself, checking it in the mirror. Dan comes in. "Christ, you're still not dressed?"

"Anything you need to tell me?" I ask, staring at him through the mirror.

He pauses, and a strange look passes over his face, one I can't place. "I don't think so."

I narrow my eyes playfully. "Nothing about a cosy dinner for two last night?" I'm teasing, of course, but he doesn't look amused, so I turn to face him and smile. "Relax, I'm kidding. But when I said grab food, I didn't mean a fancy meal in a restaurant."

"You're checking up on me?" he asks, arching a brow.

His tone is clipped, and I frown, turning back to the mirror. "Don't be ridiculous. I was checking the bank balance and transferring money into savings."

Dan comes up behind me and slips his arms around my waist. "I had dinner with a colleague. I would've told you last night, only you were snoring like a rhino when I got back," he teases.

I relax, relieved this didn't turn into a fight, and I playfully hit his arm. "Liar. Male or female colleague?" I ask, wiggling my brows at him. I don't know what made me ask. I've never been the jealous type, but something in his demeanour is alarming me.

He frowns again. "Does it matter? I didn't know you had trust issues, Meg."

He's deflecting. "You're acting weird. I only brought it up

as a joke, but now, I'm starting to worry, Dan. Should I be worried?"

He takes a breath before burying his nose into my hair. "Don't be crazy. It was a guy called Jay. He's the only one on the team who's under fifty and he was marking late too. We grabbed something on the way home." His fingers tangle with my silk robe tie and he tugs it open. He stares at my reflection in the mirror. "Umm, lace? Maybe I'm the one who should be worried. Is this new?"

I push my worries aside and force a smile. "I thought I'd treat you seeing as you're spending the evening with my insufferable friends."

His hands wrap around me and travel up my body until he's cupping my breasts. "They are insufferable," he agrees.

I slap his hands away. "You are enjoying it there, aren't you?" I ask. "the job, I mean."

He nods. "Of course. It's different to working in a school. You don't get time to speak to the other staff, which is why I made the effort last night." His explanation eases the tension.

"I know you were reluctant to accept the job . . ." I begin.

"Because I didn't want anyone thinking your father got me in there, but as it happens, I don't think anyone realises I'm related to the Vice Chancellor."

"Would it be so bad if people did?" I ask with a laugh. "He's not that bad."

"The old bastard hates me." He tugs the cup of my bra down, and then the doorbell sounds and he groans.

I laugh, pushing him away and fixing my underwear. "Go let the babysitter in. I'll be right down."

———

Sofia clutches a glass of champagne like it's gold. "I hate these parties," she hisses. "I could be sleeping right now."

"Having a newborn is hard," I say sympathetically. "But

stay an hour and then slip away. Zoe won't even notice. She'll be too busy networking."

Dan returns from the bar and hands me a drink. "How's motherhood, Sofia?" he asks.

"Don't ask. Christ, I think my nipples are leaking," she mutters, glancing down her top before handing me her glass and rushing off.

I exchange a smirk with Dan. "I remember those days well," he says.

"I was thinking about that . . . now you're at the uni and the money is better, maybe we could think about trying again?" Dan looks hesitant. "Izzy needs a sibling."

"Does she?" he asks, raising a brow.

"Don't you think so?"

"I think she's only just three and starting to sleep through. Don't you want to go back to work?"

"Do you want me to?" I ask, suddenly feeling worried at the thought of leaving Izzy.

"Christ, Meg, why are we talking about this here?" He knocks his drink back as that irritation in his voice has returned.

"Because you're never really around," I mutter.

"Which is why the money is better," he points out.

I sigh. "Fine, sorry. Look, I don't want to argue, I was just testing the waters."

His expression softens and he places an arm around me, pulling me closer. "Sorry for snapping. You caught me off guard. We'll talk about it properly, I promise, just not right now when we have an evening together without Satan, okay?"

I nod, laughing at his nickname for Izzy. He moves in for a kiss, and I close my eyes, enjoying how he tilts my head back and cradles my cheek in his large hand. "I love you," I tell him.

"I love you, too."

Three

DAN

"I'm going to find a bathroom," I tell Meg, kissing her on the cheek. I've spent the last fifteen minutes listening to Zoe tell us how amazing her new role will be, how she'll be in the same circles as celebrities, and how she plans to upgrade her already very expensive apartment to something more extravagant because, apparently, you can't run in the same circles as A-listers and not have a fancy apartment.

I make my way back through the crowd, dodging people's phone cameras as they record themselves talking about the food or the room décor. Jesus, no one lives in the moment anymore.

"Dan?"

Ashley is staring at me with a tray of drinks in her hands. She's wearing the standard black and white uniform the other serving staff have on. "Ashley," I say with surprise.

"Mixing with the up-and-coming stars?" she asks, smiling.

I look around. "Is that what this is?" I give a small laugh. "I'm supporting a friend."

"Ashley, get a move on," barks a passing waiter.

She rolls her eyes. "Nice to see you," she says before making her way into the crowd. I watch her leave, my eyes drawn to the sway of her arse, then I give my head a shake. *What the fuck am I doing?*

————

"As much as I'd love to let loose, I have a baby who will wake me in approximately," Sofia checks her watch, "one hour, and then every two hours after that."

She gives each of us a kiss on the cheek and rushes off with the promise to call Zoe tomorrow to see how the rest of the evening went.

"Since Harry, she's become a real bore," Zoe complains.

"I don't think that's very fair," says Meg, snatching another drink from a passing waiter. "Besides, they're only babies for such a short time, and what can be better than bringing life into the world?"

I can't help but feel this is Meg's way of convincing me to have another child. We haven't even discussed more kids, and I'm not sure how I feel about it. "You're not planning on kids then?" I ask Zoe to steer the conversation away from us.

She scoffs. "Christ, no."

"You'd need a relationship first," mutters Meg, and I snigger.

Zoe narrows her eyes. "I am not giving up my body to be a vessel for another human."

"To each their own," says Meg, shrugging, "but don't knock others for wanting to become mothers."

"I'm just saying you guys used to be so much fun before you had kids."

Meg's expression morphs to anger, and I place a reassuring arm around her shoulders. "That's not fair, Zoe. Priorities change when you have children," I cut in, trying to diffuse the situation.

"Exactly. So, cocktail nights and parties become an inconvenience."

"Sometimes you're so selfish," Meg tells her. "We both came here tonight to support you. We didn't have to do that. And now, you're bitching about us because we don't want to go out on your stupid binge drinking sessions."

"Stupid?" Zoe repeats angrily.

"I think you're just jealous," Meg snaps.

"Ladies, let's calm down," I whisper, noting people beginning to look over at us. "Now is not the time."

"Don't you ever get bored, Dan?" asks Zoe, tipping her head to one side. I know her next words are going to be cutting just by the look in her eye. "Being so perfect?"

"Hardly perfect," I mutter.

"See, you're jealous," snaps Meg.

"Can I interest you in sampling one of my famous cocktails?" We all turn, and Ashley gives a small smile. "Half-price to anyone willing."

"Yes," says Meg, grabbing my hand. "We'll gladly try them."

"Great, follow me," orders Ashley, and I give her a relieved smile for rescuing us before she turns to lead the way, leaving Zoe alone.

"Can you believe that bitch?" asks Meg, sitting on the bar stool.

Ashley sets about pouring spirits into a shaker cup. I can't take my eyes off her, even though I know I should. "You know what she's like," I mutter.

"Every time I make the effort for her, I regret it," Meg continues. "Are you even listening to me?"

I peel my eyes from Ashley. "Just ignore her. We both know this time tomorrow you'll be the best of friends again."

"What's that supposed to mean?"

"Just that you argue a lot and you always make up."

"Am I boring?" she asks.

I soften, tucking her hair from her face. "No, Meg, of course not."

"I remember when we'd be up all night, drinking shots and partying," she mutters.

"Those days are coming back. Izzy is more independent, and she loves the babysitter. We can start to go out again." She nods in agreement. "Unless we have another child, that is," I add.

"Wow," she snaps, glaring at me.

"I'm just saying, those days won't be possible with another newborn. The next three or four years will become about the baby again."

"Why do you say it like that's a problem?" she asks.

I take a minute, choosing my words carefully. "I'm just starting to get my wife back," I tell her. "I'm not ready to have another round of sleepless nights and," I lower my tone, "no sex."

"So, I am boring?"

"No," I rush to tell her, "that's not what I meant."

"It sounds like it. I'm sorry if the first year after Izzy was hard for me. I'm sorry our sex life hasn't been crazy, but I'm doing my best." She stands. "And if you don't want another child, fine. I'll go back to work."

I sigh heavily. "Megan, just sit down and talk to me."

"I don't want to even look at you right now," she hisses. "Don't rush home." And she storms off.

Ashley places two cocktails on the bar. "Is she coming back or—"

"Nope," I mutter, handing her my bank card. "I'll also take a whiskey."

ASHLEY

"Are you ready to swap back?" asks Annalise. "Or you can carry on working the bar. I've seen a fit bloke over there, and we're flirting."

I smile, glancing at Dan at the end of the bar, looking

sadder by the second. "I'm happy to stay on the bar," I tell her. "You go and flirt with your man." She smiles gratefully and rushes off before I can change my mind.

Dan shakes his empty glass, and I head over with the whiskey bottle. It's his fourth double, and I'm not convinced he'll walk out of here unaided. But it means my plan might come into action sooner than expected. Hearing him and his wife argue only confirmed that I might actually have a chance. They're not as happy as they pretend to be.

"Should I call you a cab?" I offer, topping up his glass. He shakes his head. "You didn't like my cocktail?" I ask, noting the two untouched glasses.

"Not my thing," he mutters, "but I like the way you broke the ice back there. Well done." He tips his glass to me before knocking it back.

"What *is* your thing?" I ask, leaning on the bar so we're closer and using my arms to push up my breasts. They're spilling out over the low-cut top, and his eyes stare longingly.

"You got tequila?" he asks, pulling his eyes away to stare at the bottles behind me.

I grab the almost empty bottle and show him. "There's not much left." I pour it into his glass.

"Join me," he insists.

I check my watch. "I can't touch a drop until I get off shift in half an hour."

He smirks. "You don't seem like the type of girl to follow rules."

I laugh. "You're right, I'm not, but I need this gig."

"How long have you been . . . doing this?"

"Are you really interested, Dan, or are you making polite conversation?" I lean closer again, and he stares at my lips. "Because I have to be honest, I'm not into the polite chitchat. I prefer a man to be blunt."

He sniggers, shaking his head and tipping the tequila back. He winces and slams the glass on the bar. "I should go."

I panic. "Are you sure? I have a full bottle of tequila back at my place."

He pushes to stand and grabs the bar edge to steady himself. "It's not appropriate," he slurs.

"No," I agree, and his eyes lock with mine. I bite my lower lip and smile. "But it's fucking exciting." I move down the bar to serve a waiting customer. I might not get to fulfil my plan tonight, but he's definitely noticing me and that's a start.

———

I grab the envelope offered to me by Elouise, my boss. I've been working at her events for a year now, and she always pays well and shares the tips amongst the staff. Tonight's wage should cover my rent. I pull on my jacket and head out to find a cab. It's hard to get one after eleven in London, and as I step out, I notice the queue and groan.

Dan waves at me. He's halfway down the line already. "You wanna share?"

I grin, joining him. "I thought it wasn't appropriate?"

He shrugs. "It's not, but we're probably both heading in the same direction so . . ."

"You live near me?"

"Are you near campus? I'm sleeping in the office tonight," he admits.

"Oh."

"It's complicated," he adds.

"It's none of my business," I tell him. The last thing I need is to hear all about his marriage problems. "Maybe we should walk," I add, looking along the row of people. "We'll be here another hour, at least. It's a twenty-minute walk." *And I get more time alone with you.*

He nods and sways as he tries to step out the line. I laugh, grabbing his arm and hooking mine through it. "Maybe it'll take slightly longer with you," I say.

"Why are you single?" he slurs.

"Why are you asking?"

"Out of interest."

"Maybe I'm too much hard work, or maybe I'm just a bitch. You'd have to ask my exes."

"Do you want to get married?"

I laugh. "What's with all the questions?"

"It's hard work," he says. "Marriage."

"You're not happy?" I ask.

He thinks it over, which gives me the real answer. A happy man wouldn't have to think about it. "I am, yes," he begins, "but it's hard work even when you're happy."

"It sounds like you miss the single life."

"God, no," he scoffs. "The thought of getting back out there and dating," he shudders, "I'm too old for that."

"Too old?" I repeat, amused. "Most people I know aren't even thinking of settling down until they're approaching forty."

"You'd be too old for kids," he points out.

"I don't want kids," I say, and after hearing the argument between him and his wife, I know he doesn't want any more either.

"Why?"

"I love my life too much. I want to travel and see the world."

"I used to say that," he mutters.

"It's not too late."

"I have responsibilities."

"Children don't stop you living your dreams."

He laughs. "You think I can just whip Izzy away and travel the world?"

"Why not?"

He shrugs. "She starts school in September."

"Children don't have to legally be in school until, what, four or five? If you want to travel, do it now. And what an amazing experience for her. She'd learn more than if she was stuck in a classroom." I feel him staring at me. "What?" I ask.

"You remind me of my wife," he says, "when we first met."

We slow down as we get to my place. "Maybe you could sleep on the couch," I offer.

"No, it's fine, I'll be okay in the office."

"Dan, my flatmate is out tonight. She's staying at her boyfriend's. It'll be nice to have some company."

"I shouldn't," he says, shaking his head.

"No one has to know."

"I could lose my job," he adds.

I grin. "I'm just offering out the couch, not sex."

He almost chokes and begins to laugh. "I guess it would save questions from colleagues."

I grab his hand before he can change his mind and pull him up the steps. We get inside, and I turn the lights on. Dan looks around. "Nice place."

"It's nothing special, but we love it."

"Who do you share with?"

"Allie. She's in her final year, studying history and politics."

I hold up a bottle of tequila from Allie's drink cabinet. She won't mind me drinking it if I replace it. "Drink?" I offer. He nods, and I unscrew the cap and pour it into two mugs, handing him one. "We don't have glasses," I explain, "and when we do buy them, they usually get broken, so we just stopped buying them."

"It's been a while since I drank alcohol from a mug," he muses.

We sit on the couch. "So, Dan, why can't you go home this evening?"

He stares glumly at his drink. "Meg wants another child."

I'm surprised he's opened up so quickly and put it down to the drink. "And you don't?"

"Meg had postnatal depression after Izzy was born. It was hard. I don't want her to go through that again."

"Understandable."

"Have you got family?" he asks, then laughs. "Of course, you have. Tell me about them."

"My parents are separated but still very close. It's weird. We still do stuff as a family, and you wouldn't guess they weren't happily married, but here we are." She shrugs. "It works for them, and I get to still see my parents together."

"No siblings?"

"No."

"Sounds lonely."

"Not really. I have some amazing friends here, and I plan to stay in London after I graduate. Have you always lived in London?"

He shakes his head. "I was born and raised in Nottingham. I moved here for work and met Meg. Her family are from here, so we stayed so she could be close to her parents."

"Do you have siblings?"

"No."

We finish our drinks, and I stand. "I'll grab a pillow and sheet for you."

I get upstairs and strip down to my underwear. I glance in the mirror and shake my head. I'm being too obvious, so I strip them off and grab my night shorts and cropped top. It only covers my breasts, but at least it looks like nightwear rather than fancy underwear.

I take a pillow from my bed and a sheet from the cupboard and head back down to find Dan standing by the window. "Do you need anything?" I ask, placing the things down on the couch. He turns to face me, and his eyes wander up and down my body. "Water maybe?" He nods, and I disappear into the kitchen.

"Maybe this is a bad idea." His voice makes me jump, and I almost drop the mug in the sink.

He leans in the doorway, and I walk over, handing him the water. "What is?" I ask.

"I don't know what the rules are, but I'm pretty sure me being here while you're half-naked is frowned upon."

I look down at my attire innocently and note my erect nipples poking through the top. "It's just pyjamas."

We fall silent, and Dan places the mug on the nearby table. "I shouldn't be here," he whispers.

I can't let him leave when I've got this far, so I run my tongue over my lower lip. He follows the movement with his eyes.

"Because you want to kiss me?" I ask, and he visibly swallows. "Because you want to see what's under my pyjamas?" His eyes darken and there's a noticeable bulge in his jeans. I decide to risk it and carefully take the edge of the bra top, lifting it slowly as my eyes burn into his. I drop the top to the floor, and his eyes move down to my chest. "I want you to kiss me," I whisper in a breathless tone.

I hook my fingers in the shorts, but before I can remove them, Dan takes my face in his large hands and moves his lips a breath away from mine. My stomach tightens, and butterflies begin to flutter inside.

"I'm married," he murmurs. I nod, not daring to speak in case I break the spell. "But, fuck, I want you so badly."

"Then have me," I whisper, and as the words leave my mouth, his lips crash against my own. He's gentle at first, kissing me softly, but as I open up to him, he becomes more desperate. His tongue sweeps into my mouth and his hands angle my head farther back, so he's practically standing over me. He walks me backwards until my backside hits the table.

I push my shorts down my legs and lift myself onto the table, not breaking the kiss. I reach for his zipper, feeling his bulge pressing against the denim as I lower it. I pop the button, and he shoves the jeans down over his backside. We break the kiss, and I glance down between us as I free him from his boxer shorts. I take his length in my hand. He's big, and when I wrap my hand around his shaft, he hisses in pleasure, letting his head fall back. I grip him, moving my hand back and forth in a slow rhythm. Precum drips from the swollen head and runs onto my hand.

He suddenly steps back, and my hand releases him. My heart hammers in my chest as I wait for him to speak, to tell me he's made a mistake, but instead, he kisses me again. He runs his mouth along my cheek and across my shoulder, down to my breast. I place my hands behind me and lean back to give him better access. The warmth of his mouth causes me to groan in delight as he takes turns teasing each nipple. He places his hand on my shoulder and pushes me to lie back, running kisses down my stomach. He parts my legs, propping one over his shoulder and running his thumb over my folds. I shudder. It's been a long time since a man's bothered to pleasure me before himself, and as he rubs circles over my clit, I close my eyes and relax into his touch.

When I feel his mouth there, my eyes shoot open and I push myself up onto my elbows, watching him lap at my entrance. His eyes connect with mine and, fuck, it's the hottest thing I've ever seen. Minutes later, I'm coming apart, shivering with pleasure as he laps up my juices.

He stands, wiping his mouth with his hand. "You taste too fucking good," he mutters, his eyes hooded as they run over my body.

I slide from the table and drop to my knees. I take his erection in both my hands and swipe my tongue over the end, licking droplets of cum. He hisses, gripping the table edge and staring down at me. I let him glide into my mouth until he touches the back of my throat and I cup his balls. "Ash, you keep doing that and I'm gonna come," he growls.

I hollow my cheeks and repeat the same movement, sucking him harder as he slides into me.

I wrap my hand around the base and grip him as I slide

him from my mouth. Running my tongue over the end, I suck him in again, this time taking him until my throat refuses to let him go any farther. He groans, and I delight in the fact I'm doing this to him.

I move faster, twisting my hand around him as my head bobs back and forth. He tenses. "I'm gonna come," he groans as I suck him in again. He murmurs the word 'fuck', gripping my head and pushing his cock farther into my mouth until I gag. He stills, holding me there and releasing into my mouth. His cum hits the back of my throat, and I desperately try to swallow as much as I can before he pulls out and spills the rest over my chin and chest.

I continue to pump his cock until the last droplet slides over my breasts. He stares down at me, his chest heaving as he pants hard. "Shit," he mutters, looking dazed.

He pulls me to stand and rubs his thumb over my chin, collecting his cum and wiping it over my erect nipple. I close my eyes as he runs his fingers through the thick white liquid on my chest, rubbing it into my skin until it's disappeared. "We just crossed a line," he admits, more to himself than me.

I take his chin and tip his head to look at me. "Don't think about it too deeply. It's just a bit of fun." I kiss him, and he lets me, and when I pull away, his cock is semi-erect. I smile, biting my lower lip and tugging his boxers up over himself. "You should sleep off the whiskey." He nods, and I take his hand, leading him back to the living room. He sits on the couch, still holding my hand and looking up at me with a million emotions on his face.

"Goodnight," I whisper, leaning down to kiss him gently on the lips.

MEG

I lie awake for most of the night, tossing and turning, going over my argument with Zoe and Dan. I finally give up on sleep at around four in the morning and throw my sheets back and stomp downstairs to make myself a hot drink. I glance at my phone for the hundredth time, but there's still no missed call or message from Dan and I wonder where he slept the night. We don't argue often, but when we do, he usually leaves me to cool down. He often crashes at our friend, Matthew's, house.

I pour myself a cup of tea and sit at the table. I know why Dan's worried about a second child. It wasn't easy for either of us after I had Izzy, and with not getting diagnosed with post-natal depression until she was almost four months old, it made things so much harder. It was only a year or so ago I stopped the anti-depressants, and the thought of going through all that again terrifies me. I pick up my phone again and send him a text.

Me: I'm sorry. I love you. Come home xx

It's six a.m. when he finally comes in. I'm on my second cup of tea and still sitting in the kitchen, wide awake. He stands in the doorway with a sheepish expression on his face. He looks just as tired as me, and my heart melts. "Why are you awake?" he asks, his voice croaky.

"I couldn't sleep. I hate it when we argue." I stand and move towards him. "I'm sorry. Zoe pissed me off, and I took it out on you." I go to take his hand, but he steps back slightly, avoiding my touch. "Dan, come on," I mutter.

"I'm feeling rough," he says, "and I stink of stale whiskey. Let me shower and brush my teeth." I give a nod. "Get back into bed. I'll come join you."

He spends a long time in the bathroom, and part of me wonders if he's hoping I'll fall to sleep so he can avoid the impending talk. When he finally appears looking refreshed, he sits on the end of the bed. I frown. "Aren't you tired?"

"I managed a few hours."

"Where did you stay?"

"In the office," he mutters, and I feel guiltier.

I crawl towards him. "I'm so sorry," I tell him again as I wrap my arms around his neck. "I ruined our date night."

His arms eventually wrap around me, and he pulls me into his lap. "You didn't. I'm sorry I didn't come home and sort it out sooner. I had a drink and then another, and before I knew it, I was wasted."

I nuzzle into his neck. "Do you want me to make it up to you?" I wiggle against him.

"Izzy will be up in half an hour," he points out. "Why don't you try and get some sleep?"

I sit up, eyeing him suspiciously. "I'm offering to have make-up sex. That never happens."

He laughs, kissing me on the forehead. "You don't need to apologise for anything, Meg. Couples argue, it happens."

I slip my silk dressing gown over my shoulders and smile coyly. "But I want to." I pull him in for a kiss, and he reluctantly kisses me back. I slip the dressing gown off and turn in his arms, throwing my leg over him. "See, I'm naked," I whisper against his mouth.

"Meg," he mutters, gripping my waist and lifting me from him. "I'm not in the mood. My hangover is in full force. Just get some rest." And he walks out, leaving me to stare at the closed door in confusion. In all the years we've been together, Dan's never turned down the opportunity for sex. Not once. I must have really upset him.

DAN

As if the guilt of last night isn't eating me alive enough, Meg is being super nice. The more I push her away, the nicer she becomes. Usually, when I'm hungover, she's pissed. She lectures me on sensible drinking because we both have a responsibility to Izzy. Today, she sent me back to bed, and when I finally woke a few hours later, she cooked a full English breakfast and then insisted I call Matthew and meet him for a drink and a catch-up.

Matthew is waiting by the bar when I arrive. He watches me with interest as I head his way then hands me a pint. "So, what's going on?"

"Huh?"

"You called me to meet for a drink. What's going on?"

I laugh. "Nothing. Can't I ring a mate and arrange a catch-up?"

"Are you getting a divorce?"

My head whips in his direction, panic filling my chest, wondering if he knows something I don't. "No."

"She's pregnant?"

"Definitely not."

"One of you are having an affair?" I almost choke on my

drink, coughing violently, and his eyes widen. "Oh shit, which one of you?"

I place the pint on the bar and grab a serviette to wipe my mouth. "Christ, Matt, I just needed a break from the normal routine. Nothing's going on."

He smiles, relieved, and slaps me on the back. "Great. Let's find a seat and you can tell me the truth." I groan. Of course, he'd know I was lying because he can read me better than anyone. We sit down, and he stares at me, waiting for me to confess all my sins.

"What's classed as cheating on your wife?" I ask, and his mouth falls open. "Don't say it," I hiss. "I already know I'm a fucking idiot."

"Are you being serious?"

"Meg and I argued," I mutter, then I groan loudly and bury my face in my hands. "Fuck."

"But you two are solid," he says, sounding shocked. "I've never met a couple matched so perfectly."

"Are you trying to make me kill myself?" I snap.

"Who the hell was this goddess you found? Because she has to be fucking amazing to top Meg."

"This was a bad idea," I mutter, standing.

He sighs. "Sorry. I'm just in shock. Sit down."

I lower back into my seat. "It's not an affair," I clarify. "We fooled around one time."

"Great. That's absolutely fine. Let Meg know it was nothing, and the world can keep on turning," he says sarcastically. I narrow my eyes in annoyance, and he leans forward. "I'm sorry, did you want me to high-five you and tell you I'm in awe? What kind of mate would I be? Meg is fucking amazing. She's gorgeous, kind, a fantastic mother—"

"Wow, do you have a thing for my wife?"

"Every man who knows her has a thing for her, you stupid son of a bitch. And you were the lucky bastard who got her. Not only that, she had your kid. She gave you a mini-

Meg, and now, you're telling me you fooled around with some fucking hoe?"

I roll my eyes. "She's not a hoe."

"Now, you're defending her?" He scrubs his hands over his face. "You're an idiot. A complete moron. Who is she? Does Meg know her?"

"No," I snap, "of course not. I just . . . we just met last night at a bar. She was the barmaid," I lie.

He looks relieved. "Great, so you won't see her again? It's hardly likely you'll bump into her, right?"

"Right," I lie again.

"So, forget it happened."

"You don't think I should tell Meg then?"

"No."

"I feel so guilty," I admit. "I don't know if I can keep it a secret."

"If this was just a one-off mistake, something you'll never repeat again, then don't tell her. You'll break her heart."

"The truth always comes out," I say with a groan, and I wish I could rewind back to yesterday. "What if she finds out later? Then she'll be hurt I lied."

"It's not lying—it's saving her from a world of pain and regret. We all fuck up. Look at me." I nod in agreement. Matt's always jumping in and out of relationships. He just can't seem to settle, and just when I think he has, he's single again. "You don't know what you've got until it's gone, trust me. Go back to being a wonderful husband and father and forget this bitch. Is there any possible way it could come out?"

I shrug. I don't think anyone saw us leave Zoe's party, and although I crept out of Ashley's place before she woke, I'm certain she's regretting it as much as I am. "I don't think so."

"And you didn't have sex with her?" I shake my head. "Good. Forget about it then." He takes a gulp of his beer. "What did you argue about anyway?"

"Meg wants another kid."

"And you don't?" I shake my head. "Why?"

"Cos of what she went through. I don't want to see her go through that again."

"You want my advice?"

"No."

He grins. "Tough. Give her what she wants. It's the least you can do. And the chances of her going through that again are low. Besides, now the doctors know what to look out for, it can be avoided."

————

Meg is already in bed when I stumble through the door. She stirs as I dance around the bedroom, trying to remove my clothing, and when I drop my shoe to the ground with a thud, she turns on the lamp. "Good time?" she asks, grinning.

"Thanks for making me go," I tell her, dropping onto the bed.

She climbs over me and begins to undress me. "Two days drunk in a row. You're going to regret it."

I grab a handful of her arse. "Right now, I don't care." She tugs my jeans down my legs. "Is your offer still on the table?" I ask, pulling her back to sit over me. I run my hands under the silk camisole top she's wearing and cup her perfect breasts. "I love you."

She laughs. "I love you too." She slides down my body and releases my erection from my boxer shorts, smiling up at me as she licks the tip. I briefly close my eyes and images of Ashley doing the exact same thing assault my brain.

"Fuck," I mutter, and she takes it as a compliment, opening wider and taking me into her mouth. "No," I add, tugging her head back by her hair. She grins, thinking we're about to rough play. "Just fuck me," I add, flopping back on the bed.

She sits over me. "So romantic," she teases.

"Let's do the whole baby thing," I add, and she stares down at me, looking concerned. It's not the sort of thing I'd usually change my mind on without an in-depth conversation. "If that's what you want, let's do it."

"You're saying that because you're drunk," she surmises.

I grab her hair again and pull her face closer so I can kiss her. "I'm saying it because I want to see you pregnant with my baby again," I whisper, and she smirks. "Because I remember how fucking hot you looked." I kiss her hard.

"Such a caveman," she whispers against my mouth. She reaches between us and takes my erection, then she lines it up at her entrance and slowly sinks down. I close my eyes. She feels so good, like home, but there's a small part of me that can't stop thinking about Ashley, and I hate myself for it.

I open my eyes, concentrating on Meg and the way she moves over me, taking her time and occasionally kissing me. This is love. It's slow and sexy and everything it should be with my wife. But then I picture Ashley's face, the way she cried out in pleasure, and the taste of her on my tongue. *Fuck.*

I grab Meg and spin us around so I'm on top. I move faster, fucking her up the bed with each thrust. "Dan," she whispers, digging her nails into the skin on my shoulders. I press my hand to her mouth. *Ash covered in my cum.* Meg moans against my hand, the sound of my name muffled. *Ash gripping my cock, choking on me.* I freeze, coming hard and releasing a growl from somewhere deep inside. I'm panting so hard, my chest hurts. Pulling from her, I replace my cock with my fingers, rubbing her swollen clit. I don't usually come before Meg, and I know she's thinking the same as she squirms beneath me, so I take her nipple in my mouth, and it sends her spiralling over the edge.

I flop down beside her, suddenly feeling sober. "Wow," she whispers. "That was . . ."

"I should drink more often," I cut in, forcing a laugh to

cover how mortified I feel. I just fucked my wife while thinking of another woman. *I feel sick.*

"Did you mean what you said?" she asks. "About another baby?"

My head is spinning, and I shrug, not really concentrating on her words. "Yeah, sure, whatever."

"Because I rang my old boss earlier, and she said I can come back to work."

I hear that and turn on my side, staring down at her flushed cheeks. "Baby, why did you do that? We didn't even discuss it."

"You said you weren't ready for another baby, so I wanted to test the waters with her. I can't sit around all day when Izzy starts school."

Guilt eats at my soul. I don't like the thought of things changing with her going back to work and Izzy starting nursery. "Let's talk tomorrow." I kiss her on the lips lightly. "Sleep."

ASHLEY

I take a seat at in the front row of the auditorium like usual. Dan hasn't arrived yet, which is odd. He's usually here early, and I often arrive twenty minutes before class so I get some alone time with him, and since our little dalliance over the weekend, I'm more than excited to see him.

"This seat taken?" asks Jaxon. He's one of the guys all the girls want to talk to. He also sits way at the back, so I'm surprised when he puts his laptop down on the table beside me. "Jaxon," he adds, holding out his hand. "Or just Jax."

I smile, taking it. "I know."

"Ashley, right?" I nod. "I know Jared and Luis."

"Right. The seat is free," I say, nodding to it, and he sits down. "You're usually at the back."

He smirks. "You watching me?"

I laugh. "No, I just always take note of the lazy students, so I can avoid them if we have group work."

"Lazy?" he repeats, also laughing.

"Isn't that why you sit at the back? To avoid being picked?"

"Actually, I just find it quieter back there."

I arch a brow. "You like peace and quiet?"

"I do."

"Funny, I heard you were a party animal and your flat are always throwing wild parties."

He cocks a brow. "You really are spying on me."

The sound of a throat being cleared brings me from the conversation. Dan is staring right at me, and I get that funny feeling in the pit of my stomach. I give a small smile, but he doesn't return it. Instead, he turns to the board and begins to write. He stays that way until the class fills.

Dan begins his lecture, and I get lost in him. The way he moves, the way he speaks, the way he shoves his hand in his pocket while waving the other around animatedly. Since Saturday night, I've had flashbacks of us and how he made me feel. I'm addicted. I need more.

"What do you think of him?" whispers Jax.

"He's good," I say. "As far as lecturers go, I've had worse."

"All the girls from my flat are mad for him. They reckon he's the best-looking teacher on campus."

I shrug. "I've not really thought about it. Besides, he's got a ring on, so he's married."

"Mr. Wright, Miss Daulton, if I'm standing at the front of class, what does that mean?" Dan barks in agitation.

I feel my face redden. "That you're teaching," Jax offers.

"Exactly. So, why are you still chatting? Is my lecture boring?"

"I was asking Miss Daulton's views on *Jane Eyre*," says Jax, smirking.

Dan's expression hardens, and I feel a panic set in. He must think I've told Jax about us. "Excellent. Maybe you could write me a ten-thousand-word essay on the topic, seeing as you're so keen?" Dan snaps. "In fact, let's have everyone's opinions on the subject. You'll all have two weeks to tell me your views on the rights and wrongs of their love story." Groans sound out, and Dan smiles. "You can thank your friends here at the front. Dismissed."

We begin to pack our things away. "What a prick," mutters Jax.

I smirk. "It was our fault for talking. See, if you'd have stayed at the back, this wouldn't have happened."

He places his hands on my table and stares down at me. "How about we work together?"

"I thought you liked silence?"

"My place, six o' clock?"

I roll my eyes. "When does a guy ever say work and his place and mean exactly that?"

He holds his hands up, grinning. "I'm not that kind of guy, Ash. I think you'll keep me focussed."

I stand. "Fine. Whatever."

He grabs my bag. "Great."

"I can carry my bag," I say, trying to take it back. He begins to lead me to the exit, still clutching my bag, and I laugh.

As we pass Dan's desk, he looks up. "Can I have a word, Miss Daulton?"

"Sure."

Jax releases his hold on my bag. "See you at six, Daulton," he says with a wink.

Dan waits until the room's cleared before fixing me with a steely glare. "You told him?"

"Christ, no," I say, firmly. "He was being an idiot."

"Have you told anyone?"

"No," I say a little more gently this time. "I'd never do that."

"Because no one can find out what happened," he continues, standing.

I nod. "I know. My lips are sealed." He visibly relaxes and leans his backside against his desk. "You left before I woke." I hate that I sound needy, but I was disappointed when I woke to find him gone.

"Ashley," he begins, and dread fills me because I know that look. He's about to tell me how he loves his wife and can't see me again. "What happened between us was a one-off. It should never have happened at all, but I was drunk and you were—"

"Easy?" I snap.

"No," he mutters, rubbing his hand along my upper arm. "That's not what I was going to say. I've never done anything like that before," he continues.

I smirk. "You're a virgin?"

He laughs, and I release a breath as the ice breaks. "I'm married," he says, looking away.

"It was good, though," I risk, peering at him through my lashes.

He brings his heated gaze back to me. "You should go and write that essay." I nod, throwing my rucksack over my shoulder. "Are you and he . . ." Dan trails off, and hope blooms inside my heart. He's bothered.

"Are you jealous?" Our eyes lock for a second, and I feel a familiar pull. He still wants me. It's a dangerous game, but he's intrigued. I step closer, glancing back at the door to make sure no one's entered the room. "What do you want to know, Dan?" I ask. "If I'm fucking him?" Our lips are close, and I feel the heat of his breath.

"Are you?"

"Not yet," I reply, running my tongue over my lower lip. "Ask me again tomorrow."

Dan's hand goes around my throat. It's gentle but commanding, and my breathing hitches in excitement. "I can't stop thinking about you," he whispers, a look of complete torment on his face.

"Same," I reply, smirking.

His lips crash hungrily against mine, and he turns us so I'm pressed against his desk. His erection presses into my thigh, and I rub my hand over it.

A knock on the door interrupts us and he immediately pulls away, rushing to his side of the desk. "Go," he hisses. "Come in," he shouts, and students begin to pile in for the next lecture. "That will be all, Miss Daulton."

———

At six, I knock on Jax's door, and he opens it, looking surprised to see me. "You actually came?"

"I feel like you're the type of guy to come find me, so I just thought I'd save you the hassle."

He opens the door wider, and I go inside and follow him to the kitchen, where three other males are sat. They look me over before continuing their conversation, and Jax grabs some large bags of crisps and two cans of Coke. He then leads me to his bedroom, where I dump my rucksack. "Do you share this place with all guys?"

"Two girls," he says, opening his laptop. "Four guys." Music begins to play from somewhere in the flat, and Jax groans. "Sorry, it's loud sometimes."

"And you thought this would be the best place to write our essay?"

"Maybe not," he admits, closing his laptop. "We could go to the library?"

"We have two weeks, so let's reschedule."

"Since you're here, why not stay and have a drink?"

"Now, I feel like I've been tricked," I say suspiciously. "Was this your plan all along?"

"Jared and Luis are coming." He checks his phone. "They've already arrived."

We head back to the kitchen, and Luis air kisses me before pulling me away from Jax. "What are you doing here?"

"He's in my English class. We were supposed to write an essay."

"Jax doesn't write essays," he says, arching a perfectly plucked brow. "He wants to sleep with you."

"How do you know that?" I ask. "Did he say that?"

"No, but it's what he does. Avoid him. You'll get a disease."

"I have no plans on sleeping with Jax, trust me."

"Is that because your heart is still set on Mr. Headford?" he sing-songs, and I laugh. "Tell me you haven't," he says, gasping.

"Of course not."

"Liar," he hisses. "I want details."

"Luis, this is top secret," I tell him, lowering my voice, and he claps in delight. "I mean it. He's married and his job would be on the line if this got out."

"Is he huge?" he asks, gripping my arm. I nod, and he groans dramatically. "Did you have sex?"

"No . . . not yet, but we will. I've got him right where I want him."

"You lucky bitch. I bet he's powerful in the bedroom."

"Not a word to anyone. Especially not Lauren. I can't deal with her judgment."

He pretends to lock his lips and throw away the key.

MEG

Sofia rushes into the café, cradling Harry. "Sorry I'm late. He filled his nappy right before I left. Typical."

I smile. "Doesn't he like the pushchair?" I ask because she's always carrying him.

She groans. "The second I put him down, he cries."

"Have you asked your health visitor for advice? It must be tiring." I tread carefully, fully aware of how I felt in these early stages. I'd hate for Sofia to think I was judging.

"She said to try controlled crying, but it breaks my heart. I can't leave him crying for me."

I nod in understanding. "You're doing amazing, Sofia, so much better than I did at this stage. And you're doing it by yourself. That's powerful." I admire that she decided to pay privately for a sperm donor. She was ready for a child and the right man hadn't come along.

"I don't know about that," she mutters. "I break down every hour."

"That's normal. If you ever need anything, even a break, I'll help. And so will Dan. He's amazing at this sort of thing."

She smiles gratefully. "You're so lucky to have him. He's perfect."

"Zoe said the same, only not like that. She said it like it was a bad thing." I'd already texted Sofia about the night of Zoe's party and the fallouts from it, which is why she insisted we meet for coffee.

"Ignore her, she's a jealous cow. We all know she fancied Daniel, but he was obsessed with you, so she didn't even get a look in and that pisses her off."

"Maybe," I mutter, shrugging.

"Hey," she says, taking my hand. "What's wrong?"

I shrug again. "I don't know. Something just feels off."

"With you or Dan?"

"I can't put my finger on it, honestly. It might all be in my head, but since our fight, things just feel weird. Like he's trying too hard to please me. He even agreed to a baby, which was the whole reason we argued in the first place."

"Maybe he had a change of heart after he'd cooled off?"

"And after that night, he came home at six in the morning. He said he stayed in his office, but he usually goes to Matt's."

"You think he did something?" she asks, looking alarmed.

I shake my head. "No. He wouldn't. It just seems weird is all."

"Meg, you guys were made for each other. Dan adores you. He'd never look elsewhere, and he'd tell you if he did because the guilt would cripple him. He loves you and Izzy, and he'd never do anything to hurt you."

I nod in agreement, needing to hear the words out loud from someone else. "I know. I'm being silly."

"So, baby number two?" she asks, grinning.

"I don't know. He agreed, but I'm not sure if that was out of guilt. And I'd already called my old boss, and she said she'd love to have me back."

"You want to go back to work?"

"I think it's time. Izzy will be going to school soon, and I'll have time on my hands. She's already so independent, and look how I'm dealing with that, making up things in my head about Dan and becoming paranoid." I laugh. "I'd drive myself crazy being home alone all day."

Zoe enters the café, and I wave her over. It didn't feel right having coffee without her. We always do these things together, and I knew it'd be the perfect time to put the argument behind us.

She gives me a sheepish look before kissing me on the cheek. "I'm sorry I upset you."

"I'm sorry too," I say, even though I still fully blame her.

She shrugs from her coat and sits down. "You missed a great night," she tells Sofia then spends the next twenty minutes filling her in. "Was Dan okay, by the way?" she asks, smirking. "He was wasted."

I laugh. "Yeah, he was fine. A sore head, the usual."

"One minute, he was in the line for the cab, and the next,

he was hooking arms with some brunette and staggering off into the night."

Sofia's eyes widen as she looks at me with worry. I feel my cheeks flushing red with panic and anxiety at the thought I might actually be right about him. "What do you mean?"

"Just that," she says, shrugging like it's nothing.

"No, Zoe, what the fuck do you mean?" I snap, and Sofia covers Harry's ears like he's going to understand me. "Are you saying he left with another woman?"

Zoe chews on her lower lip, suddenly looking unsure. "No. I mean, yes, but I don't think there was anything in it. He was wasted, and she was just helping him."

"And where were you?" asks Sofia. "If you saw he was wasted, why didn't you help him?"

"Because he already had help. Besides, I'd met someone." She leans forward excitedly. "He owns his own business and—"

"We don't care," I snap, and she slams her lips closed in surprise. "Who was Dan with?"

"A barmaid," she mutters. "I don't know her name. She had the uniform on." She glances back and forth between Sofia and me, then gives a nervous laugh. "Come on, guys, this is Dan. *Dan!* He's one hundred percent reliable and trustworthy."

"Which way were they heading?" I ask, feeling sick to my stomach.

"Towards the university."

I let out a relieved sigh. "Right, that makes sense. He slept at the office." Both women nod in agreement. "She must've helped him. He probably doesn't even remember."

"There you go then, she helped him back to his office," says Sofa, patting my hand.

DAN

Meg is dishing up dinner when I arrive home. "Steak?" I ask, my mouth watering. She cooks the best steak. "What did I do to deserve this?"

"You tell me," she says, carrying our plates to the table.

Izzy rushes through from the living room and throws herself at me. I carry her to the table and sit her on my knee. "Did you enjoy nursery today?" I ask her, and she nods as she steals one of my green beans.

"Izzy, go and watch television. You've already eaten." Meg's tone is clipped, and I place Izzy down so she can go back to the living room.

"Everything okay?" I ask.

"I met with Sofia and Zoe today," she says, fixing me with a glare.

"Why do I feel like I'm in trouble?"

"Zoe saw you leaving the party on Saturday," she continues, and my heart slams against my chest.

"So?"

"So, she said you were with someone."

I feel sick, and I'm certain my face is giving the game away. "Was I?"

"A woman."

"She's probably causing trouble so you forget about the argument."

"Who the fuck were you with, Dan?"

Meg has never questioned my loyalty to her. She's never had to. But I can't tell her the truth and risk everything over nothing, so I sigh, placing my cutlery down. "I was drunk, and the barmaid said she'd help me get back to the uni. She lived that way. I didn't tell you because it wasn't important."

"Wasn't it?"

"No. Why would it be?"

"I just feel like you're hiding something, Dan."

"We argue one time and I don't come home, and now, you think I'm cheating?"

"I didn't say that," she mutters.

"Then what exactly are you saying, Meg? Because it sounds like your witchy friends got together to poison you with ideas of me and some fucking barmaid?" Guilt tugs at my insides, but I can't back down now, the lie's already set in motion. "If Zoe thought it was an issue, why didn't she call me out?" Meg shrugs. "Because she knows it was nothing."

"You've been acting weird," she points out, and I scowl in irritation. "You turned me away for makeup sex."

I give a cold, empty laugh, knowing full well I'm about to tip this all onto her even though she's done nothing wrong. "Maybe I was still pissed at you, Meg. Maybe having slept in my office and suffering from a hangover annoyed the fuck out of me and I was still mad."

A tear slips down her cheek and she swipes it away. "Something's not right with you. I just can't put my finger on it," she says.

My mind races, and I find the perfect thing to shut this down. "Jesus. Fine. I don't want any more kids," I snap, and she stares open-mouthed. "I don't want any more at all, period." I'm distracting her from the truth, and it's a shit move, but I'm desperate.

"Why?"

"Because you can't handle it, and I don't want to be saddled with Izzy and a newborn while you're high on meds again." I clench my fists to stop me dropping to my knees and begging her to forgive me. "So, there, now we've got that out the way." I sit down and cut into my steak.

"Get out," she mutters, and I stop cutting to look up. "Get the fuck out," she repeats.

"So you can accuse me of cheating again?" I snap.

"At this point, Dan, I don't care where you go or who you're with. Just get out."

"Fine," I snap, dropping my cutlery. "Don't fucking text me in ten minutes begging me to come home because you feel guilty for causing yet another argument."

———

I go to the bar nearest the university, where some of the lecturers go. I couldn't face calling Matt, knowing he'd jump on this and call me out on my bullshit again.

I spot Jay, the only other lecturer around my age, and when he sees me, he looks relieved. "Thank the lord," he says. "I was about to head home, but now I have a friendly face, I'll have another." He signals for the barman and orders us each a double whiskey. "You look like I feel," he adds, paying for the round. "Woman trouble?"

"That obvious?" I ask.

"Wife or girlfriend?" I glance up in panic, and he laughs. "Relax, I'm kidding. Wife, obviously. How is Meg?"

"She's good. It's a long story, one I won't bore you with. What's wrong with you?" I ask, checking my watch. "Why aren't you home with the wife?"

"We're not married," he says, "and honestly, she's driving me insane."

"Have you been together long?"

"Too long," he mutters. "Coming up to six years. No kids, but a house together."

"At least it'll be a clean split with no kids involved."

He scoffs. "She's got six brothers." I wince. "Exactly. And I'm shagging her best friend."

I almost choke on my drink. "Shit. You like to live dangerously."

He smirks. "It'll be the death of me."

"How long's it been going on?"

"A year."

"And you're girlfriend has no idea?"

He shakes his head. "Do you think I'd still be alive if she knew? The thing is, I have to break it off with her now and I'm shitting myself. She's like a volcano when she's mad."

"What are you going to tell her?" I ask, signalling to the barman for another round.

"Not the truth."

I finish my drink. "Doesn't it eat away at you?"

"The guilt?" I nod. "It did in the beginning, and juggling two women hasn't been easy, but my chick on the side is pregnant, so . . ."

"Fuck!"

"Exactly. She's keeping it, and I have to step up, right?"

I nod. "I guess. If that's what you want."

He laughs. "What I want is to carry on having the best of both worlds. Natalie, my live-in girlfriend, is amazing. She's kind, thoughtful, funny—we're like best friends. And Jen, my chick on the side, is great in bed."

It's my turn to laugh. "That's it, she's just good in bed?"

"Like you wouldn't believe. She's daring, adventurous . . ." He leans closer. "She once fucked me in a restaurant full of people."

I frown. "No way. How the fuck is that possible?"

The barman sets down our new drinks, and I ask him to open a tab and give him my card. "A dark corner with her on my knee. It was the hottest thing I ever did. But now, she's pregnant and all that will stop."

I nod in agreement. The same thing happened after Meg had Izzy. The sex was still good, but it was less often. That was on both of us, though. We were tired and stressed, and with Meg suffering, sex took a backseat.

"Haven't you ever done anything like that?"

"Restaurant sex or an affair?" I ask, laughing. "No to the first, sort of to the second."

He smirks. "Tell me more."

"It wasn't an affair. I cheated." Even the words make me sick. "It wasn't sex, just fooling around."

"And Meg never found out?"

I sigh. "It was recent, like at the weekend. And since then, I've been acting off, and earlier, Meg called me out on my bullshit. We had a huge fight. She didn't ask outright if I cheated, but she implied she was thinking it, and I had the audacity to lie to her face and turn the whole thing on her. I was gaslighting her." I groan, scrubbing my hands over my face. "I should've just come clean. Maybe she would forgive me."

"And maybe she'd kick your arse out. If it was nothing, why rock the boat? Deny, deny, deny."

I nod. "Yeah, my friend said the same."

"And don't tell everyone," he adds. "How many people know?"

"Just Matt, and now you."

"Is Matt a good friend? Is his wife friends with Meg?"

I shake my head. "He's single, but he is a mutual friend to me and Meg. We all worked together."

He slaps his hand over his forehead. "To be good at this, you have to keep it to yourself."

"I don't want to be good at this," I say, knocking my drink back. "I hate feeling so guilty."

"That soon passes, trust me. The second you start fucking, all rational thought and emotion shoots out the window."

"I'm not gonna fuck anyone but Meg. What I did was a huge mistake."

"Then ride this thing out with Meg. Pull yourself together and go back to being good, reliable husband material. She can't prove anything as long as you keep denying it."

The bar door opens, and a group of students pile in. "Great," I mutter.

Jay looks over them. "I don't teach any of them. You?"

My eyes fix on Ashley, who's giggling and holding on to the back of Jaxon. Her legs are hooked through his arms, and his hands are firmly gripping her thighs. "Yeah, two of them," I mutter.

"Fuck it, they're third years, they won't want to be seen near us." He smirks. "Although the redhead at the back is hot."

"Haven't you got enough shit going on?" I ask.

He grins. "True. Looking can't hurt, though."

ASHLEY

"Great, Headford's here," mutters Jax, guiding me from his back to his front. He holds my legs around his waist and cups my arse. "Now, this is a much better position." He rubs against me suggestively, and I laugh as he lowers me to my feet.

I glance in Dan's direction and my heart stutters. He looks gorgeous, occasionally looking my way as he chats to another lecturer. "He's entitled to drink in the bar," I say.

"It's close to the uni. He must realise students come in here," Jax complains.

"Just ignore him and enjoy yourself," I mutter, placing my order at the bar.

We're a few shots in when Molly staggers over to the juke

box to select some music. "Bon Jovi," mumbles Dan from behind me, and I shiver at the sound of his voice. He presses right against me, his crotch to my backside, as he tries to get the barman's attention. "Interesting choice."

"She loves all that," I reply, staring right ahead as if I don't feel his erection against me. The bar is busy, and I love the danger in that, where we can touch and no one notices.

"You and Jax seem pretty close," he adds.

I smirk. "Are you watching me?"

"It's hard not to when you're all over each other." I note a hint of sharpness in his tone, and I smile to myself.

"Your friend seems to have taken a shine to Molly," I point out. "He hasn't taken his eyes off her. Isn't he a lecturer too?"

"History," he mutters, and I feel his hand on my waist. "You smell good."

"You're drunk."

"As are you, Miss Daulton. You seem to have lost a lot of dares during those drinking games." It confirms he's been watching me.

I turn to face him, leaning my elbows on the bar and opening my legs slightly to allow him closer. I feel his erection against me again and snigger. "What do you want, Mr. Headford?"

"You," he whispers.

"Until your conscience kicks in and you leave first thing in the morning without a word," I say, turning back to the bar. I feel his loss the minute he steps away and smile to myself. He's playing right into my hands, and I've hardly had to try.

"What did he want?" asks Jax when I hand him his drink.

"He was just waiting to get served, like me," I say, shrugging.

"He was pretty close."

"It was crowded. Don't make it weird."

"I didn't like it," he mutters.

"Now, you're acting weird. What are you talking about?"

He moves closer. "I like you, Ash."

I laugh. "You don't know me. You literally started talking to me today."

He brushes the hair from my face and cups my jaw. "I've liked you for ages, I just didn't have the courage to speak to you."

"Bullshit," I say. "You're not shy, Jax. I've seen you work your magic on girls."

"You really have been paying attention." His lips crash against mine, and for a second, I allow his kiss before pressing my hands to his shoulders and pushing him away.

"I'm afraid you'll need to work a lot harder to get me into bed, Romeo."

He grins, holding up his hands. "I like a challenge."

I glance at Dan. He's glaring at me, and his chest is heaving with what I can only describe as anger. I give a small smile, and he looks away, turning his back to me. A little jealousy will do him good.

I wait for him to go to the bathroom before following, and the second he steps out, I slam into him, knocking his breath and holding him against the wall. "Why don't you just take what you want?" I ask.

He turns us so I'm pressed against the wall, and his mouth crashes over mine in a bruising kiss. His hands travel over my body, grabbing and touching. He eventually pulls back, panting. "Not here," he says. "Meet me outside in ten minutes."

———

I slip away from the group without saying goodbye and wait outside for Dan, who follows minutes later. He looks unsure, but I'm not willing to let his doubts ruin this for me, so I grab his hand and drag him down the side of the bar.

Leaning against the wall, I pull him to me, gently kissing

him. "No one's watching us here," I whisper, taking his hand and guiding it between my legs.

He kisses me again, slipping his hand under my skirt and into my underwear. "You keep turning up when I'm weak," he murmurs between kisses.

"Maybe it's when you need me most," I counter, gripping his shoulders and allowing a small gasp to escape as he slides his finger into me.

"I tell myself it's nothing, and then you're there again, looking like you do, and I can't look away." I feel the build-up of an orgasm and close my eyes. He knows exactly how to touch me to have me coming apart in minutes. I've never had such an attentive man before.

He buries his nose against my neck and inhales. "You smell so fucking good."

"Come back to mine," I whisper.

"I can't."

"You can. No one will know."

"Someone saw us leaving the party on Saturday. They told Meg, and now, she suspects."

"What did you tell her?" He nips the skin on my neck, and I shudder against his touch.

"That she was crazy."

"So, what's the issue?"

"I'm here again, with you."

"One night," I whisper, lifting his head so I can kiss him. "Please." I don't care that I'm begging, I want this man desperately. "No one will ever know."

He removes his hand, and I want to cry out in frustration, but then he licks his finger, and I almost come right there. "One night," he confirms. My heart swells and I nod, not bothering to hide the wide smile on my face. I grab his hand before he can change his mind and peer out to check we're in the clear before rushing to where taxis are lined up at the roadside.

We jump in the nearest one, and I reel off my address before straddling Dan. I grab his face in my hands and kiss him like my life depends on it. I can't risk him getting cold feet when I'm so close. He groans each time I rub myself against him, and I smile in satisfaction.

The taxi stops, and I throw a twenty through the gap in the screen. Dan's hand feels along the door for the handle, and we spill out, still wrapped around each other. "You two enjoy your night," says the driver with a laugh.

"Condoms," mutters Dan.

"Erm . . ." I look over the road and cry in relief when I see the convenience store is still open. I drag him over just as the owner is locking the door. I knock, and he shakes his head. "Please," I beg. "We just need one thing and we'll be gone."

He sighs and unlocks the door. "What do you need?"

I smirk. "Condoms."

He rolls his eyes and opens the door wider, nodding to the front of the store where the condoms are. I grab a pack then turn to Dan. "What size?"

He grins, grabbing an XXL pack, and my insides clench. He takes them to the counter and pulls out his card to pay. I stop him and thrust over a handful of cash instead. "No trace-ability" I mutter.

As we leave the store, I can feel the sexual tension ebbing away. "I didn't think," he says, staring at the box in his hand.

I roll my eyes. "Forget it."

"I'm no good at this," he states.

I grab his hand, and he stops walking to look at me. "One night," I repeat. I stand on my tiptoes and kiss him softly. "Then we'll stay away from one another. We just need to get it out our system."

I wrap my hands around his neck, and he pulls me against him. He lifts me, pulling my legs around his waist, and walks us towards my place as I run kisses along his neck.

I unlock the door, and we fall inside, kissing passionately.

I pull away for a second to turn off the alarm. His erection presses against his jeans, and I waste no time pulling his button open to release him. He drops down on the couch, gripping his huge, thick erection in his tight fist. "Undress," he orders.

My insides clench as I stand before him and take my time lifting my top and dropping it to the floor. Next, I remove my bra. Reaching under my skirt, I shimmy from my knickers and hold them in the air. He holds out his hand for them, and when I drop them into his palm, he presses them to his nose and inhales. "Leave the skirt and heels," he says, his voice husky with need.

I watch him rip a condom packet and roll the rubber over his erection. He reaches for me, grabbing my thigh and pulling me to him. I fall over him, my legs either side of his and his cock pressing at my entrance. Leaning back, I rest my hands on his knees and watch as he guides his length into me. He's thick, and with each inch, he stretches me and a moan escapes. He leans forward, taking my nipple in his mouth and sucking as he slides deeper into me. "Now, you move," he whispers, looking between us and watching the connection. "As far as you can take."

I grip his knees and slide farther down his cock, closing my eyes as he fills me, causing sparks of pleasure. It feels so much better than I imagined.

"Fuck," he pants. His eyes are hooded and his lips are slightly apart. "You're so tight." I stop when I feel fuller than I've ever been, then he pulls me to him, kissing my shoulder. "Now, fuck me."

I lift myself, groaning as he slides out to the tip. I slowly lower myself again and repeat the motion. "Dan," I whisper, "I need you to fuck me." He nods, gripping my waist. "Hard," I add. "I like it hard and rough."

He begins to slam up into me, still watching our connection. I pinch my nipples, hardly believing the build-up is working its way through my body so quickly. It tingles from my toes until I begin to shake uncontrollably. Dan places his hands around my neck and applies pressure, and as the feeling intensifies, I shudder against him, losing my rhythm. Wetness covers us both, but he continues to move, fucking me through my orgasm.

As the sensation subsides, he wraps me in his arms and stands, lifting me with him. He kisses me before lowering my feet to the floor. His erection is dripping from my arousal, but I don't have time to feel embarrassed because he turns me away from him and guides my hands to press against the wall. He crouches slightly behind me and lines himself up again, this time slamming straight into me. I scream, the intrusion too much when I'm so sensitive down there, and he grabs a fistful of my hair.

"Are you ready?" I nod, and he pulls harder. "Words!"

"Yes," I pant, "I'm so fucking ready."

His pace is punishing, like nothing I've ever experienced. He keeps me in place as he takes what he needs. My legs feel weak, and as a second orgasm ripples through me, I almost collapse, but he wraps an arm around my waist and continues his onslaught.

Suddenly, he tenses, holding me tighter and growling as he comes. His sound is so much deeper when he's buried inside me, and I almost come a third time. He pulls out of me and immediately crouches before me, lifting one leg and burying his mouth against my opening. My hands go to his hair, gripping it as he laps my juices. "Dan," I beg, "I can't."

"You taste too good to waste," he murmurs, pressing his tongue against my clit. I cry out, shuddering harder. When he's satisfied I'm done, he rises to his feet and kisses me, and I taste myself on him. "Let's shower and do all that again."

Six

DAN

I stare up at the ceiling. I don't know the slight cracks in this one, and there's no mark where I once crushed a spider because Meg refused to sleep in the same room as it. I smile at the memory.

Ash stirs beside me, bringing me back to reality, and my smile fades. *What the fuck have I done?* There's no going back from this. This feels way worse than when I first fooled around with her. This feels bigger, heavier, and it's crushing my chest.

As if she senses me lying here awake with my heart twisting painfully, she places a hand across my stomach and snuggles into my side. I stare at her, wondering how she doesn't feel the anguish pouring from me.

My mobile phone lights up again, like it has several times since the sun rose almost two hours ago. *I can't speak to her.* I can't answer my phone and lie to my wife again because she'll hear it in my voice. She'll know what I've done, and my marriage will be over.

"You're overthinking," murmurs Ash, raking her fingers over my chest.

I roll my eyes in irritation and sit up, throwing my legs over the edge of the bed and turning my back to her. The sheets rustle behind me, and I glance back to see her sitting. "It was just sex," she adds, shrugging.

"You don't get it," I mutter, holding my head in my hands. "I cheated on my wife . . . the woman I love . . . the woman I have a child with." She stays quiet. "And on top of that, I'm your teacher."

"Don't say it like that," she mumbles. "I'm an adult, not a kid."

"It's still frowned upon. I'll still lose my job."

"No one will find out," she says, moving to her knees and pressing herself to my back. Her arms wrap around my neck. "I had a good time, and so did you. It doesn't mean anything."

"Try telling my wife that, and my father-in-law."

"What does he have to do with it?" she asks.

I groan. "He's the vice chancellor at the uni."

"Holy shit, you didn't tell me that."

"I didn't think I needed to. I didn't intend for this to happen." My phone lights up again, and we both stare at Meg's name flashing on the screen. "You should answer it," she states, releasing me and climbing from the bed. I take her wrist to stop her walking away.

"Ash, I'm sorry," I say, my voice cracking from guilt.

She turns to look at me, and my body instantly reacts to her nakedness. She smirks. "Don't look at me like that. We used the condoms." She sits over me, wrapping her arms around my neck. "Don't regret it," she whispers, gently kissing me on the lips. "I don't. And if one night was all I get, I'll savour the memory."

My erection stands between us, and I close my eyes, trying to gain control. How the hell can I still want her when all I can think about is Meg? She kisses me again, this time taking it deeper. I don't immediately push her away, not until she rubs herself against me. I break the kiss and lift her to stand.

"We can't," I mutter. My phone lights up again, and I snatch it up, cancelling the call. "I need to go."

I shower quickly and dress. When I go back into the bedroom, Ash is back in bed, staring at her phone. "I'll call." It's a lame thing to say, and she scoffs.

"When you don't have my number?"

"That was my next question," I say, pulling out my phone. I open the screen to add a new contact and pause with my thumb hovering over A. Meg doesn't check my phone, but I still feel weird putting in another woman's name, so I change it to 'Jerry – Work'. If I save it under A, it'll be the first contact in my phone and will stand out.

Ash reels off her number, and I press save. "I *will* call you," I tell her, and I'm not sure if it's a lie but she smiles anyway.

———

Once outside, I take a deep breath and check my missed calls. Ten in total, all since six this morning. I decide to walk home to clear my head.

Twenty minutes later, I unlock the door and when the alarm bleeps, I frown. It's only eight in the morning, and I doubt Meg would be out so early. I input the code and head into the kitchen. It's eerily quiet. "Meg?" I shout, then I go into the living room. There's a cold cup of coffee on the table. "Meg?" I shout again, heading for the stairs. I take them two at a time. The thought crosses my mind that she might have left me, and when I open the bedroom door and see she's not there, my heart hammers in my chest.

I pull out my phone and dial her number. She answers on the second ring. "Hold on, let me step outside," she whispers. I wait patiently, hearing a door open and close. "I've been calling and calling," she says, sounding desperate. "Where were you?"

"Where are you?" I ask. "It's eight in the morning."

"The hospital," she tells me. I'm already rushing down the stairs as she adds, "Izzy isn't well."

MEG

The second I see Dan, I throw myself at him. He holds me tight, and I bury my face into the crook of his neck. "Is she okay?"

"I don't know," I whisper, feeling the tears swell in my eyes. "She was so lifeless and . . ." I begin to cry, and he holds me at arm's length.

"What happened?"

"She had a temperature through the night. I gave her medicine, but it didn't bring it down. I tried everything. Anyway, I put her to bed with me, and this morning, when I woke to check her temperature, she was drowsy. I rang the emergency doctor, and they sent an ambulance."

"Christ," he mutters, running his hand through his hair. "I'm so sorry I wasn't there."

"You're here now." I take his hand and lead him to where Izzy is sleeping in the large hospital bed. "They gave her a room of her own," I explain, "and they're giving her antibiotics through the line in her hand."

I stand back as Dan kisses Izzy all over her face. She doesn't stir. "Baby," he whispers, "I'm so sorry."

A doctor comes in and introduces himself. He's the second one I've seen since we arrived this morning. "I've had a handover from Doctor Johnson. We're still waiting for tests to come back from the lumbar puncture—"

"The what?" asks Dan, glancing at me.

"I'll tell you later," I whisper, nodding to the doctor to continue.

"But it's not always reliable. If Isabella is in the early stages of meningitis—"

"Meningitis?" snaps Dan. "What the fuck, Meg?"

"I will fill you in. Stop making a scene."

"We've sent her bloods to the lab. These will be grown over the next couple days, and from that, we'll be able to see if that's what we're dealing with. But rest assured, we're treating Isabella as if it is that and she's on the strongest course of antibiotics."

"Will she wake up soon?" I ask.

"She clearly needs to rest, and her body is making sure that's exactly what she does. She may wake for short periods, so encourage her to drink or eat something."

I wait for him to leave and turn to Dan. "It's not confirmed. It could just be a bad infection or virus."

"A warning would've been nice."

"You answering your phone would've been nice," I snap, then sigh. "Sorry. Look, let's not argue, Dan. I don't have the strength right now. It's been a long night, and they've been talking at me since the second we arrived. My head's all over."

His frown softens and he takes my hand. "Sorry. You're right. Let's concentrate on Izzy."

———

The days blur into one. Izzy wakes for a few minutes here and there, and by day three, she's waking for longer periods and eating and drinking. The doctor returns smiling, and I hold my breath, hoping for good news.

"It's not meningitis."

I release my breath. "Thank God."

"It seems like she had a pretty nasty virus, but after looking at her observations, she's doing much better. Her temperature is back to normal, and the nurses tell me she's eating and drinking. I don't see why you can't take her home to rest."

"Home?" I repeat, scared at the thought of leaving this place where she's safe and they can watch her closely.

"She's fine, and of course, if you feel like she's deteriorating or you're worried about anything, you can bring her right back to this ward and we'll re-admit her."

Dan squeezes my hand. "That's great news, thank you."

A couple hours later, we're both staring at Izzy as she lies on the couch with her pillows and her favourite cuddly toy, watching *The Little Mermaid*, unaware of the trauma we've been through the last couple days.

"You should get some sleep," says Dan, kissing me on the cheek. Neither of us have slept well over the last few days. We refused to leave her alone in hospital, each taking turns to grab an hour in the uncomfortable chair beside Izzy's bed.

"I'm fine. You go first. I want to just sit with her."

"Actually, I need to nip into the office and grab some papers that need to be marked."

I frown. "You're on leave to be with Izzy." He'd cleared it with my dad, and they'd arranged suitable cover for a few days.

"I know," he says, grabbing his jacket, "but I thought I could do my marking from home. You know what it's like—if I get behind, I'll be working late for weeks."

There's a knock at the door and he pulls it open. "Matthew," he greets, "good to see you." He opens the door wider for Matt to step inside. He's holding a large stuffed bear and a gift bag bursting with things. I smile as he kisses me on the cheek.

"I hope you don't mind me stopping by. Dan told me she was home, so I got Izzy some gifts."

"Actually, you're right on time. Keep an eye on things while I pop into work, would yah?" asks Dan.

Matt nods. "Of course."

We head to the kitchen, and I turn on the kettle. "It's kind of you to buy her all that," I say, nodding to the things he's placed on the table.

"She's my favourite little human, and I've been worried sick."

"Yeah, it's been a tough few days."

"At least she's home now. Dan said they sent an ambulance. That must've been terrifying."

"Yeah, it was. And I couldn't get hold of Dan. I was a wreck."

Matt frowns. "Dan wasn't here?"

I shake my head, pouring the boiling water into our mugs. "We had a fight."

"Again?" I get why he sounds surprised. Dan and I never really argue.

I stir the drinks. "Sorry, I shouldn't put this on you. You're a great friend to us both."

"Exactly, so I'm here for you, Meg. What's going on?"

I hand him his coffee, and we both take a seat at the table. "I think Dan's having an affair."

Matt inhales sharply. "What?"

"I was a little suspicious before. It's why we argued, because I accused him. Zoe saw him with a waitress after one of her parties. I asked him, and he got upset, so I put the idea to the back of my mind. But when he came to the hospital," I swallow the lump in my throat, "his clothes smelt of perfume."

"That doesn't mean he's having an affair, Meg. Maybe he just saw someone he knew and hugged her?"

I shake my head. "No. To smell that strongly, he would've been rubbing against her. It was all over his shirt and jacket. His jacket still smells now. And he's been acting odd, staying out at night."

"Staying out?" he repeats.

"Twice. Both times, we'd argued, and he walked out. He said he stayed at the office the first time, and this last time, I didn't ask. Everything happened with Izzy, so we haven't talked about it."

"He loves you, Meg. I'm sure he's got an explanation."

"Is it stupid of me to ignore this? I don't have the strength to deal with it."

"You need to talk to him."

"What if he walks out again? What if he admits it all?" I burst into tears, and Matt rushes around the table to comfort me.

"Not knowing has to be so much worse than knowing. If he leaves, we'll deal with it. If he admits it, I'll kick his arse."

I smile through my tears. "Thank you."

"No problem. He'd be a complete twat to fuck things up with you."

ASHLEY

My phone rings out and I stare at the number. I don't recognise it, but I answer, hoping it's him because it's been days since he left, saying he'd call me.

"Hello?"

"It's me," says Dan.

I smile to myself. "Who?"

The line falls silent for a second before he asks, "Who are you expecting? It's Dan."

"Hey, stranger."

"Can I come and see you?"

I check my reflection in the mirror. I'm chilling at home, so my shorts and cropped top are perfect. Cute but relaxed. "Sure. When?"

"I'm outside now."

My stomach flips with excited nerves. The kind you get when you're first seeing someone and you love spending every second with them. I rush downstairs and open the door, where he stands looking tired, yet sexy as hell. I grin. "Risky, coming here in the daytime. Why haven't you been at work, Mr. Headford?" I let him in, and he follows me up to my room. I don't want my flatmate to see him here. "When you didn't show for lectures the last few days, I thought you'd left."

"I had stuff to deal with at home."

I lower onto the bed. "You told her?"

He shakes his head. "My daughter, Izzy, wasn't well."

"Sorry to hear that."

"Are you?" he asks, and I frown. "What are we doing, Ash?" He almost sounds desperate. "My daughter was lying in a hospital bed, my wife was a mess, and all I could think about was you."

I'm reeling from his confession. "I've been thinking about you too," I admit.

"But I owe it to Meg to try and make it work," he mutters, and my heart drops. "I can't give up my marriage for . . . a fling."

"A fling?" I repeat. "You know it's more. That's why we can't stay away from each other."

"I'm going to quit my job."

I stand. "You can't," I say. The thought of not seeing him again terrifies me. I take his face in my hands and force him to look at me. He's reluctant, which only proves he's upset too. "Please," I whisper, "I can't not see you again."

"I've broken the rules, Ash. If they found out about this, I'd be in so much trouble. The only way to stay away from you is to leave."

I shake my head, pulling his face lower until he's close enough to kiss. "I won't let you," I whisper, gently kissing him.

His hands go to my waist. "It's too messy. We can't keep doing this."

"We can. No one has to know." He cups my arse, and I

wrap my arms around his neck. He lifts me, and I wrap my legs around him. "It can be our little secret."

"I don't know," he mutters, looking uncertain.

I rub against him, and he groans. "You want me as much as I want you."

"You're making this impossible," he whispers between kisses. I tug my cropped top over my head, and he groans louder. "You really need to invest in underwear."

I grin. "Don't pretend this isn't what you want right now."

He lowers me to the ground and unfastens his trousers. "I need to be inside you," he mutters, turning me away from him and bending me over. "Tell me you have condoms."

I shake my head. "I'm on the pill."

"Fuck it," he mutters, easing into me. He pants hard. "Jesus, you feel so much better like this."

I press my hands against the wall, closing my eyes as he fucks me. I can't let this go. Ever.

Seven

DAN

I get home, and Matt has left. I smile tightly at Meg. "How is she?"

"Sleeping," she replies. "Dan, can we talk?"

Her face tells me this is serious, and I can't deal with whatever she wants to discuss when I already feel sick with guilt. I had every intention of breaking things off with Ash, and then I ended up fucking her again. My head's a mess.

"Sure. Can I grab a shower first?"

She nods, and I rush upstairs and strip out of my clothes. I'm rinsing the soap from my body when Meg opens the glass door and steps in behind me, wrapping her arms around my waist. It's normal and something she's always done, but I stiffen under her touch, wondering if she can sense another woman's been near me.

"Are you okay?" she asks, and I nod, reaching for the soap again and lathering it over my chest. "Here, let me," she whispers, taking it from me.

"We shouldn't leave Izzy for too long," I mutter lamely.

She places the soap back on the shelf and begins to rub her hands over my back. "I checked on her, she's fine."

Her palms slide over my buttocks and around to my front, gripping my cock. I stare down at her soapy hand and will myself to get hard. It's not that I don't fancy Meg—she's gorgeous, and I've always loved every curve of her body—but I have a limit, and I'd just reached it with Ash.

Meg moves to my front and runs her hands over my chest. "Are you stressed?" she asks lightly.

"I'm just tired and worried about Izzy."

She runs her hands over her own body, and I stare as she rubs her breasts. "I worry you're going off me," she says, looking uncertain.

I groan. "Don't be crazy, Meg. You're gorgeous, and you know I love you."

"Then touch me," she whispers. "Show me." Tears balance on her lash line, and I feel like such a prick. Running my hands over her shoulders to gather soap suds, I move them down her back and pull her to me. My cock stirs, and I relax. "I feel like we're growing apart," she admits.

"It's a blip," I tell her, turning her away from me and running my hands over her breasts. "We'll be fine."

"Promise?"

I kiss her neck, and she tips her head to give me better access. "Promise." I line my erection at her entrance and ease into her. "Nothing beats this," I say, and I mean it. Sex with the woman I love is amazing. Which begs the question, what the hell am I doing going elsewhere?

———

We spend the afternoon with Izzy, all snuggled on the couch watching films. We haven't done this enough lately, and I realise how much I've missed family time.

"So, I was thinking," Meg begins, twisting Izzy's hair around her finger while she drifts off for another nap. "We should book a holiday."

"A holiday?" I repeat, raising my brows. "I guess a summer break would be nice."

"I mean now," she corrects. "Let's book somewhere and go."

I laugh. "What about my job?"

"I'll speak to my father. I'm sure he can get more cover."

"Meg, I don't want you to call in favours. Your father already hates me."

"I just think we need some time together."

"We're together every day. What's gotten into you?"

She shrugs. "Things have felt different recently," she admits.

I groan. "Not this again, Meg. Didn't we just prove things are still on track?"

"It was just an idea," she mutters. "I guess I'm panicking."

"Why?"

"Because I'm worried you're bored," she says, looking me in the eye.

I look away. "Don't be ridiculous. I love you."

"Doesn't mean you can't get bored. I just want to spice things up a bit."

I smirk. "I'm all ears."

She smiles too. "Not just in the bedroom."

I grab her hand and kiss the back of it. "Things are fine. Stop worrying."

———

Monday comes around and I'm relieved to get back into work. I spent a lazy weekend with Meg and Izzy, and it was perfect, but routine suits me. And I can't deny I'm excited to see Ash.

She arrives for lesson twenty minutes early, like usual. She perches on the edge of my desk and runs a hand over my tie as I glance at the door. "Careful," I whisper. "Anyone could walk in."

"Isn't that the exciting part?" she asks.

Her hand travels down, rubbing my crotch. "Ash," I whisper in warning.

"Don't pretend you haven't pictured bending me over this desk and fucking me."

My cock gets harder. "A million times," I admit.

"Maybe I can call in later."

"I don't finish lectures until six today," I tell her.

"That's a long wait," she mutters, opening her legs slightly and guiding my hand between them. "Maybe you can give me something to think about."

I slip my hand into her underwear. She's already wet, and when I push my finger into her, she gasps. The door swings open, and I pull my hand free. Ash steps away, and I smirk, popping my finger into my mouth before Jax comes into view. "Good morning," he says brightly. "Mr. Headford, you're back."

"It appears so, Mr. Wright." He takes his seat next to Ash, and I push down the jealousy. Ash practically skips to her seat with a smile on her face.

"What are you so happy about?" asks Jax, and I open my laptop, pretending to ignore them.

"I'm always happy."

"Is it because you had amazing company all weekend?" he asks, grinning.

"Please," she says playfully, "you made me watch *Top Gun* . . . twice." My ears prick up. *She spent the weekend with him.*

"You made me watch *Scream*," he counters. "And I know that's just so you could cuddle up to me when you were scared."

She laughs. "Nobody gets scared watching *Scream*, Jax."

I slam my laptop closed, jealousy coursing through me. Ash glances over, and her smile fades. "Sounds like you had a good weekend," I say, my tone clipped.

"Her flatmate was away all weekend," says Jax. "And she

begged me to stay over," he teases, nudging shoulders with Ash, who's still staring at me.

"I didn't know you two were a thing," I say as casually as I can muster.

"We're not," says Ash quickly.

Jax laughs. "Way to bruise a man's ego."

The door opens and students begin to pour in. I break eye contact with Ash and turn my back to compose myself. I haven't felt jealous in a long time. Not since I first met Meg and realised just how much everyone adored her. She was a social butterfly back then, and even my jealous rages didn't dull her sparkle. She'd refused to entertain me when I got like this, and I soon learned to get my shit together and trust her. My heart twists painfully remembering how she'd spend time to reassure me she was all mine.

———

It's almost half past six when Ash shows up. She gives a small smile, and I scowl. My bad mood has stuck with me all day and it doesn't get any better seeing her. "Jax is my friend," she begins, sensing my mood.

"Your housemate was away all weekend, and you didn't think to message me and let me know?"

She narrows her eyes. "I assumed you'd be busy . . . with your wife."

"You'd rather spend time with him than me?"

"No, of course not. But you have a family, Dan, and I wasn't sure if it was safe to text you. My flatmate's away until next Wednesday. You're welcome anytime."

"As long as Jax isn't there, right?" I snap.

"If you want me to stay away from him, just say it."

"Okay, I want you to stay away from him."

She rolls her eyes. "That's unfair when I can't make the

same demands of you." She folds her arms. "Do you have sex with her?"

I wasn't expecting the question and I hesitate. She glares at me. "She's my wife," I mutter.

"When was the last time?"

"Seriously?" I snap.

"If you're going to stop me seeing other men, it's only fair I know the truth."

I march over to the door and click the lock before turning back to her. "Ash, she's my wife. It's part of the marriage," I say, and she laughs coldly. "If I start turning her down, she'll get suspicious."

"And we wouldn't want that, would we?"

I grab her hand, and she tries to tug it free, but I pull her closer. "Don't be mad." I want to laugh at how this has suddenly turned.

"Then tell me when the last time was," she hisses.

"Last night," I confess.

Hurt passes over her face. "And before that?"

"Jesus, Ash," I snap, releasing her hand. "You knew my situation. You said it was just sex."

"You sleep with her regular?"

"Yes, I have sex with my wife most nights," I growl. "I don't know what you want me to say."

"How dare you tell me I can't see other men when you're still very much in love with her? Why are you even coming to me at all?" she yells.

"Stop shouting," I warn. The last thing I need is another staff member banging the door down and finding us locked in here alone. "What do you want from me?"

She groans. "I don't know. This was a bit of fun, and suddenly, it feels serious. I never thought about you and her until now."

I grab her again and tug her against me. "It doesn't change anything between us."

Tears fill her eyes. "It does, because now I know you're having sex with her, and I hate it."

I cup her face in my hands and brush my thumbs over her cheeks. "It's a habit," I whisper. "I've been with her a long time."

"That doesn't make me feel better."

I gently kiss her. "I'll try and avoid it as much as I can."

"I want a weekend with you," she says firmly.

"I don't know if I can manage a full weekend," I reply, kissing her.

She steps away from me. "Then I don't know if this is what I want anymore."

It would be easy to let her end things and walk away. I could go back to my comfortable life and act like this never happened. But my fingers itch to hold her again, and my heart twists painfully at the thought of never seeing her again. "You don't mean that," I find myself saying.

"Maybe I do. Maybe someone like Jax, who wants to be with me, is a better choice."

My fists clench at my sides, and I feel my jaw stiffen. "He wants to be with you?"

"Yes. He's made it very clear how he feels, and I stupidly friend-zoned him because of you."

I scoff. "Fine, if he's what you want." I'm calling her bluff.

"Great, that's sorted then." She swoops down to grab her bag. "Thanks for everything."

I stare in disbelief. "You're seriously going to go to him just because I can't spend a full weekend with you?"

She heads for the door. "Yes. Goodbye, Dan." And she leaves.

ASHLEY

Lauren slides a drink towards me, and I take it gratefully, downing it in one go. "I won't say I didn't warn you," she mutters.

"Great, thanks for that, Lauren. It's exactly what I needed to hear," I snap, my voice dripping with sarcasm.

"You've been lying to me," she points out. "I'm your best friend."

"I knew you'd disapprove."

"Because I knew we'd end up here," she snaps. "Look at you, crying over another man because he chose his wife over you. When will you learn?"

I wipe my eyes. "You're right," I whisper. "And I wasn't ready to hear it, but you're right."

"Avoid him and any other man wearing a wedding band." I nod. "Although, he is pretty fine."

I groan, smirking. "Extremely."

"He gives me Tom Hardy vibes."

I nod, feeling more miserable. "You should see his wife."

She gasps. "You met his wife?"

"Briefly. She was at an event I was waitressing for. Lauren, she looks exactly like Megan Fox. She's stunning."

"I bet they'll make beautiful babies," she says wistfully.

I remain silent, still not able to bring myself to admit that I know he's got a child. "Oh well. Free and single again."

"What about Jax?"

I shake my head. "No. It's too soon."

"That boy has made his feelings clear, and we all know he's not serious about anyone. Have some fun, piss the married prick off, and move on. There's nothing wrong with a rebound fling."

"Maybe."

"Definitely." She takes my hand. "Come on, he's with the others in town. We'll meet them and get drunk."

———

A few hours later, I'm glad I listened to Lauren. Being around my friends is just what I needed. I see double of Jax and laugh. "Monday night drinking was a bad idea," I slur. He presses me against my front door and checks my pockets for the keys, and I giggle. "Careful."

"We've got an early lecture," he reminds me.

"Are you staying over?"

He smirks. "I was hoping you'd ask that."

MEG

Dan's mood has been awful since the second he walked in and tripped over Izzy's dollhouse. He spent ten minutes ranting about the state of the house before stomping off upstairs to shower. When he reappeared, he ate dinner in silence then sat in front of the television the rest of the night.

"Why are you staring at me?" he snaps.

I shake my head, not realising I was. "Sorry." I take a breath. "Are you okay?"

"Why wouldn't I be?"

"You just seem a little tense."

"Maybe because you keep staring at me."

"You've hardly spoken all evening."

"Christ, Meg, I'm fine," he snaps, standing. "I'm tired. I'm going to bed."

I lock up before heading up after him. He's tapping away on his mobile, and when he spots me, he slams it on the bedside table angrily. I undress and slip into bed naked. "Maybe you need help to relax," I suggest, moving closer and resting my head on his tense shoulder.

"I'm tired," he states.

"I'll do all the work," I promise, running my hand over his chest. I kiss his neck, and he inhales sharply. Throwing my leg over him, I pull myself to sit on his lap, and he eyes my breasts through hooded lids. I push my hand into his boxers, and he hisses when I grip him. His phone lights up, distracting him, and he reaches for it, checking a message before placing it back on the bedside table.

"Meg, I'm really tired," he mutters, lifting me from him. "Maybe tomorrow."

———

I spend the night tossing and turning, talking myself out of stealing his phone and checking it. After my conversation with Matt, I'd convinced myself that Dan and I are fine. Sex was back to normal, and he seemed to be happier, so I never bothered to bring up my concerns, despite Matt insisting on it. Maybe I just hoped it would resolve itself.

I glance over at Dan, who's sound asleep on his back with his arm over his eyes. It's been eleven years and I fancy him just as much now as the first day I saw him.

I shift over to his side of the bed and lift the sheet. Usually, Dan sleeps naked too, but his boxer shorts are firmly in place. I gently rake my nails down his torso, and he stirs. Kissing along his chest, I make my way lower until his semi-hard erection is in my grasp. He groans, and I move my hand until he gets fully hard. When I close my mouth over him, his eyes shoot open.

"Meg," he murmurs, sounding confused. His hands stroke my hair, and he watches as I suck him.

"Mummy," shouts Izzy, and I smirk, moving my mouth faster. "Mummy," she repeats.

Dan groans, grabbing my hair and pulling me from him. He guides me up his body and kisses me on the forehead. "Go and see to Izzy," he mutters.

"What?" I ask, almost laughing in disbelief. "But she's fine."

"Meg," he says, more impatiently this time, "just sort Izzy. I've got to go into work early anyway."

Eight

DAN

Ash doesn't come into class early like usual, and I find myself staring at her empty seat like that will somehow conjure her into the room. I'd text her last night apologising, and she'd sent a blurry picture of her and Jax. She wasted no time moving on, and seeing it had burned.

When the students finally file in, Ash is last, with Jax practically holding her up. She's wearing shades over her eyes, and I wait until she's seated before beginning. When she doesn't remove the shades, I pause, glaring at her. "What?" she spits.

I arch a brow. "Lose the shades."

"I've got a headache."

"Miss Daulton, lose the shades or remove yourself from my lecture," I snap.

She swipes them from her eyes, glaring at me angrily. Jax takes her hand and whispers something to her, and she relaxes back into her chair.

After the lecture, I wait until she's passing my desk and say, "A word please, Miss Daulton."

"I have another lecture," she mutters.

"I don't care," I snap.

She stops, and Jax kisses her on the head. "I'll save you a seat," he says.

When the room is empty, she looks me in the eye. "I'm seeing Jax."

"Quick work," I say, jealousy burning me.

"He's taking me away this weekend," she adds.

"Good for you, Ashley. I just wanted to say that you should leave the attitude at the door. Next time you speak to me like that, I'll ask you to leave."

She rolls her eyes. "Apologies, Mr. Headford. It won't happen again." Her voice drips with sarcasm, and I glare after her as she saunters out.

———

The rest of the week is pretty much the same. Ashley and Jax seem to be joined at the hip. He spends my lectures pawing at her, holding her hand and touching her leg. And she spends them staring at me, her eyes burning into my soul.

Meg hasn't tried to have sex with me since I turned her down on Tuesday morning, but things are fine between us. We're doing the usual things we do, like bedtime routines with Izzy and watching television, but we're getting into bed and turning our backs to one another. It's ridiculous now things are done with me and Ash, but I guess guilt is keeping me away from her.

By Saturday, my mood has improved, and we spend the day in the garden with Izzy, watching her in the paddling pool. We have a babysitter arranged for the evening because we have a charity ball that Meg's parents have arranged, and as much as I hate these things, it's a good chance to spend time with Meg and work on our marriage.

I dress in my suit and wait patiently for Meg to appear. When she finally does, dressed in a dark blue, ankle-length dress with a split up the side to her thigh, I'm reminded why

I snatched her up the second I laid eyes on her. She's gorgeous.

As we're getting in the car, my phone beeps. It's Ash. She's not texted me all week, and my heart hammers in my chest at seeing her codename light up my phone.

Jerry – Work: Hi, I just wanted to give you the heads up that I'm working an event tonight for the vice chairman. Just in case you're coming.

Me: Can't you get out of it?

Jerry – Work: No. I need the money. Sorry. I didn't realise until I arrived. I'll avoid you.

Me: Appreciate that.

"Everything okay?" asks Meg.

I nod, tucking my phone away and wondering why the hell it bothers me so much. She's moved on, and I'm happy with Meg. "Yep."

We arrive, and Meg's parents embrace her. They're both very busy people, so they don't see Meg as much as they'd like and it shows when they hold onto her until she laughs awkwardly and pulls free.

I shake hands with her father, Mark, and kiss Pam, her mum, on the cheek. We exchange polite conversation then they move on to greet other guests.

"What exactly is this for again?" I ask, taking two glasses of Champagne from a passing waiter.

"Education in some poor country," says Meg, shrugging. "They blend into one another after a while."

"We need better excuses to get out of these things."

Zoe heads over, and I groan. "What is she doing here?" I whisper.

"She helped my mother organise it," she whispers back, which explains why Ash is here as Zoe always hires the same companies.

She air-kisses us both. "Isn't it amazing?" she asks, spinning around.

"You've done a great job," Meg agrees.

"Your mother has supported me from the beginning, so I couldn't turn down her plea for help even though I'm moving forward in my career," she says.

"Of course," says Meg, smirking my way. "I'm sure she's very grateful for your time."

We sit through the three-course dinner, followed by the speeches and then the auction, and that's when I spot her. *Ash.* She's heading out the room, and I find myself desperately wanting to speak to her. "I'm going to the bathroom," I whisper to Meg, who nods absentmindedly.

I catch Ash just before she disappears into the kitchen, and she jumps in fright when I grab her wrist. "Hey," I say, dropping it immediately. "Can we talk?" I have no idea what I want to say and no plan as she nods and I lead her outside.

We move around the side of the building. "I can't be gone long. My boss is a cow when she's stressed," she mutters.

"How have you been?"

"That's what you got me out here to ask?" She looks exhausted, and I wonder if I'm the reason for that.

I sigh. "I just had this urge to see you. I thought Jax was taking you away for the weekend?"

"This came up and I needed the money more."

"Do you need help . . . with money, I mean?"

She scoffs, shaking her head. "No."

"I miss you," I blurt out before I can stop myself.

"I should get back." She tries to pass me, but I take her arm, halting her.

She looks up at me. "I'll take you away," I say. "Whatever you want."

"Don't make promises you can't keep," she whispers.

I stroke along her jaw. "All I know is I miss you, Ash. I can't stay away from you."

"Spend tonight with me." I hesitate. "If you can't, don't worry," she adds, pulling free.

I rush to wrap my arms around her waist. "Okay," I promise. "Tonight. I'll come to yours as soon as I'm done here."

She turns in my arms, and I kiss her hard, pouring all my emotion into that kiss, hoping she'll feel how much I've missed her.

As I head back inside, I feel happier than I have all week. I find Meg at the bar. She orders a glass of water for herself and a whiskey for me. "You missed the part where my father tells the room about me," she says, laughing.

"Thank God," I tease, kissing her on the cheek.

"Water?" I ask. "Aren't you wanting to let your hair down tonight?"

"Actually, there's a very good reason for that," she says. "I'm pregnant."

I stare at her open-mouthed while I process her words. "You're pregnant?"

"Very early on," she says, smiling, "but I couldn't wait to do the test."

"Wow." It's all I can think to say. My heart feels like it's beating in my throat, and my words get stuck.

She wraps her arm around me, looking up into my eyes. "That's it, just wow?"

"I wasn't expecting it," I manage to squeeze out, and she laughs.

"You said you loved it when I was pregnant," she reminds me, standing on her tiptoes and kissing me gently on the lips. "You said I was sexy."

Breathe. In. Out. In. Out. I grin against her mouth. "I did say that."

"I know you said you didn't want any more," she mutters, "and believe it or not, I didn't plan this. But sometimes things happen for a reason." I nod, words still evading me. She grins. "Remember when we used to sneak off at these things?" she whispers. "We'd find a dark corner somewhere."

I laugh. "When we were a lot younger and more flexible."

"I wore this dress on purpose. There's a long split," she says, winking.

"As tempting as that offer is—" I'm shoved forward before I can finish, almost knocking Meg off her feet.

I turn to find Ash scowling. She forces a smile. "Oops, sorry, I didn't see you there."

Meg slips her hand in mine. "You didn't see him in this crowded room?" she asks with an uncomfortable laugh.

Ash keeps her eyes trained on me. "Sorry." Then, she walks away.

"Jesus, what's her problem?" Meg asks, wiping at the water spilt on her dress.

"Maybe that's our sign to leave," I say, handing her my pocket handkerchief.

"I need to see Zoe before we go," she mutters, heading off to find her friend.

I spot Ash at the bar with an empty tray, waiting for the bar staff to fill it. I go over and push my way through the throng of people also waiting to be served and stand behind her. "What the fuck was that?"

"Aren't you busy looking for dark corners?"

"I was about to tell her no when you shoved me."

"Where exactly is this going?" she demands.

"You really want to discuss it right now?" I hiss.

"Careful, wifey's watching," she whispers, and I spot Meg over the opposite side of the bar talking to Zoe.

"We can talk later," I say, staring at the bar staff like I'm waiting to be served.

Ash presses her arse against my crotch. "I can't wait." She wiggles, and my cock instantly hardens. "Neither can you," she adds with a smirk. I grip her hips, stilling her. "Don't you like the danger?"

"If she sees us," I mutter.

She moves her hand between us and rubs my erection

through my trousers. "Imagine fucking me right now," she whispers. "No one would know."

I look around at the people all waiting to be served. The bar is busy, and we're squashed into the corner. "You're crazy," I mutter, but Jay's story of sex in public is on my mind.

She pulls my zipper down and slips her hand into my trousers. "Insane," she agrees, gripping me in her hand and moving slowly.

"Ash, not here," I beg.

Meg glances over, spotting me. She smiles, and I return it, then she gives a little wave. Ash squeezes my cock, and I jerk forward. Meg goes back to talking to Zoe. "Move my knickers to one side," she instructs.

"No."

"Now, Dan," she says more firmly. Her skirt is short, coming just under her buttocks, so it's not obvious when I slip her panties to one side. She backs onto me, removing her hand and letting me guide myself into her. I slide in with ease and still. I'm so turned on, I could come in seconds without even moving.

The barman turns to Ash. "Back so soon, gorgeous? What do you need?"

She wiggles, and I suppress my groan. "Here's my list," she says, handing over her notepad. Each movement sets off sparks between us. The barman sets about making cocktails.

Ash slides against me, moving so slowly, it's hardly noticeable. Everything in me wants to bend her over and fuck her. I feel myself building. "Ash, stop," I whisper, trying to still her hips.

"I can't," she murmurs.

"Ash, I'm serious."

It's too late, my orgasm hits me full force, and I squeeze her hip as I empty into her. Meg begins to push through the crowd towards us. "Oh shit," Ash whispers, shuddering slightly. I feel a wetness between us. I slip out of her and turn away, fastening my zipper. "I can feel your cum on my thighs," she whispers, smirking.

"Are you getting another drink? I thought you wanted to go home and ravish me," says Meg, running her hand over my back.

I feel flustered. "Erm, yeah, let's go. They're taking too long to serve anyway."

Ash slides her hand into mine and gives it a gentle squeeze right as Meg takes my other and leads me away.

———

I shower as soon as we get home. That was too close for comfort, but fuck was it exciting, and every time I think about the danger, my cock twitches.

Meg wanders in naked and stands before the mirror, examining her flat stomach. "I can't believe we're having another baby," she says.

Baby. I'd forgotten. "We need to book an appointment with the doctor straight away. And none of those NHS ones. Let's use the one your father sent the last time you got sick." I turn off the shower and step out to dry off.

"He costs a fortune," she says, grabbing my hand and placing it on her stomach. "Are you excited?"

I stare where my hand rests. "Worried."

"Don't be. We're going to enjoy this pregnancy."

———

I wait until Meg falls to sleep before I slip out. I leave a note saying I couldn't sleep and went for a walk. I'll text her later with another excuse.

I jog all the way to Ash's place, and the minute I knock, she rips the door open and drags me inside, slamming me against the wall. She pushes me to my knees, lifting her skirt to show me she's not wearing any underwear again. I bury my face against her, tasting us both. *How the fuck can I give this up when it makes me feel so alive?*

We spend the night fucking. She's relentless, never tiring, and by sunrise, I'm exhausted. "Spend the rest of the day with me," she begs, laying her head on my damp chest.

"And do what, exactly? We can't go anywhere in case we're seen."

"We'll lie here and talk all day. You can tell me everything about you."

I laugh. "There's not much to tell."

"Do you want more kids?" she asks, tracing circles on my stomach. I stiffen slightly, and she looks up at me. "I mean in general, not with me."

I don't want to tell her about Meg in case it ruins this moment, so I shrug. "I don't know."

ASHLEY

I can't get enough of him. Whenever he's not inside me, it's all I can think about. He draws mind-blowing orgasms from me, and I'm addicted to the feeling. I sit astride him, and his hands automatically go to my breasts. "You're a boob man," I state, leaning forward so he can take my nipple in his mouth.

I close my eyes, enjoying the warm feeling it evokes in me. "I'm an 'any part of the female body' type of man," he murmurs, grabbing my arse and pulling me up his body until I'm sitting on his face.

"Ashley?" comes a voice from downstairs, and I freeze. "Ashley, are you awake?"

I scramble to get off, grabbing my shirt and pulling it on. Dan watches in amusement. "It's my mother," I hiss, throwing his clothes at him.

The door rattles, and I'm relieved I remembered to lock it. "I'll be right out," I say, checking my hair in the mirror.

"What am I supposed to do?" asks Dan, fastening his jeans. I grin, grabbing his hand and reaching for the lock. He slaps my hand down. "Are you mad?"

"They won't know anything about you," I whisper, glancing at his wedding band. "Take that off."

He glares at me. "I can't."

"Well, you can't hide up here. They might stay for a drink."

He groans, pulling his wedding band off and stuffing it in his pocket. I give a satisfied smile and open the door, heading downstairs to find both my parents waiting in the kitchen. "What a surprise," I say, kissing each on the cheek. "Mum, Dad, this is Dan."

They eye him warily. "Dan, these are my parents, Kate and Adam."

Dan holds out a hand to my dad, who reluctantly takes it. They shake then Dan leans to kiss my mum on the cheek. She turns her cheek slightly, glaring at me as he gives it a quick peck.

"We thought we'd spend the day with you."

"Oh," I say, glancing at Dan.

"I'll get out your hair," he says, already edging to the door.

"Don't be silly," I say. "It would be great for you guys to get to know one another." It's risky, but if he stays, I'll know how much he really likes me.

Dan glares at me, and I smile sweetly. "I just have to make a call," he mutters, stepping out.

"How old is he?" hisses Mum the second he's gone.

"Thirty-five."

"Jesus, where did you find him, grab a grandad night?" asks Dad.

I smirk. "Don't be rude."

"Come on, Ash, what is it with you and older men?" Mum asks.

"He makes me happy," I tell them. "Be nice. Put the kettle on, and I'll go and check he's okay with all this."

Dan's talking to Meg with his back to me. "I'm being a good work friend," he says. "We can go to dinner another night." He sighs. "I know I promised. I'll make it up to you." He laughs. "Yes, fine, as long as you give me plenty of warning so I can prepare myself. I love you too. See you later." He disconnects and turns, his face paling when he sees me.

"What did you promise her?"

"To go to her friend's party next week."

"Doesn't sound too painful."

"She's a nightmare. It's Zoe. She keeps hiring the catering place you work for." He kisses me on the head. "Do they hate me?"

"They asked about your age." I laugh when he grimaces. "They're nice. You just have to get to know them."

We settle in the back garden to enjoy the sun. Dad goes to the shop to get meat for the barbeque and some beer for him and Dan. It feels nice and normal, and I picture a future like this, with Dan and me in our own place, enjoying life together.

By sunset, my parents love him, and when it's time to say our goodbyes, they invite us both to the family cottage in the countryside.

I close the door and lean against it. "That went so much better than I thought it would."

"I won your dad over by talking about cricket," says Dan, grinning.

"It felt good, didn't it?"

He pauses, looking at me warily. "What do you mean?"

"Us."

"Yeah, I had a good day." He checks his watch. "I should be getting back."

"Don't you want to do this more?" He hesitates, so I move closer, laying my hand over his chest. "It felt right today. We're good together."

"Ash," he begins.

"Don't say it," I warn. "I know you feel it too."

He sighs, brushing my hair to one side. "We can't go anywhere," he says gently. "This isn't leading to marriage and kids and a happy ever after."

"Why can't it?" I ask.

He groans, removing my hand from him, and I brace myself for his next blow. "Because it can't, Ash. Me meeting your parents wasn't planned. You sprung that on me. It won't happen again."

"They loved you. I love you."

He stares at me, open-mouthed. "Stop," he whispers.

"I do. I hate that you're going home to her. I want you here all the time with me. I want to wake in the night and make love. I want to shower together every day."

"I can't," he says, backing to the door.

"Why? You can leave her and be with me. We can be happy together."

"It's impossible."

"It's not. Just leave her."

"I can't, Ash."

"Why?" I cry desperately.

"Because . . . because she's pregnant." The world stills, and I gasp for breath. "I only found out last night at the ball." I feel behind me for a seat and lower into it. "Maybe if she wasn't . . . maybe I would've considered it, but I can't walk away now."

My throat burns with tears. "Was it planned?" I whisper.

He lowers his eyes. "Yes." I inhale sharply, my eyes filling with tears. "At first, I said no. Then I slept with you and guilt was eating me alive, so I agreed. I don't want another child," he admits. "I did it out of guilt."

"Then tell her the truth."

"I can't. She went through so much after Izzy, I can't do that to her."

"What if I'm pregnant?" I ask, and his eyes widen in panic. "We've had sex without a condom."

"You said you were on the pill."

I shrug. "It doesn't always work."

"You don't even want kids," he snaps. "Don't fucking mess with my head, Ash."

"Just get out," I mutter. "Go back to your wife and play happy family."

MEG

I wait patiently for Dan to return. He's been gone an entire day, and now, it's dark outside. The minute I hear the key in the lock, my heart rate picks up. He throws his keys on the side and stops when he spots me. "I thought you'd be asleep," he mutters.

"You were gone all day," I say accusingly.

"Not now, Meg. I need a shower." He pauses to take in my outfit. "Are you going out somewhere?"

"Yes, actually, I'm meeting a friend."

"That sounds suspicious," he says. "Who?"

"It seems we're both acting suspicious." She grabs her bag. "Don't wait up."

"Wait," he says, following me to the door, "where are you going?"

"I'm taking a night off," I snap. "A night where I don't have to sit alone and wonder where the fuck you are. A night where I don't have to be a mum or wife and I can be me."

I leave, slamming the door behind me. How dare he disappear all day and have the audacity to question me? He was always jealous. I couldn't even talk to men back when we first met without him kicking up a fuss. I'd spend hours reassuring him he was the only man for me. *And I've spent years being a good wife.* For what?

————

Matt greets me outside the restaurant and kisses each cheek. "You okay?"

I nod. "Thanks for this," I tell him. He's being such an amazing friend right now. "Just a heads up, I didn't tell him I was meeting you."

We go inside. "Can I ask why?"

"I will tell him, but I was angry, and I wanted him to feel like I feel when he goes off radar. Is that childish?" I ask as we're shown to our table.

"No, I get it, but make sure you tell him. I don't want him to think I'm taking sides."

"But you are," I say, smirking.

"I'm here to support you because he's clearly being a prick right now."

"He literally walked in at eight. Who disappears in the middle of the night and doesn't return all day?"

"So, he went for a walk in the night and somehow ended up meeting his friend from work?"

I nod. "Apparently, he's having a hard time right now and needed a friend."

"Maybe it's true."

I bury my face in my hands. "I asked my father about Jerry, this work friend. He hasn't heard of him. I mean, that doesn't prove anything because it's a big place and my father doesn't know everyone." I sigh. "I honestly thought we were back on track. He seemed to go back to himself after Izzy got sick. I convinced myself I'd imagined the weird behaviour."

We order our food, and once the waiter's gone, Matt suggests, "Maybe it's a midlife crisis."

I laugh. "Maybe. I know we need to talk, but I keep putting it off."

"You need to pin him down and have that conversation. If you're right and things are over, he should be honest with you."

"The thing is," I mutter, picking at my napkin, "I'm pregnant."

Matt gasps. "Shit."

"Thanks. That doesn't fill me with confidence," I say with a small laugh.

"I mean, shit, that's amazing," he says with a laugh, standing to round the table and hug me. "Congratulations."

"I'm eight weeks, so it's still very early."

"You only mentioned trying a few weeks ago," he says, sitting back down. "How did Dan take the news?"

"I was already pregnant before I thought about it," I say. "I'd had no hints, not even sickness. Dan seemed happy."

"Maybe his behaviour today was down to the shock?"

"Maybe. I had thought that."

"We both know he was unsure about having another because he's worried about you. Maybe he needed some space to breathe."

"Yah think?" I relax. Maybe he's right. Dan wasn't exactly jumping for joy when I told him. "I'll talk to him later. I thought maybe he's told you what's going on?" I feel bad asking and putting him in this situation, but I'm desperate.

Matt shakes his head sadly. "He's not texted me for weeks, Meg. And when I ask if he wants to meet up for a drink, he comes up with an excuse."

DAN

I open the back door and pull Ash inside. "What the hell are you doing here?" I hiss, checking my neighbours aren't curtain twitching before closing the door.

"You said she'd gone out," Ash sniffles. We'd shared a few brief texts since Meg left the house, but I didn't know Ash knew where I lived.

I take in her red nose and swollen eyes and my heart aches. I pull her to me and kiss her on the head. "Don't cry," I whisper, and another round of sobs leaves her. "I'm sorry I upset you."

"I'm sorry I got upset. Please don't end things."

"Maybe it's best to do it now, Ash, before things get too complicated."

She shakes her head, gripping my shirt. "No. I can handle it, I promise. It was a shock, but I'm okay with it now."

"It's too much to ask of you. You should be living your life, not waiting around for me."

"I don't want to live it without you in it. If I can only have you for sneaky visits, then I'll take that."

I brush away her tears. "Why is it so complicated?" I whisper, kissing her on the lips.

"I'm just so happy when I'm with you, I'm not ready to let

you go." We kiss again, this time allowing our hands to roam each other's bodies. "Will she be gone long?"

I nod. "She told me not to wait up."

Ash smiles, taking my hand. "Show me around."

"Isn't that weird?"

"I want to see where you are when you're not with me."

We step into the living room, and she immediately goes to the pictures on the wall. "You look so happy," she whispers.

I nod, moving her hair from her neck and nuzzling into her. "I was, and then I met you, and you threw it all up in the air."

"Your daughter is gorgeous." I look at Izzy's picture and my heart aches, consumed with more guilt. "I wish I could meet her."

"Maybe one day," I mutter, kissing her neck again to distract myself from the guilt.

"Is she upstairs?"

I nod, lowering onto the couch and pulling her to sit on my knee. "So, we need to be extremely quiet."

———

We're half-naked, and our bodies are slick with sweat as Ash rides me. I close my eyes, letting my head fall back as I feel my climax building.

I don't quite hear the key in the door until it's too late. I grab Ash's shirt and press it to her chest right as Matt comes into view. He stops, his mouth half-open and his eyes wide. "What are you doing?" asks Meg, laughing from behind him. My heart slams hard as she pushes him farther into the room.

Our eyes lock for a brief second before she looks to Ash and then her expression fills with pain. It's a pain I've never seen before, not even when she lost her grandmother. My world stops turning and the air around me thickens. Every breath feels tight as I wait for someone to speak.

Ash slips from my lap and pulls her shirt on quickly. I tuck myself away, thankful I'm still wearing jeans.

"You fucking piece of shit," yells Matt, lunging for me. He hauls me to my feet and punches me in the face.

I come to my senses quickly, shoving him away from me and gripping my throbbing eye. "Meg," I begin, trying to pass him to get to her. She backs away, her face full of confusion and hurt. "I'm sorry." Matt blocks me, pushing me back.

"Matt," she whispers, "get him out."

"Meg, we should talk," I try, but she ignores me, heading for the kitchen and closing the door.

"You heard her," he says. "Get out."

"I'm not fucking leaving when she's upset."

"It's not a choice," he snaps.

"Where have you been anyway?"

"I took her for dinner to cheer her up, something you should've done seeing as it's her birthday."

I frown, running the dates through my mind. "Fuck," I mutter, running my hands through my hair. With everything going on, I completely forgot. *I've never forgotten.*

Matt looks Ash up and down. "This is who you chose over your wife?" He scoffs.

"Don't be a dick," I mutter. "I can explain."

"You don't need to. I saw it with my own eyes. Jesus, you're a fucking idiot. Meg is the best thing to ever happen to you, and you're giving it all up for, what, a quick fuck with someone not even worth a tenth of your wife?"

I shove him hard. "Don't talk about her like that."

Matt laughs. "Now, you're defending her?"

I glance at Ash, who's sitting with her head in her hands. "It's complicated," I state.

"Well, let me make it easier on you, Dan. Get your whore and leave. I'll take care of your pregnant wife."

I shove him again, and he sniggers. "What the fuck does that mean?"

"She deserves a better man."

"Like you?"

"See yourself out," he snaps, heading for the kitchen.

Ash stands. "I should go."

I groan when Meg marches back in. She looks more composed, but I still see the hurt in her eyes. "How long?" she asks, looking directly at Ash.

Ash glances at me, silently begging for help. "Meg—" I begin, but without looking in my direction, she holds up her hand.

"I wasn't talking to you," she yells. "How long have you been fucking my husband?"

"A couple months," whispers Ash.

Meg turns to me with pure devastation on her face. "Months?"

"On and off," I admit.

We all glance to the stairs as Izzy shuffles down, rubbing her eyes. "Mummy, I feel sick," she whimpers. I go towards her, but Meg rushes past me, sweeping Izzy into her arms. "No," she hisses, glaring at me. "Just leave."

"She's sick," I argue. "What if it's the same as before?"

"Then I'll take care of her, just like I did before." Realisation dawns on her face. "Before . . . oh my God . . . you were with her." It's a statement more than a question, so I don't bother to respond.

Izzy coughs and vomit pours from her mouth, splattering on the floor by Meg's feet. Meg stares down at it for a few stunned seconds, and then her shoulders begin to shake and small sobs escape. I move to her again, but she steps back. "Please leave."

"Don't do this," I beg.

"Do what?" she asks, glaring at me. "I haven't done anything. You have."

"We can talk about it."

"I can't listen to this," Ash mutters, pushing past me to leave.

"Wait," I say to her, and suddenly, I feel overwhelmed. Both women are staring at me, one with anger and the other with hurt.

"I can't stand here while you beg her to forgive you," snaps Ash, pulling the door open. "Either leave with me or stay here, but either way, I'm going." And then she leaves.

"Do you love her?" Meg asks quietly.

I open my mouth to speak, but nothing comes out. I try again. "It wasn't meant to go this far."

Meg wipes Izzy's hair from her clammy forehead. "She's burning up. I need to take care of her."

"Let me stay. I can help, and then we can talk."

"Right now, I can't even look at you." And her glare is so scathing, I flinch. "Come on, sweety," she whispers against Izzy's head. "Let's get you cleaned up." She carries her into the kitchen, closing the door.

I sigh, staring at the vomit. It feels so much worse than I ever imagined, so I take the easy option and rush out the door to catch up with Ash. "Wait up."

She looks surprised. "I thought you'd stay there."

I shake my head and slip my hand into hers. "Everything's a mess."

"Maybe it's for the best," she whispers.

I want to believe her, but deep down, I think I've just made the worst mistake of my life.

ASHLEY

I can't get Meg's expression from my mind. I toss and turn, and when it's clear I'm not going to sleep anytime soon, I climb out of bed, leaving Dan to sleep.

Downstairs, I open my laptop and search Meg on social media. Up until now, I'd refrained from doing it because I didn't want to know what type of life he had with her, but now, I'm curious.

Her profile is open, and I select her photographs. There are hundreds of pictures of Izzy, starting right from when she was born, with Dan holding her in his arms and beaming down at her like a proud father. The pictures of her and Dan together are perfect, every single one. And while I know people only post the good times and the filtered pictures that don't show anything other than a smile, they look happy. *Really happy.*

When I get to their wedding pictures, I'm almost sick with jealousy and guilt rolled into one. They really are the perfect couple, both so completely stunning.

"Why are you torturing yourself?" comes Dan's voice from behind me. I jump in fright and slam the laptop closed.

"I just needed to see," I admit.

"Did it make you feel better?"

I shake my head. "It made me wonder what the hell you ever saw in me."

He sighs, taking my hand and pulling me to stand. He wraps me in his arms. "What are you talking about?"

"Look at her, Dan. She's fucking perfect. Is it a coincidence her name is Meg and she looks like Megan Fox?"

He laughs, brushing my hair from my face. "You're gorgeous, Ash. Don't compare yourself to others."

"I'm comparing myself to your wife, which is ridiculous because I don't compare myself. I never have . . . until now."

"You're beautiful, with a fantastic body." He grabs a handful of my backside. "Come back to bed."

"How can you sleep?" I ask, groaning as an image of Meg pops into my head again. "She looked so devastated."

Dan's arms drop, and he takes my seat, opening the laptop. He stares at a picture of the two of them on a beach. "I never meant to hurt her . . . or you." He glances up at me. "I don't know how it happened. Is it possible to love two women at once?"

"Love?" I repeat. After he brushed my confession off yesterday, I assumed he didn't feel the same.

"I knew it was wrong, but there's just something about you, Ash. I couldn't stop myself."

I climb onto his lap, smiling wide, and then I kiss him. "I love you too."

MEG

I'm not sure how my tiny daughter can produce so much vomit, and as I empty the sick bowl for the sixth time, I resist the urge to scream. When I go back to check on Izzy, she's fast asleep. My poor baby seems to be getting hit with every infection and stomach bug going around.

I lie beside her and run my fingers through her damp hair. I haven't cried. Not properly. Between vomit and mummy duties, I haven't had time to think about Dan. But the image of his lover riding him on our couch is imprinted on my brain forever. Why the fuck didn't I confront him before? Because I knew . . . deep down, I knew he was up to no good, and I talked myself out of demanding answers because I didn't want to argue. I scoff out loud. How fucking ridiculous is that?

An hour passes and Izzy wakes, demanding toast and acting like the vomit incident never happened. Her temperature is fine, so I take her downstairs where Matt is flicking through the television channels. He insisted on staying over in case I needed him, but I secretly think he was making sure Dan didn't come home.

The thought squeezes my heart because he didn't try to come home. He didn't call or text me. He just left. And I know that's what I wanted, but he didn't bother to fight, and that scares me more than anything else.

"The princess is awake," says Matt, standing. Izzy runs to him, and he gathers her in his arms. "Ew, you stink," he tells her, and she giggles.

"She's ready for toast," I say sceptically.

"Christ, can't we refuse to feed her? I'm not ready to deal with any more vomit."

I laugh. "Unfortunately not."

He follows me into the kitchen, turning on the small television in there and setting Izzy down in front of it. When he's happy she's glued to the pink pig on screen, he turns to me. "How are you?"

"Desperate for a shower and a strong coffee," I tell him, popping the bread in the toaster.

"You know what I mean," he says.

I turn the kettle on. "I'm okay."

He takes my wrist and stills me. "Meg?"

I sigh. "What do you want me to say, Matt? I'm hurt, angry, and I feel like an idiot."

"Why?"

"Because I knew something was going on. I should've insisted he talk to me."

"It's not your fault, Meg. He's the idiot."

I bury my face in my hands as the image of them together assaults my mind again. "On my couch," I groan. "In our home, where my daughter was sleeping."

"We'll replace the couch," says Matt. "In fact, I'll have it out of here today."

I smile at his kindness. "Thank you."

The back door opens and Sofia comes in. "Matt told me," she says, grabbing me and pulling me in for a hug. "I can't believe that shit bag."

Matt mouths the word 'sorry' and sets about making the coffee. The toast pops up and I untangle myself from her arms to butter it. "I don't want to talk about it in front of Izzy," I mutter, pushing my tears back.

Matt takes the toast. "I'll take her in the other room."

"Not on the couch," I say, and he nods.

I carry my coffee out into the back garden, and Sofia follows. "Who's looking after Harry?" I ask, as it's weird seeing her childless.

"My mum."

I frown. "I thought she wasn't going to support you?"

"She's coming around to the idea that a woman can have a child without having a man fully involved. So, what happened?"

"I came home from dinner with Matt, and he was fucking someone else on my couch." I almost choke on the last words, focussing hard on a bird hopping about on the lawn. "Or she was fucking him," I add in a whisper, letting tears fill my eyes.

Sofia stares open-mouthed. "Matt didn't tell me the details. Holy shit. What did you do?"

I shake my head and tears balance on my lower lashes. "Nothing."

"You're telling me you didn't go bat shit and beat the crap out of them?"

"I think I was in shock. I had my suspicions he was up to something, but I never expected him to bring her to our home while our daughter was upstairs. It's just not like Dan. It's like I don't even know him."

"What a piece of shit. My faith in men is completely shot. If Dan can cheat, every man can."

"You never had faith in men," I point out. "Hence, your sperm donor child."

She grins. "Good point. I thought you guys were it, yah know? If you two don't make it, what chance have any of us got?"

"Tell me she's got it wrong," says Zoe, opening the back gate and glaring at us. "Sofia texted me to say Dan's cheating on you." I nod, and her expression turns furious. "Where the fuck is he?"

"Gone," I mutter.

"Gone where?" she demands.

I shrug. "With her, I guess." And I relay the details to Zoe.

"What are you going to do now?" asks Sofia. "I think you're taking it all really well."

I give an empty laugh. "I'm still processing. I have so many things I need to ask him. I think that's when it'll hit me."

"Who is she?" asks Zoe.

"The waitress," I reply. "I recognised her from your parties."

"I'll have the whore sacked," Zoe snaps, pulling out her mobile. "What's her name?"

"Ash. I don't know her full name." Zoe wanders down the garden to make a call.

"She's a pain in the arse, but she's always got our back," mutters Sofia, and I nod in agreement. "Are you going to meet him to talk?"

I shrug. "What if he doesn't want to?"

"He owes you an explanation."

"A part of me wants to wait and see if he gets in touch first, but another part of me wants to know now. I need to know the truth about it all just to prove to myself I wasn't crazy."

Zoe returns. "Her name is Ashley Daulton, and you're not going to believe this, but she's a student at the university."

My heart hammers in my chest. "She can't be."

"Twenty-three, studying English. He's her lecturer."

My tears finally fall, wetting my cheeks and dripping from my chin. I let the pain come, twisting my heart until it hurts so bad, I want to vomit. Sofia wraps me in her arms, uttering words of comfort. After a few minutes, I pull back. "What if he loves her? When I thought she was a quick fling, it felt easier to handle, but he knows her."

"You need to confront him," says Zoe.

I shake my head. "I can't," I whisper, wiping my cheeks. "I can't face it."

"You deserve answers," Sofia says softly.

"Pack his shit up and tell him to come and get it. Then call your father and tell him what the bastard's been up to. He'll get fired. Let's see how they cope with no income," snaps Zoe.

Ten

DAN

I'm a coward. It's been three days since Meg caught me and Ash together, and I'm still hiding out at Ash's. I called in sick to work and refused to leave this place, despite Ash trying to force me. The only time I don't think about my shitshow of a life is when I'm with her, and right now, she's at uni while I'm here staring at pictures of Izzy on my phone. *Fuck, I miss her so bad.*

Ash walks in, and I shove my phone away. She smiles brightly, kissing me on the cheek. "How was your day, dear?" she asks, laughing.

"You're back early."

"Yeah, I have something to tell you." She sits beside me. "I dropped your class."

"What?"

"I just thought they might not be too fussed about us if I'm not in your class. I'll pick it up again next year with a different teacher."

"I don't think that's how it works, Ash," I mutter. "You should've spoken to me first. You were doing really well in class, you'd have aced this year."

She grins, climbing over me and beginning to unfasten her

shirt. "I want us to visit my parents at the weekend," she continues.

I shake my head, trying to focus as she guides my hands to her breasts. "No. Absolutely not. I haven't seen Izzy in days, and I have to go and talk to Meg."

Ash drops my hands. "Just text her and tell her you want to see Izzy tonight."

"The last time we spoke, she caught me fucking you. I don't think a text will cut it. I owe her more than that."

She rolls her eyes and climbs from me. "Let's go and see her together."

"She's had a chance to think it all over. She won't be as calm the next time I see her, and I don't want her to go for you."

"I can handle myself. If we're serious about being together, we should face this together."

We haven't discussed what's happening beyond this. It's the first time we've even talked about Meg because I've been desperate to avoid it. We've lived in our own little bubble, but it's time to face everything. I can't even think of me and Ash as a serious couple when I don't know what Meg's thinking.

"I'd prefer to go on my own."

She glares at me. "I've just dropped out of class for you, the least you owe me is some respect."

I scoff. "What?"

"I don't want you to be alone with her," she admits.

"I don't think you need to worry. She hates me, so she's hardly going to jump on me."

"She might be upset and beg you back."

"I know Meg, and she won't beg me back."

"Would you go if she did?"

I take her hand and lace my fingers with hers. "Of course not," I lie. "I'm here, aren't I?"

"Shall I order food in?" she asks.

I inwardly groan. If I eat another takeout, I'll scream. "Maybe we could cook," I suggest.

She laughs, and when she sees I'm serious, she groans. "I don't cook."

"You're a student. How the hell do you afford to eat takeout all the time?"

"I have a job," she points out. Then she frowns. "Actually, I haven't heard from them about working this week." She pulls out her phone. "I'm going to call them." And she disappears into the kitchen.

I pull out my phone and write out a text to Meg. It's the same text I've written several times but then deleted without sending.

Me: *We need to talk.*

Ash comes back in. "They've let me go," she says, looking shocked.

"Why?"

"She said she can't offer me work right now because one of her contractors has refused to use them if they hire me."

I groan. "Zoe. This has her written all over it." Which means Meg's spoken to her friends, and now, more people know.

"They can't do that, can they?"

"Have you got a contract?" I ask.

She shakes her head. "No, I was temporary, but I've worked for them for years."

"I'll have a word with Meg."

My phone beeps, and I open the message.

Meg: *You disappear for days and the first text isn't to ask how your daughter is?*

I sigh.

Me: *Can we talk or not, Meg?*

Meg: *Tonight. Nine.*

"I'm meeting her tonight. I'll speak to her and ask her to call off her guard dogs," I say.

"What time?"

"Nine."

"Won't Izzy be in bed by then?"

My heart sinks. I hadn't thought about that. "Probably."

"So, it'll just be you two together?"

"Don't start," I mutter. "It can't be helped."

"Meet in a bar," she insists. "Please."

I sigh. Typing the text.

Me: Can we meet in Lé Minstrel?

Meg: Some of us have children to think of, Dan. The babysitter will probably be busy.

Me: I'll ask her.

Luckily, the babysitter is free and agrees to watch Izzy. "Happy now?" I ask Ash. "Now, can we go shopping and buy food that doesn't come from a foil container?"

————

Shopping with Ash is like shopping with a child. She throws all kinds of crap in the trolley, nothing of any nutritional value, and anything sensible is on my insistence. When she reaches for the sugary cereal, I pull her away and swing her around. She laughs, sliding down my body and wrapping her arms around my neck to kiss me.

"Isn't this sweet?" I turn to see Zoe and immediately release Ash. She looks Ash up and down. "Found a new job yet?"

"You're out of order for that," I snap.

"Oh, bite me, shithead."

"How grown up," I mutter, rolling my eyes.

"Do you want to know what I've been doing the last few days, Dan?" When I don't answer, she continues. "Picking your wife up from the floor where you left her. She's a fucking mess, and you're in here with your new whore acting like you didn't just walk out on your ten-year marriage."

"Well done for being a friend, finally. It took you long enough."

She scoffs. "Izzy cried for three hours last night asking for her daddy. Do you know what Meg said? She told her Daddy was really busy with work. She covered for you after everything. That's how amazing your wife is."

"I'm going to meet Meg to talk about contact," I mutter, my heart aching with hurt knowing Izzy misses me.

"If I have my way, she'll tell Izzy the truth, that you left them for a whore. And then she'll make contact impossible."

"Good thing it's not up to you," I say, grabbing Ash's hand and walking away.

"Don't worry, Matt's taking good care of them both," she yells after me. I bristle at her words but keep walking.

MEG

I take a few deep breaths before entering the bar, and I spot Dan the second I walk in. He's wearing a white shirt I've never seen before and some jeans. I hate that he always looks this good, even in the midst of our breakup.

As I approach, he stands, and for a second, I think he's going to kiss me on the cheek. I turn my head away, and he pulls out my chair instead. "Thanks for coming," he mutters.

I shrug out of my jacket, and he eyes my low-cut top. It's the sort he'd make a fuss about if I was going out without him on my arm. I spent the entire day sorting out my wardrobe and throwing out all the clothes that make me feel dowdy and middle-aged. Then Zoe gave me this silk top, and I managed to fit into an old pair of jeans that haven't fit me since before I had Izzy. I couldn't turn up here and look like I've spent the last week crying.

I interlock my fingers and place them on the table, just like Zoe showed me. Apparently, it makes me look confident and strong, the complete opposite to how I feel inside right now.

"Sorry I haven't been in touch before now," he continues. "If I'm honest, it's because I was ashamed." I still remain silent, another tactic from Zoe. Let him do the talking. He stares at me for a moment, and when he realises I'm not going to answer, he sighs. "You must have questions."

I roll my eyes, shaking my head in annoyance. "Only one. Why?"

"It wasn't planned," he mutters, and I want to scream in his stupid, annoying face. "I'm not unhappy with you." I scoff, already pissed with his bullshit. "I wasn't even looking for anything," he continues. "But she was . . . she made it clear she was interested, and we kissed." I stare at my hands. I hate hearing this story of how they met, but I have to know the truth, and as I suspected, he's laying the blame on her. "And I knew right away it was wrong. I swore I'd make it clear to her nothing would happen, but then I got drunk again and she was there. We'd argued—"

"Wow," I say, cutting off his words. "What did we argue about?"

"Having a baby," he admits.

I frown, thinking back to that first argument. "At Zoe's party?" He nods, and pain sears my heart. "So, let me get this straight. We had a brief exchange of words, and you hopped into bed with the nearest slag?"

He narrows his eyes at my choice of words, and I arch a brow, daring him to challenge me on it. "She offered me her couch."

"You seem to prefer fucking on the couch," I hiss.

"We didn't have sex that night. It was a gradual thing."

As I suspected, this thing's been building, which makes it worse. There are feelings involved. "So, what exactly did you do that night?"

"Does it matter?"

"It matters to me, Daniel. It matters a lot."

"We fooled around," he snaps, shrugging with exasperation. "I don't see how knowing the details will help."

"It'll help me to understand how much sneaking around and lying you did before I actually caught you. Because let's face it, you were never going to confess."

"That's not true. I was trying to end things with her, but she turned up at the house—"

"And fell on your erect dick?"

"Jesus, Meg, this isn't like you. Just hear me out." I inhale sharply, resisting the urge to walk out. "After another row, I saw her in a bar and things progressed. It just felt," he rubs his brow, "easy with her."

"Great," I mutter.

"It did. I'm trying to be honest here. She wasn't on my back about another kid, and she's fun to be around. We talk about shit that's not revolving around kids and bitchy friends." The more he speaks, the more my heart splits into pieces. I think Zoe was wrong—letting him do all the talking is hurting me more.

I stand abruptly, and he stares up at me. "I know it's not easy to hear this," he says, "but how will we ever move forward if you don't hear me out?"

I shake my head sadly and walk towards the door. He actually thinks there's some way he can make all this right, and I'm not sure if that makes me angry or just sad, because he clearly doesn't realise what he's done to me . . . *to us.*

The fresh air hits me and I take a deep breath. I walk in the direction of home, needing the fresh air to clear my head, but Dan has other ideas as he follows me out and rushes to catch up with me. "Meg, please," he begs. "Don't you want to talk this through?"

"No," I state, stuffing my hands in my pockets and keeping my head down. "I thought I was ready, but I'm not."

"So, what? We just don't ever speak again? That's fucking

stupid. We're married. And what about Izzy? Think about her."

His words push me over the edge, and I spin to face him. "How fucking dare you?" I growl in a low voice. His step falters. "I have always put Izzy first. I was not the one who took off and fucked someone else." He glances around to see if anyone heard, and I almost laugh. "Christ, what am I even doing here?" I mutter, continuing to walk away. "You only care about yourself and what people think of you."

"That's not true. I wanted to clear this shit up."

I spin to face him again. "Do you realise you've not apologised?" I ask, and he frowns, like he's trying to recall his apology. "You're so desperate to tell me where I fucked up, how I pushed you to another woman, or how she somehow forced you, but not once have you said *you* fucked up and *you're* sorry."

"I am sorry," he says.

"You don't look sorry, Dan. Should you even be out here alone with me?" I ask. "Didn't little miss homewrecker set the rules of meeting in a public place?"

"No," he lies.

"I don't even know you anymore," I say. "You make me sick with your lies and excuses."

"I'm not making excuses, Meg. I just wanted to try and work out where it all went wrong."

"When you kissed another woman, that's where it went wrong. And I don't give a shit if you were drunk, unhappy, or bored. The second you kissed her, you ended our marriage. So, you can try and justify your mistakes by blaming me, but please know this is all you."

"I was never unhappy," he argues. "I told you that. But somehow, she turned my head."

"Good for you. I hope you're happy together," I spit.

"I tried to talk to you about having another child, Meg. I tried to tell you I wasn't ready."

"Boo-fucking-hoo, Dan. I was already pregnant when we had that conversation, so would you have still done all this if I'd have found out beforehand?"

"No . . . I don't know. I didn't have an affair because of the arguments. She just happened to be there, and she distracted me."

"Nothing you say is making this any better. I'm sorry you felt like I trapped you or pushed you to have another kid. I'm sorry you felt I was too full on or nagging. But you're not perfect either, Dan. I've spent years picking up your shit, cooking dinners, smiling at your shit jokes," I begin pacing, "having sex when it's the last thing I wanted to do, raising our child while you go off to work, giving up my job so you could excel at yours."

I cry out in frustration. "And at the end of it all, you get to walk away and start again. I don't. I don't get to give up on the family we started together. I have to stay and raise our beautiful babies on my own, while you get your evenings back and you get to enjoy a lie in without your children waking you. You don't have to worry about cleaning up vomit or cancelling pre-arranged plans because of childcare issues.

"So, go," I cry. "Go and be with her. Enjoy uninterrupted meals and hot cups of coffee. Watch films all day and lie about in bed naked together. Go on nights out and get so drunk that you spend the following day in bed with a hang-over. Meanwhile, I'll get to watch Izzy continue to grow. I'll give birth to our baby and raise it alone. I'll get the first smile and the first step, and do you know what, Dan? I'd rather have all that, because I committed my body and my life to my children, and that's what they are, my children. I am blessed and lucky, and I don't need you in my life." I wipe my eyes and notice Dan is also crying. I've only ever seen him cry twice, and both times it was a funeral. I take a deep breath. "I'll be in touch when I've had some time to calm down."

"Don't walk away," he whispers, swiping at his own cheeks. "Please."

"I didn't," I whisper sadly. "You did."

ASHLEY

I can't settle. I constantly check my phone for a message from Dan to tell me he's heading home. I stand at the window, waiting to see his silhouette walking down the street. When it gets to midnight, I give up and call him. He doesn't answer, so I call again and again. On the fourth call, it connects, but he doesn't speak, and I hold my breath, waiting to hear her voice. Eventually, he clears his throat. "What?"

"What do you mean, what?" I snap. "Where the hell are you?"

"I'm alone, if that's what you're asking?"

"I expected you home hours ago."

"Home," he repeats, adding a cold, empty laugh. "I needed some time on my own."

"Look, come back and we'll talk," I try, feeling on edge that he seems so distant.

"She's left me," he mutters. "Or I left her. I'm not sure which. Either way, it's over."

I breathe a sigh of relief, trying not to think too much about the pain in his voice. "Come back here, Dan. You shouldn't be alone."

"She hates me."

"Expected," I reply. "Where are you? I'll come and meet you."

"What will I tell everyone?"

"Like who?"

"Our friends, our family."

"We can tell them together. I'd love to meet your parents."

He gives an unamused laugh. "My mother won't accept you, not after what I've done to Meg. She loves her."

I roll my eyes. Everyone loves her, and it's annoying. "She'll have to get used to it, Dan. And in time, she'll accept me. Please come home."

"I'm on my way," he mutters, and I hate that he sounds upset about that.

Eleven

DAN

Every time I close my eyes, I picture Meg's face. Not her expression when she caught me with Ash, because that one was bad enough, but it was when she reeled off all the things she'll get to witness while she watches our children grow. The look of pure devastation as she spoke has scared me in a way I don't think I'll ever forget.

It got me thinking of all the things I'll miss. The little things that we did as a family, like squeezing into our bed and watching the children's channels on a Saturday morning. Or eating dinner together. And then there's the new baby. I watched Izzy come into this world, but I won't get to see my second child be born.

"Dan," Ash hisses, nudging me with her knee.

"Huh?"

"My dad asked you a question," she says, forcing a smile. "Your favourite wine?"

I shake my head to clear my mind. "Sorry, I have work on my mind," I lie. "I don't have a favourite. Anything red."

Adam smiles. "What do you do for a living?"

I glance at Ash for help. We hadn't discussed whether we'd be honest. Ash takes my hand. "He works at the university," she says, smiling.

Adam frowns, glancing at Kate. "Doing what?"

"Teaching, obviously," says Ash. "Don't worry, he isn't my lecturer," she adds with a laugh.

"And that's allowed, is it?" asks Kate.

"Not exactly," I admit. "We have to tell them we're dating, but I wanted to see if we were going anywhere. It seemed odd to tell them when we weren't sure ourselves."

"But we are now, aren't we?" asks Ash, looking at me lovingly. "Maybe we should tell them."

I can feel all eyes on me, and I swallow the lump forming in my throat. "Maybe."

"Ash tells us you're older," says Adam. "Any reason why you're not married?"

"Dad," gasps Ash, "that's so rude."

"I'm just asking, sweety. A man of his age is usually married with children. If he's not, I want to make sure you're not dating a cheat or a murderer."

I almost choke on my wine, and Ash gently rubs my back. "I'm an adult, I can ask my own questions, and Dan's past is nothing to do with you."

My mobile rings and I grab it desperately. It's Matt, and although I don't want to talk to him, I need an excuse to get out of here, so I head for the back garden and answer.

"I want to meet," he tells me bluntly.

"Why?"

"To punch you in the face," he says firmly.

I laugh. "Right. I feel like you're trying to win points with my wife."

"If you'd see what you've done to her, you wouldn't be so goddamn smart-mouthed right now. And maybe if I punch you, I'll feel a little better."

"Why are you there anyway, Matt?"

"Because she's my friend and she's hurting."

"Good old Matt, rushing in to pick up the pieces. Are you hoping you'll win her at the end?"

"You're a dick," he mutters.

"Are you forgetting that I told you about Ash? You said to keep it quiet."

"I didn't think it was a thing," he hisses. "You played it down."

"Have you just called to tell me how much you hate me? Cos I'm busy."

"When did you become such a prick, Dan? Somewhere in your fucked-up mind, you must know how much you've hurt her, yet it's like you don't give a shit. If I was you, I'd have been begging on my knees for forgiveness."

"I know Meg better than anyone. She won't forgive me, and I don't blame her." I disconnect and head back inside.

We head home that evening. After her parents questioning me, Ash decided she didn't want to spend the weekend here, and that suited me just fine because being here and playing happy couples seems alien. "Who called you earlier?" asks Ash, staring out the window.

"Matt."

"What did he want?"

"Are you always going to want to dissect every conversation I have?" I ask, irritated by her constant questions.

"Dan, you're going through a divorce, and I don't want to be kept in the dark."

"Divorce?" I repeat, frowning. "We've not spoken about that."

"But it's the next step."

I grip the steering wheel tighter. I hadn't thought that far ahead. "It's been a few nights. We're not at that stage of the breakup."

She folds her arms, and I feel the frosty attitude filling the small space between us. "Drop me off here," she says as we pass a bar.

"What?"

"I need a night away from your drama."

I pull in. "Why are you so mad with me?"

She unfastens her seatbelt. "It's just a lot," she snaps. "You, Meg, it's all just a lot."

She gets out the car, and I ask, "So, you're going to drink the night away?"

She leans in. "I'm going to be a student for one night. I miss it." Then she slams the door. I pull off angrily, cutting off another car, who beeps me until I flip him off.

I drive until I reach home. Not the home I now have with Ash, but my home. I turn off the engine and stare at the house. All the lights are out apart from the small glow of the living room lamp. It's after nine, and Izzy will be in bed. I get out and approach the door, almost putting my key in the lock before remembering. Instead, I gently knock so as not to wake Izzy. After a few seconds, the door opens and Meg gasps, clearly not expecting me.

"I know I should've called," I admit. Matt appears behind Meg and anger instantly prickles my skin. He looks smug, and my fists curl into tight balls, itching to fight. "Can we talk?"

"Now's not a good time," she replies, and I notice even her voice sounds sad.

"Because he's here?" I ask, arching a brow.

She folds her arms and rests against the doorframe. "Fine. Talk."

"I can't come in?"

She shakes her head. "No."

"I'm still paying for it," I remind her, and she rolls her eyes. "And we're still married."

"Is that all you needed to say?" she asks.

"Meg, be reasonable."

Matt scoffs, shaking his head. "I'll go," he begins.

"No," snaps Meg. "My life doesn't revolve around you anymore, Dan. You can't just drop in and expect me to change my plans."

"I didn't know you'd be busy."

"Of course, why would you think for one minute I'd have a life? Because I'm always here, aren't I? Ready for you to pick up and drop whenever you feel like it."

"Jesus," I mutter, shaking my head to myself. "This is what I mean, I can't talk to you."

"Then stop trying," she says clearly. "Take a hint."

"We have shit to talk about," I yell, and she glances around to check there's nobody about. "I want to see my daughter. And we have to talk about a divorce." The words tumble out before I register them, and Meg gasps again, her eyes filling with more pain.

"Daddy?" Izzy stands on the bottom step, rubbing her eyes. "Why are you yelling?"

I shove past Meg and pull Izzy to me, burying my nose into her hair and inhaling. I missed her baby smell. "I'm sorry," I whisper, and she wraps her arms around me too. "I'm so sorry."

I hear Meg tell Matt that she'll be fine, and then the door closes. I'm relieved when I turn around to find him gone.

ASHLEY

"You're mad at the guy for being sad he's lost his wife?" asks Lauren, arching her brow.

"I love him," I argue, "and he loves me. This isn't just a fling anymore." She rolls her eyes. "Stop fucking judging me," I yell.

"What do you want me to say, Ashley? You stomped into his marriage and ripped him away from it. His life's falling apart and that's on you."

"That's a little harsh," says Luis. "You can't take a married man who's happy."

"Jesus, don't make excuses. If she hadn't come along and flirted her arse off, he'd still be very happy."

"Luis has a point," says Molly. "If he was truly happy, he wouldn't have entertained Ash."

"Thank you," I say, giving Lauren a smug smile.

"Fine, whatever, but don't sit here crying because he's trying to navigate his way through a messy breakup."

"It wouldn't be messy if she just did the decent thing and threw his clothes out, then hit him with divorce papers like a normal scorned wife," I mutter with a tone of bitterness.

"It's the kid I feel sorry for," says Jared, and I glare at him. Everyone is now silent.

"You didn't say he had a kid," snaps Lauren accusingly.

"I didn't know," I argue.

"Bullshit." Jared laughs. "He talks about his kid in lectures. Plus, he's got a photo on his desk."

"Well, I didn't notice," I hiss.

"Wow. You really are a piece of work," Lauren mutters. "And what about Jax? Weren't you sleeping with him a few weeks ago?"

"Dan got jealous, and that's how we ended up here. It pushed us closer together."

"No, you ended up here because his wife caught you fucking on his couch," snaps Lauren. "Do you think she'd know if she hadn't walked in on you?"

"He'd have told her eventually."

"No, he wouldn't," she screeches, laughing. "You're so fucking stupid. He'd still be very much married while sleeping with you on the side. He had his cake, and he was eating it. How the fuck his wife didn't beat the shit out of you is a miracle."

"Do you think he'll keep his job?" asks Molly, and I shrug.

"His bitch wife had me sacked from the waitressing job I had," I tell her.

Lauren shakes her head. "Poor you, how awful that his wife was upset you were screwing her husband." Her voice is dripping in sarcasm.

"Stop trying to play down our relationship, Lauren. I love him, and he loves me. We didn't mean to hurt her, but sometimes love is cruel."

She scoffs. "You really believe the bullshit you spout."

"If you can't be happy for us, stop taking my calls. I don't need your negativity."

She laughs, picking up her bag. "You know what, Ash? Fine, and for the record, it's not negativity, it's realism. I am a realist, and your relationship will not last. He's using you because he's been kicked out of his home. That doesn't mean he's going to set up home with you. Once he recovers from this nightmare, he'll either go back to his wife or move on. Don't come crying to me when that happens." She storms out.

"I need shots, and lots of them," I mutter.

MEG

Dan takes Izzy back to bed and reads her another story, while I take the time to relax and gather my thoughts. Him turning up unexpected threw me, and unlike our last meeting, I have to remain calm and get the answers I need.

I hear him approach and turn off the television. "You got a new couch," he mutters, running his fingers over the back of it.

I nod. "I didn't want Izzy sitting on it."

"I'm so sorry," he says. "If I could take it back—"

"Sit down, Dan." My voice sounds strong, way stronger than I'm currently feeling. He lowers into the armchair. "Start from the beginning. I need it all." He shifts uncomfortably. "I'm not going to get mad," I add, "I just need to get it all straight in my head because you caught me so off guard, I haven't processed any of it."

"What exactly do you want to know?"

I pause, thinking over his question. "Did you make the first move? And be honest. I don't need any more lies."

He shakes his head. "No. I don't think I did." He frowns. "She was a little flirty after class sometimes, but I didn't think anything of it. Some of the girls that age are like that. We ended up going for some dinner after class. It felt weird, but after a few glasses of wine, I relaxed. After dinner, she kissed me on the cheek, and I told her I was happily married. I said she was out of order." He sighs. "But I can't deny I felt a buzz," he admits. "She's young, attractive, and she came on to me. I was flattered, I guess, but I pushed it to the back of my mind. Then me and you argued at Zoe's party, and I was going to the office, I swear, but I had a few more drinks, and Ash was waitressing-"

"I asked about the dinner, and you lied to me. You knew right from that moment it was more, Dan, or else why would you lie? She was the waitress Zoe told me about, the one you left with?"

He nods and more hurt fills my already broken heart. I knew back then something wasn't right. "It was just friendly chatter and she offered me the couch. One thing led to another." He looks away, his expression one of shame. "We didn't have sex. We just fooled around, and I left before she woke up because I couldn't face her. I was ashamed and guilty. I came home, and we made up."

"I knew," I whisper, clutching my hands to my chest. "I had this feeling, but I couldn't bring myself to just ask. So, I sent you back to bed to sleep off your hangover, and I made you breakfast when you woke. Then I sent you off to meet with Matt because I thought maybe he could talk to you about whatever was making you act weird." I groan, burying my face in my hands as those memories come flooding back and I realise how deep his lies were running.

He stares down at his feet. "I told Matt, and he said to keep it to myself."

My head snaps up to glare at him. "What?" My heart hammers harder in my chest.

"He said it would only cause you hurt, and because I didn't plan on doing anything with Ash, there was no point."

I take a shaky breath and release it slowly. *Why are all the men around me betraying me?* "Then you told me you wanted another child," I say, and he nods, wincing. "But you didn't. Not really?" He shakes his head. "It was out of guilt?" He nods and a sob escapes me. I cover my mouth and try to get myself together. Dan moves to sit closer, but I shake my head. "No," I say firmly, "you don't get to comfort me."

He nods once and falls back into his seat. "I'm not fucking proud, Meg. I hate myself for what I've done."

"What happened next?" I feel ill from the torment of knowing, but a sick part of me needs it all.

"We argued again, and Zoe told you about seeing me and Ash together-"

"Which you denied, told me I was acting crazy. You narcissistic shitbag."

"I panicked. I didn't plan on seeing her like that again. It was just a mistake, and I couldn't lose you over it, so I lied. I went to a bar near the uni and met with a colleague, Jay."

"At least that wasn't a lie," I mutter.

"But Ash came into that bar with her friends, and we got talking. We ended up back at hers." He buries his face in his hands.

I nod slowly, realising what he means. "So, the night I tried to call you because our daughter was ill, you were having sex with her?"

"I hate myself for it," he repeats, hanging his head in what looks like shame. I can't stop the tears as they flow freely down my cheeks. "I vowed I'd end it. I was determined to stop and concentrate on you and Izzy. So, I went to see her—"

"When?"

He briefly closes his eyes like he knows I'm not going to like the answer. "When we got home." It dawns on me it was the time he left to pick up papers from work. "The guilt was eating me alive, and I had to see her to tell her . . . but then I . . . well, it didn't go to plan."

"Things felt better after then," I say, frowning. "I'd convinced myself it was all in my head and you were back to normal."

"Ash made it clear she was happy to be the other woman," he mutters.

I cry harder, rubbing my chest. "Wow, how accommodating. And so, you carried on with her, and I was blissfully unaware. After the charity function with my parents, you went to her?" I think back to that night and frown. "You were at the bar with her," I say, and his expression changes to something I don't recognise. Embarrassment? "You were standing so close to her, and I thought it was weird." My mind races to picture them together. "I didn't really think too much about it because she was so young. Really young. Her face was flushed, and you were . . ." My mouth falls open. "Did you . . . oh my god, were you and her . . . at the bar, were you two doing something?"

"Meg, I am so sorry," he cries, diving from the chair to grab my hand. I pull it away, recoiling with disgust.

"I feel sick," I mutter, getting up and rushing into the kitchen. I lean over the sink, heaving, but nothing comes out as I sob uncontrollably. I feel him in the doorway watching me as I wipe my mouth on the back of my hand. "I told you I was pregnant that night."

"I know. I went to her house to tell her I couldn't carry on seeing her."

"Have you ever fucking heard of a text message?" I snap. "Because every time you went to her, you never managed to end things. It just progressed more."

"I ended it, Meg. I told her you were pregnant, and she was angry. She kicked me out."

"So, she ended it," I cry, "not you."

"No."

"You spent the entire day with her, Dan, so you never went there to end it," I say, recalling how he told me he was helping a friend. "Stop fucking lying to me."

"Her parents turned up, and I was roped into staying there. But after they left, it became apparent she was looking at us differently. She wanted more than I could give, so I told her about the baby, and we ended it."

"You met her parents?" I wail.

"Not intentionally."

I take a steadying breath and pinch the bridge of my nose before asking, "How did she end up in my house on my couch with my husband?"

"She came to talk to me, to convince me we could still work."

"And she convinced you well enough to fuck her in our marital home with my daughter right up there," I yell, pointing to the ceiling.

"Meg, I know I've messed up. I am so fucking stupid, and I don't deserve another chance but—"

"Don't say it," I hiss. "Don't fucking ask me to forgive you."

"We're having a baby," he says. "And we have Iz."

"Having Izzy didn't stop you before and another child won't stop you again. Christ, Dan, you just sat there and told me you were planning on keeping the whole thing a secret because she was willing to be your bit on the side. That's not fucking okay. I deserve a man who loves me."

He walks towards me. "I love you. I have always loved you."

"No," I snap, shoving him back. "If you did, this would never have happened."

"Baby, please don't do this."

"There you go again," I shout, "blaming me. I haven't done this to us, Dan. You have. You cheated on me and Izzy. You left us for her. I can't imagine my life without you," I say, a sob escaping, "but because of what you've done, I have no choice."

"This can't be it," he whispers desperately. "I fucked up one time."

"Jesus, Dan, you're living with her. You got caught and you fucking left with her," I cry.

"You asked me to leave. I didn't want to go."

I shake my head in anger. "You must've known it would be over the second you broke our vows."

"I know it's going to be hard to get you to trust me again, Meg. I am fully prepared to do whatever it takes to make this right."

I can't believe the audacity of him right now. I frown, taking a breath before trying to lay this all out clearly for him. "Are you seriously asking me for another chance after everything you've just told me?" I give an empty laugh. "I caught you having sex with another woman in our home," I add, shaking my head in disbelief. "You've spent the last few months sneaking around, making me think I was the crazy one. You even turned it around on me, fully gaslighted me knowing I was getting closer to the truth. And even if I wanted to forgive you, I can't, because I will never get the image of you and her fucking on my couch out of my head. You are not the man I married. I don't know you anymore."

He grabs my arm. "You do," he says, wiping a stray tear from his own cheek. "I'm still me. I just fucked up." He pulls me closer and places his hand on my stomach. I stare at it, letting the tears flow down my face. My body shakes from exhaustion and pain. and right now, I feel the urge to curl up in bed and never come out. "I betrayed you in the worst possible way," he continues, but I've already shut his words out because I don't want to hear them anymore. "But you do know me, I just got a little lost."

I scoff. "The Dan I married would have never in a million years made me hurt the way I am right now. He wouldn't have lied. In fact, he wouldn't have even looked at another woman." I pull free. "You should go now."

He straightens, squaring his shoulder and wiping his face with his hands. "I spoke to a guy who went through divorce," he says, "and I don't have to leave this house."

I smile sadly. "Fine. Stay. But I won't be here, and neither will Izzy."

"You'd rather tear her from her home than stay here with me?"

"I don't want to be near you right now. I don't want to look at you, and I certainly don't want to hear your fucking excuses and bullshit apologies."

"Maybe I won't let you take Izzy," he threatens, arching a brow.

I laugh, and it's cold and empty. "Try it, Dan. Try taking my daughter. You'll see a whole different side to me." I take a step closer, anger coursing through my veins. He gives me a wary look. "Don't threaten me because I refuse to fall at your feet and take you back."

"I just want us to go back to how we were," he mumbles, hanging his head.

I sigh. "I'm tired. I want you to leave. I'm seeing my parents tomorrow and I have to be up early."

"Have you told them?"

I shake my head. "But I will. And you should call your mother. She keeps ringing me and asking for you because you're ignoring her calls. I'm running out of excuses."

I walk him to the door, and he turns, taking my chin in his fingers and forcing me to look at him. "I'm not giving up on us." He kisses my cheek, and I recoil, shuddering. I know without a doubt, I can never let him touch me again.

Twelve

DAN

Ash crawls into bed, and I glance at the clock. It's almost four in the morning. She slides her hand up my back and over my waist, snuggling behind me. "I'm sorry," she whispers, but I remain silent. She pushes her hand into my boxers, and I grab her wrist, removing it. "Come on, Dan. I said I'm sorry."

"Go to sleep," I mutter, pulling the sheet farther up my body.

———

I'm making breakfast when Ash surfaces looking worse for wear. She grabs a glass of water and downs it. "Eggs?" I ask, and she glares at me, shuddering. I smirk. "Maybe next time, don't drink so much."

She rolls her eyes. "I thought we could do something together today?"

"I just want to watch films and chill." My life is falling apart, and the last thing I want to do is play happy families with Ashley.

"You always want to hide away," she mutters. "Why can't we do something away from this house?"

"Like?" I ask, sighing.

"I need to go into town and get an outfit."

I groan. I've never been a fan of shopping—Meg always did that shit alone. "I'd rather not."

"We're going out tonight, so maybe you could grab a new outfit too."

I frown. "Going out?"

"It's Jared's birthday."

I laugh. "You want me to go to a birthday party for a student from the uni? We still have to hide our relationship, Ash. I can't flaunt us around."

"Why? I'm not your student anymore, and you've left your wife."

"I need this job if I've got to provide for Meg, Izzy, and a newborn."

"And you think perfect Meg isn't going to tell her father?" She laughs. I hadn't thought of that, and I pull out my mobile to text her. Ash snatches it. "Fuck, Dan, we're having a conversation here. There's only a small group of my friends going, and they already know about us, and it's not a party, it's drinks in a bar. So, we're going shopping, you're buying me a new outfit, and we're going together because, quite frankly, I'm sick of staying home like a boring married couple." She stomps off, taking my phone with her.

I sigh heavily. She's forgetting that's exactly what I am—a boring married father of one, soon to be two. I groan. *What the hell have I done?*

————

We go from shop to shop, where Ash tries on hundreds of outfits that all look similar. I'm slowly losing my mind when she calls me into another change room. I pull back the curtain, and she spins slowly, showing off the purple lace bra and panties she's wearing. "I'm not ready," she whispers, laughing. I step in, pulling the curtain across.

"If you're going to continue to torture me, the least you could do is make it worth my while," I say, pushing her against the mirror. She wastes no time pulling my erection free from my jeans and hooking her leg around my waist. I reach into my back pocket, pulling my wallet. "I'm prepared," I joke, taking out the condom.

She frowns. "I'm on the pill."

"I know, but we should still take precautions."

"We've had sex without a condom before."

"Right, but now we have one, so let's use it. You don't want kids, remember?"

She rubs my cock, and I close my eyes. "Maybe kids with you wouldn't be so bad."

Alarm bells ring in my head and my eyes shoot open. "Ash, we're using the condom," I say clearly.

She drops her leg to the floor, releasing my erection. "I've changed my mind," she mutters, turning away from me and reaching for the dress she was about to try on. I tuck myself away and step out, leaving the shop completely. *Fuck this bullshit.*

I head in the direction of the pub Matt and I used to meet up in. I spot him at the bar drinking a pint and watching football. I stand beside him as the barman pours my pint without asking me, and Matt groans. "I wanted a quiet pint on my own."

"Liar. You miss our Saturday catch-ups."

"Like a fucking hole in the head."

I pay for my drink. "I told Meg everything."

"I know," he says, staring at the television. It pisses me off she rushed to tell him, but I push the feeling down. If I ever want Meg to forgive me, I need him on side.

"What did she say?"

He glances at me. "You mean between sobbing and vomiting?"

"She's sick?"

"No, dickhead, she's pregnant. I don't want to have this conversation with you, Dan. I won't be your spy or your way back into her heart, so if that's why you're here, fuck off."

"I thought you'd be with her."

"I would," he says, turning to face me, "but some fucker told her I knew everything."

"I never said you knew everything," I tell him, smirking. "I told her the truth."

"Making her even sadder than she already was, because now, she doesn't trust me either."

I shrug. "You told me to keep it from her." I don't see his fist coming until it's already connected, knocking me on my arse. I grip my jaw and give my head a shake. "Fuck."

He towers over me. "I was trying to stop you breaking her heart, but you did it anyway, and you couldn't stand the thought of me comforting her, so you screwed me over too. Fuck you, Dan."

The barman looks over the bar, and I hold up my hand to show I'm fine. "No more," he mutters before going back to serving.

"She's my wife, Matt. You're all over her like a disease."

"You're scared I'll steal her?" He sneers. "You're a joke. Do you think she'll spend her life single? There will always be someone waiting to jump in there to be the man you couldn't be, because she's fucking it, Dan. She's the woman you settle down with. She's the woman you make your wife and hold on to. You fucked up, and now, you get to watch her life play out without you. And I can't fucking wait."

I push to stand. "I'm going to win her back," I say with confidence, and he laughs hard. "I am."

"You don't stand a chance."

"Because you're going to get there first?" I ask, glaring at him.

"Some of us are respectful. I don't want to jump in the bed

you just vacated. I want to be there for her because she's my friend and you destroyed her life."

He sits down, taking a drink from his pint, and I take the stool beside him. "I know I fucked up, Matt . . . and I know I'm a dick." I take a drink.

"I won't tell you anything about Meg."

"I know."

"And I don't want to know about Ash. Don't put me in the middle of this."

"I won't." And just like that, we've reached a new kind of calm.

———

I watch Ash as she slips into her new dress. She looks good, even though it's aluminous yellow, super short, and has a chuck missing at her waist. She checks herself in the mirror. "What do you think?"

"You look amazing." She called me right after she finished at the clothes stores, and we met back up for lunch. Neither of us mentioned our earlier spat, and I don't intend to.

"Are you sure you won't wear the shirt?" she asks. I smirk, shaking my head. She got me a shirt to match her dress, and it was a definite no. "Thank you," she adds, standing before me and taking my hands. "For making the effort with my friends."

"No problem. Just know, if they start chugging beer kegs, I'm done."

She laughs, and I stand. "You're going to relive your youth," she says, grinning and adding a cheeky wink. I swat her arse for her cheek, and we head out.

MEG

I answer the door to find Matt holding up a takeout bag. "I come with apologies and Chinese."

I open the door wider and stomp back into the living room. I'm upset he lied to me and encouraged Dan to lie. I hear him banging plates in the kitchen but remain seated. Morning sickness has hit me hard today, and I don't have the energy to do anything.

He returns, handing me a tray piled up with food. It smells delicious and my stomach growls in appreciation. "Before we eat," he begins, "I want to say how sorry I am."

"You already said that," I mutter.

"But I am, Meg. I honestly did it with the best intentions to protect you. I thought he'd just kissed her and fooled around a bit. He swore it was nothing and he wasn't going back there. I didn't know anything about the affair. I told him he was an idiot."

"You hurt me, Matt. I thought you had my back."

"I do, Meg. I swear, I do. Which is why I should tell you I saw him today."

My heart skips a beat. "Where?"

"He turned up at the pub. I hit him."

I smirk. "You did?"

"Hard enough to knock him on his arse."

I smile wide. "For me?"

"I hate what he's done to you and Izzy, and I hate I was a small part of that. I won't ever lie to you again, and I won't ever cover for him."

"At the end of the day, he was the one who lied and cheated. I get you were trying to protect me."

"I just hate the thought of you guys ending. You were solid. It gave me hope that I'd find that one day."

I tuck into the Chinese and hum in approval. "One day, Matt, you'll meet the perfect woman for you."

"That might be quite hard actually," he mutters, and I wait for him to explain as he fidgets. "I'm gay."

I almost choke on the rice, coughing violently. "Huh?"

He laughs nervously. "Not quite the reaction I hoped for."

I move my tray to the table. "Sorry," I say, wiping my eyes. "You caught me off guard. Shit, Matt, I never knew."

"I've been in denial a long time," he admits.

"Am I a shit friend?" I ask. "That you weren't able to come and tell me?"

He grabs my hand and gives it a gentle squeeze. "Not at all. Like I said, it's taken me a while to accept it myself."

"How did you know?" I ask, and he laughs. "Sorry, is that a stupid question?"

"No, it's a popular one. I think I've always known, but I ignored it. I had a few flings back in university, but I always felt ashamed after, worried what everyone would think and too afraid to be different. My parents are old fashioned. They hate the modern world and often comment that kids are confused because we allow them to be. They see it as a phase."

"You've told them?"

He shakes his head. "No. I can't bring myself too. But I've met someone."

I gasp. "Matt, that's fantastic."

"It's made me realise what I want. My parents may never know. They're in their seventies, and I'm happy letting them believe I'm just single. But Carl . . . well, he thinks I should be honest, so I can be happy."

"Would you be happier if they knew? Honestly?"

"Maybe." He shrugs. "I hate the lies and secrets, and I would love for them to meet Carl."

ASHLEY

I throw my arms around Dan, and he pulls away slightly. "Don't be boring," I complain, but I know I'm pushing his buttons. He's uncomfortable and it shows. He's hardly spoken a word all evening, and he's made no effort to interact with anyone.

"You go and dance. It's not my thing."

I scowl. "Fine." I go over to where the girls are dancing and groan when Jax comes stumbling over.

"You didn't call," he says accusingly.

I glance in Dan's direction, relieved to see him talking to Luis. "Sorry, I've been preoccupied."

"And you're never in class anymore."

"I dropped it," I say. "Sort of. I changed to another."

"Because of me?"

"Don't be silly. I just wasn't feeling that class."

Molly giggles, leaning in. "She was feeling the teacher instead."

I nudge her, and Jax glares at me. "You and Headford?"

"It's not a big deal."

"Like hell it isn't. I thought we were a thing?" he yells, and a few people nearby look our way. I catch Dan's eye, who's now watching us with concern. Jax follows my line of sight and growls angrily, marching towards Dan, who rises to his feet. Jax tries to punch him but misses, crashing into the table and knocking drinks everywhere.

I groan, rushing over. "What the hell?" I cry as Jax climbs to his feet.

"You fucking used me," he yells.

"Now is not the time," I hiss, fully aware that he's about to tell Dan what happened between us.

"I thought you liked me," he continues, and I see Dan stiffen out the corner of my eye.

"It was nothing," I say to Dan.

"You told me you liked me, Ash," snaps Jax. "And then you ghost me for this old fucker?"

"Careful," Dan warns.

"Fuck you, pervert," spits Jax.

Dan shoves him. "Go home, Jaxon. You're drunk."

Jax laughs. "It's the weekend. It's what us young'uns do."

"I'm warning you, walk away," Dan says firmly.

"Fuck off, grandad." Dan rears back and punches Jax, knocking him back onto the table and into the broken glass. He storms off, ignoring me when I call his name.

Jax's hands are bleeding, and I crouch down to check them. "Jesus," I mutter, "you need to get these checked."

"Don't worry about me. Go after lover boy."

I glance over my shoulder, and Dan is nowhere to be seen. "I think I'll leave him to cool off. Come on, up you get."

––––––––

The hospital accident and emergency department is busy, mainly with idiots like us who drank too much and got injured. Back at the bar, the doormen gave first aid and wrapped Jax's hands, but they need washing properly to remove the small shards of glass. "Thanks for waiting with me," he says.

"What were you thinking?"

He shrugs. "I just really like you, Ash. I mean, what do you see in him anyway?"

"I'm not going to talk about me and Dan with you," I mutter. "Just be happy for me."

"He'll lose his job."

"Not if no one tells the vice chancellor."

"You mean his father-in-law doesn't know?"

I shake my head. "I don't think his ex will say anything. She needs Dan's money."

"Well, when he breaks your heart, which he will, I'll be here."

––––––––

By the time I walk in the front door, it's five in the morning. I'm tired and pissed-off, and I'm not surprised when I find Dan waiting up for me in the kitchen. "Where have you been?" he asks, rushing to me and cupping my face in his hands. "I've been worried sick."

I throw my bag to the side. "At the hospital."

"Why? Are you hurt?" he asks, looking concerned.

"No, Jax was, remember?"

His hands drop to his sides. "You went to the hospital with him?"

"Yes. What the hell were you thinking shoving him like that and then punching him in the face?"

"He deserved it."

I pinch the bridge of my nose. "Do you know why I never settle for boys my own age, Dan? Because they're immature. And right now, you remind me of them."

"You forgot to mention you were sleeping with him," he says, grabbing my bag and searching through it. I try to snatch it, but he pulls out my mobile.

"Now, you're checking my phone?" I snap.

"You've clearly not been honest."

"Coming from you?" I ask, laughing. "The guy who got his wife pregnant while sleeping with me?"

"Is that why you did it, to pay me back?"

"No!" I snap, angrily.

Allie pads into the kitchen, rubbing her eyes and yawning. "Can you guys keep it down?"

"Gladly," snaps Dan, storming off upstairs, and I roll my eyes.

"Look, Ash, we really need to talk about this situation," she says, sitting down at the table.

"I know it's not ideal—"

"You never asked if he could move in."

"He hasn't," I mutter. "That's not what's happening. He just needed a place to stay."

"Look, his time is up. I've tried to be nice, but I'm sick of being woken in the night by you either fighting or fucking."

"I'll talk to him. We'll be more considerate." The last thing I want is to send him back to his wife.

She shakes her head. "Either he goes alone or you go together, either way, I want a quiet house by this evening."

———

Dan's in bed. I sit on the edge, and he opens his eyes. "Allie wants us out."

"Us or me?"

"Either or," I mutter, shrugging. "I don't blame her. All we do is fight."

"I'll try and find somewhere to stay," he says.

"I was thinking we could find a place together." There's hope in my voice, but he quashes my idea by shaking his head with a smirk.

"Not happening. You just said yourself that all we do is fight."

"We need our own space," I try.

"We need space," he corrects. "The fun has suddenly gone, and we'll never get that back if we rush things."

"I feel like you're trying to break up with me."

He sighs, gently wrapping his hand around my neck and pulling me in for a kiss. "I'm mad you fucked Jax. I haven't been that jealous in a long time, Ash, but last night, I realised we're rushing this because of my situation. But we can slow it down and get things back on track." I climb over him. "That's a good start," he says, grinning.

DAN

I shower and dress in record time, but it's not quick enough to escape Ash's clutches. She stretches out on the bed, letting the sheets slide down her naked body. "Where are you sneaking off to?"

I can't tell her the truth because I don't need the argument right now, but knowing I have to find somewhere to live means I have to get my arse in gear and sort my shit out. "The gym," I tell her.

"Shall we meet for lunch after?" I nod, kissing her on the cheek and heading out.

I drive over to Meg's, noting Matt's car is parked outside. I pull onto the driveway, loving how familiar it feels. Meg answers the door, and I take in the silk night dress and her messed-up hair. I've always found her sexy first thing in the morning. "You're back so soon," she mutters with no enthusiasm.

"I need a place to stay," I tell her, and she laughs.

Her smile fades when she sees I'm serious. "And you expect me to let you come back here?"

"No, of course not, but we need to think about how we're going to move forward."

"It's nine in the morning, Dan. Can we do this some other time?"

"The house is worth a fortune. We could sell and split it, or I could buy you out." Matt appears behind Meg in his boxers and a T-shirt. I scowl. "This looks cosy." Matt smirks. "So, he's staying over to support you now?"

"I'm not doing this," says Meg, starting to push the door closed.

Seeing them together has pissed me off. The thought she might have moved on scares the hell out of me, so I stick my foot in, and she glares at me. "Your bed isn't even cold yet," I snap.

She grins. "Yours was never cold, was it, Dan?"

"I deserve to know if you two are a thing."

Matt rolls his eyes. "Get a grip, Dan."

"I don't owe you anything," she snaps. "You left, remember? Text me your address," she says, changing the subject. "I'll have the divorce papers drawn up."

"Just like that?" I ask angrily, my hope vanishing fast. "I'm going to see a solicitor for advice tomorrow, Meg. You're not kicking me out of a house I'm paying for, only to move him in."

————

By the time I get back to Ash's, I'm raging. She takes one look at me and sighs. "You didn't go to the gym."

"I went to see Meg," I admit, grabbing a bottle of water from the fridge. "She's got Matt sleeping there."

"So?"

"So, he's our friend, and now, he's in my wife's bed." She arches a brow, and I'm aware it sounds bad, but I'm too angry to stop the words flowing. "She can't keep me out of that house. I pay for it."

"So, you're gonna move back in?"

"Yes." I go upstairs and grab my bag from under Ash's bed. She stands in the doorway, watching as I pack my clothes.

"This is crazy. I don't know how I feel about you going back there."

I turn to her, pulling her close and kissing her with everything I have. "Why should I pay for it and have to go flat hunting for myself?"

"Because you cheated?"

"Marriages break up all the time. I'm missing Izzy, I have no home, all because I fell for someone else. I'm taking that house back. There are two spare rooms."

"I don't want you to go back there."

"I'll spend most of my time here with you," I promise. "It doesn't change anything." I kiss her again and grab my bag. "I'll call you later, and we'll meet for dinner." I rush off before she can protest anymore.

I find my spare house key in the glove compartment of the car, and I smile triumphantly. Let's see how Meg moves on with me breathing down her neck twenty-four-seven.

I let myself in to find the house empty, so I go upstairs and unpack my shit in the spare room next to Izzy's. Then I head downstairs and prepare dinner. I never cooked, only on special occasions like Mother's Day or Meg's birthday, but this is my chance to show Meg I can change.

By the time she walks in, the roast dinner is fully under way. Izzy rushes to me, throwing herself into my arms, as Meg stands in the doorway glaring at me. "Izzy, go and wash your hands," she says firmly, and I place her down so she can go to the bathroom. "What are you doing here?"

I point to the oven. "I'm cooking dinner."

"Why?"

"I've moved back in."

She inhales sharply. "Tell me this is a joke, Dan, because I know you wouldn't just do that without talking to me first."

"I tried to talk to you earlier."

She moves closer, bracing her hands on the worktop. "You are *not* moving back in here."

"I already have. Don't worry, I took a spare room."

Tears fill her eyes. "It's like you enjoy torturing me," she almost whispers.

I feel a pang of guilt, but she'll soon see I'm not here to hurt her but to heal her. "That's not what I'm trying to do, Meg."

"Then leave," she hisses.

"I can't do that."

"You had no trouble doing that a few days ago." She takes a shaky breath. "My heart is in tiny pieces because of you, and now, you want to live here like we're best friends?"

"We were once."

She squeezes her eyes shut, and when she opens them, tears trickle down her cheeks. "I'm begging you . . . leave."

"No."

She sighs, pushing off the counter and heading upstairs. I wait a few beats before following, curious to what her next move will be. She grabs a suitcase from the top of her wardrobe. "Don't do that," I say, moving quick to take it from her.

"Dan," she hisses, trying to remain calm for Izzy's sake.

"Please," I beg. "Don't do that."

"What choice do I have?" she whispers angrily.

"Just stay. I know everything is raw right now, but it won't always feel like that."

She stares at me in disbelief, and my braveness wavers. "I don't think you even realise what you've done," she whispers. "You're fucking delusional."

I grab her hands. "I'm not, I swear. I know exactly what I've done, but it makes sense to be around each other. We can see how we really feel about one another."

She rips her hands from mine. "Are you serious? I don't

need to be around you to know I fucking hate you, Daniel. I absolutely, one hundred percent, hate you."

I shake my head. "You're hurt and angry."

"Damn right, I am. And then you walk back in here like everything is going to be fine. I don't want to look at you. I don't want to breathe the same air as you, and if you dropped dead tomorrow, I'd dance on your grave."

"You don't mean that."

"Try me."

"Izzy is used to having me around."

"Izzy doesn't know what you did."

I kick the bedroom door closed in case she wanders in. "I am trying," I growl. "I want to make this right."

She wipes her eyes and forces a cold smile. "Okay," she says, nodding. "So, you've finished things with her?"

I hesitate, and she laughs. "Of course," I lie.

She holds out her hand. "Let me call her."

"Don't be stupid."

"You said those words to me before," she mutters, sniffling. "When I asked you if you were up to no good. And guess what, I was right."

"Fine, I haven't exactly told her because I was avoiding the headache, but in my mind, it's done with. I'll tell her later." She slaps me. It's hard, and I wince as it burns my cheek.

She clutches her hand to her chest and more tears fall. "You must think I'm fucking stupid. You're keeping her on in case we don't work out. In case I send you packing," she hisses.

I take a calming breath. Meg doesn't have a violent bone in her body, so the slap was completely out of character. It dawns on me that I've pushed her to this, and I sigh. "Look, I don't want to hurt you anymore," I say, raising my hand carefully to cup her jaw. I stroke my thumb over her wet cheek, and she briefly closes her eyes, leaning into my touch. "But please don't make any rash decisions tonight when you're upset. Let's sleep on this and talk tomorrow."

She steps away from my touch. "I have a headache. I need to lie down."

I nod, placing the suitcase back in its place, relieved she's staying put for now. I back out the room, adding, "I'll save you some dinner."

"Don't bother."

MEG

I lie in my bed, wondering when this pain will end. Or when I'll stop feeling the sickness in the pit of my stomach whenever I see Dan or hear his name. I hate him, I'm certain of that. I can't sleep without seeing his hands gripping her waist, covering her modesty after she'd fucked him on our couch.

His words run on repeat in my head, and I spend hours analysing them, coming up with new things I need to say or questions I still have, so I can torture my heart a little more. He's consuming my every thought and feeling, and I hate it.

And I also hate that I don't want to hear from him, yet I check my phone a hundred times a day or more to see if he's texted me, even though when he does, it makes me feel sick again. And most of all, I hate that I can't stop picturing their life together. Do they watch television like we used to? Does he still watch the same things we did? Do they argue in the supermarket over the amount of sweet treats in the shopping basket?

Those are the times my heart cries out for him to come back, and it promises me we can forgive him if he'd just come home. And now he's here, in my home, and I'm kicking myself, wondering why the fuck I didn't change the locks or take his key. Because now he's here, I want him gone. He makes my skin crawl and my heart ache. He says all the wrong things and makes me feel ten times worse. And he didn't drop to his knees and cling to my legs, begging me for forgiveness and promising to stay faithful. And worst of all, he didn't dump her and make her heart ache like mine does.

I fall into a restless sleep, unable to get comfortable. Somewhere in my subconscious, I feel a dull ache in my stomach and I dream of vines growing there, tearing my body open. I wake with a start, half-sitting and looking around the room. It's dark outside, but I can hear Dan in the next room, reading Izzy a story. I grab my phone and see it's six o'clock.

I throw my legs over the edge of the bed and notice blood on the white bedsheets. A dread fills me as I check between my legs and realise I'm drenched there. I rush to the en-suite bathroom and remove my underwear, sitting on the toilet and grabbing a handful of tissue to wipe myself. I stare at the red tissue with a hand over my mouth. This can't be happening. Not on top of everything else.

I shower and dress in comfortable clothes before calling my mum. She always sounds so pleased to hear from me, but this evening, she sounds worried when she answers, probably because I never call her in the evening. "Hey, Mum," I mutter. "Can I ask a favour?"

"Of course. Are you okay?"

"I think I'm having a miscarriage and I need a ride to the hospital."

"Oh my god, are you sure?" I never got to announce my pregnancy. What with everything else going on, I haven't had a chance.

"I did a test a couple weeks back, but now, I'm bleeding. I don't think the hospital can do anything, but I don't know what else to do."

"Sit tight, I'm on my way."

I head downstairs and push my feet into my trainers. Dan comes down minutes later. "I saved you some dinner."

"I'm going out."

He frowns. "Where?"

"That's none of your business anymore. Watch Izzy for me. I'll be back in a few hours." I step outside, as I'd rather wait out here than in there with him.

———

The hospital pretty much confirms my fears. Although they can't be certain until they check my bloods, the chances are it's a miscarriage. They do an internal scan and can't find a small bean with a flicker of a heartbeat, but my womb shows signs there was a pregnancy. They take my bloods to check my hormone levels and tell me to go home and rest.

Mum insists we grab a coffee on our way out, and as we're walking back to the car, she takes a seat on a wooden bench.

"So, what's going on?" I stare blankly, and she tips her head to one side in that knowing way all mums have. "I can tell something's wrong."

Tears threaten to fall again. God, I'm so sick of crying. I sigh. "I just lost my baby."

"That's not it, that hasn't even hit you yet. You look sad and lost. Are things okay with you and Dan?"

I burst into tears, and she quickly places the coffees on the ground and pulls me to her. She stays silent while I sob. "He . . . left . . . me."

She finds a tissue in her pocket and stuffs it in my hand, waiting while I try to compose myself. "What the hell's going on, Meg? What do you mean he's left?"

"Well, he's back now, but he did leave. I caught him with another woman. Today, he came back and moved into the spare room."

"Oh Meg," she whispers, rubbing my back. "Why didn't you tell me?"

"I was trying to process it, and I guess a small part of me didn't want to say it out loud because then it would be true."

"How's Izzy coping?"

"She cried the first few nights. She was just starting to settle again, and he decided to come back."

"Does he want to try again? Do you?"

I shake my head. "No and no. He's still with her while telling me he's sorry."

"Do you think all this is why . . ." She nods to my stomach, and I gently rub it. "The stress and all?"

I shrug. "I guess we'll never know."

We drive back to my house in silence, and when she pulls up outside, she asks if I'd like her to come in and remove Dan from the house. I smile because for a short woman, she's feisty. "How about I come over tomorrow and have lunch with you? We can talk about it more?" I suggest, and she nods, kissing me on the cheek.

Dan is watching the television when I get in. He glances my way in irritation. "It's almost two in the morning," he says, arching a brow.

"I'm surprised you didn't move your girlfriend in while I was gone," I mutter, kicking off my trainers.

"Where does a pregnant woman go until this time?" he asks.

"I really can't do this with you now," I tell him, heading to the stairs.

I feel him rush up behind me and turn just as he makes a grab for my wrist. I frown. He's never been aggressive, although he would get into jealous rages back when we first dated. "I know you weren't with Matt. I called him."

I sigh heavily. "Why are you checking up on me, Dan? We're not together, remember?"

"Because you're pregnant with my child, and you left me babysitting Izzy with no notice or explanation."

A small laugh escapes me. "Babysitting?" I repeat. "She's your daughter. You did your fucking job," I snap. "The same job I'm expected to do every second of the day, so you can go about your business uninterrupted, something you've certainly been utilizing well."

"I just want to know who you were with," he says, his tone pleading. It crosses my mind to drag out his curiosity, but then it would make me as childish as him, so I pull out the leaflet the hospital gave me from my bag and shove it hard into his chest. Then I march up to my room, lock the door, and fall onto the bed. Tears don't come—I feel like I've cried them all away over the last few days.

Fourteen

DAN

I stare at the leaflet entitled 'What is miscarriage?' in disbelief before going upstairs and trying the bedroom door. I'm not surprised when I find it locked. My heart hammers in my chest, and I rest my forehead against the cool wood. "Meg, talk to me."

"And say what?" she asks.

"You've lost the baby?"

"Yes, Dan, so you're off the hook. Free to fuck about with who you want, not that it stopped you anyway."

It's hard to breathe, the guilt of everything on top of this choking me. I turn, sliding down the door until my arse hits the floor. "Why didn't you tell me? I would've taken you to the hospital."

"It's not your responsibility. Besides, you were the *babysitter*, remember?"

"Of course, it's my responsibility. You're still my wife, and that's still my baby."

She laughs and it's cold. "Not anymore."

"I'm so sorry," I mumble. My arms itch to hold her and comfort her. "Do you need anything?"

"For you to leave."

"No, Meg. You need me here now more than ever."

The door opens and I fall back, staring up at her enraged face. "I don't need you. Don't pretend you're here for me or Izzy. You're here for yourself because you needed somewhere to stay."

"You should be in bed," I say, ignoring her anger as I push to stand. "Get some rest." She shrugs away from my hand as I try to guide her.

"What's the point? The baby's already gone."

"You're upset—"

"I'm fine."

"You're not fine," I snap, and she jumps at my harsh tone. "You're not fine," I say more calmly, "and that's okay. I'm here to help. I'll take care of Izzy while you rest."

"Izzy," she whispers, frowning. And then she moves around me and goes to Izzy's room. She climbs into bed behind her and curls her body around our daughter, burying her nose in her loose curls. I pull the door closed and head to the spare room with a heavy heart.

————

Morning comes and I go for my run, returning just as Meg is carrying Izzy down the stairs with a pained look on her face. I rush to take her. "You should be resting," I hiss, angry she'd carry Izzy. "Sit down and I'll get you a drink."

"No, thanks. I can manage."

I sigh. I hate the way she's shutting me out. "How are you feeling?" I ask, placing Izzy at the table and grabbing the bread. I pop a slice in the toaster as Meg turns on the coffee machine.

"I slept well for the first time since I caught you," she says, side-eyeing me. "Does that mean I'm healing?"

She keeps trying to pull me into these arguments, but I

refuse to engage. "We should talk," I tell her, "about what's happened."

"There's nothing to discuss."

"Well, do you have to go back to the hospital? Are there more checks, or is there anything they can do?"

"I don't want to talk about this with you. All you need to know is there is no baby."

"This was my child too, Meg. Don't shut me out."

"You shut yourself out, Dan. Don't play the concerned husband now."

"Of course, I'm concerned," I hiss, glancing at Izzy to make sure she's not paying attention. I butter her toast and take it to her, placing the iPad in front of her with her favourite show playing. "I'm hurting too. I've lost a baby too," I say, stepping closer to her.

"You can go and make a new one," she says, her eyes filling with pain. "She's younger than me."

"I'm meeting Ash today. I'm going to make it clear we're done."

Meg shakes her head. "It won't change things between us. The damage is done."

"Couples recover from affairs all the time," I tell her, grabbing her hand. "We can get through this."

"I don't want to recover. I don't want to move forward. Not with you."

Her words burn me, and I drop her hand. She sounds so final. "I told you before, I'm not giving up."

She groans, frustration radiating from her. "Stop trying, Dan. I fucking hate you."

MEG

Izzy takes her last bite of toast, and I take the plate, placing it in the sink. "Let's get you dressed for nursery," I tell her.

"You shouldn't be running around. I'll take Izzy."

"No, thanks. I've got places to be, so I've got it covered."

"There you go again with the 'places to be'," Dan mutters.

"Why do you care all of a sudden?" I ask, scooping Izzy up in my arms. "You didn't care before where I was or who I was with. Do you think I'd be out there, up to no good, after everything that's happened in the last twenty-four hours?"

"No, of course not."

"My life is carrying on the exact same as when you were here. Nothing's changed for me except you're no longer a part of it." I carry Izzy upstairs, only wincing from pain a few times before I set her down in the bathroom and fill the sink with warm water.

"Are you cross with Daddy?" she asks, staring up at me with her beautiful innocent eyes.

I smile sadly, twisting a curl of her hair around my finger. "No, sweety. I'm cross with myself."

ASHLEY

Dan hasn't been into work. I've been past his office numerous times, and I've called at least a dozen times, but every single one went to voicemail. Lindsey gives me a sympathetic smile as her eyes scan the dining room for her new boyfriend. "It's all going to be okay," she mutters, looking disinterested.

"Can Miss Ashley Daulton come to the vice chancellor's office, please?" The Tannoy announcement startles me, and Lindsey's eyes widen.

"Shit. Do you think they'll ask about Dan?"

I'm already shaking as I push to stand. "Surely, he'd have called me. Right?" She shrugs helplessly. "Oh fuck," I mutter.

I get to the office and tell the stern-faced secretary I was asked to come. She checks her notepad and nods, pointing to the office door. "Knock and enter. He's waiting," she says.

Sickness burns my throat as I raise my hand to knock.

"Come in," a voice bellows. It's full of authority, and I can't seem to calm my racing heart as I push the door open.

The vice chancellor is sitting behind his desk. He smiles warmly, then my eyes fall to Jaxon and, suddenly, this all makes sense. "Please, come in and take a seat," says the chancellor, pointing to the leather chair beside Jaxon's. I lower into it. "Don't look so worried, Miss Daulton. You're not in any trouble."

Jaxon's hands are still bandaged and a pang of guilt hits me. "Mr. Wright has brought something to my attention which I need to ask you about. Apparently, you witnessed this assault by one of our faculty members, Mr. Headford."

I glance at Jax, my eyes silently pleading with him not to do this. He shrugs, and I realise he's not going to take this back. I swallow and give a slight nod, focussing my eyes back on the chancellor. "Yes."

He sits a little straighter. "Can you explain what happened?"

"Jax, erm, Mr. Wright was drunk. He yelled at Mr. Headford and fell into a table of glasses."

"Really, Ash, you're just gonna lie for him?"

"You were drunk," I whisper.

"Did you see Mr. Headford push Mr. Wright?" the chancellor asks, more firmly this time. "It's very important you tell me the truth."

Tears burn my eyes as I nod. "But if Jax hadn't been drunk, he wouldn't have fell so hard. Dan . . . I mean, Mr. Headford was just protecting me."

The chancellor narrows his eyes. "Mr. Wright, I need to speak alone with Miss Daulton. I'll call you back in once I've spoken to all the witnesses, but this is a serious accusation, and you should keep it to yourself while I investigate."

Once Jax leaves, the chancellor fixes me with a stare that tells me he's feeling very serious right now. "Is there anything you need to tell me?" I shake my head. "Because now would be the perfect time."

"There's nothing," I lie.

He nods once before dismissing me. The second I step out the office, I breathe a sigh of relief. I head outside and send a text off to Dan.

Me: The chancellor called me into the office. Jax made a complaint about you.

Seconds later, it rings and Dan's name flashes on the screen. I cancel the call. How fucking dare he respond to that but not my other messages?

———

I get home and Allie is cooking dinner. "Lover boy is upstairs waiting for you," she tells me, and a thrill goes through me. I know he's only here about my meeting, but still, he's here, and I have a better chance of him listening to me if we're face-to-face.

He's pacing the room when I enter, stopping when his eyes land on me. "What the fuck, Ash?" he snaps.

"I think you mean, 'Hi, babe, I've missed you'," I spit. "I don't hear from you for days and you want to talk now?"

"This is serious. It's my life falling apart."

"Didn't wifey give you the heads up?"

He shakes his head. "I haven't seen her much."

I roll my eyes. "Hard to believe when you've moved back in there. I thought you said you'd still be here all the time, Dan? Why haven't you called or answered my messages?"

"Meg . . . well, she's not been well."

"I don't care," I scream. "I don't care about your fucking wife."

He places his hands on his hips and stares hard at the ground. I've learned it's his way of staying calm, but I want him to lose his shit. It's when he speaks the truth. "She lost the baby," he mutters.

My mouth falls open in surprise, and I almost smile in relief before remembering myself. "Oh, Dan," I whisper, rushing to him and throwing my arms around his neck. "Are you okay?"

He wraps me in his strong arms, and I smile to myself. It feels good. "I just need some calm," he murmurs against my neck. "Everything's so fucking messed-up."

I move my lips to the skin just behind his ear and kiss gently. "I'm so sorry," I whisper, holding him tighter. Seconds later, we're ripping off each other's clothes. He growls when he removes my top to find me braless. "Why are you out in public without underwear?" he murmurs, kissing down my chest. We fall back on the bed, and he shoves my skirt up. "Fuck, Ash," he growls, seeing I'm naked down there too.

"I was praying I'd bump into you at uni," I whisper, guiding his hand between my legs.

MEG

I take the cup of coffee from my mother and offer a weak smile. It's nice not having to pretend I'm fine now she knows the truth. "So, there's no hope of you two sorting it out?" she asks after I finish telling her.

I shake my head. "I always thought I'd take him back no matter what. I mean, it's Dan, for god's sake, he's perfect. But now it's happened, I can't even bare to look at him. I don't think I've ever hated anyone so much."

She offers a sympathetic smile and gently squeezes my hand. "Good for you, Meg. You deserve so much better."

"I thought you'd be heartbroken. You love Dan," I say with a sad smile. She loved him the second I brought him home. My father wasn't so keen, but I'm a daddy's girl, so no one was ever going to be good enough in his eyes.

"I am, mainly for you and Izzy. I just can't believe he's done this. He was always so infatuated with you. I used to watch how he looked at you and swoon. And after everything you went through after Izzy's birth, I thought you'd be forever."

The door swings open and my father walks in, marching right over to me and wrapping me in his arms. I immediately begin to cry, half laughing at how silly I feel and half sobbing. He eventually pulls back, holding me at arm's length. "Your mother told me what he did. But you should know a student placed a complaint against him today."

I stiffen slightly, wondering if Ashley would have done that. "Really?" I ask, patting my cheeks dry with my jumper sleeve and sitting down.

"He lashed out at a male student over the weekend. Did he mention that to you?"

I shake my head, but the news doesn't surprise me. It's just another thing I don't know anymore. "Do you know why?"

He shakes his head, placing his briefcase down and giving Mum a kiss on her head. "I haven't gotten to the bottom of it, but I have a sneaky suspicion there's another student involved . . ." He pauses and looks directly at me. "A female student." My heart hammers hard. "Is there anything I should know, Meg?"

"Have you asked him?" I should tell them everything, but I can't bring myself to say the words out loud. I was the reason my father gave him a chance.

"Megan, this is serious, if it's what I think it is."

I take a deep breath. "If having a student-teacher relation-ship is what you're thinking, then you're spot-on," I say, and I hear a sharp intake of breath from my mother. "I'm sorry, I just couldn't bring myself to say it."

My father groans, snatching up his mobile and leaving the room. "Oh Meg, Jesus," Mum whispers. "What a mess."

I nod in agreement. "Tell me about it. I feel like a fool. You should see her, Mum. She's gorgeous and young, and did I mention gorgeous?"

"They always are, dear. But she isn't you, and he'll regret that."

I shrug. *Somehow, I doubt he will.*

DAN

When I arrive home, Meg is in the kitchen stirring a pan of curry and staring at her phone. She doesn't bother to look up as I take a seat at the kitchen island and watch her. "Are you feeling okay?" I ask.

"Yes."

"Are your parents good?"

She finally looks at me, placing her phone down on the counter. "Yes."

"Did you tell them?"

"I'm looking for a place to live," she announces.

I groan. "Please don't do that, Meg. Being here with Izzy is perfect for us both."

"Perfect for you," she corrects.

"Not true. She's been so happy to have me back home. She's clinging to me in case I leave again. Don't do that to her." Her eyes widen, and I instantly regret my choice of words. "I did this," I rush to correct. "I did this, but please don't come between me and Izzy."

Hurt replaces the angry look on her face. "How dare you?" Her voice is low, like her energy just suddenly left. "You expect me to live here after what you've done, and then you use our daughter to emotionally bully me into doing what you want?"

"I didn't mean to," I whisper desperately. "I just don't want to lose her."

"I would never stop you seeing her, but we can't live together like we're one big happy family."

"Why?" I ask. "Exes become friends and blended families exist."

She almost chokes on a sob. "I never thought we'd be having this conversation, and here you are, presenting your ideas like you've said the words a thousand times. I guess you've had months to practise, but it's all too fresh for me, Dan. I'm still playing catch-up, remember?" She looks me in the eye, and I brace myself for her next words. "Who did you hurt the other night, a student apparently?"

I lower my eyes to avoid her accusing gaze. I should have known her father would tell her. "A guy from my class. He was drunk."

"Was it over her?" When I don't answer, she shakes her head in disgust. "Wow, she must be really something if you're losing your family and your job over her." She adds a cold, empty laugh. "I remember when you used to feel that strongly about me."

"I still do," I admit. "Is it possible to love you both?"

She takes a plate from the cupboard and then Izzy's plate from the drawer. I watch as she serves up the home-made curry, my stomach growling in hunger. She doesn't leave anything for me, pouring way more than she'd usually have on her plate. "Izzy," she shouts, "dinner is ready."

"I take it I'm not invited?" I ask. She scoffs, taking the plates to the table. "Where will you go?" I ask, watching as Izzy runs in and Meg lifts her, wincing. I rush over, taking Izzy and placing her in the highchair. "You're doing too much."

Meg gently rubs her stomach and falls into the chair. "This would all be a lot easier if you just left."

"Fine," I mutter. She eyes me with hope, and I decide I can't put her through anything else. Besides, letting her stay here means I know where Izzy is. "I'll go. I'll find somewhere else to live."

———

It's seven a.m. when my phone rings, bringing me from a troubled sleep. I answer without checking the caller I.D. "Mr. Headford?" The lady sounds official, and I immediately sit up.

"Uh-huh." I rub sleep from my eyes and pull the phone away to glance at the screen. Seeing it's the university, I wince. "Yes, sorry, that's me."

"The vice chancellor would like to see you first thing in his office."

"There's a mistake. I'm off sick right now."

"No mistake. He was very insistent I move all his appointments this morning to get you in at eight."

I check my watch. "That's an hour," I mutter, my brain kicking into overdrive. They must be taking Jax's statement seriously. "Okay, I'll be there."

———

I've always hated this part of the building. The university's been here for over a hundred years, but a lot of it was rebuilt over time. Yet where the offices are is very much the old building with antique-looking wood and the smell of old, dusty books.

I tap on the office door, and he barks for me to come in.

Mark Stirk lives up to his reputation as a hard-faced bulldog, and he's never liked me. When Meg raised the idea of me working here, he dismissed it right away, despite me getting a first in English language and literature. I think he just hated the thought of having me around—or maybe it was the fact I might actually prove him wrong and be good at something.

He doesn't smile when I enter. In fact, he hardly looks at me and goes right back to staring at some paperwork on his desk. I wait patiently before him, like a lamb to the slaughter, and when he eventually pushes the papers away and removes his reading glasses, he points to the chair. I sit. "Tell me, *Dan*," I hate the way he says my name, like it leaves a bad taste in his mouth. "What possessed you to not only drink in a campus bar but to assault one of your own students?"

I stare him in the eye, wanting him to know he doesn't intimidate me. Ash told me what she said, and I think between us, we can convince him it was all Jax's fault. "Assault is a strong word."

He smirks like this is the way he knew it would go. "Don't tell me he fell."

"Actually, yes. I only shoved him to move him out of my face. That's legal. He was being aggressive to a fellow student, and when I tried to intervene, he got agitated."

Mark glances at the paperwork. "The fellow student being Miss Ashley Daulton?" I nod once, and he arches a brow, leaning back in his chair. "And what's your relationship with Miss Daulton?"

I frown. "What are you asking?"

"Well, you felt it necessary to intervene in a lovers spat."

"They're not lovers," I mutter.

"That's not what Mr. Wright said."

"And Miss. Daulton? Did you bother to ask her?"

He leans forward, resting his elbows on the desk and clasping his hands out in front of him. "The proper procedure would be for me to escalate this further," he says, "but I'm going to make you an offer."

I bristle at his words. "Proper procedure for what?"

"For a teacher-student indiscretion."

"Look, I know you're aware of my split from Meg," I begin, "but you're not pinning anything on me that'll jeopardise my career."

He laughs. It's cold, and when he finally stops, he glares angrily. "You were never good enough for Megan. You never will be, and the only good thing to come from any of this is that little girl. She's the reason I'm not hauling you before the governors. A fucking affair, Dan, with a student," he hisses. "What the hell were you thinking?"

I'm surprised by his language. I've never heard him curse, but it's enough to make me see he knows and the game is up. "Did Meg tell you?"

"It doesn't matter who the hell told me. I want you out of that house."

"Or?" I'm leaving anyway, but I want to know what he's threatening to do exactly.

"I'll ruin you."

"And what will Izzy think of that? Her grandpa chasing her dad away, out of her life?"

"She won't notice because we'll give her all the love she'll ever need."

I scoff. "Because you're always around, aren't you? You don't see Meg from one week to the next in between your golf, tennis, and holidays to Egypt. And let's not forget the three cruises a year."

"Now you're out the picture, I'll be taking Meg and Izzy with us. Do you even see what you're doing to her?" he asks. "She's in pieces, and you're dragging this out. For what? In the hope she'll take you back? I can promise you now, that will never happen."

"I just wanted to be near Izzy. I've already told Meg I'll leave the house. I just need time to find somewhere. I didn't mean to hurt her," I add, my words laced with regret. "I know I'm an idiot."

"You realise you can't keep your job here," he says firmly, and I nod. It's what I expected. "And Miss Daulton will be kicked from her course."

"No," I say, almost jumping to my feet. "That's not fair."

"You're getting off lightly."

I hold my hand out in a placating manner. "I know," I mutter. "I know, but she didn't do anything wrong, and actually, if you kick her off because of your personal feelings, you could get into trouble."

"She instigated an affair with my daughter's weak and pathetic husband. You need to agree to a divorce, sell the house, and give Meg a bigger cut than what you take."

"I can't do that, Mark, and you can't kick Ash off her course. Even if you went through the proper channels, she wouldn't get kicked off."

He laughs. "If I went through the proper channels, you'd be in a lot more trouble, with your career in tatters."

I stand. "Then go through the proper channels," I snap. "We both know you won't want to drag all this up in front of the board, because whether you like it or not, I'm related to you. It won't look good." I storm out the office, frustrated when I can't slam the heavy wooden door on my exit.

MEG

I take the coffee from the barista and smile gratefully. I don't remember the last time I enjoyed a posh coffee from a shop that asks a thousand questions about how I'd like it, but as I back out the heavy door, I'm looking forward to finding a place in the park and watching the world go by.

Mum insisted I take some time to myself today and collected Izzy right after breakfast so they could spend the day together. Dan was also up and out early, but I didn't want to stick around the house in case he came home. Being there alone without Izzy would feel awkward.

My mobile rings and I groan when I see Dan's name. "Hello?" I say, accepting the call.

"What the fuck are you trying to do to me, Meg?" he yells, and I frown. "Telling your father about Ashley was a fucking low blow."

"Actually," I hiss, checking no one is listening, "I didn't. He'd guessed after your little boxing match with your student. But I'm glad he knows. Hopefully, you'll get what you deserve."

"Have you really thought this through, Meg? What happens when I can't pay the mortgage on the ridiculously big house you insisted we buy?"

I scowl. "We both loved that house." I loved the area and wanted to be closer to my parents, but we both fell in love the second we stepped into the house. "We'll have to sell it and split the profit," I add.

"What profit? We re-mortgaged after your little break-down," he spits bitterly. "And there'll hardly be enough to lay down a deposit on another place."

"Why the hell are you ringing me to yell about something you did?" I snap, turning into the park. "Next time, don't fuck your student, arsehole." I disconnect right as I crash against a hard chest, bouncing back and falling onto my arse. My coffee falls beside me, spilling over the stone. I watch it run into the cracks and burst into tears. Hot, angry tears.

"Shit, I'm so sorry." I look up to find a tall man staring at me with wide eyes. "I was lost in . . ." He holds up his mobile like that explains it. "Are you okay?"

I rest my arms on my knees. "Everything's going wrong," I whisper through tears. He crouches down so we're eye level, and I blush, wondering why the hell I'm telling this hand-some stranger anything. I brush my tears away. "Sorry, I wasn't paying attention either."

He holds out a hand. "Hugo," he introduces.

I take his hand, and he pulls me up to stand. "Megan."

"Let me replace the coffee. There's a stand just back there," he says, pointing behind him.

I nod because I was really looking forward to that coffee. We walk silently through the park until we come to a small shack, and Hugo points to a wooden bench. "Take a seat."

I watch as he places our order. He's tall, maybe six-foot-two, with brown hair cut short and a neatly trimmed beard. He's got a good physique, and I decide he's probably a runner. He looks the type.

He returns, handing me the coffee. "Sugar?" he asks, pulling some white packets from his pocket. I shake my head, and he takes a seat beside me. "Me either."

"Sorry about that outburst of emotion back there." I wince, feeling embarrassed. "It's been a really bad few weeks."

"Don't worry, I completely understand."

We fall silent again, and I sip my coffee. "Do you run?" I ask and wince again. *Where the hell did that come from?*

He gives a small laugh. "No. You?"

I shake my head. "I used to go to the gym."

"I work out every day."

"I can tell." My cheeks burn with embarrassment. *Why does it sound like I'm flirting . . . badly?* "Oh Christ, I don't get out much," I admit, adding a nervous laugh.

"Let's play a game," he says, easing back against the bench. "Tell me a lie, something you wish was real but isn't."

"That's easy," I say. "I'm happily married." He side-eyes me. "I'm not flirting," I blurt out, and my cheeks burn brighter. "Just in case you were wondering." I inhale, trying to compose myself. "Your turn."

"My wife wasn't dead." He stares out across the park, but I feel the sadness radiating from him. "Next," he adds, a little quieter than before.

"Recently?" I ask, unable to stop myself because I suddenly have the urge to know this stranger's story.

"Recent enough for me to still walk this park because we used to come here every lunchtime and meet, no matter what."

I smile. "Even in the snow?"

"No matter what," he repeats. "Even if we argued and refused to speak to one another."

I laugh. "You'd walk around in silence?"

He nods. "A happy, yet angry silence."

My heart aches for him and his wife. "Were you married long?"

He shakes his head, rubbing a hand over his beard. "Not long enough. I wanted eternity."

I nod in agreement. "Me too."

He turns to me. "So, tell me your sad sack story."

"Well, it doesn't seem as sad as yours, so I don't think I should," I say, keeping my tone light-hearted. I relax when he laughs, glad he gets my sense my humour. "He cheated."

Hugo rests his arms across the back of the bench, holding his coffee loosely in one hand and the other resting behind me. He stares straight ahead again. "You're right, it's not as sad as mine. I win."

It's my turn to laugh. "I didn't know it was a competition or I'd have chosen something else that's tragic in my fucked-up life."

"There's no point. You'll never beat a man with a dead wife."

I grin, not really thinking over my next words until they fall from my mouth. "I lost my baby at twelve weeks." I press my lips closed. "Shit, sorry, that was so inappropriate. I wasn't trying to out-do you." I groan. "Oh God, I feel awful."

I catch him staring at my side profile, and his eyes are full of sympathy. "I'm so sorry for your loss, Megan."

Tears spring to my eyes again. "No one's said sorry," I whisper. "Not even the nurse."

"Sorry is all I keep getting and I fucking hate that word," he says, taking a sip of his coffee. "I don't know why I just said it to you." He gives another empty laugh. "Sorry your wife died. Why? Why is everyone sorry?"

"I guess it's just what people say."

"It doesn't make it better. I'd rather someone be real and say it's fucking outrageous your wife died, Hugo. Let's smash shit up."

I laugh a little louder than expected and slap my hand over my mouth. "Would smashing shit help?"

He shrugs, smirking. "Probably not. Nothing helps."

"Smash my husband up. That'd make us both feel better," I suggest.

He grins again. "So, give me the details. Who was the other woman? Did you know her?"

I shake my head. "Nope. She crept into our marriage, and I didn't know until it was too late. He knew her through . . ." I pause, choosing my words. "Work."

"Ouch. How did you find out?"

"Now, this will score me sad sack points," I say, arching a brow. He sits straighter, waiting eagerly. "I found them together."

He shrugs. "Um, a little disappointed by that reveal, I can't lie."

"In my house," I add, "on my couch."

His eyes widen. "Fuck, that is brutal. Okay, extra points for that one."

"The worst part," I add, sadness returning to my heart, "our daughter was upstairs sleeping."

"It sounds to me like you're better off without him, Megan." I like the way he says my name, curling it round his tongue like it's special.

I drink the last of my coffee. "I should go."

He nods, standing. "Me too."

I smile. "Thanks for the coffee."

He takes my empty cup and nods. "Sorry I spilt your first one. It was nice to meet you. Take care." And then he walks away.

Sixteen

DAN

Ashley stares wide-eyed, waiting for me to tell her this isn't happening. Only I can't because it is. "My parents will kill me," she says. "Isn't there anything you can do?"

I shake my head. "I tried."

"How hard?" she snaps accusingly.

"I told you before, the bloke hates me. He's been waiting for this day to come, and I bet Meg broke her neck to tell him everything." I run my hands through my hair, feeling the stress mounting. "I can't believe she'd do that to me. I can't afford to just hand the house over. I've lost enough already."

"Wait," says Ash, narrowing her eyes. "He asked you to hand the house over?" I nod. "What did he offer in return?" I chew on my lower lip, debating what exactly I should tell her without upsetting her. She pinches the bridge of her nose. "Did he offer to drop everything regarding us?"

"Ash, you have to understand, I worked hard for that house, years of blood, sweat and tears—"

"I don't care," she suddenly screams. "Take the fucking deal, Dan."

"And lose it all?"

"Yes." She stands, pushing her face right into my own. "Because you get to have me, and I am worth it."

I swallow the words I want to say cos I know they will send her over the edge. "Of course, you are," I try, "but where will we live if I have no money? That house is worth so much, it could get us a really nice place together."

She relaxes slightly, thinking over my words. "How nice a place?"

I take her hands and smile, pulling her against me. "Nice enough you won't want to leave it to go to lectures." I kiss her on the nose, feeling her calming by the second. "And you can enroll to another university and do your last year in September."

She pouts. "That's months away. What am I going to tell my dad?"

"Gap year?" I ask, shrugging.

"What, leaving three months into the course?"

"I know it's not ideal, baby," I whisper, running my fingers through her hair, "but it'll work out in the end. I'm going to find a small place to rent for now, get the house on the market, and then we can look for somewhere."

"Wait, you're renting?"

I nod. "Meg is struggling having me around. She was going to move out—"

"Then why didn't you let her? I could have moved in, and we could've been together until the house sale."

I inwardly shudder at the thought of moving Ash into my marital home. "I can't let her take Izzy. Who knows how far she'd move away."

"You drive," she mutters.

"I know, but it's not the same as being able to tuck her into bed every night. I'll push for the sale so we're not waiting too long," I lie.

She looks slightly appeased. "Why don't we rent a flat together?"

My mind races to find an excuse. "I can only afford somewhere small, especially now I don't have a job."

"Dan, it makes more sense for us to get a small place together, so I can help with the rent and bills."

"I need to think about Izzy," I explain. "She might want to stop over."

"Well, she can."

"It'll be a one-bed. If I'm living alone, she can come anytime and share with me." I kiss her, trying to distract her. "Look, we'll find a place as soon as the house is sold, okay?" She reluctantly nods.

―――――

I get home to the sound of Christmas music blaring out. I stand for a moment, listening to Izzy giggling, and as I move into the living room, I can't help but smile as I watch Meg swinging our little girl around, singing badly to Mariah Carey's 'All I Want for Christmas', surrounded by boxes of Christmas decorations.

I lean against the door frame and watch as they dance together. Usually, we'd agree on a date to put up the decorations together as a family. Meg always wanted to do it at the beginning of December, and I always made her wait until as late as possible, wanting to avoid the mess. *Why did I make her wait?*

"Wow, we're doing this now?" I ask, smiling.

Meg stops spinning and fixes her eyes on me. She's breathless and it takes her a second to gather herself. "I've already told Izzy how you're busy," she says.

"Nonsense," I say, smiling wider as I slip out my coat. "I never miss decorating the tree."

Meg places Izzy down. "Go and get yourself another cookie from the kitchen and eat it at the table," she says, kissing her on the head. Once she's gone, she turns to me. "I'd rather you didn't get involved."

"Meg," I say, my tone pleading, "don't shut me out."

She growls. "God, you're such a prick," she hisses. "You don't get to be a part of the family when you feel like it. You don't get to show up to all the fun things and then leave again."

"Is this because I yelled earlier?" I ask. She grabs handfuls of her hair, glaring at me with wide eyes. "Okay, so it's not," I add quickly.

"Just go away, Dan. Let me and Izzy have one night without me having to think about this breakup. Please."

MEG

I'm relieved when he nods and goes up to his room. I exhale and shake the stress from my shoulders as I go into the kitchen, where Izzy is munching on the cookies we made together when she came home from my parents'.

"Is Daddy helping us?" she asks.

I shake my head, and she looks sad. I tuck her hair behind her ears and crouch down so we're at eye level. "Daddy isn't going to be here as much as normal," I say, thinking now's as good a time as ever to try and explain things. "But he loves you very, very much. That hasn't changed and it never will. So, no matter where Daddy is, he will always love you. Okay?"

She nods. "I love you, Mummy," she whispers, and I kiss her on the nose.

"I love you so much."

We go back to the living room, and I push everything else to the back of my mind as we spend the next hour hanging Christmas decorations on the tree.

————

The following day, Dan insists on taking Izzy for lunch. It's another great opportunity to spend some time on my own, something I never really had a chance to do before. I guess I always felt I had to spend every minute of the day with Izzy, seeing as I gave up work to be with her. And I've enjoyed every second of it, but it's also nice to have some 'me' time and remember who I am now I'm no longer someone's wife.

I go straight to the park and purchase two coffees from the kiosk. I spent all morning wondering if it would look weird, me turning up here like this, but then I decided I wanted to repay Hugo for the coffee. He was nice and somehow made me feel lighter about the whole situation, even though he's clearly going through stuff himself, and if I happen to see him again, I'm prepared. Besides, the park is a public place, and the chance of me seeing him again is very slim.

I sit on the same bench from yesterday and take out a paperback from my bag. If I'm reading, it looks less weird . . . right?

It's not long before Hugo drops down beside me, and I can't help but smile. "Are you stalking me, Meg?" I like the way he's automatically shortened my name.

"I just thought I should repay you for the coffee yester-day," I say, closing my book.

He takes the book from me, and I blush, knowing he'll open the damn thing. I realise I should maybe have chosen something different as he scans his eyes over the blurb. He arches a brow. "Umm, lady porn."

A laugh escapes me. "It is not," I deny.

He scoffs, flicking through the pages and coming to stop about halfway through. "His throbbing—" he begins, and I quickly remove it from his hands and slam it closed.

"You made that up," I hiss, unable to stop smiling as I put it in my bag. "Take your coffee and get your mind out the gutter," I add, sliding the paper cup towards him.

He rests his arm over the back of the bench again. "You're here for a second day," he says, staring out over the park.

"How do you have so much time on your hands with a toddler?"

"She's with her dad today," I say, hating how the words sound out loud.

"How's that feel?"

I shrug. "Pretty crap. I never thought I'd be here saying those words. It makes it real that we're separate now, no longer a family unit."

He nods in understanding. "That must be hard."

"Tell me about your wife," I say. "That must be so much harder. I still get to see Dan, as much as I hate him right now, but the thought of never seeing him again, and that choice being out of my hands, kills me."

He gives a sad smile. "She was perfect." He laughs to himself. "People must roll their eyes when I say that, because it's something people say after death isn't it—she was great, she was kind, she was wonderful." He pauses, sighing. "But it's true. She really was perfect. She was easy-going and relaxed about everything. We laughed so hard, every single day. I fucking hate that I don't laugh like that anymore."

My heart feels heavy for him, and I feel bad bringing the subject up. "What do you do apart from walk around the park at lunch and talk to emotionally wrecked strangers?"

His lips tug into a small smile. "I have brothers and crazy parents who follow me around to make sure I don't hang myself. I've got friends, but they're all couples who knew us both. It just reminds me I'm single."

"Huh, single," I mutter, adding a groan. "I hate that word."

"Me too. This other woman . . ." he starts, then adds, "Now, this is not a pick-up line, it's an honest question. But what the fuck does she look like? Because you," he pauses, grinning, "are hot. I'm just putting it out there. So, she's gotta be a supermodel."

I blush, staring down at my feet. "No. Actually, she was his student."

His grin fades immediately. "His student?" he repeats, and I realise how bad that sounds, so I rush to correct it.

"He works at a university. He's a lecturer. She's twenty-something."

He relaxes slightly. "Still not allowed, though, right?"

"So, this is where you go when you don't have Izzy?" I spin to the sound of Dan's angry voice and pale slightly when I see he's marching over with Izzy in his arms. All kinds of emotions pass through me, and I wonder why guilt is one of them when I'm not doing anything wrong. "You didn't waste any time," he spits. Izzy reaches for me, but Dan keeps her in his arms. "No, sweety, Mummy is busy."

"Dan, this is Hugo, my . . ." I pause, not knowing what Hugo is really, apart from a stranger I share coffee with. "Friend," I say stiffly, praying he doesn't embarrass me any more than he already is.

"Hugo," Dan repeats, like the word is dirty in his mouth.

I sigh, turning to Hugo. "I am so sorry about this."

He gives an easy smile. "I'll leave you to it," he says, standing.

"Yeah, you do that, Hugo," Dan spits.

I wait a few seconds for him to walk out of earshot before glaring at Dan. "What the hell was that?"

"I'd prefer we didn't argue in front of Izzy," he snaps, marching off in the direction of the exit.

"Daddy," she squeals, "I want to play at the park."

"Well, Mummy ruined it," Dan replies, and I squeeze my hands into angry, tight balls, following them back to the house.

He sits Izzy in front of the television, then goes into the kitchen as I follow. "Why are you so angry?" I ask, watching as he slams pots and pans about, emptying the dishwasher.

"How long have you been screwing Hugo?"

I laugh. "I haven't."

"You've been playing the victim, making out you're the one who's hurting, and all along, you've been seeing him."

"Are you serious right now?" I hiss, trying to keep my voice down. "I met him yesterday in the park, and we got talking after he knocked my coffee from my hand."

"Likely story."

"And quite honestly, I don't know why I'm even explaining myself to you. I don't owe you anything."

"You've been holding the moral high ground, making me out to be the bad guy."

"That's it," I snap, marching upstairs. I can't take it anymore. I burst into the spare room and take his bag from under the bed. I begin to throw his things in the bag as I feel him lingering in the doorway. "I'm done. You're leaving."

"You can't kick me out," he snaps.

"Watch me. I should never have let you back."

"It's my home too."

"No," I yell, spinning to look him in the eye. "No, you negated the right to our home when you cheated. And I will not have you speaking to me like that ever again. And I will certainly not let you make me out to be the bad person to our daughter. If you ever blame me again, I'll tell her exactly why Daddy no longer lives with us."

"You're acting crazy."

"You make me crazy, Dan. Who the fuck do you think you are? You cheated and ruined our marriage. You ruined my life. Everything we had, all our memories, are tainted forever because of you. And now, you accuse me of being like you? How fucking dare you? I've always been faithful. Don't you think men have tried to turn my head? And not once," I yell, stepping closer and pointing my finger in his face, "have I ever been unfaithful."

His expression softens. "I shouldn't have said that."

"No, damn right. And Hugo just lost the love of his life,

and he is grieving." I grab the bag and shove it hard against his chest. "Get out."

"You don't mean that," he pleads.

"Get the fuck out now, and don't you dare come back. We'll sell the house. Get yourself a solicitor."

I shove past him and go back downstairs, turning off the television. "Come on, Izzy," I say, picking her up. Dan stands on the bottom step with his bag in his hand. "Don't be here when we get home," I warn, leaving.

I'm shaking all the way to Sofia's. I couldn't stay and watch him leave because, finally, it's for the last time. Dan will no longer live with us. We have officially separated, and even after everything, that makes me sad.

Seventeen

ASHLEY

I stare wide-eyed at the white plastic stick, the small word 'pregnant' staring back at me. "Fuck," I whisper to myself. "Fuck, fuck, fuck."

"Ashley, you have a visitor," Allie calls from downstairs.

I stuff the stick under my pillow and rush downstairs. Dan is waiting at the bottom with a bag in his hand. "You okay?" I ask, because he doesn't look okay. His shoulders are hunched in a defeated kind of way, and he looks tired and maybe a little older than usual.

"She kicked me out." The news surprises me, but I can't help the little happy dance my heart is doing. When he went back there, I fully expected them to work their shit out. She looks the type to forgive and forget.

I go to him and wrap my arms around him. "What happened?" I ask, kissing him gently.

"I saw her with another man." I pull back and notice his eyes have darkened. "In the park. I was babysitting our daughter," he pulls from my embrace, dropping his bag at his feet, "and she was on a fucking date." The way he spits the words screams jealousy.

I put some distance between us before folding my arms over my chest. "So?"

"What do you mean, so?" he snaps.

"So, why do you care?"

His expression suddenly softens. "I don't," he says with a shrug that tells me he really does. "It was a shock. Besides, I had Izzy with me, and she shouldn't have seen her mother with another man."

"You realise that will happen, right?" I ask, narrowing my eyes in annoyance. "Megan will meet someone and move on." There's no hiding the devastation on Dan's face as my words sink in, and I roll my eyes. "Fuck's sake, Dan, get out," I mutter, turning my back on him and going into the kitchen.

He rushes after me. "Don't be like that, Ash," he says desperately, grabbing my wrist and turning me to face him. He tucks my hair behind my ear and smiles. "Sorry, I'm just all over the place, what with work and being homeless." He adds a small, uncertain laugh.

"You can't stay here," I mutter. Allie will flip her shit if I even dare to ask, and besides, I need to process my recent news and I can't do that with Dan here distracting me.

"Right," he mutters, nodding, "of course." His hands drop to his sides and that defeated look returns.

"Don't you have friends or family who can help you out till you find a place?" I suggest, guilt creeping in.

He nods overenthusiastically as he makes his way back to the hall. "Of course, I wasn't asking to stay here, I was just letting you know." He grabs his bag and pulls open the front door. "I'll text you later and let you know where I'm staying." He turns to place a quick kiss on my cheek before leaving.

I close the door and lean against it, letting out a heavy sigh. Allie appears in the living room doorway holding a mug of coffee. "Everything okay?" I nod, feeling an overwhelming urge to cry. She smiles sympathetically. "Here if you need a chat," she tells me then disappears back into the living room.

Technically, now I know I'm pregnant, I should have cancelled the night out I had planned with Lauren and the rest of the group, but I couldn't face a night home thinking about my situation. I have no idea what to do about any of it, it's all such a mess.

I take the margarita being offered to me from Jared. It's the third one I've had, and a nagging voice in the back of my head keeps warning me this will end badly, but I'm in no mood to listen.

"You've had a face like a slapped arse all night," says Lauren. I glance around the table, and all eyes are on me.

"I'm fine," I lie.

"Bullshit," singsongs Jared. "Is it Dishy Dan or Jaded Jaxon?"

I roll my eyes at his nicknames. "I haven't heard from Jaxon, but he made a complaint against Dan," I say, and they all lean in closer.

"Oh shit," Molly gasps. "He went to the top?"

I nod. "The chancellor called Dan in, and he's currently suspended or some shit."

"Holy fucking cow," whispers Jared. "I didn't think Jaxon had it in him."

"He's clearly way more upset over you than you thought," Lauren adds, arching a brow. "I told you this wouldn't end well."

"I don't need to hear 'I told you so' right now, Lauren," I snap. "Everything's a fucking mess and I don't know how to fix it."

"Try putting yourself in his wife's shoes," says Lauren, and I growl in frustration.

"Fuck his wife," I almost yell. "I don't give a fucking shit about his perfect wife or his daughter."

Lauren leans back in her chair with a disgusted look. "That about sums you up, doesn't it? A selfish bitch."

I nod in agreement and tears slip down my face. "Yep, that's me,"

"And you're not even sorry about it," she yells.

"I'm pregnant," I cry, and the table falls silent. Everyone is staring at me wide-eyed with mouths hanging open. "I'm fucking pregnant and my life's falling apart." I bury my face in my hands and sob. I feel Molly slide closer and wrap her arms around me. Someone else pushes some napkins into my hand, and I wipe my face.

"How far along are you?" Molly asks gently.

I shrug. "I just bought a cheap test."

"Maybe it's wrong," suggests Luis. "That shit happens."

"I've been feeling sick, and I can't eat."

"But margaritas are going down a treat," says Lauren, lifting hers in the air in a silent cheer before knocking it back angrily.

"Give it a rest, Laur," mutters Molly.

"I'm sorry, but she's done this to herself," she continues, and I bury my face back in my hands. "You ripped his marriage apart, and now, you're saddled with his kid."

"Thanks for the recap," I mumble.

"You want sympathy? Well, I'm sorry, but you won't find it from me. Your tears won't make this better, Ashley. You need to fix up and sort this out. Work out if you actually want to be with him now he's free and available, and if you do, tell him. How he responds is how he truly feels."

MEG

Matt tops up both our wine glasses and slides one to me. "You look good, mama," he says, and I smile. I couldn't face going home tonight in case Dan was still around, so after Sofia's, I dropped Izzy off to my parents and came here.

"So do you. It must be that new man?"

He smiles and it lights up his whole face. "I can honestly say I'm so happy, Meg. Like, really happy."

His smile is infectious, and I follow him into the living room, where we both sit on the couch. I turn to him and tuck my legs under my arse. "You deserve to be."

"And so do you. What's happening with you and Dan?"

My heart aches at his question. "I finally found the balls to kick him out today," I say, and he gives a knowing smile.

"That explains why he's been calling me all afternoon. Don't worry, I turned my phone off."

"He accused me of cheating," I tell him. "Can you believe it?"

"Why?"

I bite my lower lip. "He saw me talking to a man in the park."

Matt sits straighter. "What man?"

I can't help the small smile that creeps onto my face as I picture Hugo. "There's nothing going on," I say, and Matt grins like he doesn't believe me. "No, really, he literally ran into me, or I ran into him," I shrug, "and he spilt my coffee, so he got me another. Then I returned the favour the next day, and Dan saw us."

Matt frowns. "Hold on, so you bumped into one another in the park?" I nod. "And he replaced your coffee?" I nod again. "And then you got him another?"

"The next day," I say.

He smirks. "You went back the next day and had a second coffee with a stranger?"

"Why are you saying it like that's something?" I wail, laughing. "The guy lost his wife. I feel bad for him."

He arches a brow. "So, it's like a pity thing?"

"Yes . . . no . . . I don't know."

"It sounds like a thing," he teases, "or at least the start of a thing."

"I doubt he'll ever speak to me again after meeting Dan today. He acted crazy."

"Don't let Dan ruin this—whatever this is—because he doesn't deserve to have a say. He cheated, so fuck him."

"It's not that easy, is it? He's begging me back one minute, then running to her. The lines are so blurred."

"But you're not considering taking him back . . . are you?" I sigh, and he glares at me. "Come on, Meg, tell me you're not."

"No, I don't think so. I just feel so sad, and I know if I forgive him, I won't be sad anymore."

"Bullshit," he says, drinking a big gulp of wine. "You'll be sad and paranoid because you'll never know if he's cheating or not. He's ruined your trust, and that's hard to get back."

"I know, I know," I mutter, rubbing my tired face. "You're right. It's the easy option."

"And you're strong."

"Am I?"

He taps the bottom of my glass, forcing me to take a drink. "You are. Meet the stranger for more than coffee. Get Dan off your mind."

"I could never," I say, shaking my head. "No, I'm going to concentrate on Izzy and leave men well alone."

"Aren't you just a little curious about where this could lead?" he asks, wiggling his brows.

I laugh. "No, not in the slightest. We're just two sad people who had a coffee. It felt good to talk to someone who didn't know Dan, no offence. The fact we were both sad gave us a small connection."

"Is he good looking?" he asks, topping up my glass again.

I groan. "Extremely."

Matt laughs. "You know, no one would judge you for having a fling to get over your marriage breakup."

"Absolutely not," I screech. "My marriage might be fucked, but I'm not ready to move on." The thought of being with anyone other than Dan in an intimate way scares the crap out of me. It's only ever been Dan, and at this rate, it might only ever be Dan, because I can't see myself ever loving anyone the way I love him.

"Relax, Meg, no one's suggesting you meet a guy and move him right in like Dan never existed. But you're human, and you're free and single, and no one expects you to stay home and be sad forever."

I drink the glass of wine in one go, letting his words sink in. I don't know why I suddenly feel so sad. Maybe the thought of moving on hurts me way more than it should.

DAN

Why won't he just pick up the damn phone? I've been calling Matt all afternoon, and he's not bothered to call me back. Jay wasn't available, and Matt's my last hope unless I want to disgrace my parents with my presence, and seeing as I've been avoiding them and delaying telling them about my marriage breakdown, Matt is my only option.

I knock on the door and wait patiently. When he finally opens it, he looks smashed. "Dan," he slurs, sounding surprised. He glances over his shoulder before bringing his attention back to me. "You okay?"

"I've been trying to get hold of you all afternoon," I snap, pushing my way in. "I know we've not been seeing eye to eye, but I'm desperate." I drop my bag in the hall. "I need a place to stay. Can you believe Meg kicked me out?"

"Erm, now's not a great time," he says, frowning at my dumped bag.

"You're not listening. I need a place to crash until we sell the house, which will be fucking soon if I have my way," I say, kicking off my shoes. "I'm contacting the estate agent tomorrow. The sooner we deal with the house, the quicker we can both move on. Speaking of which, did you know she's met someone . . ." I trail off as I walk into the living room and stare right at Meg. Her lips are pressed together in a tight line, and by the flush of her cheeks, I see she's drunk too. "Great," I mutter.

"As I was trying to explain, I'm busy right now," says Matt, appearing behind me.

"Well, she's got a house to stay in so . . ." I shrug.

"Wow, when did you get so petty?" she asks with a laugh. "It's a real ick."

I arch a brow. "An ick? You sound like a teenager."

She grins. "You'd know what they sound like, wouldn't you?" Matt bursts into laughter.

"She's not a teenager," I correct, sitting down and draining Matt's glass of wine.

"She's not an adult either," says Meg, sniggering behind her own glass.

"I really don't need this right now," I say, topping up the glass.

"Why aren't you there tonight?" asks Matt, taking his glass back.

"Maybe the thrill of the chase is over," Meg suggests, and Matt taps his glass against hers. "She won, and now, she's bored."

"That's not it," I snap, taking the bottle and drinking a mouthful of wine. "And I'm not discussing it with you."

Meg grabs her bag and places her glass on the table. "Good, because I don't want to hear it."

"Don't go," says Matt as she stands on wobbly legs.

I briefly close my eyes before also standing. "I'll walk you home." I can't let her walk home alone in this state, even if it's just a five-minute journey.

"I'm fine," she says, waving her hand around. "And I don't need you to walk me anyway."

"You're still the mother of my child, Meg. I can't let you walk home in this state."

She kisses Matt on the cheek and stumbles out the house with me close behind. I leave the door off the latch in case Matt falls to sleep. I'm a few steps behind Meg, but as she sways from side to side, I take her arm and force her to hook it through my own. It's painful feeling her so close when she's so far away from me emotionally. I've never not been able to talk her around to my way of thinking, but with this cluster-fuck, I know I've lost her.

"We should see someone together about selling the house," I say. "Decide who we want to sell it through."

"Whatever, just pick anyone and get it on the market."

"Really?"

"Were you expecting me to kick up a fuss?" she asks. "Truth is, Dan, I hate that house now. I can't be there without you. And there are a thousand memories haunting me. It's like living with a ghost."

"I wish you'd fight for us," I mutter, and I feel her eyes on me. I turn to her, and we come to a stop. "You're letting us go so easily."

"I didn't have a choice," she whispers. "You didn't give me a choice." She tugs on my arm, and we begin to walk again. "If you'd have told me you were unhappy, gave me a chance to fix things, maybe we wouldn't be here now."

"I wasn't unhappy," I say, and I hate that she thinks I was. "I really wasn't."

We come to a stop outside the house, and she fumbles in her bag to find the keys. It's the bag I always complained about because she can never find anything in it. "One day, you'll sort that thing out," I tease.

She pulls out the keys and holds them up triumphantly. "Ah-ha," she announces.

I find myself smiling. I miss this side of Meg, the fun side. I help her along the garden path and take the keys from her, inserting them in the lock and pushing open the door. She stops in the doorway, turning to face me, and places her hand on my chest. "Stop right there," she says with a grin. "You can't come in."

"Are you sure you don't need my help? I know what you're like on red wine."

"I can handle myself," she says, her hand still against my chest. She's looking at me, her eyes flicking between my eyes and lips, like she wants to kiss me. "You should worry about Matt. You know he's way worse than me."

I groan while grinning. "Shit, I forgot about that. You sure you wanna kick me out?"

She smiles, nodding. "It's what you deserve."

I nod in agreement. "I do."

"When it's like this," she whispers, taking a handful of my shirt, "I almost forget." I remain still, terrified if I so much as breathe wrong, it'll break the spell she's currently under. She moves closer, her eyes fixed on my mouth. "And I need to forget," she adds. I close my eyes as she presses her lips against my own and a million feelings flood me. We're hungry as our mouths clash together, and I feel hope building. She breaks free and our heavy pants fill the silence. She still has my shirt screwed up in her hands as she rests her forehead against my chest. "Fuck," she whispers.

Before she can tell me her regrets, I tilt her head up to look at me and place a chaste kiss on her cheek. "Goodnight, Meg."

Eighteen

MEG

I feel around blindly for my alarm as the shrill sound of my wakeup call rocks my skull. I slam my hand against the button to shut the damn thing off, then I slowly push myself to sit, groaning aloud when my head spins. *Why do I drink red wine when it always leaves me feeling like crap the next day?*

I snatch my mobile off the side and check for messages. There's just one, and I open it and smile. My parents are taking Izzy out for the day, which will give me a chance to go and see someone about getting the house on the market. I groan again when I think about Dan and our kiss last night. Remembering I practically threw myself at him, I bury my face in my hands. I regretted it the instant my lips touched his.

I still remember the first time I kissed Dan, and it felt so right, like I was home. Last night, it felt far from that. He didn't feel like my Dan anymore. It didn't feel like home.

I force myself to get out of bed and shower. Then I pick out my outfit and head downstairs to grab a coffee. I text my mum back to confirm I'm happy for her to take Izzy for the day, and then I grab my bag and head out.

I find three different estate agents who all agree to come out to the house and valuate it, so we can decide who to put it on the market with. I then head to Sofia's, because when I stopped by yesterday, I sensed she was struggling. I feel like I've spent the last few weeks so lost in my own misery, I've neglected her.

When she opens the door, she has a screaming Harry on her hip and a harassed look about her. I offer a sympathetic smile, and she opens the door wider for me to go in. "He's been like this all night," she says, and I swear there's a wobble in her voice.

"He's probably teething," I suggest. "Do you want me to take him?"

She hands him to me without me having to ask twice and busies herself making a drink. Harry begins to quiet down, and I see the hurt in her expression. "It's just a change of face," I say. "Izzy used to do this to me all the time."

She sits opposite me. "I feel so useless. I didn't think it would be so hard."

I grab her hand over the table and give it a gentle squeeze. "I promise it gets easier."

"He hates me."

"He does not. You're his mother."

"I don't feel like I know him at all. I don't know why he's crying. I don't know what he wants." She breaks down, sobbing. "My parents were right—I can't do this."

"Sofia, it's just the baby blues. Everyone goes through it. You've never done this before, and it's not easy, so it's okay to feel like you've not got this. But you will. You'll find your way, and I'm here to help."

She dries her eyes, nodding. "I'm just tired," she whispers. "I don't remember the last time I slept properly."

"How about I take Harry out for a walk while you get some rest?"

She glances at Harry and begins to shake her head. "I don't know."

"It will do you both some good. I'll just go for an hour and come back."

She gives a small smile. "If you're sure." I'm already standing and walking towards the pushchair. "Everything you'll need is in the changing bag," she says as I lay Harry into it.

I give her a hug. "Rest. And don't worry, he'll be fine."

I head towards the park. It's becoming a habit. As I approach the bench where I sat with Hugo, I see him already there. Only he isn't alone. There's a brunette next to him, and they're each holding a coffee and chatting animatedly. I know it's stupid to be jealous, I don't even know the guy, but seeing him with her, doing what we did, somehow feels like a betrayal.

I'm too close to turn back without drawing attention, so I continue to walk, keeping my eyes fixed ahead. As I pass, Hugo looks up, and I feel his eyes on me. It seems silly to ignore him, but I'm embarrassed to be caught here, like I'm his number one fan, so I just keep walking.

By the time I get back to Sofia's, Harry is passed out and sound asleep in his pushchair. Sofia is also sleeping on the couch. I decided to grab something simple from the super-market on our way home to cook for her, so I take the pushchair into the kitchen and set about making chicken pasta.

It's almost an hour later when Sofia pads into the kitchen looking a little less stressed. She smiles, peering into the pushchair where Harry has been happily kicking away for the last twenty minutes. I push the newspaper I was reading away as she takes a seat at the table next to me. "You make it look so easy."

"Sofia, I've been watching him for maybe two hours, you have him twenty-four-seven. You have it so much harder."

"Where did you go?"

"Just to the park and then the supermarket."

She eyes me "The park?"

I nod. "Yes, where people walk and take their kids."

"And meet handsome strangers."

I roll my eyes. "That's not why I went." When she arches her brow with a playful smile, I let out a dramatic groan. "Okay, maybe it is, but I really wish I hadn't. I blame Matt for putting silly ideas in my head."

"What happened?"

I stand, grabbing a cup and placing it under the coffee machine. "He was there . . . chatting to another woman."

Sofia gasps but in a mocking way, "Oh lord, call the cheat police, the stranger is cheating on you."

"I know I sound crazy, okay, you don't need to take the piss out of me. I just felt," I stare out of the kitchen window, "less special."

"Jesus, you've been out of the dating loop for way too long, Meg. These days, you can hook up and still see other people. It's not official until someone makes it official. Until then, you can kiss, talk to, and sleep with anyone you want."

"That's disgusting."

"It's how it is now. Why'd yah think I didn't bother going down the traditional route to get Harry? There is no traditional route."

"I just had a coffee with the guy a couple times. It's no big deal. I'm totally overreacting, and I think it's because last night," I hand her the coffee and rejoin her at the table, "I kissed Dan."

This time, she gasps for real. "Why?"

I shrug. "Because he's still my husband, still very familiar, and maybe I just needed comfort. He was an easy option."

"I hope you washed your dirty mouth out. Lord knows where he's been."

"I was drunk. It was a mistake, and he knows that. He doesn't want me anymore, but it's hard turning off my feelings."

"Well, turn them the fudge off, okay, because Dan is old news. What did Matt say about your stranger?"

I wave my hand like it's nothing, adding, "Just that he might help me get over Dan."

"Totally agree."

I stare wide-eyed. "I thought you'd be against that idea."

"Why? It makes perfect sense. He's grieving, and you're sad. A perfect setting for a one-night stand."

I shake my head. "No, that's not me."

"How would you know?"

"I just hate the idea of having sex with no feelings. And I'm still married."

"To a cheating, lying wanker. He does *not* deserve your loyalty right now. Look, why not ask him out on a date, at least put yourself out there?"

I shake my head again. "No, I'm not ready. I'm *so* not ready." I don't know why everyone assumes I'd want to just move on like Dan and I never happened. It's hard to erase your memories, and yeah, he's tainted them with all the shit he's done lately, but I have good memories of our marriage too. Why would I even think about ever trusting a man again? If Dan let me down, anyone can. "Besides, maybe it's his thing. Knock into stressed-out women in the park, feed them a bullshit story to make them feel sorry for him, and bam, get them into bed. No, I'm happy as I am."

DAN

Nothing can beat my happy mood today. After everything, Meg kissed me. I never thought in a million years she'd let me near her ever again. It's given me hope.

I take two coffees from the counter and carry them over to where Ashley is waiting. I need to make it clear we're over, so I can concentrate on repairing my marriage.

"So, where did you stay last night?" she asks.

"With Matt."

"Any luck finding a place?"

I shake my head. Honestly, I haven't even looked at lettings today. My head's been too full of ideas that Meg will take me back. "We should talk," I begin. Ashley immediately pales, and it makes me feel like shit. It's like she senses what's coming. "Everything's been so crazy," I add.

"I have some news of my own," she says, glancing around nervously.

"Let me just get this out, Ash, or I'll get distracted, and it's just delaying the inevitable." It's the reason I arranged to meet here, in public, because I get so easily distracted by her, I end up not saying anything.

"I really think you need to hear this," she says firmly.

"You never listen," I snap.

"It's important."

"So is what I want to say," I argue. And as I say my next sentence, she also blurts out hers. "I kissed Meg last night."

"I'm pregnant."

We stare at each other for a few seconds. My heart hammers hard in my chest, and as her words penetrate my brain, she slaps me hard across the face. "You fucking prick," she hisses. Nearby customers glance over, but I'm still too stunned to speak.

"Pregnant?" I repeat, my voice trembling from shock. Meg will never forgive me now. The hope I felt moments ago ebbs away, along with my good mood.

"I don't know why I put up with your shit," she mutters, and I notice she's crying. "I deserve so much better." She stands, grabbing her bag and storming from the café.

It takes a minute for me to gather my thoughts before I run after her, catching her at the end of the street. I walk behind her as I ask, "How far along?"

"Did you sleep with her?" she asks, spinning to face me and bringing us both to an abrupt stop. "Are you back with her?" I shake my head. "So, what? You just kissed and it meant nothing?" I shake my head again, and she screams angrily, shoving me hard in my chest. I take a step back. "You still love her, don't you?"

How do I tell her that I never stopped? "Let's go somewhere and talk like adults."

"You condescending shithead," she hisses.

I groan as she begins to march ahead of me again and I chase after her. "That's not what I meant."

"You think you're so much bigger and better than me because you're older? Didn't mind fucking me, though, did you?"

"Jesus, Meg . . ." I trail off as the name leaves my mouth, and Ash spins around again, but this time, I see her hand coming and halt it mid-air by grabbing her wrist. "Sorry, it was an accident," I mutter.

"Like us, one big fucking accident."

"No. Don't say that."

"Just answer me this," she snaps, pulling her wrist free from my grip. "Were you about to end things with me back there?"

"No," I lie, the word almost choking me. "I just wanted to be honest."

"So, you still want to be with me?" I nod, not trusting myself to say the lie out loud. "And the baby?"

I keep nodding, willing my brain to catch up. "Uh-huh," I squeeze out. "Let's talk."

We find a wooden bench just across the street and both sit down. My palms are sweating, and I feel like my throat's tightening. I pull at my shirt, already knowing that's not the reason. I'm choking on fear.

"I did the test yesterday. I needed time to get my head around it."

"I just didn't think you wanted . . ." I trail off, unsure if my words will earn me another slap, but Ashley doesn't seem the maternal type. In fact, she stated more than once she never wanted children.

"This was an accident," she says, "but I'm coming around to the idea."

"How far along are you?" I'm asking textbook questions because I still have no idea what I'm supposed to say or feel right now.

"I think I'm around six weeks, maybe."

"And you want to keep it?" I ask, carefully glancing at her before staring out ahead.

"I think so, if that's what you want."

"It's your body," I shrug, "your choice, right?"

"I can't do this without you, Dan. I want you by my side."

My heart twists so painfully, I rub my chest. If I agree to stick around, that's Meg and I over forever. My family as I know it will forever change. But if I say no, she'll destroy an innocent life, and I just lost one of those. I inhale sharply and twist to face her, taking her hands in my own. "If this is what you want, I'm here." The words burn my throat, and my chest tightens again.

She smiles. "Really?" I nod. "Because I'm terrified," she admits. I give a weak smile and pull her to me. *You and me both.*

ASHLEY

My talk with Dan went better than I thought. We went back to my place and spent the afternoon in bed. It put things right between us, and I feel like we're back on track. And even though I decided last night that I didn't want the baby, I knew Dan was about to leave me and I don't want that either. But my snap decision to tell him and keep it felt right. Which brings me here.

I run my fingers through my hair and take a deep breath as I reach for the doorbell. "Hold on," Meg calls from inside. I slowly release my nervous breath and take another. When the door finally opens, her smile fades the second she sees me. "What are you doing here?" she asks, looking past me, probably wondering where Dan is.

"I need to talk to you."

She folds her arms over her chest. "Does Dan know you're here?" I shake my head, and she smirks, rolling her eyes. "If you think I'm inviting you in, think again."

"I'd rather we didn't do this on the doorstep. It's about your kiss."

She falters and takes a step back, holding the door open for me to go inside. I step in, noticing the new couch. There are still photographs on display of her and Dan together, which immediately pisses me off, but I follow her through to the kitchen.

"Make it quick," she mutters, leaning against the worktop and glaring at me.

"I want you to stay away from Dan," I say firmly.

She laughs, and it's cold and empty. "You want me to stay away from my own husband?" I nod, my confidence slipping away. "Does Dan want that?" she asks, arching a brow.

"You just need to do the decent thing and back off," I snap.

She places her hands on the counter behind her, and I hate how confident and beautiful she is. "Pity you didn't take your own advice when you began pursuing my husband."

"That's not how it was," I mutter.

"So, he pursued you? Because that's not how he tells it."

"Why can't you just let him walk away?" I almost wail. "You don't want him after what he's done, surely?"

"I would love nothing more than to walk away, trust me, but we have a daughter together, a commitment. So, whether you like it or not, we'll always be in each other's life."

"And what if we have children?" I ask.

She laughs again. "Dan didn't want the baby I just lost,

and that was with his own wife, so what makes you think he'll have one with you?"

"He didn't want another child with you, maybe you were the problem."

She looks a little less confident. "Is that what he said?"

"Pretty much," I lie. "We're happy, and we want to make a real go of things. We can't do that if you're hanging off him, kissing him, trying to lure him back."

She scoffs. "You have no idea what you're talking about, little girl. We were very happily married for ten years. He was my first and only love. And then you came along with your sights set on him and made it your mission to take him away. I did all the hard work, I made him a loveable, respectable man, a father, and you came along with your tight vagina and stretchmark-free backside and decided he was going to be yours. But you can't erase ten years and a child with great sex and blowjobs on tap.

"But for the record, I don't want Dan back. That kiss was a drunken mistake. I hate him, and I hate who he is now, so you're more than welcome to him. Enjoy the snoring, the trail of mess he leaves around, the weekend visits from a tantruming three-year-old, the bitter ex-wife, and everything else that comes with a middle-aged married father of one. Because you, dear sweet, innocent Ashley, are fucking welcome to him." She points to the door. "Now, get the hell out of my home and don't come back here."

MEG

It's been four weeks since my run-in with Ashley and things have been okay. Dan is quiet and less in my face, so maybe she had a chat with him too. He collects Izzy on Friday evening and stays at Matt's with her until Sunday morning. The house is on the market, and we've had two offers, which means we can both start looking for a new place.

Matt shakes hands with the stone-faced woman, Alison, who's about to show me around a nice apartment that's just within my budget. It's my last hope as all the others have been a washout. But when I saw this place online, I fell in love. Not only do they have a concierge with security twenty-four-seven, but it's a fairly new building with a gym and pool downstairs.

We take the elevator to the second floor, and when we step out, there are three apartments on this floor. The excitement bubbles away as she unlocks the door and we step into a large hallway. "There's controlled access downstairs. The concierge will call with visitors, and you can choose if you'd like them to come up or not," says Alison, tapping the telephone on the wall.

We go through to the lounge. It's the perfect size, with large floor-to-ceiling windows looking out over London. Next is the smaller of the bedrooms, which is perfect for Izzy and I know she'll love it. My room is bigger and there's a small balcony. The kitchen is small compared to what I have now, but it's enough for the two of us, as is the bathroom with a walk-in shower. I smile wide as Alison steps away for us to talk. "I love it," I tell Matt, and he sags in relief. I think he's just as exhausted from all this house hunting.

"Love it enough to take it right now?"

I nod eagerly. "I can't miss out on this place, Matt. I can see me and Izzy here."

———

We step out into the fresh air, and I squeal with delight and break out into a happy dance. Matt laughs and hugs me. "You just got a place." Luckily, my parents loaned me some of the deposit until the house sale goes through, plus I had some savings for the holiday I'd wanted to surprise Dan with before the breakup.

We head to a nearby bar for lunch and to celebrate. "Thanks so much for helping me," I say as we stare at the menu.

"What's next?" he asks.

"I have an interview," I announce, and he drops his menu down on the table. "For a school right around the corner from here."

"That's amazing, Meg. You're really putting your life back together."

I smile under his praise. "Thanks. I feel like I am. How's Dan?" I always ask because apart from us dropping off or collecting Izzy, we don't speak unless it's about her.

"He's not much better," he says, picking up the menu again. Matt told me Dan's been quiet and down for weeks. "But he found a place too."

"He did?"

He nods. "He's renting like you, just until the sale goes through, but it looks like a nice place."

"With her?" I ask, bracing myself for more heartache. Matt nods, staring hard at his menu. I told Matt about her visit, but Dan hasn't mentioned it to either of us, so I'm still not sure if he knows.

"Meg?" I look up into the smiling face of Hugo. "I thought that was you," he adds.

I glance around, but there's no one with him. "Hi, Hugo. How are you? This is my friend, Matt." I add it in because it occurs to me, he might think I'm dating, and then I inwardly groan because why should I care?

He nods at Matt, and they shake hands. "I'm good. You?"

"Join us," Matt offers.

"I'm sure he's busy," I cut in, kicking him under the table.

"I'd love to," says Hugo, and Matt slides along his bench so he can sit down. "I've been looking out for you at the park," he says.

"I've been busy," I say. "Do you still go?"

He nods. "Every day."

A silence falls over the table and Matt clears his throat. "Are you single, Hugo?" he asks.

I almost choke and kick him again under the table. This time, Hugo grunts and reaches under the table to rub his leg. "Sorry," I mutter, "I had a cramp."

Matt smirks, taking a drink of his wine while waving the waiter over for a top-up. Hugo orders a bottle. "I am," he says, finally answering his question.

"Matt's gay," I say, arching a brow. "He's always on the prowl."

Matt narrows his eyes in a playful manner. "Oh, I'm not gay," says Hugo, looking apologetic.

"Shame," says Matt. He makes a performance of checking his phone and gasping, "Oh shit, I've got to shoot," he says.

My eyes widen. "What?"

"I'm so sorry, Meg. Here," he stuffs some cash into my hand, "buy Champagne on me." He turns to Hugo, who stands to let him out the booth. "Make her celebrate—she's just got her own place." And then he rushes off, and I silently vow to kill him.

Hugo sits back down, and we smile awkwardly. "You bought a house?"

I shake my head. "An apartment and it's rented."

"Fantastic. Well, congratulations. I assume that means you didn't sort things with your husband?"

I shake my head again. "He's moved on and so have I."

He looks disappointed. "Oh, you met someone?"

"No, god, no," I say with a small laugh. "Just that I've got a new place and we're selling our marital home. It's all going great and these things happen for a reason." I'm rambling, and I inwardly cringe for the second time. "So, what's happening in your life?"

The wine arrives and he tops up both our glasses. "It's all

going good on my end. Haven't killed myself yet," he adds with a laugh.

"Congratulations. Seems we're both celebrating."

We clink glasses. "I saw you," he says in a quieter voice. "A few weeks back, you were in the park and I was talking to someone, but you walked past us."

"I did?" I ask, playing dumb.

"Just in case you were wondering, she's my wife's sister."

"Oh."

"I just wanted to explain in case you thought I was chatting to lots of women in the park." He shifts nervously in his seat, a blush spreading over his cheeks.

"It's none of my business," I say with a shrug, but I'm secretly happy to hear it.

"When I didn't see you again, I thought maybe you were upset with me."

I suddenly feel silly and shake my head. "Of course not." Then I sigh, realising I don't want to lie. "Maybe a little."

He looks relieved. "She turned up at my wife's grave, so we grabbed a coffee. They weren't close and didn't see eye to eye."

"She doesn't live around here?"

He shakes his head. "She was here on business. It happens once in a blue moon. I wanted to chase after you and explain," he says, "but I felt weird about it, like I was reading too much into it and . . ." He trails off. "You make me nervous," he admits, laughing.

I smile too. "I felt embarrassed, like I was maybe coming across stalkerish. I felt like I was one in a long line of coffee-drinking park lovers you were chatting to." I bury my face in my hands. "I'm so embarrassed."

He tugs my hands away, grinning. "My brothers are hounding me to meet with them," he says. "Come with me." I begin to object, but he keeps hold of my hands and gently rubs his thumbs over the backs. It's the most touch I've had since Dan, and my heart swells. "It's Friday, what else are you doing?"

"It's a lot," I tease, "meeting your family on our third date."

He laughs loudly, throwing his head back. "Third date? Were they dates?" I blush. "Now, your stalker tendencies are showing."

DAN

I open the front door, and Ashley smiles back at me. We'd agreed that Izzy should meet her this weekend so she's got some time to adjust before the baby arrives. We have a scan in two weeks, then I plan on telling Meg.

"You ready?" I ask.

She nods, but she looks nervous as she steps inside. I take her through to the living room, where Izzy is bouncing on the couch. She stops, eyeing Ashley with caution. "Iz, remember I said I wanted to introduce you to my friend?" When she doesn't respond, I take Ashley's hand. "This is Ashley."

"Hi," says Ash, giving a little wave. "You must be Izzy. I've heard so much about you."

"When's Mummy coming?" Izzy asks, turning to me and reaching up until I take her in my arms.

"On Sunday, remember?" I've been having her over at Matt's place for the last few weeks, but it's still taking time to adjust. It doesn't help she doesn't have her own room and sleeps in with me. "Next week, when you come to stay, it'll be in our new house."

"With Mummy?"

I sigh. "No, baby, we talked about this. Mummy is getting her own place for you and her, and I'm getting a new place for when you come to stay with me."

"I want our old house."

"How about a game of snap?" Ashley asks, pulling a card deck from her pocket.

I frown. "She doesn't know how."

"We can teach her."

"I want to watch television," says Izzy, and I place her back on the couch and turn on the television.

Ashley follows me into the kitchen. "I don't feel it went well."

"She's still confused," I explain. "Since she's been coming to stay here, she's been asking for us to all be together in the old house. It's hard for her."

"From next week, she'll be seeing me a lot more."

"I know, and then she'll get used to it."

"What if she doesn't?"

I gently kiss her on the head. "She will. Parents separate all the time and the kids survive."

"Did you tell Meg I was meeting Izzy today?" she asks, shrugging from her coat. I notice a small bump showing because she's wearing a short top to show off her midriff.

"I didn't have a chance. She was rushing to get to some viewings."

"Dan," she mutters, "she might not be okay with this."

"Two more weeks and she'll know everything, so it won't matter. You could have hidden this," I add, pulling her to me and placing my hand over her stomach. "I don't need Izzy guessing and telling Meg before I get a chance."

She tugs me close and wraps her arms around my neck. "Can't we sneak off upstairs?"

I groan when she rubs her hand over my cock. "No. She can't be left for a second, she'll destroy something."

Ashley kisses me. "Are you sure?" she whispers against my lips.

"Daddy?" We break apart, and Izzy stares at me through wide eyes.

"Hey, I thought you were watching television." I sweep

her up in my arms and carry her back through to the living room. "Shall we watch this pesky pig together?"

ASHLEY

I watch Dan as he bounces Izzy around on his lap. She giggles, and I can't help but smile. I can't wait to see what he's like with our baby. I subconsciously rub a hand over my tiny bump. I didn't think I wanted this, but seeing how happy he is right now makes me want it.

Two more weeks and we'll know for sure how far along I am, and then we can tell everyone, including Meg.

"Can we call Mummy?" Izzy asks.

Dan glances at me nervously. "We can call her tomorrow."

"But I want to call her now."

He sighs. "Maybe just on a voice call."

"But we always see her face," Izzy complains.

He looks at me. "Do you mind if we call her?" I shake my head, even though I do mind.

"Izzy, we can't tell Mummy about Ashley right now, okay?"

I feel myself bristle at his words. "Why not?" she asks.

"Yeah, why not?" I add.

"Because it might upset her," he tells Izzy, then he turns to me. "Because I didn't clear it with her, and I can't be arsed with the argument."

I shrug. "Fine, whatever."

Dan places his phone on a stand on the table, and he and Izzy lean in close. He presses call, and when she answers, I watch his face light up. "Izzy wanted to see you," he tells her.

"Okay, let me just step outside." It sounds like she's in a bar, but I can't see the screen from where I am. "How are you, baby girl?" she asks once she's outside.

"I want to come home," Izzy announces.

Dan glances at her. "You don't wanna stay with me?" He sounds hurt.

"Baby, we talked about this. It's Daddy's turn to spend some time with you. And you missed him all week, we had to call every night." It's news to me, and I glare at him.

"I don't like his new friend."

Dan groans. "What new friend?" asks Meg, and I hear the anger in her voice already.

Izzy turns the phone stand towards me, and I give a small wave. "Izzy, put Daddy on the phone," she orders.

Dan grabs the phone and changes the call to a voice call. "I should've told you, but you were in a rush this morning," he explains, heading into the kitchen.

I follow and can hear her yelling about co-parenting and making decisions together, and I roll my eyes. She's so uptight. Dan nods, even though she can't see him, and that irritates me more. He's basically agreeing. "Okay, I'm sorry. We'll talk about it on Sunday." There's a man's voice, and Dan stiffens. "Who's that?" he asks. "Meg, are you out with a man?"

I snatch the phone and disconnect the call. He glares at me. "Why do you care who she's with?" I snap, slamming it on the side. "And why are you letting her call all the shots?"

"Because she's Izzy's mum."

"So, you don't get a say in anything? She's your daughter too, and when she's in your care, you should make the decisions."

"You'll understand when you have the baby," he mutters.

"I understand perfectly," I snap. "When you have your little chat on Sunday, I'll be there."

"No," he says firmly. "That's not a good idea."

"We're telling her about the baby, Dan. And we're laying down new rules." I stomp out the house, slamming the door behind me.

MEG

Hugo's brothers are amazing to be around. From the second we arrived, I was swept up in strong arms. Together, they are all very similar. There's a Viking kind of vibe going on with the beards and messy hair, but it's their eyes that show their connection. Hugo is the eldest of the four at thirty-seven years old, then there's Eric, who's thirty-five, James—or Jimmy, as he likes to be called—is thirty-one, and the youngest at twenty-eight is Sebastian.

The sports bar we're in is crammed with rugby fans, and the three large screens around the bar are playing an England versus Wales match. I've never been a sports fan, but I can't help but join in the cheers each time England scores.

"I'm sorry about this," Hugo yells in my ear. "I didn't think it would be so busy."

"It's fine, I'm having fun." And I am. I don't remember a time when I came out like this to let my hair down. Any dates with Dan had all but disappeared after we'd had Izzy, except the odd charity event where we hired a babysitter. And whenever I meet the girls for a drink, it's always nice and civilised, never rowdy and chaotic like this.

"Did you speak to your daughter?" he asks. My smile fades at the mention of the video call I just had with Izzy. He gently takes my hand, as if sensing my anger, and leads me out the bar to the garden area out back. It's a lot quieter out here, with only the odd smoker taking a quick cigarette break. We settle at a wooden table. "Is everything okay?"

"I guess. Izzy is finding things difficult having two houses to stay at. She's confused. And then tonight, Dan decided to introduce his girlfriend to her. He didn't discuss it with me, and I didn't even prepare Izzy for it."

He winces. "Shit move."

"Is it?" I ask. "Because I don't know if I overreacted. I don't know how to deal with any of this." I groan. "Sorry, you don't want to hear about this crap."

"Hey, I like hearing other people's shit. It takes my mind off my own." He gives me a small smile. "He should've spoke to you first, checked how you'd feel."

"Maybe. He understood why I was upset, and he didn't fight me on it like he normally would, but then I think he's been a little depressed lately."

"I'd be depressed if I walked out on you," he says with a wink, and I blush. "It's happened now, so all you can do is speak to him about it and ensure it doesn't happen again."

I nod in agreement. "I like your brothers."

"Should I be worried?"

I laugh. "Do you always get on so well with them?"

He nods. "Generally. They drive me mad most of the time, but they've all been amazing since . . ." He trails off, leaving the sentence hanging. "Anyway, let's get back in there before they cause havoc."

Once inside, he leans in close again, and I get the impression he quite likes being this close. "I forgot to ask, who's baby were you looking after in the park that day?"

"My friend's son, Harry. She just had him and she's finding it hard."

"You're a good friend, Meg."

My phone illuminates in my hand and I answer, pressing

it to my ear and shouting "Hello" as I make my way back outside. "I managed to get Sofia out the house," Zoe says, "and we called round yours with a bottle of wine, but you're not here."

I smile. "Nope. I'm out."

"Out where, and with who?"

"Come and find out," I say. "I'm in the . . ." I look around, but there's no sign out the back, so I turn to a man nearby. "What bar is this?"

"Cooper's Brook," he tells me, and I relay it to Zoe.

Back inside, Eric grabs my hand and pulls me through the crowds to the back of the bar where it's slightly quieter. He points to the table. "You have to lie down."

I glance at Hugo, who shrugs, but he's smiling, so I'm sensing this is some kind of game. I lie back on the table. "Hugo, you're up," says James, slapping his brother on the back.

Hugo comes close. "Are you sure about this?" I smile, nodding. I have no idea what's about to happen, but my drunken mind is telling me to go with it.

Hugo gently moves my hair away from my neck. "Nuh-uh, brother, where we can see," says Eric.

Hugo rolls his eyes, then brings his face so close to my own, I have to restrain myself from inching closer and kissing him. My eyes fix on his lips, and he smirks. "Lie still," he whispers. He places his hands either side of me, leans down, and drags his tongue slowly over the skin just above my breast. I inhale sharply as my skin breaks out in goosebumps. He produces a salt pot, though I have no idea from where, as I'm too focussed on his mouth. He sprinkles salt over the wet patch he left on my chest, then he produces a lemon wedge. "Open," he whispers, tapping it against my lips. I open, and he places it skin down between my lips. "Ready?" I nod.

His brothers count down from three, and Hugo tips a tequila shot into his mouth. He moves over me once again, licking the salt from my skin, taking his time like he's snatching up each individual grain at a time, and then he's staring into my eyes, his lips inches from my own. He takes the lemon between his lips and sucks before gripping it in his mouth and stepping back. He spits it out, takes a second shot, and tips it back. I watch, mesmerised by his every move, and then he sweeps down over me a third time and places his lips against my own. I instinctively open and liquid trickles into my mouth. I wince at the bitter taste, and as Hugo goes to pull back, he swipes his tongue into my mouth, sending a shiver down my spine, right to my toes. He winks, and his brothers cheer.

"Why do I feel like I'm part of some kind of fraternity?" I ask, pushing to sit.

"Your turn," says Jimmy. "Pick a victim."

Hugo's eyes are fixed on me, but out the corner of my eye, I see Zoe waving frantically as she pushes through the crowd with Sofia right behind her. "I choose her," I say, pointing to Zoe.

"Hey," she greets. "I didn't know this place was here." She kisses me on the cheek.

"Gentlemen, meet Zoe and Sofia, my very best friends." I turn to the men. "Ladies, this is Hugo, Eric, Jimmy, and Seb."

"Oh my," mutters Zoe as each takes a turn to kiss her and then Sofia on the cheek.

"Let's just pause the game for a second," Hugo announces, grabbing hold of my hand. "We'll be right back." He pulls me from the bar, this time leading me out the front. "I just have to . . ." He backs me against the wall, placing an arm above my head and leaning close. He's staring at me with curiosity, and maybe a hint of trepidation. "Just one time," he says, and then he kisses me. His fingers gently take my chin, tilting my head, and his tongue expertly sweeps into my mouth while his lips brush my own. He leans his body in, moving closer until he's pressed against me. The way he towers over me, so commanding and strong, makes me feel weak at the knees.

When he finally pulls back, his eyes are dark with need. "We should . . . get back inside," he murmurs.

"Right," I whisper, nodding. My body is alight with excitement, and all I really want is to feel his lips on me again, but I can see in his eyes he's conflicted.

"You go ahead," he mutters, turning his back to me. "I just need a minute."

Zoe grabs me the second I walk back inside. "Oh my god, is that park guy?" I nod. "He's gorgeous."

Sofia is right behind her. "What happened out there?"

"Nothing," I say with a shrug. "We just kissed."

They both squeal in excitement, and I rush to shush them, glancing around to make sure Hugo isn't nearby. Luckily, there's no sign of him.

"Just calm down. Remember, he's grieving, so it was probably just a one-time thing." As I say the words, I'm silently hoping it isn't.

"Ah man," says Jimmy, staring at his phone, "Hugo's left."

My ears prick up and my heart beats rapidly in my chest. "What do you mean he's gone?" asks Eric. Jimmy holds his mobile up for his brothers to read, and Eric laughs, "Bloody lightweight, can't handle the shots."

"Hugo's left?" I ask.

"Yeah. What did you do to him out there?" Jimmy teases.

I blush and turn away. "Shots anyone?" I ask, heading for the bar.

DAN

Sunday rolls around far too quickly. I changed the pickup plans with Meg, so we're meeting in the park. It's a copout. I know Ashley is coming over in the hope we'll tell Meg about the baby, but that isn't going to happen, and this was the only way I knew how to avoid it.

As I stroll across the park hand-in-hand with Izzy, I spot Meg walking towards us. She's looking good, just how I remember her pre-Izzy. Her hair hangs in loose curls, and she's even wearing a light dusting of makeup, giving her a glow.

When she reaches us, she swipes Izzy up in her arms and spins her, planting kisses all over her face. I smile, wishing I'd taken more time to immerse myself in these kinds of moments when we were together. "You look good," I say, the words tumbling out before I can stop them.

Her smile fades slightly as she places Izzy back on her feet and takes her hand. "You thought the park would save you from having the talk we so desperately need?" she asks.

I shake my head. "Not at all. Let's grab a coffee. There's a great little shack back there," I say, pointing behind her.

She glances back. "Let's just sit over there," she mutters, pointing to a bench overlooking the play area. "Izzy can go off and play."

We sit down, and Izzy rushes off towards the slide.

"I just want to start by apologising," I say. She looks surprised, and I smile. "I can admit when I'm wrong."

"It just would've been nice to talk about something like that. Izzy meeting Ashley is a huge step, for her and us."

"I know," I agree. "I wasn't thinking."

"What's the urgency anyway? Why rush it?" I stare down at my feet. "I mean, if you two are the real thing," she pauses, and I hear the pain in her voice, "then you have plenty of time to introduce them."

"It's just . . . well, Ashley will be around a lot more when I move into the new house."

"Okay," she says, also staring down at the ground, "but wouldn't it have made more sense to wait until you'd moved in, then have Izzy over for dinner? She'd probably handle it better if the introductions are small and short. She's only three."

"You're right. You're always right."

"Was that a dig?"

I sigh, shaking my head. "No, not at all. I should've spoken to you about it, then we could've decided what was best for Iz. I'm sorry."

She smiles. "Look at us, working together like adults."

I grin too. "We're getting good at it."

"So, I need to ask a favour. I'm moving into the new place tomorrow." My head whips around. I knew she was looking at places, but I didn't expect it to be so quick. "I had savings," she explains, "and my parents helped with the deposit. I just thought it'd be nice to make a fresh start, and I hate being in that house without . . ."

"Me?" I ask, and she nods.

"It's weird being in our family home where we made so many memories and not having you there." She sighs. "Izzy does something and I want to tell you about it, then I remember you're not around anymore and it hurts all over again. Maybe in my new place, that won't happen. So, can you collect Izzy from school and keep her for dinner? I can come by and collect her about six-thirty?"

"Sure. Not a problem."

"Have you sorted a job?" she asks.

Since losing my job at the university, I've been using savings to live off. "I've got an interview on Wednesday."

"Wow, me too," she says with a smile. "I hope it all goes well. Still in education?" I nod. Luckily, her father hasn't reported me for any kind of breech on the understanding I left quietly, taking Ashley with me. He didn't want bad press for the university, and I needed to continue doing what I love.

Meg stands. "I have to shoot. I'll see you tomorrow."

ASHLEY

I pace outside Matt's house. There's nobody in, despite Dan telling me to be here for ten o' clock. I'm about to give up and leave when Dan walks around the corner. He spots me and his step falters, but he forces a smile as he gets closer. "Sorry, I forgot to text you and tell you we had a change of plan."

"Really?" I snap, glaring at him.

"Meg was out, so we met at the park. It was all last minute, so I forgot to text you. Sorry." He leans in to kiss me, and I turn my head so it lands on my temple.

I follow him inside. "Have you told her about the baby?"

"Not yet."

We go into the kitchen. "Why?"

"Because we agreed to do it after the scan."

"What difference does it make?"

He gently rubs my arm. "After what Meg went through, I don't want to risk anything bad happening." He's referring to her miscarriage, which pisses me off, but how can I argue with that? "We'll tell her, I promise."

"You'll have to soon. I'm beginning to show. It can't be a secret forever."

"I know." He turns on the kettle. "I heard from the estate agent. We can move into the house next week."

The news lightens my mood. "We can? That's great. I can't wait to decorate the baby's room."

He bites his lower lip. "It's only two bedrooms."

I nod. "I know." I haven't seen it yet. Dan went to look at it and said it was perfect for us, so he accepted it right there.

"So, Izzy will need a room."

I frown. "And our baby won't?"

"Of course, but initially, it'll be Izzy's room because the baby will sleep in with us."

I shake my head. "No. It will be the baby's room and Izzy can stay in there when she sleeps over."

He groans. "Don't make this a thing. The baby doesn't

need a fucking room for months. I need Izzy to feel settled with us, or she'll be forever crying for her mum."

"Then stop forcing her to stay with you," I snap.

He pinches the bridge of his nose. "You don't get it. Izzy has to be my priority right now while she's still upset over me and her mum separating. My time with her is precious, and I want her to stay over and see this place as her second home."

"What should we do with our baby then? Stick it in the cupboard every weekend?"

"Now, you're just being ridiculous. The baby will sleep in our room for the first few months, and then Izzy and the baby will share."

"Not happening."

"Why?"

"Because . . ." I throw my arms up in the air. "I don't even know Izzy and I'm supposed to let her share a room with my baby."

He frowns. "She's just a little girl, and this baby with be her half-sibling."

"Don't remind me," I mutter.

"We can't do this if you can't accept Izzy is a huge part of my life," he snaps.

"What are you saying?"

"I'm saying, either accept my daughter as part of the package or forget us."

Twenty

MEG

It's been a mad rush to pack up everything I want to take from the house and move it into a smaller apartment. I left most of the furniture for Dan, apart from Izzy's bedroom furniture, just because I thought she'd settle better with her own things. And as I stand in my new living room, watching everyone putting together a flat pack unit, I smile. Zoe is bossing Matt and Sofia around. Carl, Matt's lover, is rocking Harry to sleep in his pushchair, and my parents are in the bedroom, putting together my new bed.

I place the tray of drinks on the glass coffee table. "Right, how are we getting on?"

———

Dan insists on bringing Izzy to the new place rather than letting me collect her like we'd agreed. I think he probably just wants to check it out. I don't blame him, as I'd want to see where my daughter was going to be living, so when the concierge calls me to announce his arrival, I unlock the door and wait for the lift to open. I smile wide as Izzy runs into my arms. "She's been so excited," he tells me.

The others only left ten minutes ago, and there's still a few stacked-up flat packs waiting to be built. "Ignore the mess, there's still a lot to do."

I walk from room to room, showing them. I feel proud as Izzy excitedly bounces on her bed. She's happy, and that's all I was worried about.

Dan leans against the door frame, watching her. "It's a nice place," he says.

"I love it. And with the added security, it gives me peace of mind. I didn't realise how relaxed I felt having a man around the place."

Dan rolls his eyes. "I feel like these little digs are getting old."

I frown in confusion. "It wasn't a dig." Things have been better between us, but I can tell he's angling for a fight, and I don't want him to ruin my happy mood.

"Christmas is just over a week away," he states. "What are we doing with Izzy?"

"Well, she'll be here with me on Christmas day."

"That's not fair," he snaps.

I sigh, knowing I can't avoid an argument now. "Izzy, play nicely. I'll come back in a minute, I just need to talk to Daddy."

I close the bedroom door, and we go back down the hall and into the living room. "So, you just get her on Christmas day with no discussion?" he snaps.

"Yes."

"Why?"

I grit my teeth. "Because I didn't leave."

"You can't punish me forever. So, we broke up, I wasn't happy, did you expect me to stick around?"

I arch a brow. "Wow. Get it all off your chest, Dan."

"Well, what do you expect? That I'll just roll over while you get to take all the best bits of our daughter?"

"Yah know, I was going to suggest you come over and see

her open her presents, but maybe that's not such a good idea."

"I want my own time with her, Meg. If I wanted to sit with you and see her open her presents, I wouldn't have left you."

Tears fill my eyes, and I blink them away. I'm determined not to cry in front of him. "I can see you're not in a good mood," I begin, heading towards the door. "Maybe you should go, and we can talk about this another time."

"I want her Christmas night."

"We watch movies together Christmas night," I argue. We've always done it. We get all the blankets and pillows from our beds, throw them on the living room floor, wear our Christmas pyjamas, and watch movies.

"Well, you were so keen to start afresh, maybe you should get new traditions."

His words hurt, and I press my lips in a tight line to stop me screaming at him. "Is that why you're upset, because of this place?"

"No, I'm glad you're starting over. I am too."

"So, what's the problem?"

"The problem is, I deserve quality time with Izzy too, and you can't punish me because I chose to leave you. I should still get to see her at Christmas."

"Christmas night?" I ask, and he nods. I shrug. "Fine. What time?"

"And Boxing Day. I'll pick her up at four and keep her for two nights."

"Hold on, four? That's way too early."

"Four," he snaps.

"Whatever, Dan. I just want you to leave."

DAN

Ashley refuses to speak to me. She cancels my calls and ignores me knocking at her door. I don't know what to say to make things better because I can't back down on Izzy's bedroom. It's non-negotiable. I'm about to go into the school for my interview, so I shoot her a text telling her we have the keys for the house and asking if she'd like me to pick her up later to have a look around, then I turn off my phone and head inside.

The receptionist smiles brightly as I sign my name into the large book on her desk, then I take a seat. I hate having to come back to a secondary school, but Ashley wasn't keen on me moving to another university, so to keep the peace, I applied for English teacher. *Maybe she doesn't trust me.*

The doors slide open, and I hear heels clicking on the polished floor. I bristle at the sound of Meg's voice as she tells the receptionist she's here for a job interview. I inwardly groan as she signs in then heads towards me. Her eyes widen as she hisses, "What are you doing here?"

"Same as you, apparently."

"This is the school? Why aren't you applying to a university?"

"Because . . . never mind that. We can't both interview for a job here. What if we get it?"

"I need this," she hisses, taking a seat.

"So do I, but we can't work together."

The office door opens, and Meg takes a sharp breath. It's the guy from the park I saw her with a few weeks back. He looks just as shocked to see her, but he pulls himself together quickly, straightens his tie, and turns to me. "Mr. Headford?" I nod, standing, and he shakes my hand. "I'm Hugo Chadwick, the headteacher."

HUGO

Why is my heart hammering so hard at seeing her? The fact she's sitting right next to her ex is a strange coincidence. When I saw the matching surnames on the applications, I was intrigued, assuming a married couple had come for a job in the same school. We don't often get that, but when I saw the different addresses, I thought it was a coincidence. It never occurred to me that it was the same Megan I'd been thinking about for the last few weeks, or her stupid arse of an ex, Daniel. I inwardly groan at my own stupidity as I show him into my office.

The school governor shakes Daniel's hand. "Can I just grab a drink?" I ask. "Anyone else?" They both shake their heads. "Start without me," I say, leaving the office and closing the door.

Meg stands as I stride over to her. "Hey," I say, giving a half-smile, half-grimace. I totally did a runner right after I kissed her, and now, I feel like a prick. I'd even avoided going to that end of the park, just in case I bumped into her, and now, she's here standing right in front of me. If I believed in angels, I'd think Elizabeth was bringing us together in some cruel form of torture, because I'm so not ready to move on. "You're here," I add.

"Your school?" she asks, still looking shocked. "You never said what you did for a living."

It's true, I didn't, because people seem to think head-teachers are boring, and I didn't want to give her that impression. "Don't let it put you off. You're here for the assistant's job, and teaching assistants are the heart of our school."

She glances at the exit, and I brace myself for her excuse to get the hell out of here. Not that I blame her—this must be the most awkward situation ever. "Meg, is that you?" I groan as my brother rounds the corner.

Meg turns to Jimmy and smiles. "Jimmy, you work here too?"

"P.E. teacher. What are you doing here?"

"Interviewing for a T.A. position."

"Fantastic, we're desperate for some fresh blood around

here. Don't tell them I said this, but all the T.A.s here are over fifty."

Meg laughs, and her sound warms my heart. "They're waiting in the office," I tell him pointedly.

"Just need the bathroom," he says with a wink as he rushes off.

"It's a bit of a family affair," I explain. "Eric is my assistant head too."

"Wow," she says, smiling, "that really is a family affair. Look, if this is weird or awkward, I can just . . ." She points to the exit.

"No, not at all. Erm, did you know about Daniel applying?" Maybe they get along really well these days and want to work together. I don't know how I feel about that.

"No," she says, rolling her eyes, "I didn't."

"There's no marker on his file. I'd have thought after what he did at the university, he'd have been struck off."

She blushes. "Oh shit, I told you about that. He's good at what he does," she says, "and technically, he didn't break the law."

She shrugs helplessly, and I leave it there. There's a reason he's not been reported, but I don't have time to delve into that now. I give a nod. "I'll keep that in mind."

Back in the office, Dan is wowing Peter with his tales of university life. The door opens and Eric comes in, taking a seat behind the desk beside me. "Sorry I'm late. Year elevens are crazy today," he says, shaking Dan's hand. "I'm Eric Chadwick, assistant head."

"Chadwick?" Dan repeats.

"Brothers," Eric confirms. "There're three of us here. It can get confusing, but the kids are fine with it."

I glance at Dan's application form. It's extremely impressive when you don't know his history. "Why did you leave your last job?" I ask. It's going off the listed questions we came up with, but I want to know if he'll be honest, and by the look on his face, I can tell he's going to lie.

"University life isn't for me."

"Why?" I feel Eric glance at me, but I stare right at Daniel.

"I like to be busy. I miss the hectic schedule of teaching eleven- to sixteen-year-olds," he says with a nervous laugh.

"The stacks of marking and planning?" Eric jokes.

Dan nods. "Exactly."

The others question him according to the list we have, both scribbling notes. I don't bother because I already know he isn't who we're going to hire today.

"Eric will observe you for the next half-hour teaching our year nines," I say with a smug smile as I feel Eric glaring in my direction. We'd previously discussed sticking to our year seven or eleven, just because they're a little easier. Year nines are our hardest group. "Nine B should be in English right now," I say, and Eric leans close to my ear.

"Seriously?"

I nod. "Yes. I'll get on with the next interview."

Once Eric and Dan have gone, Pete turns to me. "Nine B? What the hell, Hugo?"

I smile as I head for the door. "He'll be fine. He's worked in a university. I want to see what he's got."

"Those kids will scare him off before we've even made a decision."

"Then he's not the guy for the job," I say simply. "Mrs. Headford," I say out into the hall, "we're ready for you." We have one day left before we break for Christmas, and I'd like to get the interviews wrapped up, so I can enjoy the holiday break.

MEG

I breeze the interview and I'm prepared for a test run, like the letter I received inviting me for this interview had explained.

But Hugo stands and holds out his hand for me to shake. "It was great to meet you. We'll be in touch."

My heart sinks a little. "Oh, you don't want to see what I can do?"

He shakes his head, giving an awkward smile. "We have enough to go on, and I can see from your resume that you have previous experience."

I give a knowing nod and head for the door after shaking the hand of the governor. "Thanks for seeing me today. I hope to hear from you."

Dan is already signing out at the desk, and he glares at me as I approach to do the same. "Well, that was a fucking disaster," he whispers close to my ear. "I don't think lover boy liked me so much." I sign out and leave with Dan hot on my tail. "Did you know he worked here?"

"No," I mutter. "I told you, we don't know each other that well."

"This job is well below my pay grade," he mutters angrily.

"Then why did you go for it?"

"Because I wasn't left with a fucking choice, thanks to your father."

"Don't blame him because you screwed a student."

His face pales. "Oh my god, does he know about that?" he asks, glancing back at the school.

"No," I say a little too quickly. I hate to lie, but how was I supposed to know they'd ever meet when I spilled the secret to Hugo? Besides, it's true. "Have you packed everything you need from the house?" I ask, changing the subject.

He narrows his eyes but lets me get away with it and nods. "Yes, I'll have it all out by tomorrow evening."

"Would you like me to keep Izzy so you can settle in?"

"No. It's my day," he snaps.

I sigh heavily and turn out of the school gates and head for the park. I see why Hugo comes here so often—it's literally across the road. "I was just trying to help you out, Dan."

"You should know Ashley is moving in with me tomorrow," he adds.

"I thought she would be," I answer. I lower onto the nearest bench, just by the park gates, and Dan stands before me. "Are you sure about this?" I ask. It's moving very fast considering he was begging me back not so long ago.

"Why wouldn't I be? She's gorgeous, young, clever." He forces a smile, and I nod.

"Well, as long as you're happy."

"I am. Very. In fact, it's the happiest I've ever been."

I want to roll my eyes but instead stare out across the park. I'm getting used to the bitterness in his voice and the way he keeps digging at me. I've put it down to anger that I haven't forgiven him and taken him back. Now we've both found new places to live, it's becoming real. "We should talk to Izzy about it, so she understands."

"Actually, I'm glad you've raised that because I do need to run something by you before I tell Izzy next week," he says, and there's a steely look in his eye.

I brace myself for whatever he's going to throw at me next. "Okay."

He sits beside me and rubs the palms of his hands over his knees a few times, like he's nervous, and suddenly, I feel a dread come over me. His eyes reach mine, and I just know from the pain in them that he's about to break me all over again. "Ash and I are . . . well, we're having a baby." I inhale sharply and curl my fingers under the edge of the bench, digging my nails into the rotting wood. My vision blurs, and the group of people I was just watching across the park blend into one. It's not the news I expected to hear.

"I know this is hard for you to hear, but there was no easy way to tell you. I'd really like your support when I tell Iz. She should be encouraged to be excited. This will be her half-sibling." I find myself wondering if he means to be so cruel or if he's just trying to fill the silence. "Say something," he urges, and I feel his eyes burning into the side of my head.

But there are no words that immediately rush to my mind. All I want to do right now is scream, but instead, I push to stand. "Baby," he whispers, his tone pleading, and a choked sob leaves my throat. It's almost a glimpse of the Dan I used to know. "Please talk to me."

I walk away, thankful when he doesn't bother to follow me.

HUGO

I sigh with relief when the lunch bell sounds. The day is dragging, and I can't think straight since seeing Meg earlier. I had a battle on my hands with Pete, who wanted to hire both Dan and Meg. It was a job convincing him that neither where right for the position.

I grab my coat and head straight out the building and across to the park. It's the only place where I feel I can truly breathe. "Hey, handsome," Sonia greets me. She's been working at the coffee hut in the park for as long as I've been coming here, and every day, she greets me the same. She hands over my coffee, and I throw the extra change I have into her collection pot to pay for the homeless to grab a coffee.

"Have a great afternoon," I tell her as I head towards the bench.

My step falters when I spot Meg hunched over. She looks upset, and it's the only reason my feet continue toward her. "Meg?" She jumps in fright, looking up and blinking through tears. "Jesus, are you okay?" I wonder if the office has already begun making calls about the job.

"Shit, is that the time already?" She sniffles, standing and wiping her cheeks with the sleeves of her coat. "I didn't realise. Sorry," she says, and she turns to walk away.

"Hey," I take her hand, and she freezes, looking down at our connection, "you don't need to leave."

She uses her free hand to point to the bench. "This is your place," she says, choking on a sob.

"I don't own it," I say, offering a small smile. "Besides, this is the best bench in the park to cry on."

"Yeah?" she asks, wiping her cheek again.

I nod. "It's rotting away with people's tears. Come, sit." She lets me tug her down beside me, and for some reason, I don't release her hand. "Is it the job?"

She stares through wide eyes. "Oh shit, I didn't get the job?"

I falter. "Erm, we haven't made a decision yet," I lie, "but I wondered if I'd upset you in some way."

She shakes her head. "No, nothing like that. I'm being silly."

"Why not tell me and I'll decide if you're being silly."

She takes a deep breath, releasing it slowly. "Dan and his new girlfriend are having a baby."

"Shit," I mutter. "He just told you?"

Meg nods, a fresh set of tears streaking down her cheeks. "And I know it's nothing to do with me now, but it fucking hurts."

"Of course, it does," I agree, pulling her into my side and wrapping an arm around her shoulders. She leans her head against my chest.

"He wants me to be all happy in front of Izzy so she's excited."

"Jesus, the guy's got no shame."

"It's like he forgot we lost a baby," she sobs. "A baby he never even wanted, and now, he's doing it with her."

"Oh Meg," I whisper, kissing her head and inhaling the scent of her shampoo. I briefly close my eyes and picture wrapping it around my fist and kissing her so she'll forget that prick.

"It's like I don't even know him anymore."

"I guess you stopped knowing him the second he began sneaking about," I say, gently stroking my hand down her silky hair. "He's not worth your tears."

"How does he do it? How does he just turn off his feelings for me and move on like what we had for eleven years was nothing? I can't even kiss a guy without giving him the creeps . . ." She trails off, wincing. "Sorry."

"Hey," I say, brushing a hand down her damp cheek and tipping her head back to look at me, "you didn't give me the creeps."

"You legged it," she says, laughing through her tears.

"I did, but not because of you. Well, not totally." I twist so I'm facing her. "I haven't liked anyone since Elizabeth," I admit, and her expression softens. "It freaked me out because I had this overwhelming need to . . . well, it doesn't matter. But it wasn't anything you did. I'm sorry if I made you feel like it was."

She shrugs, wiping her face again. "It doesn't matter anyway. I'm sorry for crying on your shoulder . . . again. You must think I'm crazy."

She stands, and I rise to my feet, not ready for her to leave. "Why don't I chuck a sicky this afternoon and we go for dinner and a drink?"

She shakes her head. "I have to pick Izzy up in a couple hours." She begins to walk away. "Thanks for being so nice, Hugo." She turns to me, walking backwards. "If only it was a different time."

It's seconds before I'm marching towards her. I can't ignore the effect she's having on me, and she stops, staring wide-eyed as I approach. "Fuck a different time," I murmur, and I wrap my hand in her hair and kiss her with everything I have. Her tiny hands grip the lapels of my jacket as our mouths hungrily move together. We pull apart, both breathless.

"My place?" I ask, and she nods. "Great," I say, elation spreading through my body. I grab her hand, and we march towards my place. As we walk with urgency, I call Mandy, my receptionist. "I'm sick," I say, "so I won't be back this afternoon. Call me if anything urgent comes up." I disconnect before she can call me out on my shit—she knows me too well and knows I'm never sick.

MEG

I stare in shock at the large building as we head for the entrance. "You live here?" I squeak. He leads us inside, and the man on the concierge, Ted, looks up. "Mr. Chadwick," he greets, then brings his eyes to me. "Ms.—" I shake my head, and he clamps his mouth shut. The last thing I need is for Hugo to realise I've moved into his building.

"Headford," I finish for him, like we don't know each other and I don't bring him a cinnamon roll every morning when I return from the school run.

"Ms. Headford." He nods, looking confused.

"Ted," Hugo says back, nodding in greeting and clearly not noticing the awkwardness between me and his concierge guy. He presses for the elevator, watching each floor light impatiently as it rides down to us.

We step inside, and I almost choke on fresh air when he presses for floor two. *Fuck, fuck, fuck.*

I don't have time to process because as the doors close, Hugo pushes me up against the elevator wall and kisses me until my toes curl. I mentally thank the universe that I put on nice underwear this morning because good underwear makes me feel nice and I had to walk into that interview with confidence. It's all happening so fast. I give my head a shake as he pulls back, then the doors slide open. "You sure about this?" he asks, pulling his jacket over his obvious erection.

I grin, nodding as he rams the key into the lock of his door, the one that's maybe five strides away from my own.

The second we get inside, he's ripping his coat off and pulling me to him. His lips are gentler this time, and he walks me backwards as he loosens his tie, followed by a short pause to kick off his shoes. I take that second to glance around and realise his apartment is a direct match of my own. "Bedroom's through there," he whispers against my mouth. "I'll grab us a drink."

I shake my head, taking his collar in my hands and pulling him back for another kiss. I don't need to be alone to reevaluate or overthink what I'm about to do. This is so irresponsible of me and something I've never done in my life, but Dan's words ring in my ears about our boring sex life and it drives me forward.

Hugo smiles and leads me to his bedroom. There's a large bed, perfectly made with the sheets tucked in, and it's surprisingly clean and tidy. He steps back as I sit down on the edge. "It's been a long time since I," he glances down at the floor, "well, since I've had sex."

I nod. "Same." I want to add that I am so inexperienced, I'm currently panicking, but he moves towards me, caging me in with an arm either side of me. I lie back slightly, resting up on my elbows. "Should we close the curtains?" I ask.

He shakes his head. "I don't have any."

I glance back at the windows. "How do you sleep?"

He grins. "I let the light wake me naturally. I hate alarms."

"You don't set an alarm?"

He shakes his head again, swooping down to kiss me. I lie back fully, and he hovers over me, trailing kisses across my cheek and down my neck. He takes his time, and I don't mean to compare the two, but it feels nice being with a man who's looking at me like he wants to give me the world while making me his last meal.

He slides my top up, placing kisses along my stomach,

and when he reaches my bra, he unclips the front fasten with ease. I ignore the self-conscious voice in my head wondering if he's noticed the stretch marks across my stomach. "Relax," he whispers against my skin. "You're beautiful." It's like he's read my mind as he takes my nipple into his warm mouth, humming in approval.

Hugo licks and kisses as he moves down my body, working the buttons free on my pencil skirt and rolling it down my thighs until it's off completely. He hooks his fingers in my knickers, removing them too. I waxed just last week, but I'm sure it's not as neat as I'd have done it had I known this handsome man would have his head between my legs. I feel myself blush and glance down to watch in case his reaction is one of disgust.

His eyes are full of heat, and they connect with mine right as he licks along my opening. I gasp, arching my back when he does it again. My worries are instantly forgotten and replaced with need.

His finger enters me, and with the pressure of his mouth, I feel my orgasm building. It's been too long since I've felt this alive just from a touch, and I come apart, gasping and screwing the sheets up in my hands, amazed at my body's reaction.

I'm panting as Hugo slides up my body. He somehow got naked in the seconds between my mind-blowing orgasm and this moment, and I resist the urge to look between us to see what he looks like down there. Smiling to myself, I feel like a teenager. "You good?" he asks, and I nod. "You taste fucking amazing," he adds, smirking right before he kisses me, forcing me to taste myself on his lips. Somehow, it doesn't turn my stomach like it used to when Dan did it.

Hugo makes it sexy with his hungry eyes and dimpled smirk. He takes my hands and pushes them above my head. "Anyone ever tell you, you're gorgeous?" he asks, staring hard into my eyes. The way he stares me down makes me feel more confident, like I'm beautiful. He kisses me again, slow and sexy, then he pauses to rip open a condom and sheath himself.

I feel his erection pressing at my entrance. He slides in carefully, stretching me an inch at a time, occasionally stopping to give me time to open for him. He drops kisses on my lips, and no matter how hard I want to, he doesn't let me look away. There's something hot about being forced to stare into his heated eyes, and when he's in as far as I can take him, he groans. It's deep and guttural, almost primal. "I need to watch you ride me," he murmurs against my lips.

I hesitate, not confident fucking a stranger in the daylight, but before I can object, he rolls us so I'm on top.

He laces our fingers together, his eyes roaming my body. "Don't be shy," he encourages. "You're hot."

"I'm really not," I mutter, my confidence dipping.

He frowns. "Are you shitting me? Meg, you're gorgeous."

I give a small, unsure shrug, and he sits, causing me to lean back slightly. "I don't usually do this sort of thing," I admit, "and especially like this."

"Like what?"

"In the daylight. I'm a lights off kind of girl."

He pushes us to the edge of the bed, and I climb from him. He stands and turns me so my back is to his front, then he walks me over to a full-length mirror. I turn my head slightly, but he takes my chin, forcing me to look in the mirror. He's taller than me, towering over me as we stare at one another through the glass. "You're perfect, Meg." He sounds so sincere, and I find myself staring at my body. He runs his fingers down my arm, up my stomach, and over my breasts. "You're sexy."

"I have bumps and marks," I whisper, my voice sounding unsure, and he shakes his head. "Stretch marks," I add, like that confirms it all.

"They add to your beauty," he tells me, burying his face

into the crook of my neck and kissing there. He bends me slightly, slipping back into me. I gasp, reaching behind to grip onto his thighs. We lock eyes in the mirror, and he moves, the friction sending sparks through my body. "Jesus," he groans, wrapping my hair around his fist. "I've thought about this moment so many times," he pants, moving faster.

He holds my hip with his other hand, his pace jerky, then he slips his hand between my legs, rubbing circles over my swollen clit. I lift my arms over my head and grip his, running my fingers through his hair. We're still locked in a heated stare as we both come apart. It's the hottest thing I've ever watched as he growls, gritting his teeth as his body stiffens and he climaxes.

The only sound in the room is our heavy breathing. He slips from me but continues to kiss my neck and run his hands over my body.

"I hate to break the spell," I murmur.

He pulls me closer. "Don't say it," he whispers.

I smile at our reflection. "I have to go and get Izzy."

"It's two-thirty," he murmurs. "I'll drive you."

"It's a five-minute walk," I tell him, "but I need to change."

"I need your number," he says, releasing me.

I begin to dress, and he disappears into the bathroom to remove the condom. When he returns, he looks uncomfortable, and his eyes wander to a picture laying face down on his bedside table. I never noticed it before, but I can only assume it's of him and his wife. Guilt suddenly hits me, and I dress quicker, slipping my feet into my heels. "Thanks for . . ." I stop talking, not knowing what to say. "I'll see myself out."

"Meg, wait," he mutters, but I'm already rushing down the hall and through the living room. I get to the front door and glance behind to make sure he isn't watching me, then I leave, pressing for the elevator, just in case he's listening, before letting myself into my apartment.

I lean back against the door and release the breath I'm holding. I thought I'd feel good, and I did, for a short time. Being with Hugo was different, and maybe even better than with Dan, but I can't shake the guilt I feel. And he clearly felt the same, enough to place the picture of his wife face down while we had sex. *Oh my god, did we have sex in their bedroom? He never said whether they'd lived there together or he'd moved since her death.*

I send a text to Zoe and Sofia, asking for drinks tomorrow night. I'll need them to help me take my mind off Izzy not being here. I hate it when she's with Dan—the place seems so quiet without her. Zoe agrees, and Sofia tells us she'll try to find a sitter for Harry. I take a deep, cleansing breath and release it slowly. At least I made the first step to get over my marriage breakup. No one said it would be easy.

Twenty-Two

ASHLEY

I've been ignoring Dan ever since our argument over the bedroom. He even texted me to say he had the keys for the new house, asking if I wanted to see it. I immediately called Molly and asked her to meet me for a drink. She doesn't judge me like Lauren. But when Molly walks into the bar followed by Lauren, I groan in annoyance. They take a seat, and Molly gives me an apologetic smile.

"Look, you might not like what I have to say," Lauren begins, "but at least I don't sugar-coat it." She grabs my hand and gently gives it a squeeze. "I love you, and you're my best friend. I'm still here for you."

"I'm keeping the baby," I announce, and they exchange a look that tells me they think I'm crazy.

"Congratulations," says Molly, wincing as the word leaves her mouth. "Right?"

"I'm still getting used to the idea."

"How does Dan feel?" asks Lauren.

"He's excited," I lie, because he hasn't really shown the slightest interest in the baby, and all we've really done since I told him is argue.

"Really?" she queries. My smile faulters, and she grabs my hand again. "Oh Ash, what the fuck's going on?"

"He kissed her . . . his wife," I admit, "and I think he was going to break it off with me."

"Wait, you are pregnant, aren't you?" Lauren asks. "It's not a lie to keep him?"

"I wouldn't lie about that," I snap, outraged she thinks I'd stoop so low. "But I said I was keeping it because I panicked, thinking he was going to end things with me. And now, I'm kind of going along with it."

"Shit, Ash. Is this what you really want?" asks Molly.

I nod. "He said he'd stick by me whatever I decided, so this is what I decided."

"So, why do you look so sad?"

I bury my head in my hands. "I'm supposed to be moving in with him tomorrow, and his three-year-old daughter hates me. He doesn't want the baby to have the only other bedroom, insisting Izzy should have it to make her feel welcome, but what about me and my child?" When I look up, they're both staring at me like I've lost my mind. "What?" I ask.

"It's just weird," says Molly, shrugging. "A few months ago, before you met him, we were drinking every night and your only worry was how to fund a night of tequila shots. Now, you're talking about a house and kids."

Sadness fills my chest at the life I used to have. "I know."

"Don't you miss it?" asks Lauren. I nod because I do miss how simple things were before Dan. "Do you really want this baby?"

I shrug. My gut tells me no, but the thought of losing Dan hurts. "I fought so hard for him," I mutter.

"And look how miserable you are," Lauren points out.

"Maybe you need to talk to Dan and find out how he really feels," Molly says gently. "You might discover neither of you are truly happy."

———

Dan turns up the following morning at my door, and Allie refuses to lie for me again, so I step outside to where he's pacing back and forth. He stops when he sees me. "You haven't answered my messages. I was worried," he says, wrapping his arms around me. "I told her . . . I told Meg about the baby."

My heart skips a beat. I didn't expect him to say that. "What did she say?" I ask.

"Don't worry about it. Today, we're moving into our new place, and I don't want anything to ruin it." He looks so happy that I begin to question whether I should raise my worries at all. "And I have Izzy from three o' clock, so we need to get a move on."

My heart sinks again. "We need to talk."

"Later," he says, grabbing my hand. "I can't wait for you to see the house. And I've been thinking, you're right about the bedroom. Izzy will love it however you decorate it, and she's only there for two nights a week. It's important the baby has somewhere."

DAN

I feel a resistance as I lead Ashley up the path towards our new home. I glance back and smile reassuringly. "We really do need to talk," she whispers, and I can't stand the look on her face, like she's changed her mind. I ignore her and open the front door, then I bend at the knee and scoop her into my arms. "Dan, what are you doing?" she whisper-hisses as I carry her over the threshold.

"Wait until you see the bedroom," I tell her, carrying her straight upstairs. "It's so big, I've ordered a super king-sized bed. There'll be enough room for me, you, the baby, and Izzy," I say with a laugh. I check my watch as I place her back on her feet. "And it's arriving any minute."

"But we need to talk."

I pull her to me and kiss her hard. "Don't ruin this, Ash. Not today, please." The doorbell sounds, and I smile. "That's the bed. I'll be right back."

The delivery men carry the bed upstairs, and while they set it up, I show Ash around the rest of the house. She doesn't mention the talk again, but she's still quiet as I try to drum up some enthusiasm.

Once the delivery men have left, we return to the bedroom. There's plastic covering the mattress and Ash begins to pull it off. I wrap my arms around her waist and snuggle into her. "I love you," I whisper.

"I don't think I should move in straight away," she mutters. I still but keep her in my arms. "It's not that I don't want to, but Izzy needs to get used to me first."

I feel like she's pulling away. "She can do that whilst you're here."

"And I have to get used to her," she adds, and I realise that's the real problem. "It's a lot," she whispers, "and it's all moving so fast."

———

Matt laughs when I tell him why Ash isn't setting up home. I invited him around for a beer and to help me unpack. Izzy loves the house and has already claimed the bedroom, which might not be an issue if I can't get Ash to move in.

"I hope you're not looking for sympathy."

"I'm looking for advice," I say, rolling my eyes.

"Don't leave your wife," he says, adding another laugh.

"Great, thanks," I mutter, wondering why the hell I didn't call Jay.

"Look, she's just a kid herself." I glare at him, and he shrugs. "She is. Twenty-three-year-olds shouldn't be settling down with married men who have commitments. She knew what she was getting into, and now, she's got cold feet?"

"She said it was for Izzy, so she could settle in."

"Bullshit. This bitch didn't give two craps about Izzy when she started bonking her dad."

"Jesus, Matt," I hiss. "And don't call her a bitch."

"You've given up your marriage for her, Dan, and now, she's decided she wants to live like a twenty-three-year-old. Well, too fucking late."

"That's not what she said," I argue.

"It's what she meant."

"You think?"

"Have you checked she's not lying about the baby?"

I shake my head. "But I am a little worried," I admit. "She slept with a guy when I first split from Meg. What if the kid's his?"

"Christ, you don't half mess shit up. You were fucking happy with Meg and Izzy, and now, look at your shitshow of a life."

"I don't need you to remind me, thanks."

"Did you hear about the job?" he asks, changing the subject.

"I didn't get it. I knew I wouldn't the second that knob stepped from the office."

"By knob, you mean that gorgeous hunk of a man, Hugo?"

"I wouldn't say gorgeous," I mutter, hating how accurate his description is. He just missed the words 'Viking' and 'god'.

"Then you're blind. I hope Meg goes after him and shags his brains out."

"Just what I want an image of, my wife shagging that Adonis," I snap.

Matt laughs harder. "It's what you deserve."

"He's probably got a tiny knob anyway. Men who look like that usually do." It only makes him snort with more laughter.

MEG

I arrive at the bar to find Zoe and Sofia waiting with mojitos lined up. I take one and down it before kissing them both on the cheek. "You made it," I say to Sofia, and she smiles.

"I made up with my parents properly," she says, and I hug her.

"That's amazing."

"I went to see them earlier today, and when I admitted I was struggling, Mum broke down. We talked it all through—how I felt, why I made the decision to conceive like I did. It felt good, like a huge weight was lifted. They insisted I have a night off so they can spend some time with him, and they've promised to be around a lot more."

"That's such great news, Sofia. Well done for reaching out."

"Never mind that," Zoe butts in, and Sofia and I share a knowing smile. "Tell us what got your panties in a twist."

"I took your advice," I say, shrugging. "I used Hugo to get over Dan."

"You did?" screeches Zoe. "Oh my god, no one ever takes my advice."

"I kind of said the same," says Sofia.

"I took *both* your advice and shagged Hugo."

"Wow," says Sofia, looking shocked. "You actually had sex with another man?"

I nod smugly and fill them in on the job interview, the park, and the sex. I leave out the part where Dan broke my heart all over again.

"You must feel great," says Zoe.

"I did, for a short while, but then he went weird, and I noticed he'd laid a photograph face down on the side."

"Of his wife?" Sofia asks.

I shrug. "I don't know, but I'm pretty certain it was."

"I'd do the same," says Zoe. "No one wants to stare at the

picture of a dead person while they're fucking." A nervous laugh escapes me, and the girls join in. "You're overthinking it," she adds. "It was probably hard for him. Take it for what it was, an afternoon of fun to get over the pain you're both feeling."

"The worst thing is," I continue, "he lives in my building."

"Oh shit," says Sofia.

"I'll bump into him at some point."

"It's a big building, I doubt it," Zoe says, shrugging.

I shake my head. "He's my neighbour, literally."

Zoe breaks out into a fit of giggles, and Sofia looks mortified for me. "That could only happen to you."

"He's going to think I'm a fucking stalker. I turn up at the park, at his work, and then in his building, next fucking door!" I wail, and the girls are both laughing hysterically.

"Why didn't you just tell him?" asks Zoe, wiping her eyes.

"I don't know. I thought it might put him off. No one wants to shag their neighbour."

"You've made it ten times worse," says Sofia. "Now, he'll wonder why you didn't tell him. He's going to think you're batshit crazy."

"Maybe I can keep avoiding him," I suggest, sounding hopeful.

"Good luck with that," says Zoe, rolling her eyes.

HUGO

The last day of term was as manic as it always is. Christmas and children don't mix well. I went for a quick drink with the staff after work then slipped out unnoticed, so I could come home, take a bath, and relax. I'm exhausted.

As I sink into the hot water, groaning in delight as the warmth relaxes me, I hear a key in my door and Eric shouting my name. I mutter a few choice curse words and slide under the bubbles.

A second later, I hear the bathroom door swing open. I surface, wiping my face. "You went without saying goodbye."

"Christ, Eric, I'm not gonna break," I snap. He eyes me in that way he has that's silently warning me to change my tone, and I sigh. "I didn't want a fuss."

"It's gonna be hard," he says, and I want to yell at the top of my lungs that I'm okay. "But last Christmas was shit, the least we can do this year to honour Liz's memory is have a good one."

"And I will. I just need to relax and get my head out of work, and I can't do that in a bar with colleagues."

"I'll pour us a drink, big brother. Jump out that girly bath and come talk to me."

There's no point in arguing. He's persistent, so I do as he says and join him in the living room once I'm dressed again.

"Mum's going all out this year," he tells me. "She's got enough food for an army."

We always have Christmas with our parents, and last year was no exception, even though I'd just received the worst news in the world, that Elizabeth was dying from cancer and there was nothing anyone could do.

"How soon is too soon to move on?" I blurt, and he pauses with his drink halfway to his mouth. "Like in an intimate way?" I clarify.

"Why do you ask? Have you met someone?"

"It's just a question."

"Megan, right? This is about Megan."

"It's just a fucking question," I snap, grabbing my beer and taking a drink.

"Chill, brother. She's gorgeous, I get it. And only you know when you're ready."

"I feel like a fucking cheat," I admit, rubbing my tired face. "I feel like I cheated on my wife with a really hot woman who consumes my every thought."

Eric smiles. "She does?"

"And I hate feeling like this. It makes me sick to my stomach because if Liz was here, would I still have slept with Meg?"

"You slept with her? After the interview?" he guesses, and I nod.

"And I placed my wedding picture face down. How sick does that make me?"

"Hue, it was just a picture."

I stand, pacing. "It wasn't just a picture," I snap. "It was the happiest day of my life, and now, I'm starting to forget what she sounded like, how she laughed, how her body felt. I'm replacing the memories with Meg."

"You can't hold on to Liz forever, man. She's gone." He gives me a sad smile. "She wouldn't want you to grieve forever."

"Six months and I fucked someone else," I yell, throwing my beer across the room. It hits the wall and shatters, sending shards of glass across the wooden floor. I stare at the brown liquid dripping down the white wall. "I miss her, Ric. I miss her so fucking much."

He stands, moving quickly towards me and wrapping me in his arms. And for the first time in months, I break down.

Twenty-Three

ASHLEY

I wipe myself for a second time and stare at the bloody tissue. My heart slams harder in my chest. There's no pain, no cramps, just blood, and I don't know what that means exactly, so I pick up my mobile and call Dan. He answers straight away. "Are you okay?"

"I'm bleeding," I announce. "I don't know what to do."

"Shit, we need to go to the hospital."

I check my watch. "It's eleven, and accident and emergency will be full of drunks. I don't want to sit there for hours waiting to be seen."

"You need a doctor," he argues.

"What can they do, Dan? Nothing. Can I come over and stay with you instead?"

"Of course."

We disconnect the call, and I get a bag together and head over. He's just a five-minute walk, so it doesn't take long, and he's waiting for me on the doorstep. He pulls me to him and holds me tight. "How are you feeling?"

"There's no pain, just a bit of blood."

"Let's get you inside. You need bed rest."

Once I'm in my pyjamas and tucked up in bed, he brings

me a cup of tea and hands me the television remote. "There're no channels yet, just Netflix," he tells me.

The door creaks open and Izzy appears rubbing her eyes. "I had a bad dream," she whispers. Dan glances at me, but Izzy doesn't seem to pay any attention as she climbs onto the bed. "Can I lay with you?" she asks me.

I stare at Dan in alarm, and he gives a soft, reassuring smile. "Yeah, sure," I say, lifting my arm. She tucks herself into my side, and I wrap my arm around her tiny, warm body. My heart swells as I stare down in wonder. She's cute. A random tear slowly falls down my cheek, and when I look at Dan, he's watching us both with so much love, it brings a lump to my throat. "I don't want to lose it," I whisper, and I realise it's true. I want this baby. I want Dan's baby.

He reaches over and wipes my tear away. "Everything will be fine."

MEG

We stumble back to my apartment, as it's the closest and we're way drunker than we meant to get. The second we step from the elevator, I place a finger to my lips, indicating to the girls to be quiet. We creep across the landing like thieves, and I point at Hugo's door, so they know which place is his.

I push my key in the lock just as Hugo's door swings open. I scream in surprise and shove my door so hard, I tumble inside, falling flat on my face. The girls fall about in a fit of giggles, and I hear Hugo ask if they're okay.

"You're Meg's friends," he says, a realisation in his tone.

I crawl farther into the apartment, trying to kick the door shut, but Zoe sticks her hand out. "Yeah, she's right here," she says, laughing harder.

I roll onto my back, groaning as Hugo pokes his head inside. "Meg?" I give a small wave.

"She's your new neighbour," Sofia announces, doing jazz

hands and trying her best to look enthusiastic. "Surprise," she adds.

A range of emotions passes over Hugo's face, and I hate that I don't recognise a single one. I do notice he doesn't smile. "Right, I was told we had a new neighbour," he mutters.

"I swear I'm not stalking you," I say, my words slightly slurred.

"What's the hold up?" comes another voice, and Eric appears. "Hey, Meg, why are you on the floor?"

"She's my new neighbour," says Hugo, and they exchange a look that tells me they've talked about me.

"We gotta run," says Eric, slapping Hugo's back. "Nice to see you again, Meg. Sorry you didn't get the job."

"I didn't?" I ask, and Hugo groans.

"You were getting a letter in the post," he mutters.

I try to recover my shock quickly. "Right, okay. No bother. Thanks."

"Sorry, Meg, I thought he'd called to tell you," Eric adds, wincing.

I push to my knees, and Hugo holds out a hand for me to grab. I ignore it, reaching for the wall and climbing to my feet. "It's for the best anyway. See you around." I practically bustle him out the door then drag the girls in and close it a little harder than I mean to.

"Holy shit," Sofia whispers. "That was so awkward."

"At least he knows where you live now," adds Zoe, laughing.

"Fuck," I mutter, covering my embarrassed face with my hands. "Do you think he thinks I'm crazy?"

"Yes," they answer in unison.

———

I'm so hungover, I can hardly open my eyes, because each time I do, the room spins until I want to vomit. The girls left first thing. Sofia was panicking after being away from Harry the entire night, even though her parents had insisted she take the break, and Zoe mentioned something about work.

There's a knock on the door, and I groan aloud. Before I can get up off the couch, the door opens and Hugo shouts, "Hello." I wince as he's the last person I want to see, especially right now, when I'm certain I look like death. I feel him standing over me and open one eye, immediately regretting it. He holds up a paper bag. "Peace offering."

"Are we at war?" I ask, my voice raspy and dry.

"You look in no fit state to battle anyone."

"I think I hit the vodka way too hard," I admit, slowly pushing to sit and groaning out loud again.

"Lucky for you, I make the best hangover cures. I'll be right back." He disappears, leaving the paper bag on the table. I take it cautiously and peer inside, slamming it closed when the sickly-sweet aroma of cinnamon hits my nostrils.

He returns with a glass containing a green liquid. I shake my head, glaring at the gloop like it's poison. "I'm not kidding, this stuff really works. In five minutes, you'll feel like you could go get right back on the vodka."

I take it warily and sniff it, screwing up my face in protest. "I should've told you I'd moved in next door," I admit. "I was in shock when you brought me back here, and then I didn't want to break the spell."

"The spell?" he cuts in, smirking.

I narrow my eyes. "The spell you were clearly under."

He laughs. "Of course, your stunning beauty definitely placed me under a spell."

"I just felt silly telling you. First, I showed up in the park, then at the school, and then, bam, I'm your neighbour."

He nods, a smile still playing on his lips. "It does scream stalker."

"Well, you'll be pleased to know I'm not stalking you."

"Why?"

I frown. "Why?" I repeat.

"I'm clearly hot, single as fuck, great in bed . . ."

I laugh, wincing as pain shoots through my delicate skull. "We're neighbours. We should box up whatever this is," I wave my hand between us, "and stick to being neighbours."

A strange look passes over his face, and I think he looks bothered by that. Before I can ask, my phone shrills to life, and I see Dan's name. "I should take this," I mutter, grabbing it and placing it to my ear. "Yeah?"

"I tried to call you," he snaps. I push to stand, panicked by the urgency in his voice.

"Is Izzy okay?" Hugo senses my unease and watches me with concern.

"It's not Izzy, but I need you to come grab her."

"Erm, okay."

"Ashley isn't well."

I roll my eyes. "If she's going to be a mother, she needs to realise you can't palm a kid off when you get ill."

"She's bleeding," he cuts in, and I bite my lower lip.

"Right. Okay, I'll be there in ten minutes."

I disconnect. "Everything okay?" asks Hugo.

I nod. "I have to collect Izzy." I have a sudden wave of sickness and shove past Hugo to make a run for the bathroom. I get there just in time to empty last night's liquid into the toilet bowl. I cough violently, blindly feeling for the towel. Hugo appears with a glass of water and some tissue. I take it and wipe my face, feeling my cheeks burn with embarrassment.

"Good job we're not fucking cos that might really turn a man off," he teases.

I shove him playfully, taking the water. "Ashley is bleeding," I whisper.

"Shit. That must be tough on you, bringing back memories?" I love how he always thinks about my feelings. "Let me drive you."

I shake my head. "No, I don't want to put you out. It's a short walk."

"So, an even quicker drive. You're in no state to walk anywhere. And you can drink my hangover cure on the way."

Minutes later, I'm in the passenger seat of Hugo's flashy car with the glass of green gunk in my hand. He takes my seatbelt and fastens it for me, and I watch in wonderment as he pulls back and tugs on the belt to make sure I'm secure. He suddenly looks embarrassed. "Sorry, force of habit," he mutters, gently closing my door and going to the driver's side. He climbs in and fastens his own seatbelt. "I only have a booster seat," he explains. "Is that okay?"

I glance in the back to the child booster seat and nod. "Why do you have that?" I never asked him if he had children.

"Sebastian has a son. He's six and crazy, just like Seb."

"Seb's the youngest brother, right?"

He grins, starting the engine. "Now, you sound like my mother. Four sons and her youngest is the only one to give her a grandchild."

"She's kinda got a point."

"Drink," he orders, pulling out into the traffic.

We arrive at Dan's new place just a few minutes later. I stare at the outside of the small semi-detached, and my heart aches a little. When we bought our house together, we were so excited, Dan insisted on carrying me over the threshold. It's a happy memory. "You want me to come?" Hugo offers.

I shake my head and unfasten my seatbelt. "Are you sure you don't want to go? I can walk back."

"We're friends, right?" he asks. I nod, and he smiles. "Then go get your girl and I'll drive you home."

I knock on the door, and Dan answers with Izzy in his

arms. "Thanks for this," he mutters, handing me her bag. Izzy comes to me, and I set her on her feet. Dan glances past me to the road where Hugo's car is still running. "What's he doing here?"

"He gave me a lift."

"You were with him when I called? Is that why you weren't answering all morning, cos you were busy with him?" he snaps bitterly.

I roll my eyes. "I hope everything is okay with Ashley," I mutter, turning away and heading back to the car.

"Wait," he snaps, rushing after me. "You didn't tell me you were seeing him."

I open the back door and lift Izzy into the seat. I strap her in then close the door, and Dan is still waiting for a reply, so I sigh heavily. "Fuck you, Dan," I mutter, then I get in the front and close the door, staring straight ahead without looking at him.

Once we drive away, I turn back to Izzy. "Are you okay?" I ask.

She nods. "Ashley is sick," she tells me.

"I know. I'm sure she will feel better soon. Did you have fun?" She nods again. "This is Hugo, my friend," I add.

"Hey, Izzy," Hugo says, smiling at her through the rearview mirror. "I love your hair."

She touches her plaits. "Ashley is good at hair," she tells him with a smile.

Hugo glances at me, and I force a smile. "Perfect Ashley," I mutter quietly, and he smirks.

ASHLEY

I stare at the grainy image on the ultrasound machine. "See the heartbeat there?" asks the technician, pointing to a small flicker.

I lean a little closer and squint. "I think so."

"Let's have a listen," she adds, pressing a button. She rolls the wand across my stomach and the room is filled with the sound of a fast-beating heart. "Everything is fine."

I release a long breath, and Dan squeezes my hand. "See, I told you."

"And you're certain?" I ask.

The technician smiles. "Absolutely. Strong heartbeat and you're measuring at eleven weeks. All looks fine. I suggest you rest, take it easy for a few days, and the bleeding should stop. It's normal for some new mothers to have slight bleeding in the beginning. If it gets heavier, or persists between now and your next scan, come back."

She prints off a few pictures and hands them to me. "Lots of rest," she reiterates to Dan as I fasten my jeans.

By the time we get home, I'm exhausted. I hardly slept all night. The dread that I was about to lose the baby I'd been wishing away made the guilt ten times worse. Dan points to my jeans. "Get those off. No more restricting clothes," he says, pulling a blanket from the back of the couch. I smile at his concern and take them off. "Lie down," he orders, pointing to the couch. I do as I'm told and relax back as he places the blanket over me. "Do not move. If you need anything, call for me."

"Where are you going?" I ask.

"To do some shopping. I'm going to cook for you this evening. You need something involving vegetables." I screw up my nose, and he smiles. "I'm going to look after you, Ash. No more arguments. We're having a baby, and that's amazing. We're going to be a happy family."

My heart swells. "I love you," I tell him.

"I love you too."

DAN

I do a healthy food shop. Ashley always eats takeout, and I'm determined to make sure she eats well, especially while she's pregnant. Last night scared the shit out of me, and I think it made us both realise this baby is a blessing and it's about time we treated it as such.

On the way back from the supermarket, I stop at Meg's place. The concierge calls up to her apartment, and she allows me up, but she's waiting at the door, a sign she's not about to let me inside.

"I want to apologise," I say. When she doesn't reply, I continue. "For everything. I never meant to hurt you the way I did."

She rolls her eyes, glancing down the corridor. "Come in," she mutters, moving to one side so I can pass.

"It looks great in here," I say, looking around the organised living room. "You did the flat packs," I add, nodding to the television cabinet. The thought her new man might have done them brings out my jealousy and I take a calming breath. I can't fuck this up.

"What are you doing here, Dan? I literally just saw you."

"The baby is fine," I say, and she nods, biting hard on her lower lip.

"That's good."

"It was the wake-up call I needed," I add, "and I realised I can't fuck this up with Ash." Hurt passes over her face and she folds her arms over her chest like she's putting a wall between us. "After we kissed," I begin, and she groans. "Just hear me out," I rush to say. "I was going to tell her it was over. I realised I hadn't put any effort into getting you back. I fucked it all up and just left like you were nothing." A tear rolls down her cheek. "And when we kissed, it reminded me of how we were . . . before Izzy . . . before bills and stress." She remains quiet, her mistrusting eyes staring at me. They're so full of sadness, it breaks me all over again. "And I wanted to get that back. So, I went to tell her I wanted you and I was going to fight, and she told me she was pregnant. She asked me outright what I wanted, and I knew if I chose you, she'd terminate an innocent life."

"Dan," she whispers, her tone pleading, "why are you telling me all this?"

I shrug. "Because I want you to know, I was going to fight for us, but then she told me about the baby and it was almost like the universe was interfering. I saw it as a sign. And today, when they told us there was a strong heartbeat, I decided it probably was a sign and walking away from another family wasn't an option for me. But you need to know that I'm sorry for fucking it all up."

"I'm glad the baby is okay," she mutters. "You should go."

"I am sorry," I repeat.

"And I appreciate your apology, but it doesn't change anything. My heart still hurts for me, for Izzy, and for everything we've lost. And maybe that's selfish of me," her voice breaks with emotion and more tears fall down her cheeks, "but I can't just forgive you for blowing up our lives into a million pieces and walking away like we meant nothing, like eleven years were nothing. We were happy, I know we were, and you never said any different."

"We were happy," I admit. "I fucked it all up. It's all on me."

"So, I'm glad you got a sign and your life is full of excitement and a new shiny family, but you can't keep turning up in my life with a kiss or to tell me you thought about making us work, because it makes me feel like the bad guy when I have to tell you I'm still very much broken and I don't forgive you. I don't like giving my daughter away for long weekends. I hate that I won't ever have another Christmas with us as a family. I can't stand the fact that your lover did my daughter's hair and that she cuddled her after her nightmare last night," she sobs, her whole body shaking, and my heart twists harder, causing a pain in my chest.

"And I don't get a say in that because you decided we weren't enough, that I wasn't enough. I got older, Dan. It happens. So, yes, things weren't like they used to be before Izzy, but when a woman gives birth, her life changes. And I know yours did too, but not like mine. I had to do all the stuff required to keep a baby alive, and you came in for the cuddles and the fun parts. I had to give up my job to raise her while you continued with yours. I sorted childcare and did all the important stuff like appointments and parent meetings. So, yes, things changed, but that happens when a baby comes along. It takes hard work and commitment. And conversation. Why didn't you fucking talk to me about how you felt? You can't just get bored and leave."

"Meg," I whisper. She lets me pull her to my chest, crying so hard, she's gulping big gasps of air.

"Meg?" I glance back over my shoulder to find Hugo in the doorway, his face full of concern. Meg pulls away from me and goes to him. He looks surprised as he takes her into his arms and wraps them around her. He buries his nose into her hair and whispers reassuring words that I can't quite make out.

I force myself to watch them as he tilts her head back and uses his thumbs to wipe her tears. I wonder if her face looked that small in my hands, or if I ever looked at her the way he looks at her, like she's enough. Hugo eventually looks at me. "I think you should go."

Meg keeps her eyes to the ground, and I realise this isn't a battle, because I've already left her and he's already saving her, picking up the mess I've made. I nod once and step out the door. He follows me out onto the landing, and I press for the elevator.

"It's like you enjoy prolonging her pain," he says, his voice cold.

"That's not what I want to do. I was just trying to apologise."

"How can you apologise for what you did?" he asks. "She can't ever forgive that, so stop finding excuses to see her and drag out this bullshit."

"You've made yourself clear," I mutter, stepping into the elevator. "Consider me warned."

He scoffs. "This isn't a warning. This is me telling you she's had enough and she can't take any more. If you ever loved her, you'll stop dragging this out at every opportunity and let her move on. She's trying so hard to pick herself up and keep going for Izzy's sake. So, instead of trying harder to break her completely, walk away properly and concentrate on your new life. This one's gone."

Twenty-Four

MEG

Christmas morning has always been a big affair in my life. When I was a child, my parents made it special with traditions like making sure I always chose the breakfast option. We'd open stockings stuffed with mini gifts in bed before going downstairs and opening a mountain of presents. We'd have breakfast, and a turkey dinner would come right before the Queen's speech, and in the evening, we'd have family over for a huge celebration. More gifts would be exchanged, and it felt magical and exciting.

Once Izzy was born, I took on the same traditions. Dan, Izzy, and I would spend the morning at home, we'd have dinner together, and then we'd head to my parents' for their annual party. Dan's family would also come down from Nottingham, and we'd be one big, happy family.

This year, I lied to my parents and told them I was spending Christmas with just me and Izzy, in our new place, to celebrate our new start. In reality, Dan is picking Izzy up any minute, and she's having a turkey dinner with him and Ashley and Dan's family. And for the first time today, I realised Dan's actions haven't just hurt me but our families too, because our parents loved getting together at Christmas, and that's no longer possible because we're all pulled apart and trying to spend Christmas where we think we belong. And right now, I belong here, because the thought of facing my extended family and explaining over and over that Dan and I are now separated makes me sick to my stomach.

The buzzer goes and I wait outside the apartment for Dan to come up and collect Izzy. She insisted on wearing her new Christmas Minnie Mouse dress, and I had to plait her hair perfectly. *Just like Ashley does it.*

Dan smiles wide and opens his arms. Izzy runs into them, and he kisses her on each cheek. "Happy Christmas, baby," he whispers, stepping out the elevator. He looks to me and his expression softens. "Happy Christmas."

"She's got everything in this bag," I say, handing him the holdall. "She insisted on bringing all her new clothes, but I could really do with you sending them back because she's grown out of so much, I'm struggling."

He nods. "Of course. I think we've got her some new clothes too, so it's fine."

"Great. So, are you bringing her home tomorrow evening or should I collect her?" I hate how robotic I sound and how all this seems normal now.

"I'll drop her back. Say, seven?" My heart sinks a little, as I was hoping to have her earlier, but I find myself nodding because I can't face another argument. "Are you going to your parents'?" he asks.

I shake my head. "I'm feeling like a quiet one, to be honest."

His smile fades. "You're staying here?" I nod again. "Alone?"

I force an awkward smile. "Thanks for pointing that out."

"Sorry," he winces, "I just thought you'd make plans."

"I don't feel like seeing anyone," I admit.

"Meg, it'll make you feel better seeing people. It's Christmas."

"Don't worry about me, Dan. I'm fine."

He looks torn. "What about Hugo?"

"We're not together," I say, and he almost looks relieved.

"Well, should I bring Izzy home sooner?" he asks.

I shake my head, pressing the call button for the elevator. It opens straight away. "Be good for Daddy and Ashley," I tell Izzy, kissing her on the head. "I love you."

"I love you too, Mummy," she says.

"We'll call you later, so Izzy can show you what Santa left for her." Izzy jumps up and down with excitement.

"Great, I'll look forward to it," I lie, because the last thing I want to see is all the wonderful things another woman's bought for my child. I hate how bitter it makes me, but I wave and blow kisses to Izzy as the elevator door closes.

I release a long breath, and as I turn back to go inside, Hugo's door opens. He looks up in surprise. I haven't seen him for a few days, since I broke apart in his arms in front of Dan. He knocked a couple times to check on me, but I ignored it because I felt stupid—or maybe I'm just tired of him seeing me in some crazy kind of state.

"Merry Christmas," he says.

"You, too."

He glances at the elevator. "Was that Izzy leaving?" I nod. "Must be hard. What are you doing now?"

"I have a box of chocolates and *P.S. I Love You* waiting for me."

"And dinner?"

"Did you know they do microwave Christmas dinners?" I ask. "There's a whole world of wonders for singletons like us."

He grins. "Well, you're absolutely not spending today eating shit food and watching crap films."

"You underestimate how badly I want to eat wafer-thin turkey," I joke. "Seriously, I'm okay."

"I'm not taking no for an answer. Get dressed."

"Hugo, I'm terrible company. I just want to sleep the day away and miss my baby girl."

"Fine," he says.

I smile in relief. "Thanks. Have a great day." I turn to go inside but stop when I hear Hugo talking on his mobile phone. "Hey, Ric, tell Mum I can't make it. I'm so sorry," he says. My eyes widen, and I wave my hands frantically to get his attention. He turns his back to me. "Something came up. I'll call her later." I jump on his back, and he begins to laugh as I fight him for the phone.

I grab it and press it to my ear. "Eric," I pant, "ignore him, he's on his way."

Hugo tugs me around to his front. "Tell Mum to set another place. I'm bringing a guest," he shouts into the phone.

I disconnect the call, and he takes it from me. He's still holding me against him, and there's a brief moment where I think he's going to kiss me. Instead, he slides me down his body until my feet hit the ground. "Get dressed. You can't attend dinner wearing your Lilo and Stitch pyjamas."

––––––––

The second we walk into his parents' house, a warm, homely feeling wraps around me like a huge blanket. There's a real sense of love, and it pours from each and every wall. As we step through the front door, I notice hundreds of framed photographs, all different shapes and sizes and all filled with the loving faces of happy boys and proud parents. Hugo sees me looking and begins a crazy dance to stop me. "Ignore the wall of doom."

I laugh, pulling him out the way. "This is amazing," I comment. My eyes land on a picture of four boys, all under the age of fifteen at least. "Is that you?" I ask, grinning at the eldest-looking child in the photograph. His hair is overgrown, and he looks like a typical moody teenager.

"It was my goth phase," he admits, pushing me along the hall to rush me along.

He opens a door and noise bursts out. It's a happy sound, full of laughter and excited chatter, and as we step into view, it stops. Everyone turns to look at us, and it's so quiet, we'd probably hear a pin drop. I take a large swallow, wishing the ground would open up and suck me inside.

An older woman pushes through, smiling wide, and I instantly know it's Hugo's mum. They all have the same eyes. "You must be Megan. Eric was just telling me about you."

I return her smile and blush. "Yes. Lovely to meet you, and thank you so much for letting me come to dinner. Hugo kind of insisted."

"Please don't apologise. This woman cooked enough to feed an army and then some." A man steps forward, placing his arm around the shoulders of Hugo's mum.

"This is Harry, and I'm Charlotte."

I hold out my hand, but Charlotte rolls her eyes and pulls me in for a hug. "Please, we don't do civilised around here."

Harry kisses me on the cheek and places his arm around my shoulder, leading me farther into the room. "Apparently, you already know the motley crew," he says, and I smile at Eric, James, and Seb. "Over there is my father, Hugo, but to save confusion, we all just call him Grandpops. You call him Hugo and he won't answer. He's practically deaf anyway." I give the elderly man a wave, and he returns it with a slight nod of the head. "He's ninety-two."

"Wow."

"I know. We love him dearly, but he's hanging on for dear life, literally." He laughs to show he's joking. "This is Katie, Seb's significant other." Katie also hugs me, and I instantly warm to her. "And that little terror is their son, Chester." The young boy glances up from his gaming device and gives a small smile.

"You'll have to excuse him. He just got that Nintendo thing for Christmas and it's been glued to his hand ever since," Katie says, rolling her eyes.

"No need to explain. I have a daughter, so I know exactly what they're like."

"Fabulous. Is she here?" Katie asks.

I shake my head, sadness hurting my chest again. "She's with her dad for Christmas."

"Oh, I'm so sorry," she whispers. "That must be awful."

"The first one, so it's weird, but I'm dealing with it."

"You need wine," she declares, grabbing my hand. "Charlotte, we need wine," she shouts louder as she pulls me back through the kitchen to where Charlotte is stirring gravy.

HUGO

Eric tops up my whiskey and leans closer. "What happened to keeping your distance?" he asks, smirking.

"She was on her own, man, I couldn't leave her like that."

"You don't think you're giving mixed signals?"

"Nah, she was the one who friend zoned me," I say, shrugging. The truth is, since I held her sobbing in my arms, I felt something change between us. Everything in me wanted to smack that smug prick right in the face and tell him to stay the fuck away from her because I don't want to ever see her that hurt again. But I saw it today, just hidden better. Her eyes are brimming with pain, and I just want to make it better.

"The family loves her," he says, as we watch Meg, Seb, Katie, and James laughing like little kids over some drawing game they've spent the last half-hour playing. It reminds me of Elizabeth and how Christmas used to be.

"They love everyone. Mum just likes to make a fuss of anyone new."

"But it feels good, doesn't it, to hear laughter again? We haven't had so much of that since Liz."

I nod in agreement. "Life goes on, doesn't it?" I mutter.

"It's good to see you smile too, brother. We've missed it."

Guilt hits me once again. Smiling without Liz doesn't seem right, but with Meg, I find it happens and I don't even realise. I don't spend so much time thinking about Liz when Meg's around, which makes my heart ache a little less but my guilt double.

"Dinner is served," Dad announces like some waiter, and we all rush to get a place at the table.

I dive to the seat on the left of Dad, who always occupies the head of the table, and I pull the chair beside me out for Meg, who smiles as she lowers into it. "You okay?" I ask. Since we got here, she's been kept busy by everyone but me.

"Yes. Thank you so much for making me come. I'm really enjoying it."

"Good. What do you usually do at Christmas?"

"We'd spend it at home and then head to my parents' in the evenings for a family get-together."

"And you didn't fancy that this year?"

She shakes her head sadly. "And have to explain over and over that Dan left me for a woman younger and prettier?" She scoffs, "No, thanks."

"Hey, she's not prettier."

"How do you know? You've not met her."

I grin. "Because no one is prettier than you."

She laughs hard, making a gagging sound. "Smooth."

"But seriously, stop comparing yourself to her. You're perfect just the way you are."

We get stuck into dinner, and there's happy chatter around the table. Times like this make me grateful for my family. Without them, I wouldn't have survived the last few months.

"What do you do for work?" Dad asks Meg, and she glances at me, almost laughing.

"I was a stay-at-home mum to my daughter, Izzy, but she's in nursery now, so I'm looking for work as a teaching assistant."

Dad looks at me. "Well, can't you help her out, son?"

Eric grins at me from across the table. "Yeah, Hue, help the girl out."

I roll my eyes, and Meg reaches for my hand under the table, giving it a gentle squeeze. "It's fine. We already live next door to one another, and we have a great friendship, I'd hate to ruin that."

"Actually," I say, placing my cutlery down, "we do have a position."

I feel her eyes on me, and she smiles. "You do?"

"Yeah. I think you'd be perfect for it."

"Well, maybe I'll consider it," she almost whispers.

———

We spend the evening playing games, laughing and drinking. It's perfect. It's almost ten in the evening when Meg leans closer. "I need to call a cab. It's getting late, and I don't want to outstay my welcome."

I throw my arm around her shoulder. "You're staying. No arguments." She leans into me and smiles before joining back in with the game.

At eleven, I stretch and push to stand. "We're going to bed," I announce.

"Okay. Remember, first one up makes breakfast," says Mum as I swoop down to kiss her on the cheek.

"Thanks for today," I whisper.

She smiles, placing her hand on my cheek. "It's so good to see you smile again, baby boy."

I fist-bump Grandpops and turn back to Meg. "You coming?" I ask, and she blushes before standing and following me.

My childhood bedroom is no longer adorned with super-hero wallpaper and Page Three naked models. Mum redeco-rated it in case guests decided to stop over. I hold the door open for Meg to step inside.

"Are you sure this is okay? I don't mind going home," she says. I close the door, and she eyes it. "Where are you sleeping?"

"In here, with you," I say matter-of-factly.

"Oh my god, Hugo, no," she hisses, covering her face. "Your parents will think we're . . . yah know."

I grin. "Relax. I'm an adult, they know I've had sex."

Her eyes widen. "But they don't know you've had it with me."

I laugh. "I feel like they suspect."

Her face burns red with embarrassment. "Oh shit, I can't stay now."

"No funny business, I promise," I say, holding my hands up. "You said yourself, we're neighbours, let's not complicate it."

She watches with unease as I strip from my clothes, leaving just my boxers in place. I climb into the double bed and turn on the television. When she doesn't move, I glance her way. "Are you getting ready for bed?"

"I don't have my pyjamas," she mutters feebly.

I grin wide. "Looks like you'll have to sleep naked." When she looks borderline hysterical again, I hold up my hands. "I'm kidding. Here, take my shirt." I throw it to her, and she holds it to her chest.

"Close your eyes."

I close them. "I feel like a naughty teenager," I mutter. "You're making this a deal when it doesn't need to be one."

I hear her rustling, then the bed dips and she slides in beside me. "Dan didn't call me," she whispers.

"Was he supposed to?"

"He told Izzy she could call me to show her presents."

"Maybe they were having fun and just forgot?"

She nods. "Yeah, that's what worries me."

"It'll take a lot of getting used to. You'll have to work out every holiday to suit you all, but it'll fall into place."

"I hope so."

"Liz's parents split when she was small too. She hated cutting herself down the middle, but when she was old enough, she refused and told them to either get along or she'd spend the holidays alone."

"I can't ever imagine spending the holidays with Dan and Ashley."

"You can't right now because you're still hurting. But one day, you'll be happy again, and it won't hurt so much to see them together."

"You offered me a job," she states, changing the subject.

"I did."

"Were you serious?"

"Yeah, but it comes with conditions."

She arches a brow. "If it involves sleeping with the boss, forget it, I already did that."

I laugh. "You have to have coffee in the park with me every day."

DAN

Christmas day passed by in a blur. Ashley is still resting, but the bleeding has stopped. I spent the day in the kitchen, given that Ash doesn't really know how to cook, and her parents joined us for dinner. It was awkward and different to what I'm used to. For a start, Meg and I always shared cooking duties, and our dinners were intimate with just the three of us.

Apparently, Ashley always has dinner with her parents, and I wanted to make her feel relaxed, so I invited them over. They were taken with Izzy and even got her a gift, and they seem happy about the baby.

Izzy woke several times through the night, until eventually, I climbed into bed with her so we could both get some sleep. I'm not surprised when she wakes in the morning sniffling and coughing. Her temperature is high, and she's refusing to eat or drink.

"Maybe she should go home," Ash gently suggests over breakfast.

"My parents are coming today," I snap. "It's not an option." It's been weeks since they've seen Izzy, and they'll be heartbroken if I send her home.

"I can't risk getting sick, Dan. What if it starts the bleeding again?"

I ignore her, but as the morning goes on, Izzy cries for Meg, making it impossible to bring her temperature down.

By the time my parents arrive, Izzy clings to me like her life depends on it. Mum feels her forehead. "She's burning up," she states.

"I know. I tried Calpol, but she spat half of it out."

"You have to sing the song," Mum says. "The one Meg made up."

"Huh?"

She rolls her eyes and takes Izzy from me. "It distracts her." I follow them into the kitchen and watch as Mum sings a song I've never heard and Izzy takes her Calpol.

I make tea and then we gather in the living room. "Mum, Dad, this is Ashley." Mum gives a curt nod, and Dad offers a small smile. "Ashley, this is James and Hannah."

"Great to finally meet you," says Ash nervously. "Did you have a nice Christmas?"

"We spent it alone," says Mum coldly. "For the first time in ten years."

"Mum," I mutter, "don't start."

"Dan didn't tell us about you, yah know," she adds, and I groan. "Meg did. He didn't have the balls."

"Mum, language," I hiss.

"Do you know how much that hurt me?" Mum asks me. "My own son couldn't talk to me."

"I didn't want to hurt you."

"Hannah, not now," Dad mutters.

"Then when? Because he ignores my calls, and I have no idea what's happening."

"She's right," says Ashley gently, "you owe them an explanation."

"But today isn't the day," I snap.

"We're having a baby," says Ashley, and Izzy lifts her head from Mum's shoulder.

"A baby?" she asks.

I glare at Ash, and she has the decency to look guilty. "Yes, sweetheart, you're going to have a baby brother or sister."

She smiles but lays her head back down and closes her eyes. "And when were you going to tell us?" Mum snaps.

"I'm telling you now."

"Last time we saw you properly, you were happy with Meg, and now, you're in a new house and your bit on the side is pregnant," she hisses.

"She's not my bit on the side," I snap. "Not anymore. In fact, I was going to wait for dinner, but seeing as you're so keen to know everything . . ." I reach into my pocket and pull out the ring box I'd found when I was packing my things. I drop to one knee before Ash, and she watches through surprised eyes. "I love you, Ash, and I know we can't get married right away, but when we can, will you marry me?"

"Oh my god," she cries, covering her mouth. "Yes! A million times yes!"

I place the diamond ring on her finger, and she throws her arms around me. "I love you," I whisper.

"I love you too."

"Jesus," Mum mutters in annoyance.

"Congratulations, son," says Dad, shaking my hand before kissing Ash on the cheek. "Ignore your mother, she'll come around."

ASHLEY

We eat dinner in silence. It's not what I'd pictured our day to be, especially now we have something else to celebrate. The second his parents leave, I pull Dan to me and wrap my legs around his waist. "We need to celebrate."

"Sick child, remember?"

I groan. "My parents invited us to their party. Can't you send Izzy home early? Besides, I don't want to get sick."

He glances at Izzy, who's spent the day sleeping on the couch. "I don't know. We could take her at seven like planned and then go to your parents."

"But I wanted to celebrate together first," I whisper, rubbing myself against him. He's instantly hard, and I grin. "We could sneak upstairs for a minute."

I kiss him to seal the deal, and he carries me upstairs. "You can't tell anyone yet," he says against my mouth as he pushes me up against our bedroom wall.

I lift my skirt, and he unfastens his trousers. "Why?"

"I should tell Meg first."

"And ask her for that divorce while you're at it."

I move my knickers to one side, and he slides into me. "Exactly."

"Daddy," Izzy wails.

I groan. "Just keep moving," I mutter, kissing his neck.

He moves faster. "Daddy."

"I need to check on her."

"Just a few minutes. She'll be fine." I move against him, and he groans, slamming into me. "That's it," I whisper. "Harder."

"Daddddddyyyyy," she screams.

Dan pulls from me, fastening his trousers and rushing downstairs before I can protest. I roll my eyes and drop onto the bed, pulling out my mobile and snapping a picture of my diamond ring. I smile as it glints in the light.

I open social media and post the picture with the caption, 'I said yes', making sure to tag Dan in it.

MEG

Sleeping next to a man as hot as Hugo for an entire night while he's semi-naked is one of the hardest things I've ever done. I lost count of the number of times our limbs brushed, and as we eat lunch, my body hums with need.

My mobile lights up and I mutter an apology to Charlotte as I step out into the hall to take it. "Sorry to do this," says Dan, "but can I bring Izzy home now?"

"No, I'm not there."

"Where are you?"

I'm irritated by his question, especially with my recent frustrations. "None of your business."

"She's sick," he mutters.

I stand straighter. "Sick?"

"She woke a lot in the night, and now, she's coughing and sniffling and her temperature is high."

"Have you given her Calpol?"

"Of course, but she wants her mum, like all kids when they're sick."

"You don't get to hand her back when it gets hard, Dan. You insisted on having her until seven."

"I know, but she's crying for you, Meg. I feel bad for her."

"I'll come and get her," I snap.

"No, I'll bring her to you, just send me the address." I reel it off and disconnect right as Hugo walks in.

"Dan's bringing Izzy here, then I'll get out of your hair. Sorry, he insisted on driving her to me."

"It's fine. You don't have to leave."

"Izzy is sick."

"Mum loves to fuss over kids. She'll have a remedy for that in a second."

"No, I already crashed Christmas and I can't put you or your family out anymore. Besides, I don't want Izzy to pass on her germs."

When Dan arrives twenty minutes later, Izzy is sleeping in his arms. "She had Calpol this morning," he begins to tell me.

"This morning?" I snap. "She needs it every four hours," I say, feeling her forehead. "Christ, Dan, she's burning up."

"Look, I'm no good at this shit," he whisper-hisses. "You did all this, and she wouldn't take the Calpol from me."

"Did you sing the song?" I ask.

"No, I didn't know about the damn song. Mum did it when she came over."

I take Izzy from him, and he places her bag on the floor. "Whose is this place anyway?" he asks, glancing behind me to try and see inside the house. "I thought you had no plans."

"What's your mum think about the baby?" I ask with a smirk, knowing full well Hannah will be furious. She hated the fact Dan and I split, and she's made it perfectly clear she's pissed with him. "You shouldn't have avoided her for so long."

"You know, it would probably help if you weren't in her ear bitching about Ashley."

I scoff. "Please, I haven't wasted a word on Ashley, or you, for that matter. When she calls, it's to ask about her grand-daughter, and the only time I mentioned you was when I was forced to tell her about our split because you didn't have the backbone to and she kept calling to ask what was going on."

I feel Hugo step behind me, and he places his hand on my shoulder. "Everything okay?"

"Yeah, all good," I mutter.

"Is she here?" comes Charlotte's voice. I turn slightly to show her Izzy, and she gasps. "My god, she's burning up. Here, let me take her and get her settled." She gently lifts her from me, and Izzy stirs. "It's okay, baby girl. It's all going to be okay," she coos as she whisks her away.

"Wow, you're meeting the entire family," mutters Dan.

"The deal was you return her at seven, your rule, not mine. I would've been home at seven. Did you expect me to drop my plans because you couldn't care for our daughter?"

"Why are you in a suit?" Hugo asks. It's a good point, one I didn't think to raise. I stare past him to the car, where I see Ashley waiting.

"You have plans," I say more as a statement than a question.

"Meg, it's not like that . . ." he begins.

"I'll take it from here, Dan," says Hugo, wrapping his arm around my shoulder and slamming the door in Dan's face.

I smile. "That was mean."

He shrugs. "The guy's a dick."

Charlotte already has Izzy sitting on the couch in her vest and pants, sipping a drink and listening to Katie read a story. My heart swells. They don't even know us and they're treating us like we're a part of their family.

Harry steps beside me, nudging me with his arm. "You have a gorgeous little girl there," he says.

"And you have the most wonderful family," I tell him.

DAN

I'm pissed. Who the fuck does that Hugo guy think he is to slam the door in my face? It's my family he's trying to piss all over in some kind of macho contest, and I'm not going to stand for it. I'll be speaking to Meg the second I get her alone.

"It's nice having Izzy over," says Ash as she pulls down the sun visor and begins to apply lipstick. "But it's nice to be alone together too."

"There won't be much of that when the baby comes," I say, sounding snippier than I mean to. I feel her pause to look at me. "We won't be able to dump the kid on someone when you wanna go out."

"Dan, we took her back a couple hours earlier, what's the big deal? Was Megan pissed about it?"

"Of course, she was pissed, Ash. She doesn't call me up when Izzy's ill. She gets on with it, which is what mums do."

"And when I have my own child, I'll do that too, but Izzy isn't mine and she wanted her mum."

I grip the steering wheel tighter. "It was just another

reason for that prick to get all smug with me."

"Who?" she asks, sounding irritated.

"Meg's new boyfriend."

She slams the sun visor shut and turns to me. "Meg has a boyfriend?"

"Yes," I snap. "Hugo. I told you about him."

"Oh, I thought they were just friends."

"I'm not stupid. He's always around, and now, she's spending Christmas with his family. You should've seen the way his mum just whisked Iz off, like she was her actual grandmother."

"Then maybe it's a good time to mention a divorce?"

I fidget uncomfortably. "I'll speak to her in my own time. Don't push me."

"You were the one to propose to me, remember? Besides, if your mother doesn't beat you to it, someone else might."

I glance at her as we pull into her parents' driveway. "What's that supposed to mean?" My mobile rings and I groan when Meg's name flashes up. "What have you done, Ash?"

She gives a coy smile. "I might have accidentally put it on social media."

"What?" I yell. "I asked you not to tell anyone yet." I cancel Meg's call and open the app. I groan at the picture Ash posted, announcing to the world we're engaged. I never go on social media, I don't even know why I've kept my profile, but I never deleted Meg from my friends list, so she will have seen this post. It turns my stomach, especially as it was a last-minute thing and completely unplanned.

"I know, but I didn't think you meant I had to hide it from my friends. How would Meg have seen it? I'm not friends with her."

I groan, burying my face in my hands. "You stupid little girl," I hiss.

"What the fuck?" she snaps.

"You have no idea what you've done. I'm trying to be sensitive towards Meg because I've put her through enough, but you couldn't just let me do this my way, could you?"

"What about being sensitive towards me?" she demands. "What about how I feel having to sneak around still, even though we're together now? I'm tired of treading on eggshells so we don't upset Meg. You're not together anymore."

"And don't I fucking know it," I mutter, resting my forehead against my hands on the steering wheel.

"This was supposed to be the happiest day of my life, and so far, you're ruining it."

I suddenly feel exhausted. "Get out," I demand, not bothering to lift my head.

"What are you talking about? We have a party to go to. My parents are expecting us."

"I'm tired, Ash. These past few months, the lies and the sneaking around, have near enough killed me, and I'm tired."

"What are you saying?"

I shrug, finally looking at her. "I need a break. I'll call you in a few days."

"What?" she screeches.

"I just need some time, Ash."

She scowls as she scrambles to get out the car before marching around to the boot to get her bag. When she comes back to the passenger door, she's got the ring in her hand. "Fuck you and your break, you spineless piece of shit." She throws the ring in my face, then she slams the car door and marches into her parents' house.

I groan, taking the tiny ring and staring at the sparkling diamond I once presented to Meg. "I knew you were a bad idea," I mutter, stuffing it in my pocket. I wanted to make a statement in front of my mother, but I hadn't thought it through. I was going to replace the ring, of course I was, as I had no intention of letting her walk around with my ex-wife's old engagement ring.

Twenty-Six

MEG

Hugo drives us home after the most amazing two days with his family. When it was time to leave, his mum insisted I take her number as well as Katie's. She even suggested I join them for a coffee sometime soon. And when I asked Hugo if he'd feel weird about me staying in contact, he assured me he had no issue with it.

I can't stop smiling as he carries Izzy up to the apartment. "Just through there," I tell him, pointing to Izzy's bedroom.

He carefully lays her down, and she stirs, gripping his shirt. "Story," she whispers. He looks to me for permission, and I nod.

"She loves this one," I say, passing him Izzy's favourite book.

I go through to the kitchen to make us a drink, and while the kettle boils, I open my social media account and click on the picture of Ash's hand showing off my old engagement ring. It was a shock when I saw it earlier, and for a second, I was raging and called Dan, but I soon hung up because it's a natural progression, right? She's having his baby, they're living together, so of course, he's going to marry her. And so what if he was tacky enough to use the ring he once presented to me? We'd since replaced it with a much nicer one anyway, and lately, nothing surprises me when it comes to that man and how low he'll sink.

"You still thinking about that?" asks Hugo, leaning against the door frame.

I shrug. "It doesn't hurt as much as I thought it would," I admit. "At first, I was shocked, and maybe a little hurt he didn't speak to me first, but he doesn't have to, does he? He's not my Dan anymore, so why the fuck would he run things like this by me?"

"Still a shitty move to use your ring," he says.

I nod. "Yeah. But in some ways, that makes it easier because I realise how much he's changed. He's not the man I married. He's not even the man I fell for. That man's gone, and this Dan is thoughtless and unkind. He's wrapped up in himself and doesn't care about anyone else. This Dan, I can hate."

"Fancy watching a film?" asks Hugo.

"How are you?" I ask, making the coffee.

"Me?" he asks, sounding surprised.

"Eric might've mentioned Christmas brings back bad memories for you."

Hugo rolls his eyes. "It wasn't his place to."

"You've spent the last few months picking me up, and I've been selfish."

He moves to me, placing his hands on my shoulders. He stares right into my soul with his piercing eyes. "Liz was sick for such a short time, and then she was gone, and the pain was the worst thing I've ever felt. But now, I just feel sad. Dan hurt you so badly, and you never saw it coming. You didn't get a chance to adjust before he was leaving and flaunting his new woman in your face. And since then, he's made it impossible for you to pick yourself up and move on. I'm not comparing our heart ache, but I feel like you've had a really shitty deal. If Liz had left me for another man and I still had to see her every week, I don't think I could've handled it nearly as well as you do."

It's the first time anyone's seen my pain from the exact same way I see it, and I can't help letting a few tears escape down my cheeks. He rubs them away with his thumbs, and I lean into his touch and close my eyes. I love how he's so attentive and the way he makes me feel so special. I will him to kiss me, and when he steps away, my heart sinks with disappointment. "Now, are we watching a film or not?" he asks, reaching past me to grab the coffees.

HUGO

The day after Boxing Day is when I always meet with my brothers for drinks, which is crazy seeing as we've spent the whole of Christmas so far doing exactly this. But there's something about the sports bar we all love that relaxes us into comfortable conversation. We've been doing this since the year I married Liz. Eric was worried that as we grew up, we'd grow apart, so we made a pact that we'd meet once a month and the day after Boxing Day. It's now an unwritten rule that none of us are allowed to break, no matter what. They dragged me out my bed after Liz died, refusing to give me a pass. I hated them for it at the time, but now, when I look back, it's exactly what I'd needed.

"I just want to put this out there," says Jimmy, placing the tray holding four pints of beer onto the table, "that Mum is besotted with Meg and Izzy."

"She isn't the only one," says Seb, nudging me.

"It's not like that," I say. "She wants us to be friends."

"Bullshit," says Jimmy. "She's crazy about you."

I shake my head, laughing. "Even if she was, she's made it clear we're neighbours. She friend zoned me." I don't mention the way she leant into me last night, or how she kept looking at my lips, hinting that she wanted me to kiss her.

"What if she changed her mind?" asks Eric.

I take a drink. "She won't. Besides, things are still raw from her breakup, and Liz hasn't been gone a year. It's too soon for both of us."

"There's no set time to move on. If someone comes along, maybe that's a sign," says Jimmy. "I gotta go speak to someone," he adds, winking before heading off back to the bar.

"She comes with baggage, and I don't know if I want to deal with all that," I continue, but as the words leave my mouth, I know they're a lie. Izzy is amazing, and apart from Dan, who I can deal with, there's nothing to stop me wanting to be with Meg, and that's what scares me. She's perfect.

"Make a list," says Seb, grabbing a paper napkin from the bar and asking to borrow a pen. He returns and writes 'pros' and 'cons' at the top of the napkin.

I laugh. "No. I'm not listing anything, don't be ridiculous."

"It works," he argues. "It's a good way to rationalise your worries."

"I don't need a list," I say, still amused by his crazy idea.

"I think it's a good idea," adds Eric. "It can't hurt." I roll my eyes.

"She's got a kid," says Seb, writing it as a con.

"Is that a con?" I query. "She's a cute kid."

"But she comes with her dad, who sounds like a total twat," says Eric.

"True point," says Seb, pointing his pen at Eric before writing 'twatty ex' on the con side.

"She's been married, so she knows all the tricks. You won't get away with shit," adds Eric, and Seb writes down 'married' as a con.

"Soon to be divorced," I cut in, because she mentioned last night she'd be looking for a good divorce solicitor.

"Again, it's a con. Married and divorced before forty." Seb adds it to the growing list.

"She's still heartbroken," says Eric, "You can see the pain in her eyes."

"Is that a con?" I ask, grabbing the pen before Seb can write it down.

"Yes. It means she's still thinking of her ex." He snatches it back and writes it down.

"Which means she's an emotional wreck," says Eric.

I groan as the list grows. "She's not an emotional wreck. She's hurting, and that's okay."

"But that means she's going to rely on you to be there for her. Do you want to listen to her cry over her ex?" asks Seb.

"Another reason why she's not ready to move on," I reason, "which is why I'm not making a move."

"So, she cries?" asks Eric, and I nod. Seb adds it to the list.

"Cross that out," I order. "You can't use her emotions against her." He laughs, putting a line through it. "Can we move to pros?" I ask. "There are more pros."

"See," Seb smiles, "you're getting into it now."

"I'm only doing this because, otherwise, you'll make it up." I take a breath. "She's gorgeous, kind, she makes me laugh—"

Seb scribbles away. "Hold on, not so fast."

"She's a great mum."

"Oh, I have another con," Eric cuts in, and I groan. "She'll be working at the school."

"How is that a con?" I ask.

"Working together, what if you don't work out? She's still gotta work there."

"Good point," I mutter, and it gets added to the list. "This list is a bad idea," I finally say, snatching it and stuffing it in my pocket. "Meg and I aren't ever going to get together, at least not until we're both fully healed. Now, shut the fuck up about my life and get another round of drinks."

ASHLEY

Lauren drops down onto my bed and runs her fingers through the ratty ends of my hair. "You can't hide away forever." It's been four days since I threw the ring back in Dan's face and I've heard nothing from him. I at least expected him to check in on me seeing as we had a scare. "Why don't you just call him?"

I shake my head. "You didn't see the defeated look in his eyes. I did all the chasing and I refuse to keep doing it."

"But look how sad you are," she whispers.

"I'd rather be sad than a mug."

"We could go out for dinner. Maybe if you get out, you'll feel better."

"You sure I can't just stay in here forever?"

She smiles, shaking her head. "Nope. You gotta eat. You have a baby to grow."

———

We meet Molly at the restaurant. Lauren was right—I feel much better having showered, dressed, and put on makeup. "You're looking more like you," Molly comments.

"It was becoming stressful," I admit, "the commitment thing."

"I thought that's why you liked married men," says Lauren, "because there was no commitment."

I nod in agreement. "I lost my way."

"And now, you're having a baby. It's the biggest commitment of all. How did your parents react?"

"Not great. They're worried, but it meant I didn't have to tell them the real reason I'd been kicked from uni."

I spot Jared and Luis, and behind them, Jaxon appears. He avoids eye contact as they come over to say hello. "We're going for a few drinks. You coming?" Jared asks.

Lauren glances at me, and I shrug. "Yeah, sure, why not?"

We pay the bill and leave, heading for the nearest bar,

where I order a Coke. Jaxon stands beside me, waiting to order. "I never see you in lectures," he comments.

"I got kicked out," I say coldly. "Your little vendetta to punish Dan got me kicked."

"Shit, you're kidding?"

"You think Dan's wife's father would let me off?"

"I didn't think he'd screw you over like that."

"I slept with his daughter's husband. Of course, he was going to screw me over, Jaxon. Look, forget it, it doesn't matter."

"Are you and Dan still . . ."

"Sort of," I mutter. "It's complicated."

"Then maybe for tonight, we can forget complications and just be how it used to be." He slides me a shot. "For old times' sake?"

I stare at it longingly. "Don't even think about it." I spin to find Dan there. He's glaring at my hand, reaching for the shot. "We need to talk."

DAN

I was passing the bar when I saw Ash's friends in the window, and gut instinct told me she was here too. Seeing her about to drink that shot made me realise how badly I'm fucking everything up. Not that I needed to see that. I've spent the last few days on my own, trying to get control of my life.

Ash follows me from the bar, and we sit outside. "I wasn't going to drink it," she mutters. "I was going to give it to Lauren."

"How have you been?" I ask.

"Not great. You?"

"Me either," I admit, "but I needed that time to clear my head. I had a job interview today," I say. "They just called me to say I got it."

"That's great." She looks genuinely pleased.

"A secondary school not far from the house." Not having a job was stressing me out. I felt like I was losing purpose in life, and getting that call was like a weight had been lifted. "I missed you," I tell her.

"You did?"

I nod. "I know it's been hard for you too, getting used to Izzy and putting up with the way I've behaved. There have been times when I've questioned what the hell I'm doing because this is so unlike me, but we'd be crazy to just walk away from what we have."

She knots her fingers together. "I'm sorry I posted our private business on social media."

"No," I say, "don't be. You were happy and you had every right to be excited. But you have to remember that I come with baggage, so that's what I want to talk about. Our relationship will never be like anything you've had with previous boyfriends. I have to consider Izzy, and sometimes Meg, when I make huge decisions. I can't change that. And when you have our baby, whether we're together or not, I'll be the exact same with you. That's so hard for you to accept, and I get it, so if you think that'll be an issue, just say the word and we'll call it a day."

"And the baby?" she asks.

"I'll always be here for the baby, and for you, if you need support. I'm not walking away. I'm just trying to establish some rules. Izzy comes as part of my package. It's non-negotiable."

"Do you even want to be with me, or is this about the baby?"

I take her hands across the table. "I want us to try. I don't know how it'll work cos I've never done this sort of thing whilst having other responsibilities, but I want us to try."

"The engagement isn't back on," she says firmly. "The next time you ask me to marry you, it'll be because you really want to be my husband. You'll make the effort to ask me properly and at a time when we don't have to hide it."

I nod in agreement. "Is that a yes?"

"We can try, one last time."

MEG

It's been a long week with Izzy hanging on to this cough and cold, so when Zoe drops by, it's a relief to have some adult conversation. Hugo has knocked each evening, but he hasn't come inside for a chat. It's become a little joke because it started when he stopped by to bring Izzy a chocolate rabbit. I made a joke about him not getting me anything, and every night since, he's dropped round with a treat for us both. It's sweet that he checked in on Izzy, and each time I think about it, I smile.

"Earth to Meg." Zoe clicks her fingers in front of my face, and I blink away all thoughts of Hugo.

"Sorry," I mutter, blushing.

"Hugo's on your mind," she guesses.

"I can't help it," I say with a grin, and I tell her about his daily visits. "He's just so sweet to think about her."

"Why don't you ask him out this weekend?"

I shake my head. "No, it's New Year's Eve, he'll be busy."

"Your parents are throwing the best party this side of London. Invite him." Zoe organised the entire thing, and from what she's been saying, it's going to be a lavish affair.

"Definitely not. I'm not going to stick him in a room with my parents, so they can pull him apart and put me off him."

"I don't understand why you're putting this off. You clearly like the guy and . . ." There's a knock at the door, and she trails off.

"That'll be him," I say, glaring at her. "Do not say anything that will embarrass me, or I'll ruin you," I warn, narrowing my eyes. She grins, saluting as I go to open the door.

"How are my two favourite ladies?" Hugo asks, holding up two chocolate hearts.

"You really don't have to do this anymore. She's pretty much back to her usual self," I say, smiling. "Izzy, Hugo's here."

Izzy comes barrelling through the hall, full of excitement. She hurls herself at Hugo, who picks her up. "You look much better," he says.

"I got a new doll," she says excitedly. "Come and see." I open the door wider, and he steps inside.

Izzy drags him through to her bedroom to show off her new toy from Zoe, and when he returns, he's minus one chocolate heart. "She told me she'd had her dinner," he says, placing the other on the side. "Hey, Zoe."

"What are you doing tomorrow evening?" she asks, ignoring my warning glare.

"New Year's Eve, so probably seeing my brothers. Why?"

"That sounds great," I cut in. "Have a great night."

"Because Meg needs a date for a black-tie event."

"I really do not," I hiss.

Hugo smiles at my obvious discomfort. "You need a date? Why didn't you say?"

"I don't need a date."

"She does. I can get tickets for your brothers too."

"Do they need to bring dates?"

"No. Meg needs a date because it's her parents' bash. How many extra tickets should I get?"

"Four—three for my brothers and one for Katie." I relax at the thought of seeing Katie.

"Great. I'll stick your name on the door for all tickets. Arrive with Meg at eight." She stands, kisses me on the cheek, and leaves.

"You don't have to come if you don't want to," I mutter, humiliated. "I don't need a pity date."

"Yeah, you do," he teases, "and I'm good at pity dates."

————

My parents send a limousine to collect us all. I'm embarrassed at their little show of frivolous behaviour, but then I console myself with the fact it was probably Zoe's idea.

Hugo pops his head into my bedroom, where I'm putting the finishing touches to my hair. "You curled it," he says, smiling, "You look beautiful."

I subconsciously run my hands over the black sequined dress I chose. It's a little looser than I remember, but I have dropped a few pounds since the breakup. I slip my feet into my black heels and grab my clutch. "You scrub up nice for a pity date," I say, admiring his tuxedo. He fills it well, and his large frame looks good in a suit.

"I tried," he says, winking. "I don't wanna let you down."

We go through to the living room, where his brothers are waiting, and Katie hugs me. "You look amazing," I tell her, admiring her little black dress.

"I don't get a chance to wear this often," she tells me, slowly spinning. The back is open, and Seb places his arm around her waist, pulling her into his side.

"Apparently, you can't wear a bra in this dress," he mutters, not looking pleased.

I laugh. "But she looks amazing, right?"

"Too good," he mumbles, and she kisses him on the cheek, laughing herself.

"The car's waiting," says Hugo, ushering us out the door.

We waste no time popping open the Champagne in the back of the limo. It turns out everyone but me has had sex in one of these things. The brothers share tales of prom dates, which have me and Katie in stitches. The journey goes so quickly, I'm disappointed when the car comes to a stop and I realise we've arrived at the large, stately home my parents hired out for the evening.

A butler greets us, taking our bags and handing them to staff standing behind him waiting on instruction. "I feel a little intimidated," Katie whispers.

I take her hand and give it a reassuring squeeze. "It's really not as formal as it looks. My mum curses like a sailor, and she only does all this to piss off the wives on the committee. It's like a competition that none of them admit to taking part in."

Inside, my parents are hanging around the entrance to greet guests. They see me and both wrap their arms around me. "We missed you at Christmas," says Mum.

"I'm here now," I say, kissing her on the cheek. "I've brought some guests," I add, turning. "This is Hugo and his brothers, Eric, James, Sebastian, and Seb's wife, Katie." They shake hands as I sign everyone in and collect our room cards, handing them out.

"Zoe has really gone to town this evening," says Mum. "Go and get yourselves a drink and we'll catch up shortly."

There must be over two hundred people gathered inside. We each take a glass of Champagne from a passing waitress. "Your parents seem lovely," says Hugo. "Have you told them anything about me?"

I shake my head. "No. My mum would be pushing us together, especially when she realises your job."

"That would be awkward, especially when I have to tell her I'm only here because you couldn't get a date."

I give an amused nod. "I was fine about coming alone," I lie. I've never been to such a big event alone—Dan's always been with me.

Zoe rushes over, looking stressed as she takes the drink out my hand and downs it before handing back the empty glass. "Christ, the chef is a pig," she whispers, "and he's done nothing but complain."

"You've done an amazing job," I tell her. "I don't know how you do all this and still look so fabulous."

A passing photographer pauses, aiming his camera at Zoe, who waves her hand in objection. "Not a chance will you get a picture of me looking like this," she warns. "But this is Megan, daughter of Mr. and Mrs. Stirk." She then pushes me and Hugo closer together and steps back, and we stand awkwardly while he snaps a picture. "Christ, Meg, make an effort to look less constipated," says Zoe. "Take another one," she orders the photographer.

Hugo gives a laugh before placing his arm around my shoulders and pulling me closer. I glance up at him, and we smile at each other before turning to the camera. Zoe leans over his shoulder as he checks the pictures back. "Yes, that one. Print that one," she tells him.

———

We're seated at a large table for ten. My parents are already settled, and I take the vacant seat next to Mum. Dad leans towards us. "So, Hugo, what do you do for a living?" It's his go-to question, and I roll my eyes. "What?" he asks. "I can't show an interest in a man who turns up with my daughter?"

"I'm a headteacher at a local secondary school," Hugo answers confidently.

I can tell my parents are instantly impressed, and Dad jumps into a million different questions while dinner is served.

"What's happening with you and Dan?" Mum whispers quietly, but Dad overhears and slams his fork down.

"Is it true what they're saying at the university?" he demands to know.

"Do we really need to have this conversation now?" I ask.

"Your dad heard that the girl is pregnant."

I give a slight nod and make a grab for my wine. "So, you're getting divorced?" asks Dad.

"I guess," I say, shrugging.

"You guess?" he repeats, looking astounded. "You want to stay married to a man who not only embarrassed you but who got his lover pregnant?" Mum glares at him, and his face softens. "Sorry, sweetheart. He makes my blood boil is all."

"Mine too," I admit. "Divorce solicitors are expensive," I add, "but I'm looking into it."

"Consider it done," says Dad. "I'll make sure it's rushed through and you get the best deal."

"I don't want the best deal," I say. "I just want to be free of him."

"You need money for Izzy, and my solicitor will make sure you get it, with extra."

"Dad," I say warily, reaching over to place my hand over his, "I don't want a battle. I just want to sign the papers and get him out my life. We'll split everything down the middle."

"I think your dad's right," says Hugo. "He broke your marriage vows, and he shouldn't get half of everything."

"Maybe not, but I can't face the arguments that'll follow if I try to get more than what we talked about."

"I just want to see you happy," says Mum. "You'll be a Stirk again."

I smile. It's been so long since I was Megan Stirk. My heart squeezes at the thought of changing my name back and being different to Izzy and my smile fades. "I might keep the surname."

"Over my dead body," snaps Dad.

"I need the bathroom," I mutter, pushing to stand.

Hugo takes my hand and gives it a gentle squeeze. "You okay?" he asks, his face laced with concern. I nod and walk off.

Twenty-Seven

HUGO

Meg's been gone for a while, and I excuse myself and head off to check on her. It's clear something about the whole name change bothered her, or maybe I overstepped when I gave my opinion.

I spot her sitting at the bar nursing a drink. The seat next to her is taken, and as I move closer, I realise the man beside her is chatting her up. I'm instantly jealous. I don't like this prick sitting so close.

I stand the other side of her and signal to the barman. "Whiskey, neat," I order. "Can I get you anything?" I ask her.

"We got it covered," the man snaps.

Meg smiles at me, her cheeks slightly pink and her eyes full of mischief. "Apparently, we have it covered."

"Is this seat taken?" I ask her, pulling it out and sliding onto it.

"Mate, not to be rude or anything, but do you mind?" the man asks, looking exasperated. "We were having a private conversation."

"Actually, I do mind," I say, placing my arm around the back of Meg's chair and stroking my thumb against her shoulder. "You're wasting your time, she's with me."

He sighs heavily, grabbing his drink and marching off. "Did you just cock-block me?" she asks, smirking.

"I believe I did," I say, taking a sip of my drink. "Cos if anyone's getting lucky tonight, it's going to be me."

She laughs, throwing her head back. "Is that right?" The sound makes my heart leap, and without wasting another second, I press my lips to hers and kiss her. She freezes for a second before placing her arms around my neck and kissing me back. The background noise fades away, and I cup her face in my hands, stroking my thumbs over her cheeks. When we pull apart, we're both breathless. "I'm tired of pretend-ing," I whisper.

"What if we fuck it up?"

"Then at least we'll have had great sex."

She laughs again, tipping her head back and exposing her throat. I nip the delicate skin, and she gasps. "We have sepa-rate rooms," she murmurs.

"Pick one," I say, grabbing her hand.

"Zoe is staying in mine," she points out.

"Mine it is," I mutter, pulling her towards the elevators.

The second we're in it, I slam her against the wall and kiss her again. My erection is straining against my trousers and I'm not even embarrassed. She does things to me that remind me of when I was a horny teenager.

We spill out from the elevator, still wrapped in one another, and I feel in my pocket for my room card. I retrieve it and blindly press it against the door to my room until I hear the click, allowing me to push it open. We spill inside, and I kick off my shoes while she unzips her dress, letting it pool to the floor.

I step back and stare in awe at her black lace underwear. "Jesus, are you trying to kill me?" I pant, fighting with my bowtie. I throw it across the room and begin trying to unfasten the buttons on my shirt. They're small and fiddly and I lose patience, gripping it and pulling hard, sending the buttons scattering across the floor. Meg giggles then goes to take off her heels. I stop her, pressing her against the wall and kissing her again. "Leave them on."

She smiles against my lips. "Kinky bastard."

I feel her hands pulling at my belt before she rips it from the loops and drops it to the floor. Then she lowers to her knees and pulls the button open. I watch as she slides my trousers down my legs before reaching for my boxers. My erection springs free and the heat in her eyes intensifies. She wraps her hand around the base of my cock and trails her tongue from the base to the tip before enveloping the head with her warm mouth. I hiss, letting my head fall back as she sucks.

She works my cock until I'm ready to burst, and I reach under her arms and lift her. "I need to be inside you," I pant, grabbing my overnight bag and pulling out a condom.

She arches a brow. "You came prepared."

"I came with hope," I correct, ripping the packet open as she slides back on the bed. "I was trying to be respectful to your wishes," I add, sheathing myself.

"Oh yeah, how's that working out?"

I grin, crawling over her and planting random kisses along her body. "I saw another man near you and damn near lost my mind. I can't sit back while you get with someone else."

"I'm not getting with anyone else," she murmurs, running her hands over my back.

"Tell me how you feel, Meg."

I part her legs and line myself at her entrance. "I like you," she whispers.

"Louder," I say, inching into her.

Her nails dig into my skin as I stretch her open. "I like you," she repeats, louder this time. Fuck, she feels good. I close my eyes, enjoying the way she squeezes my cock each time I move.

"We're doing this," I tell her, kissing her slowly.

MEG

Sex with Hugo is mind-blowing. If anyone else told me their sex life was like this, I'd think they were lying or exaggerating, but he knows my body better than I do. I'm not saying Dan was bad, because he wasn't, but Hugo does things to me that make me feel like the most wanted woman in the world. He's so attentive and meticulous. The way he touches me sets me on fire, and he can bring me off with his sexy mouth alone.

I glance down between my legs, where his mouth is currently working its magic. We're both coated in a sheen of sweat and in desperate need of another shower, which we had not half an hour ago and it led us back here. I shiver involuntarily as he pulls another orgasm from my exhausted body.

He lies beside me, throwing his arm around my waist and tugging me against him. There's no regret this time when I look into his eyes. He's not thinking about anything but me. "You okay?" he mumbles sleepily.

"Yes. Are you?" I run my fingers over his arm.

"I'm on top of the world."

I grin. "Me too."

We drift off to sleep, and it's another few hours before he's waking me by sliding into me again. At midnight, he leads me to the window, where he wraps his arms around me and we watch the sky light up with fireworks as others celebrate. "Should we go back down to the party?" he asks.

I shake my head. "Definitely not." The thought of us breaking this little bubble makes me shudder, so we climb back into bed and sleep wrapped around one another.

The next time I wake, the sun is streaming through a gap in the curtains directly onto my face. I groan, turning over and coming face to face with Hugo. He smiles, and I return it, blinking the sleep away as I stretch out. "Do you think we were missed last night?"

I shrug. "Probably not. I texted Zoe to tell her I was here."

"Did she approve?"

"I think she was relieved. She said she'd found her own hookup."

"Hookup?" he asks, smirking. "That's not what this is."

I shrug. I didn't want to label us and scare him off. "What is this?"

He leans over, taking my nipple in his mouth, and I close my eyes. "This is a thing."

"A thing?"

"Do we have to go back to reality?" he asks, resting his head against my stomach.

I run my fingers through his hair. "What about your brothers?" I ask, suddenly remembering we left them to fend for themselves last night.

"Why are you thinking about my brothers?" he asks, gently nipping the skin on my stomach.

I yelp, giggling. "We left them last night."

"They're big enough to look after themselves."

"I should go and shower and pack my bag," I say with a sigh. "Dan will drop Izzy home soon."

He jumps from the bed and holds out his hand. "Let's shower together, then I'll come back to your room with you to get your things."

———

Twenty minutes later, we're entering my room. It's still bathed in darkness, so I turn the light on, coming to an abrupt stop when I spot Zoe in a Chadwick brother sandwich. Hugo almost crashes into my back, laughing as he wraps his arms around my waist and nuzzles my neck. When I don't respond, he follows my gaze to the bed, where Zoe is sound asleep between Eric and James. "Holy shit," he murmurs.

"What do we do?" I whisper. "Pretend we didn't see?"

"Just get changed," he mutters, releasing me. I grab my bag and head into the bathroom. When I return minutes later, all three are awake and sitting up in bed.

"Morning," I say as breezily as I can manage.

Zoe presses her lips together to hold in a laugh. I get the impression Hugo's just finished ranting because both brothers look pissed as I grab my bag. "Ready?" Hugo asks. His features are hard, and I imagine this is the same face he uses when he's cross with his pupils.

I nod, heading for the door. "See you later, Zo," I tell her with a wink.

We wait for the elevator in silence, and when we step inside, I let out a small laugh. "That was awkward."

"Yeah, I'm really sorry about those two."

"Don't be. They're living life, and Zoe is an adult."

"Not the point."

"Hey," I say, taking his hand and trying to catch his eye, "it's fine. I'm not bothered."

"I am," he snaps. "You invited them to your parents' party, and they shag your friend."

I laugh. "What's wrong with that?"

"It's disrespectful."

"It's human nature. They fancied each other, so let them have their fun. And Zoe is no innocent little flower. She's a vixen with the libido of a rabbit."

His features soften and he smiles slightly. "I just want to see where this goes with you, and I don't need those clowns upsetting your friend."

"It would take a lot to upset Zoe."

"Just don't hold me responsible for that pair of twats."

I reach up on my tiptoes. "I promise."

———

We stand outside my apartment twenty minutes later, both smiling wide. "Are you free later?" he asks. "I could pop over?"

I nod. "I'd like that." He places a gentle kiss on my nose then goes to his apartment as I go into mine.

Half an hour later, the concierge calls up to tell me Dan is on his way up with Izzy. I open the door just as they're getting out the elevator. My smile falters when I see Ashley is with them, hand in hand with Dan.

"Good morning," I say, before sweeping Izzy into my arms and kissing her all over. "Did you have a nice time?"

"Yes. I stayed up really late," she tells me, and I place her back on the floor so she can run off inside.

I fold my arms over my chest. "Thanks for dropping her off." I don't know why I always thank him, like having his own daughter is doing me a favour.

"Actually, we wanted to talk to you," says Dan.

I hesitate before opening the door wider, glancing out at Hugo's door and wishing to God he hadn't left me so soon. We go into the kitchen, and Dan gives Ash a reassuring smile. "Now the house sale is going through and things are more settled—"

"Sorry I'm late," shouts Hugo, and I almost sag in relief. Dan frowns as Hugo bustles in with a carton of milk. He looks at Dan and Ash like he's surprised they're here, but I suspect he was watching through his spy hole and saw my desperate face. He places the milk on the side and kisses me on the cheek. "I didn't know we were expecting visitors, or I would've grabbed more," he says, casually nodding to the carton.

"It's fine, we're not staying," says Dan tightly. "Are you two . . ." He trails off.

Hugo wraps his arms around my waist and rests his chin on my shoulder. "New year, new start, right?"

Dan has the audacity to look pissed. "Actually, can Meg and I speak alone for a second?"

"I don't think that's necessary," I say.

"This man is going to be around our daughter more than me, so we need to talk," he says firmly.

"Your choice," says Hugo. "Do you expect Meg to stay single forever?"

"I don't know anything about you," Dan snaps.

I scoff. "I'm not doing this, Dan. It's got nothing to do with you. Like Hugo said, you made your choice, and now, I'm moving on. I can't have you kicking off every time you get jealous."

Ash shifts uncomfortably beside him. "I'm not fucking jealous," he spits, grabbing her hand. "I love Ash."

"Good for you."

"Let's just talk about why we came," Ash politely suggests.

"I want a divorce," says Dan bluntly. I'm not blindsided, as it's something I expected him to say, but I resent him coming here with the woman he left me for to discuss it, especially as he fully expected me to be alone.

"Great. I have a solicitor in place. I'll get his details over to you later, and you can share them with your solicitor."

"Solicitor?" he repeats. "I thought we were gonna split everything. We can have the marriage dissolved without all the cost of a solicitor." Hugo shakes his head in annoyance. "You got something to say?" snaps Dan.

Hugo arches his brow. "You want to split everything fifty-fifty after you broke the marriage up with your infidelity?"

"Hugo," I mutter, giving his hand a gentle squeeze, hoping he'll drop it.

"I'm just giving my opinion. He asked."

"Your opinion doesn't matter," snaps Dan. "You've been on the scene a few days."

"Weeks," Hugo corrects.

"Still, we were married for eleven years, so we don't need your input."

"Hugo's right," I cut in, and I feel all eyes on me. "I want it done properly and fairly, and I don't know if fifty-fifty is fair after everything."

"What?" he yells.

"I'm not saying I want more. I'm just saying I want to speak to a professional and get some advice."

"So they can talk you into taking me to the cleaners? Fuck, Meg, you've changed."

His remark gets my back up, and I snap. "I've had to, Dan. You didn't give me any choice."

"Here we go again," he mutters. "Let's hear how I'm the wanker."

"Just get out," I snap. "I can't speak to you when you're like this."

"You're being unreasonable," he complains.

"Because I want legal advice?" I yell. "I've never done this before, and thanks to you, I've got to do it now and I want a legal guide to tell me what to do. So, excuse me if I don't want to listen to Dan's top tips for a divorce."

"See what she's like?" he asks, looking at Ashley. "Do you see what I have to put up with?"

"You're a prick," mutters Hugo, and Dan squares his shoulders.

"Say it again."

"Prick," says Hugo more clearly.

"Enough," I snap. "Dan, get the fuck out. I don't want to talk to you again. Let's do it through solicitors. And Ashley, good luck. I told you you'd need it."

"When?" snaps Dan, looking between us. "When did you two talk?"

I grin. "She didn't tell you about her little visit?" The room is silent, and I can't help feeling smug as Ashley stares down at her feet. "She came to see me to beg me to stay away from you." Dan's eyes burn into Ash. "Apparently, she thought after our kiss, I'd want to take you back." I laugh. "You know, secrets aren't good in a new relationship. Maybe you two should talk."

Dan grabs her hand and storms out. I smile when I hear the door slam. "Dickhead," I mutter.

"What did you see in him?" asks Hugo, kissing me.

"Were you spying on me?" I ask, wrapping my arms around his neck.

"I hate him being around you because he makes you sad." My heart swells, and I kiss him harder. I love how he cares so much.

"Thank you," I whisper against his lips.

Hugo sticks around for dinner, and then Izzy insists he read her a bedtime story again. It's becoming a habit, but one I love. It's just another thing to add to the list of things I love about him.

The last week's been hectic with all the celebrations, so I take the chance to curl up on the couch and enjoy the peace.

HUGO

I finish the fifth story and glance over to see Izzy fast asleep. I smile to myself and gently lay the blanket over her before turning on her night lamp and backing out the room. "She was tough tonight," I say as I go into the living room. I stop, seeing Meg is also fast asleep. "Like mother, like daughter," I whisper in amusement, pulling a blanket from the back of the couch and laying it over her.

Meg deserves a rest, so I decide to stick around in case Izzy wakes.

―――――

I stir, groaning when my neck aches in protest. I rub it and push myself to sit up. Meg is still asleep on the couch, and I must have nodded off in the armchair. I stretch out as Meg stirs, then her eyes flutter open and she smiles when she sees me. "What time is it?" she whispers.

I check my watch. "Two in the morning."

She pushes to sit, and a groan escapes her. "Gosh, I don't feel so good." I help her to stand, and she clutches her head. "I feel dizzy."

"Not a problem," I whisper, scooping her into my arms and carrying her to bed. She slides under the sheets. "I'll get you some paracetamol. You're too hot."

When I return, she's fast asleep again, so I place the tablets on the side with a glass of water and climb in behind her, snuggling against her warm body and drifting off to sleep.

―――――

The room feels bright when I peel my eyes open to find Izzy tapping my face. I blink a few times until her cute face becomes clearer. "I'm hungry," she announces.

I glance back at Meg, who's still asleep. "Okay, let's sneak out, so we don't wake your mummy."

We go to the kitchen, and I lift Izzy onto the counter. "Okay, what do you want for breakfast?"

"Chocolate twists," she says, like I have a clue what that is.

"Um . . ." I open a few cupboards, and Izzy giggles.

"You have to make them."

I arch a brow. "Of course, I do . . . how?"

She points to the fridge. "With the pastry."

I nod. "Pastry. Got it." I rummage in the fridge and

retrieve a pack of ready-rolled puff pastry and hold it up for her approval. She nods. "Now what?"

"Chocolate spread," she says with exasperation.

I laugh. "You're the sassiest three-year-old I know."

She shows me how Meg takes a spoon of chocolate and spreads it over the rolled-out pastry, then she directs me to cut it into long strips, twist, and place it in the oven. I make myself a coffee and pour her a glass of milk, and we both sit at the table to wait for the chocolate twists to cook. She tells me all her favourite things to play with and occasionally asks me a random question like, do I have a cat, to which I answer no and she pouts.

When the twists are looking hot and golden, I take them out and carefully place each one on a cooling rack. Then I sit Izzy in front of the television to watch her favourite morning show while I check in on Meg.

She's still out cold, but her face is flushed red, and I feel her forehead. She's still burning up, so I gently shake her awake, and she groans in protest. "You gotta take these meds," I tell her. "You're running a temperature. You must have what Izzy had."

She slowly pushes to sit, and I pop the pills into her mouth. She sips the water and swallows, wincing. "My throat is sore," she croaks.

"Rest."

"I can't, I have Izzy," she mutters, throwing back the covers.

I shake my head and place them back over her. "She's fine. I've got it. We're just about to eat chocolate twists and watch that spoilt pig show she loves."

"I can't ask you to watch Izzy," she murmurs.

"You're not asking, I'm insisting. Now, get some rest."

Twenty-Eight

MEG

Sofia stares wide-eyed. "So, you're telling me Hugo spent the last four days caring for you and Izzy?" I nod, unable to stop my happy smile. Hugo refused to leave my side the entire time I was sick. He gave me regular meds and kept Izzy occupied while I napped. He even cooked for us all every day, breakfast, lunch, and dinner. "Where did you find him, and how do I get one?" she demands.

I laugh. "He's just . . ." I sigh wistfully, and she throws a napkin at me.

"I don't need to hear it," she says. "It'll make me sick with jealousy."

Zoe rushes over, shimmying out her coat and passing it to the waiter before flopping into the chair. It's the first chance I've had to speak to her since the awkward morning on New Year's Day. "Sorry I'm late, I was busy."

"I bet," I smirk, and she narrows her eyes in on me.

"Not like that."

"Like what?" asks Sofia.

I smirk. "Zoe met someone . . . actually, not one but—"

"Thank you," Zoe cuts in. "I don't think we need to discuss my private life over dinner." She opens her menu and pretends to read it.

"I want to discuss it," Sofia insists.

"Me too," I add.

The waiter returns. "I'll take the steak," says Zoe before turning to me.

"We've ordered," I tell her. "Now, get explaining." The waiter takes her menu and leaves.

"We drank a lot and got talking about fantasies," she says, shrugging.

"Start at the beginning," says Sofia.

"I caught her in bed with two men," I rush to explain, and her eyes widen. "I know, kinky bitch."

"Haven't you two ever wondered what it'd be like?" asks Zoe.

I laugh, and Sofia rolls her eyes. "I had to get artificially inseminated, so I had trouble getting one man to show interest, let alone two."

"This was purely sex," says Zoe. "Apparently, they've done it before."

I lean closer. "Was it good?"

She grins wide, nodding, and I sigh. "All the brothers are hot, but those two together . . ." She trails off, fanning her face.

"Brothers?" asks Sofia.

"New Year's Eve," I explain, "Hugo brought his brothers to the party."

"Oh shit, I knew I should've come."

I eye her. "You wanted to join in the threesome?"

She immediately blushes. "No," she hisses, "I just meant I wish I hadn't missed all the gossip."

"Like when Meg disappeared . . . all night," says Zoe, clearly pleased to get her own back.

"Don't even start. She was just telling me all about the wonderful Hugo," says Sofia, pretending to stick her finger down her throat.

"I don't know what love potion you cast on that man, but he's got it bad," says Zoe.

"We're just seeing where things go."

"From what Eric was telling me, Hugo is diving all in. He adores Izzy, just in case you didn't know."

"There has to be something wrong with him," I say. "He can't be this perfect. He went back to work today, and this morning, he dropped us breakfast. And every evening, on his way home, he gets us a treat and leaves it outside my door."

"Enjoy it while it lasts. It's a new relationship, and he'll soon be leaving the toilet lid up or pissing on the seat," Zoe warns.

I smile. "We're not in a relationship, or at least we haven't said the words out loud."

"So, ask him," suggests Sofia.

"She can't ask him." Zoe laughs, shaking her head. "It's rule number one."

"So, how will she know if they're in a relationship?"

I lean closer, waiting for Zoe's answer, because frankly, all this dating stuff seems hard these days. There are so many rules, I've lost track. "I dunno, maybe flirt with another guy?"

I shake my head. "I'm not a game player. Anyway, I spoke to someone at the party, and he kind of told me he was jealous, but it doesn't make the relationship thing any clearer."

"Tell him you've met someone?"

"No, what if he gets upset? Or worse, isn't bothered?"

"At least you'll know."

"I don't think I want to," I mutter.

Dinner arrives and we order a second bottle of wine. "Why is dating so difficult?" I ask. "I just want to know if we're going somewhere and if we're exclusive. What if I'm fully invested and he's out there shagging other women?"

"Zoe just told you he sounds crazy about you and Izzy," Sofia reminds me.

"Doesn't mean he's not seeing anyone else," Zoe points out.

"How can things change so much since I last dated?"

"You didn't date," Zoe reminds me. "You met Dan, lost your virginity, and married him. Maybe you should get yourself out there, get some more experience." I hate the thought of that, so I don't bother to answer.

After dinner, Zoe insists we hit a few bars and make the most of Sofia being free for the evening. With Izzy at Dan's again, I'm free, so we head out and find the nearest bar.

HUGO

I'm surrounded by unmarked schoolbooks as I glance over to Eric, who is lost in marking. "Thanks for helping me out," I tell him. I've spent the last week covering the English classes since we still don't have a teacher.

"No problem," he mutters. "You need to find someone ASAP, though." I nod in agreement. "And what about Meg? Is she coming to work with us?"

"I'm getting the contract drawn up, and she's starting in a week," I tell him. It took some extra convincing as she thought my offer was because I was drunk, but Meg finally agreed to take the teaching assistant role.

"Will it be weird, working with her?"

I shake my head. "I did it with Elizabeth."

He looks up. "Does she know that?"

I'd thought about mentioning the fact that she'll be filling Liz's role, but I didn't want to make it weird, so I shake my head again. "It doesn't make a difference."

"She might not agree," he says. "I mean, first you're sleeping with her and then getting her to take Liz's role, she might feel weird about it."

"I'm not just sleeping with her." I resent my brother

treating this like some experiment to get me to move on from my dead wife. "We're a thing."

"What does that even mean?"

"Yah know, seeing each other."

"These days, that just means it's sex."

"We're both on the same page," I tell him as his phone buzzes and he opens the screen. "You sure?" He turns it to me and there's a picture of Zoe.

"Why are you showing me a picture of the poor woman you're using?"

"Behind her," he says, and I look closer to see Meg talking to another man. I clench my jaw, trying not to look bothered, even though I am.

"She's allowed to talk to other men."

"But if she doesn't know you're exclusive, she might do other shit. You gotta lock it down before you lose her."

"How am I supposed to do that?" The last thing I want to do is lose her. She's turning out to be more amazing than I ever thought, and I hate she's out there with men circling her like sharks.

"Let's go and see them?"

I shake my head. "No way am I turning up on her girls' night out like some psycho trying to claim her. I'll talk to her tomorrow."

"And what if she's already slept with him by them?"

"Christ, Eric, they're just talking." But I'm already heading to my bedroom to change.

MEG

I try to lean back to avoid the way this guy keeps almost trying to kiss me every time he talks to me. I've been trying to signal to the girls for the last ten minutes to come save me, but they're too busy chatting to his friends to notice.

"And I told him, he can fucking leave the job if he hates it so bad," he slurs in my ear. I give a small smile and take another drink of my sours. "What do you do again?"

"Teaching assistant," I say for the fourth time.

"Bet you look good in a pencil skirt." He grins. "Do you wear those sexy glasses that teachers wear?"

I frown. "You're confusing reality and porn." I sigh heavily and stand. "I need the bathroom."

He grins. "Is that code?" He wiggles his eyebrows in a suggestive manner.

"Again, you're confusing the reality and porn thing," I say. "Women don't do that sort of thing in real life." I march away. He's the third man to chat to me tonight and give me the ick with his terrible banter and flirting.

I go to the bathroom, and as I head back over to the table, I spot Eric by the bar. I search the faces around him until my eyes connect with Hugo's. My heart speeds up in delight as he makes a beeline for me. "I was gonna lie," he says, leaning close to my ear to shout over the music, "and tell you it's a coincidence I'm here, but it's not. I'm fully stalking you because of a picture Zoe sent to Eric."

I can't hide my smile. "What picture?"

"One where a man was talking to you in the background."

I bite my lower lip and think back to what Zoe said about feeling him out. "Yeah, that was . . . Dean," I lie. "He asked me out."

"I bet he did," he says seriously, "but you can't accept."

"I can't?"

He places a finger under my chin to tilt my head back so I'm looking at him. He shakes his head slowly, and my heart does a happy dance. "No. I don't know if I made it clear before, but this thing we've got going on leaves no room for anyone else."

"It's just us?" I clarify.

He nods. "Me, you, and Izzy." He kisses me until my toes curl and I'm breathless. "Are we clear?"

"Crystal."

We stay for a few more drinks then leave. We walk Sofia home, leaving Zoe and Eric in the bar, then we walk hand-in-hand back to his apartment, where he spends the night showing me how exclusive we are.

———

By the morning, my body is sore, but in the most delightful way. Hugo is still out cold, so I sneak out of bed to make him breakfast. He's spent the last week looking after me, and it's the least I can do.

I rustle together some eggs and bacon, and as I'm plating up, Hugo appears. He's completely naked and not at all embarrassed as he moves towards me with a glint in his eye. I laugh, backing away. "We got the whole day," I say. "Can we please eat first? I'm so hungry."

He grabs me, pulling me into his arms. "If we must." He kisses me then lowers onto a stool, holding me against him and grabbing a fork. "Open," he orders, taking a forkful of egg from the nearest plate and feeding it to me.

"I can feed myself." I laugh, but he keeps me against him and eats a mouthful himself.

"I wanna take care of you," he says, "all the time."

"You're doing a good job," I tell him.

"You deserve to be treated like a queen, Meg. I'm gonna make sure that happens."

"You'll have to dial it down come Monday," I say. I'm nervous about working at the school. I don't want it to become too much if we're always together, and I don't want my new colleagues to look at me differently because of my relationship with him.

"Of course. The last thing you need is for the kids to give you a hard time."

"And the other staff," I point out.

"They need to know you're mine," he says, kissing my neck.

I laugh. "And why's that?"

"So they know they can't have you. There's a sixty-five percent male-to-female staff ratio."

I turn in his arms. "I'm serious. Let me settle in without everyone gossiping about me."

HUGO

I enter the staff room, and everyone quiets down. We have a staff meeting every Monday morning, but today feels different because I have Meg here. I try to keep my face neutral as I scan the room for her. She's sitting on her own at the back and it instantly pisses me off.

"Monday is here again," I say with a small smile, and there're a few groans around the room. "Which means a fresh start and clean slate. Whatever we dealt with last week stays there. Jane, that means Hunter Skellington is out of detention. I spoke with his mum on Friday, and she's insistent we integrate him back to lessons." Jane sighs, shaking her head but making a note in her pad. "Let's all be extra supportive for him today. In other news, we have a new member of staff joining us." I see Meg's eyes widen in panic. "Megan Stirk," I say, pretending to scan the room like I don't know exactly where she is. "Right at the back," I add, smiling at her. The staff turn and offer small greetings. "She's our new teaching assistant. Lisa, take her under your wing this week." Lisa's worked here for many years and will be able to show her everything.

"Have we found a new teacher to fill English yet?" asks Arthur, one of the eldest staff members.

I shake my head. "We're reposting later today. If that's all, you can get off to sort your heads out and get ready for the day ahead."

I wait for the room to almost clear before cornering Meg. "That was embarrassing," she hisses.

"Lunch. The park." I walk away without looking back.

By the time lunch arrives, I'm bursting to see Meg. The fact she's been in the same building all morning and I've been unable to see her, touch her, or kiss her has about killed me off. I grab the lunch bag full of food for us both and rush out. Everyone knows I'm out the building at lunch. It started with Liz, and we'd always come to the park, but after she left, I couldn't break the routine. I felt closer to her here.

Meg arrives five minutes after me. She's smiling, so that's a good sign. I hand her a salad as she places a light kiss on my lips. "How was your morning?"

"Really good," she says, nodding enthusiastically. "I think I'm going to love it here."

I'm relieved. I want her to stick around. We eat lunch in a comfortable silence, and after, we take a walk hand-in-hand. It's been a while since I've felt such peace.

MEG

My week passes in a blur of juggling work and Izzy. It's not easy, and I've relied heavily on my parents for support as Dan started his new job too, but I have to find another way.

So, when I drop Izzy off Friday evening, I broach the subject. "We really need to share childcare," I say, "now we're both at work."

"Impossible," he mutters, taking Izzy's bag. She heads inside, and Dan goes to close the door. We haven't spoken since he came to mine last week with Ashley.

"That's it?" I ask. "That's all you're going to say?"

"I'm a teacher," he snaps. "I can't take time off or leave early."

"Why? I have to."

"I just can't. It's a new job."

"So is mine," I argue, "and it's not fair I have to bear all the responsibilities when it comes to Izzy."

"That's what mums do, Meg. Sorry, but I can't help."

I sigh, hating my next sentence before it's even left my mouth. "What about Ashley?"

He almost laughs. "What about her?"

"Well, she's free during the day, isn't she?"

"I'm not asking her to have Izzy all day."

"It wouldn't be all day, just where she can. Izzy's at nursery every morning now." I had to up her hours when I took the job. "So, just the pickup and until I finish at four."

"Jesus, Meg, listen to yourself. You want the woman you hate to take care of our daughter?"

"Well, you don't hate her, and she's carrying Izzy's half-sibling."

"It doesn't mean she's ready to become step-mum of the year overnight. Besides, she's having a rough time of the pregnancy. She's not up to it."

"Then we'll need to find a babysitter."

"You're not sticking Izzy with a stranger," he snaps. He's always been against the idea of putting Iz into a childcare setting. It took a lot to convince him she needed nursery to be around other kids.

"There's no other option."

"There is, Meg. Stay at home and look after her like before."

"I can't do that. Where am I supposed to get money to pay the rent and bills?"

"You said yourself it's just half a day, so cut your hours at work. Why did you even take a full-time position when you had no childcare?"

"Because I stupidly thought you'd help me out," I snap. "Forget it. I'll sort it myself."

I check my watch as I get in the car. I have a meeting with my solicitor in ten minutes, and my dad is meeting me there.

He's waiting outside when I arrive, and he kisses me on each cheek as he ushers me inside. The office is the sort of place I'd never think of coming because it's way out of my price range.

We sit behind a large desk as Walter Wainright sits opposite. Dad briefly explains the split between me and Dan. He seems to think I've lost my voice and rambles on. Walter makes notes, occasionally asking me a question about finances or roles within the marriage.

"Take the bastard for everything he's worth," Dad tells him.

"Actually," I cut in, "I just want what I'm owed."

Walter taps his lower lip with a pen. "If this was the other way around, do you think he'd be so lenient?" I shrug. "I see men like him all the time. If the shoe was on the other foot, you'd be on the bare bones of your arse by the time he'd finish with you. Look, we can get exactly what you're owed and more. He's basically forced you to give up the role you love."

I frown. "He has?"

"You were a stay-at-home mum to your daughter. Now, you've had to go back to work full-time to pay the bills. He broke the marriage contract, and had he not, you'd still be at home, raising your daughter."

"He's got another child on the way. I don't want to ruin him."

"Stop thinking about him," snaps Dad. "He's a scumbag."

"I'm so sick of men bossing me around," I mutter, standing. "I've had enough. I'm going home." I walk out, ignoring my dad as he calls my name.

I get home ten minutes later, and I'm just putting the key

in my door when Hugo sticks his head out. "You okay?" he asks.

I shake my head, and he holds out his hand for me to take. I do, and he leads me inside. "Dan refused to help with childcare then gave me a lecture on staying at home to raise her. Now, I feel like a shit mum. Dad spoke for me at the solicitor's, which made me feel like a teenager again. I left them to plot out their attack on Dan, even though it's not what I want." I sigh heavily. "I'm just tired of it all."

I sit down as he goes to the table, where a bottle of wine is chilling. He pours us each a glass, and I contemplate my next question. I don't want to annoy him, but I have to know the truth.

"Hugo, did Elizabeth work at your school?"

He hands me the wine. "Yes."

I wasn't expecting him to be so honest, and I really wanted the answer to be no. "Why didn't you tell me?"

"I didn't think it was important."

"I saw her picture on the trophy wall. She was smiling with a bunch of girls as they held up a trophy." Hugo smiles.

"They won the netball championship two years in a row."

"She was a P.E. teacher?" I ask.

He shakes his head. "No."

"What was her role?" His smile fades and he fiddles with his glass. I suddenly feel nervous about his answer. "Hugo, what was her role?" I repeat more firmly.

"Remember, you came for the job before I really knew you."

"Hugo?"

"She was a teaching assistant."

I feel numb as my mind races with questions. "Okay, but that's not the reason you hired me, I wasn't her replacement?" He doesn't answer, and I place my glass on the table. "Hugo, I wasn't her replacement?"

"It's not as bad as it sounds," he mutters. "She's been dead a while, and I couldn't bring myself to rehire."

"So, you thought you'd hire the woman you've been sleeping with?" I stand, covering my mouth. "Oh god," I mutter through my hands. "I'm in her bed . . . I've taken her job."

"You didn't take it," he mutters, looking irritated. "There was a position, and you needed a job. If you didn't take it, someone else would have."

"That's not the point," I snap. "You know what I mean, Hugo. What will people think when they find out about us?"

"Who cares?"

"I care," I yell. "I fucking care. I have enough going on right now without worrying everyone at work is going to be talking about me like I'm some kind of weirdo taking Liz's husband and then her job."

He sighs. "Meg, people aren't going to think that."

"I just need to . . ." I head for the door, and he dives up to follow, looking worried.

"Please don't go like this."

"I need to think."

"You'll overthink and it'll be bad," he mutters. He looks panicked, and I almost feel bad as I walk out, closing the door behind me.

I release a long breath and go into my apartment. Maybe Dan is right. Maybe the job is all wrong for me. Maybe I need something with less hours and away from Hugo. That way, things won't get messy between us.

I shower and get into my pyjamas, then I make a coffee, and as I go back into the living room with plans to watch a chick flick, I spot Hugo's hoody on the back of the chair. My heart twists, and I place my coffee down on the table and take the hoody, holding it to my nose and inhaling his spicy after-shave. I smile. His scent makes me safe and feel warm inside. And in this exact moment, I realise I can't give him up.

I wrap the hoody around me and grab the coffee, deciding to send him a text to come over. We'll worry about everything else another day, but right now, I need him.

HUGO

I feel relieved when the text message comes through from Meg.

Meg: I'm sorry. I hate that we fought. Forgive me?

Me: Yes. One hundred percent yes.

Meg: Wanna watch P.S. I love You?

I groan. We've watched it a hundred times since we started hanging out, but I'm finding I don't mind as long as I'm with her. I grab the half-drunk bottle of wine and head next door, where I find her curled up on the couch with a coffee. She's wearing my hoody, and I like that. She looks good.

She reaches for me, and I bend to kiss her. "Sorry," she mutters.

"Don't be. I should've told you. We'll work it out." I hold up the bottle. "Wine?"

She shakes her head. "I'm good with coffee."

"Mind if I grab a glass?" She shakes her head, and I go into the kitchen. I pour a large glass, drinking half of it before re-joining her. I need a good buzz of alcohol if she's going to make me watch this film again. "You look good in my hoody," I tell her, sitting beside her.

She smirks. "I was cold."

"Liar. You missed me," I tease.

She pulls her hand from the pocket, holding up a piece of folded paper. "Love notes?" she asks, wiggling her brows. She places her coffee on the table.

"Probably a shopping list."

I watch as she begins to unfold the paper, and the second I see Seb's handwriting, I freeze. The next few seconds seem to go in slow motion as she opens it completely and scans it, a frown adoring her perfect face. "What is this?"

My brain races to find the answer. One that will make this sound much better than it currently looks. I try to grab it, scoffing and waving my hand like it's nothing, but she moves it out of reach, keeping a firm grip as she continues to read.

"It was a stupid list that Seb forced—"

She looks up and there's hurt in her expression. "Seb?"

I groan, burying my head in my hands as she stands and begins to pace. "Baggage," she reads out.

"That's not a bad thing," I argue.

"It's on the cons side," she mutters. "Twatty ex." She shrugs like she agrees with that one. "Married and divorced before forty." She looks up again and the pain in her eyes is worse. "That's not my choice."

"I know. Ignore it, it's a stupid list that Seb wrote. It doesn't mean anything, and it doesn't reflect what I'm thinking or feeling right now. We're in a good place."

She ignores me. "Heartbroken. How is that bad?" Realisation passes over her face as she spots the next few, and she almost chokes on her next words. "Emotional wreck . . . really?"

"Again, I'd like to point out that I didn't write this."

"Why did you cross out 'cries'?"

"If it was up to me, I'd cross them all out." *Fuck, why didn't I rip it up and throw it away?* With each word that falls from her lips, I feel sick. The thought of causing her any more pain racks me with guilt.

"Work together?" she almost screeches. "You pushed me into it."

"I know. Eric said—"

"Eric was there too?"

"Oh god, Meg, I'm not explaining this very well. There are pros right? He wrote pros?"

She arches a brow. "Four. Four pros, and one, two, three,

four, five, six, seven, eight, nine cons, if you count 'cries' which was crossed off."

"We won't count that," I say in a hushed tone. "Seb thought it would be a good idea to write down the pros and cons. I didn't say those exact words. We were talking, and I was expressing my worries. Seb twisted them and wrote them down."

She growls, and I flinch slightly. I haven't seen her angry before, but she suddenly looks raging. "I am so tired of men not taking responsibility for their actions. You were there, yes?"

"Yes, but—"

"And you watched while Seb wrote this shit, yes?"

"It wasn't like that."

"It was exactly like that," she suddenly screams, and I press my lips together to stop from speaking. "You spoke about me to your brothers, and they wrote down all my bad points. And I can't even argue with some of them. You're right, I am heartbroken, and I do cry a lot. I have baggage and a twatty ex. But it's my life, Hugo, and you knew it all before you kissed me, before we had sex. So, take responsibility for this bullshit," she hisses, holding the paper up.

"Fine," I mutter, shrugging. "You're right, it was my fault too, I was there. But I didn't want to write the list. He just started—"

"There you go again," she snaps. "Just accept you fucked up, Hugo."

"Okay," I snap, pushing to stand. "I fucked up. Is that better? I wanted to get everything clear in my head, so I dug around to find shit that would make me stop wanting you. But guess what, it didn't fucking work because I wanted you anyway."

She hands the list back and shrugs out of the hoody. When she holds that out to me also, I refuse to take it. "You should go."

"No," I snap. "We need to talk about this."

"There's nothing to say. Your cons list far outweighs the pros."

"Ignore the fucking list," I yell, as fear envelopes me like a heavy weight. I can't let her end this over a stupid fucking list.

"I can't," she mutters. A tear rolls down her cheek, and she swipes it away. "You took all the things I worry about and wrote them down in a list. And your top pro was that I'm gorgeous. That's your top one." She says it like it's a bad thing.

"You're so much more than a pretty face," I rush to say, trying to grab her hand.

She pulls it away and folds her arms over her chest in that way she does whenever Dan is around, like she's putting her armour up. "Yet you didn't write those."

"Because I made him stop. I hated the fucking list."

"But you kept it in your pocket. Was that to remind you?"

"Christ, no," I snap. "I forgot it was there. I took it from Seb and stuffed it there, so he couldn't add anything else."

She sighs heavily. "Just go."

"I don't want to," I admit. "Because I know if I leave, it'll be the last time you let me back in."

Her eyes are downcast as she places my hoody on the couch. "Don't make me call security."

My heart aches as I pick up the hoody. She follows me to the door, and as I turn back to speak, she closes it gently in my face. I place my hand against it and rest my forehead there. *Fuck.*

Thirty

MEG

I will not cry . . . I will not cry . . . I will not cry. I repeat it like a mantra as I empty the wine down the sink. I can't cry because, apparently, it's a fucking con. I growl out loud and slam the glass on the side. I'm a fucking idiot. I knew I should have been more cautious, and I knew he was too good to be true. Damn me and my crap judgement.

I go to bed, even though it's still early, and I make a promise to myself that from now on, I'll stay single.

———

The following day is Saturday. I wake feeling like shit, but I refuse to sit around and be sad, so I go shopping. It's not my favourite thing to do, but I needed to get out of the apartment. I didn't want to risk Hugo popping round with his bullshit apologies.

When I get back, there's a bunch of flowers leaning against my door and the usual breakfast croissant. I unlock the door, stepping over them to go inside.

I arrange to meet Zoe for dinner, but Sofia can't make it. She doesn't want to take the piss by using her parents to babysit yet again, but I feel like she would probably be the better person to tell this to, so I change our plans last minute and we all meet at Sofia's.

They're already halfway through a bottle of wine when I arrive. "Oh no," whispers Sofia the second she lays eyes on me. Her face is full of sympathy, and it takes everything I have not to break down. "You have that sad look in your eye."

"I'm fine," I say briskly. "Absolutely fine."

"You and Hugo broke up?" she asks, ignoring my lies.

"Were we ever really together?" I shrug like it's no biggie.

Zoe pours me a glass of wine. "What did he do?"

I take it and sit down between them. "I told you he was too good to be true."

"Tell me he didn't cheat," snaps Sofia.

I shake my head sadly. Maybe if he had, it would hurt less. "He wrote a list."

Zoe frowns. "Like a shopping list?"

"No, like a pros and cons list. He basically wrote down everything that gives him the ick about me, and I found it."

"Oh Jesus," murmurs Sofia. "Why did he do that?"

"Because he's a man and they're all like grown children," says Zoe.

"It just hurt, yah know, seeing the things I hate about myself right now listed like some fucking . . ." I sigh. "I dunno. It just hurt."

"What was on the list?" asks Zoe.

Sofia scowls. "Don't make her relive it."

"How can we advise if we don't know what was on it?"

"He said I'm too heartbroken, I cry too much, and I'm an emotional wreck." Anger builds and I take a gulp of wine. "Who the fuck does he think he is? My marriage broke down, of course, I'm going to be emotional, but I'm hardly a wreck."

Zoe bites her lip in that way she does before she's about to disagree, and I brace myself. "You make a valid point," she begins, trying to soften her blow, "but are these things really that bad? He was stating the obvious," she says. "Apart from the wreck bit," she adds quickly before I can say anything.

"Okay, but he also listed 'married and divorced before forty', like that's my fault."

"Again, he's stating the obvious."

"He put 'working together', yet he pushed me to take the bloody job," I argue.

"All I'm saying is these aren't things like . . ." She thinks over her words and adds, "fat arse or big nose. Eats too loudly or is crap in bed."

"No, they're worse because they're all the things I hate about myself. I cried in front of him so many times and regretted it, thinking he was going to run a mile from my broken ass. But he stuck around, and now, I find out those things irritated him. I'll never be able to cry in front of him again."

"What was on the pros?" asks Sofia.

I roll my eyes. "Standard stuff. Gorgeous, makes me laugh, kind, good mum. I want a man who thinks I'm his world. That list doesn't scream that he's in love with me."

"In love?" repeats Zoe, laughing. "You think a list is what you need to see if he loves you?"

"It would've made the blow a little easier," I mutter.

"Meg, the guy worships you. He brings you and your daughter pastries every morning. He brings you a chocolate treat every night after he finishes work. He checks in on you. He reads your baby bedtime stories. He took care of you when you were sick. That's how you know how he truly feels, not some bullshit list."

"There's something else," I say, because I'm clutching at straws now she's made me feel silly for getting upset. "His wife used to work at his school."

"So?"

"So, I took her position as teaching assistant."

Zoe winces. "That is a little weird."

"And now, if our colleagues find out we're together, it's going to look gross, like I'm some fucked-up, crazy bitch trying to replace his dead wife."

"Someone had to fill the position," Sofia reasons.

"But not me. Not the woman who's jumped into bed with her husband."

"Maybe you should take some time to work on you," Sofia suggests gently, placing her hand over mine. "You've had so much going on. Hugo came along and took your mind off Dan, which is great, but maybe some time to figure out who you are without Dan or Hugo will be good for you and Izzy."

I nod in agreement. "You're right."

———

When I get home, there's more flowers and a box of chocolates. I sigh, stepping over them and going inside. Hugo knocks on the door a few minutes later. I know when it's him because anyone else would have to go through security and be buzzed up. I open the door, and he's holding the flowers and chocolates. "Peace offering."

"Take a hint."

"I can't walk away, Meg. This feels wrong."

"And just a heads up, I won't be back to work on Monday. I quit."

"No," he groans. "No, no, no."

"It's for the best."

"Please, just give me a chance to make it up to you."

"I saw the girls tonight, and Sofia said something that made sense. She said I need to find out who I am before I even think about getting with anyone else. Maybe you need to do the same too."

"I know who I am, Meg, and I know I'm better when I'm with you."

HUGO

There's a lost look in her eyes, and I hate I'm the reason for that. I never in a million years thought for one second that I'd be the one to cause her pain.

"But I don't think I'm better with you," she admits, her voice breaking slightly. She recovers, squaring her shoulders and staring me dead in the eyes.

"You're wrong. And you're wrong about us. We came together when we were both so lost." Tears form in her eyes, balancing delicately on her lower lashes. "That wasn't a coincidence. We were meant to bump into each other that day."

"You're right," she agrees, and I relax a little. "And you were great in helping me move forward. You distracted me from the shit I had going on with Dan." Her words burn me, and I stare in disbelief. "You helped me get over my heartbreak." I wait silently for her to take the words back, but she doesn't. Instead, she stares at me with disappointment. I give a slight nod and back away. She's lashing out, pretending what we had was nothing more than a hookup so she could get over Dan. But it's not true, and she's just hurting. So, I choose to go quietly, heading back to my apartment and throwing the gifts in the bin.

———

"What do you mean it's done?" asks Eric.

"Thanks to you and Seb for the great idea of listing the pros and cons of dating her. She found it, by the way."

He cringes, glancing at Seb, who looks just as awkward. "Shit. Why did you keep it?" asks Seb.

"I didn't keep it on purpose, dickhead," I snap. "I put it in my pocket when I took it from you, and I forgot about it."

"What did she say?" asks Jimmy.

"Nothing good."

"We can fix this," says Seb, taking a drink of his pint.

"It's not fixable," I say, staring up at the large screen in the bar that's showcasing rugby. "She hates me."

"Bullshit. You can't walk away because of a stupid list," says Eric.

"What was on it?" Jimmy asks.

I pull the crumpled piece of paper from my pocket and place it on the table. He straightens it out, giving a low whistle as his eyes scan the list. "Fuck, what were you thinking?"

"It was my fault," mutters Seb. "Shit, man, I'm so sorry. I was trying to help."

I sigh, taking the paper and ripping it into tiny pieces. "It wasn't your fault. I shouldn't have let you write it. I was trying to find reasons not to move on from Liz. Fat lot of good it did."

Jimmy slaps me on the shoulder. "Hey, you've had your first heartbreak since Liz. It's another step to recovery."

I nod sadly, staring down at the paper. "I guess."

"You're not giving up?" Eric asks. "Surely, you're not just gonna walk away."

I shrug. "I tried, but she gave this speech about needing to move forward on her own to discover who she really is without Dan or me."

"Fuck that, Hue. If you like the woman as much as I think you do, make her see you're good together."

"Maybe," I mutter.

"It's the first time we've seen you smile in ages. You have to get her back," adds Seb. "Besides, if Katie finds out, she'll rip my nuts off."

We all laugh at that. Katie's taken a real shine to Meg. "You have to tell her, or she might contact Meg for that coffee. If she finds out through Meg and we didn't tell her, she'll rip all our nuts off," says Jimmy.

I get home an hour later with my usual chocolate treat for

Izzy. I thought about getting Meg one like normal, but she's already refused my flowers and I don't want to give her another reason to look at me with those sad eyes. When the elevator opens to my floor, Dan's at Meg's door dropping Izzy off. Usually, I'd hang around because Meg hates being alone with him, but this time, I walk past, keeping hold of Izzy's chocolate. I'll leave it at the door later.

"Wait a minute," says Dan, sounding amused. "Have you two fallen out?"

"You can go now," Meg mutters.

"Which one fucked it up?" Dan asks, laughing again. "Let me guess, he got bored of shagging a single mum and moved on?"

"That's your trait, right?" I say, pausing with my door half-open.

"What did you say?" he snaps.

"You heard. For your information, it was me who fucked up, but not because I got bored or cheated. I wouldn't do that to her."

"Cos you're so fucking perfect," he scoffs, rolling his eyes.

"I'm better than you," I snap, squaring my shoulders, and he does the same. "You left your wife and kid for your student. You can't get much lower."

"Leave it," hisses Meg.

"You don't know anything about my life," Dan yells.

"I know you fucked up and you'll live to regret it, because you had the world and gave it up for a quick fuck."

"Jesus, stop," Meg shouts, moving between us as we take a step closer.

Dan ignores her, shoving me. "Who the fuck are you to judge me?" he roars.

I do something I've wanted to do for months. I bring my fist back and smash it right into his smug face. He groans, bending over and holding his nose. "You broke my face," he moans.

"Are you happy now?" Meg yells, glaring at me.

"Me?" I shout, my eyes wide in shock. "He started it."

"Listen to yourself," she snaps, shaking her head in disgust.

Dan straightens. There's a red mark on his cheek but no blood, unfortunately. "I should report you to the police."

"Grow up," snaps Meg. "Get inside. You need ice on that." Dan glances back over his shoulder and smirks at me as Meg goes to follow.

"Meg—" I begin, my tone laced with regret, not for punching him but for doing it in front of her. She pauses in the doorway. "I'm sorry, I—"

"Pray to God he doesn't press charges," she whisper-hisses. "You could lose your job." And then she goes inside, slamming the door.

DAN

Meg presses an ice pack to my cheek. It's the sort of thing she always has on hand after years of bumped heads or scraped knees with Izzy. It's something I told Ashley we'd need, and she rolled her eyes like I was a dinosaur.

She stands between my legs, and I'm eye level with her chest, a place I was once familiar with. Since our split, she's lost weight and her whole body seems to have changed. I hate that I don't know it anymore. "You shouldn't have bated him," she lectures.

"I couldn't resist."

"Well, try. He's my neighbour, and I can't leave this place for another six months, so be civil."

"Why'd yah break up?"

"None of your business."

"Did he hurt you?" I ask, because she's got that same defeated look in her eye that I put there when she caught me with Ash.

"How's Ash coping with the pregnancy?" she asks, changing the subject.

"She's struggling," I admit. When she's not sick, she's complaining she feels it. "It's like she's the first pregnant woman in the world." I don't mean it to sound so criticising, but she complains an awful lot, and some days, she refuses to move off the couch.

"She's young," says Meg, and then she sighs. "I didn't mean that as an insult."

"I know," I say, because it's not often Meg insults anyone. "I wasn't around much when you were pregnant, was I?"

"You had to work to pay the bills."

"So, I don't remember you suffering with sickness."

"It's the worst thing ever, like being seasick twenty-four-seven and nothing helps. Try and be sympathetic towards her, she's got it rough right now. Growing a human isn't easy."

I grin. "You're giving me advice on how to take care of my lover?"

She smiles. "I know what a dick you can be."

I bite my lower lip and carefully run my finger over her stomach. She watches me, her eyes burning with curiosity. "I'm sorry," I whisper.

"It's fine. Hugo's just hurting. He's not usually like that." She steps away, handing me the ice pack.

"I mean I'm sorry for what I did to you." She rests against the counter and lowers her head. "I put you through hell, and I still am. I know it's not easy for you to see me with Ash, and I'm sure it'll only get harder when she has the baby. If I'd known back then what I was about to ruin, I wouldn't have done it. I was so distracted with the danger and flirting, I didn't stop to think. So, I'm sorry." I feel like it's the first time I've said it and meant it.

She gives a nod. "I appreciate that. And just so you know, I'm seeing the solicitor tomorrow."

I stand. "It's fine. Whatever you want, you can have, Meg. You deserve it." I head for the door.

"No," she says, following me. "I'm going to stick to what we agreed. You have a new baby on the way, and I don't want to take more than what I need for Izzy. Despite everything, you're a good dad. You were always a good dad."

I smile, resting my hand against the doorknob. "You were a good wife, Meg. A damn good wife. I didn't appreciate that until it was too late." I open the door and almost step on a chocolate bunny. I swoop down and pick it up, holding it out to Meg. "This belong to you?"

She gives a sad smile and takes it. "It's for Izzy."

"Ahh, the treat he always leaves for Iz," I say, glancing over at Hugo's door. "She told me about that." I press for the elevator. "Don't tell him I said this, but I hated the smile he put on your face. You looked happier with him." I pull her to me and wrap my arms around her. I'm surprised when she lets me, resting her head against my chest. "Whatever he did, it wasn't as bad as what I did. Surely, it can be forgiven."

I feel her smiling. "You want me to forgive the man who just punched you?"

"I want you to be happy, and he made you happy. And as much as it grates me to say this, Izzy loves the guy." Something passes between us, like a sense of calm we've not really had since I left.

I place a lingering kiss on her head, inhaling the scent of her fruity shampoo. "I'll always love you, Meg." I step away and push the button for the elevator again. "See you Friday?"

She nods. "Yeah."

Thirty-One

MEG

The weeks pass and things seem easier somehow. I felt better after Dan's apology. It felt sincere, and it came at a time when I was finally ready to hear it. The divorce is going through smoothly, and we've even agreed on holiday contact, taking it in turns to spend our Christmases with Izzy.

The house sale was split down the middle once legal costs were taken out, and with a nice healthy chunk in the bank, I can take my time to get a new job before I decide on where I want to buy a house.

I haven't seen Hugo, not even in passing. He still leaves a treat every evening for Izzy, and each time he does, she asks if she can see him. It's hard getting her to understand that he's not a part of our life anymore, and sometimes, I regret ever introducing them because she misses him. When I next meet someone, I've vowed to wait until at least six months, but it'll be hard when she spends most of her time here with me, which is why I'm trying to enjoy single life.

I take one last glimpse in the mirror and smile. I look quite nice in the tight-fit leather leggings low-cut vest Zoe insisted I buy . I pull on a blazer-style jacket and slip my feet into my heels. I give my hair one last tussle so that the curls fall over each shoulder, then I grab my bag.

I'm locking my door when Hugo's door opens. I give a little side glance and watch as he steps out, unaware I'm here. I can feel my heart beating wildly in my chest. It's our first encounter since the split, and although I'd pictured this a thousand times, I'd never really thought about what I'd say.

I press for the elevator, and he turns to see me, but it's too late for either of us to go back inside without being obvious, so we stand side-by-side waiting for it to open.

We step in together, and I press for the ground floor. My heart slams harder in my chest as silence wraps around us. It's weird to be so close to the man I've had great sex with and not interact. "Going anywhere nice?" I eventually ask, wincing when my words come out high-pitched from nerves.

"Erm, yeah, I've got a date."

His words twist my heart painfully, but I recover quickly. "Great."

"You?" he asks.

"Meeting the girls for a few cocktails."

The elevator opens and I breathe a sigh of relief as we step out. "Have a great night," he tells me, rushing off.

Ted glances up from his newspaper. "Good evening, Ms. Megan."

"Hey, Ted," I say, unable to hide the glumness in my voice.

"Was that Mr. Hugo I saw rushing out of here?"

I nod. "He couldn't wait to get away."

"I don't think that's true." I'd spent many hours sitting this side of Ted's desk and boring him with my terrible love life. He's a good listener.

"Oh yeah, apparently, he's going on a date."

He gives a knowing smile. "She'll never match up to you."

I grin, "Thanks, Ted. Have a quiet shift," I say as I step out into the cool spring evening.

———

The girls give me a sympathetic hug when I tell them about Hugo. It's shit that the first time I see him in weeks is when he's already met someone else. "It's a sign for you to move on," says Zoe.

"I don't think so. I'm not putting myself through another minute of heartache."

Sofia checks her watch. "We're going to be late," she tells us, downing the rest of her drink and encouraging us to do the same.

"Late?" I ask, confused. "I thought we were just having a few drinks."

"I said we'd meet Matt," she tells me, gathering her bag and coat. Matt's been so busy playing house with Carl, he's hardly had time to see us.

We follow Sofia from the bar, and she leads us towards the park. "What are we doing here?" I ask.

"It's a cut-through," she says. "We're meeting him in Blue Bar. This way is quicker."

I groan. I've avoided the park for weeks because it reminds me of Hugo.

Zoe hooks her arm in mine. "I'm meeting Eric later," she tells me, pulling out her mobile and showing me a couple pictures with them together.

I grin. "Are you two a thing?"

"Maybe," she says with a shy smile.

When I look up from her mobile, I gasp. Sofia has stopped and is watching me closely for my reaction. Behind her is a table with a flickering candle in the centre. It's surrounded by fairy lights, laid neatly on the grass. Hugo stands, his smile unsure.

"Oh great," I hiss, "he's bringing his date to the park."

Zoe giggles. "You're adorable."

"We should go," says Sofia, grabbing Zoe by the hand. "Call if you need us."

I stare wide-eyed as it dawns on me. "You set me up?" She blows me a kiss, and they rush off.

I turn to where Hugo is still standing. "You're my date," he confirms. He pulls out my seat, and I carefully sit down, staring in disbelief at the pretty lights and the wine on ice.

A bike stops beside us, and a man gets off, opening a bag. "I ordered us Chinese. I hope that's okay," says Hugo with an apologetic smile. The man hands Hugo the bag, and he gives him some cash. Once he's gone, Hugo takes a seat. "I wanted to ask you properly, but I was worried you'd turn me down."

"So, you approached Zoe?"

He laughs. "God, no. She'd never have agreed. I took the easy option and went for Sofia." I can't help the smile playing on my lips. "You needed space," he continues, opening some of the containers and placing them on the table, "and I respected that." He hands me a fork. "But now, I need to show you how much I love you." I almost choke on fresh air. *He said he loves me.* "And I miss you, Meg . . . so much." I open my mouth to speak, but he shakes his head. "No, don't say anything. Just listen to me, then we can eat, and I'll walk you home, so you can think about what I've said."

I give a nod, and he relaxes slightly. I wouldn't know what to say anyway, I'm in shock. "I didn't bring plates, so just dive in when you're ready," he says, nodding at the food. I don't bother to tell him that all this has stolen my appetite. I grab a fork and take small bites of noodles.

"When I met Liz, I knew right away she was the one for me." He opens the wine and pours us a small amount each. "I couldn't even look at another woman. She was it, and we had the best marriage. When she got sick, it knocked us both on our arses. We didn't expect it, and we weren't prepared. They gave us a matter of weeks to say goodbye, and I remember sitting there thinking, it's not enough time to show her how much I love her. But I didn't need to show her because she knew. She knew because she felt the exact same."

A tear rolls down my cheek. Hearing him be so open and honest makes my heart swell. "She got bad real quick. I think another two weeks passed before she was bedbound, and every time I looked at her face, I saw another piece of her slipping away. We had plans—we wanted to visit Rome, get a dog, build a house in the country, and we wanted kids. We wanted all the things everyone else had, but in those final days, I would've given it all up if I could just keep her. Nothing was more important than her."

HUGO

It's the first time I've spoken like this to anyone about Liz. Meg silently wipes her tears on her sleeve, and I hate that it's upsetting her, but I have to be honest, so she can see how she's saved me.

"In her final hours, she knew she was leaving me. She told me to gather everyone so she could say her goodbyes. She wanted to be able to say what she had to say before she got too weak. So, we did the whole goodbye thing, people came and left in floods of tears, and I stood beside that bed and never shed a single tear because I really thought deep down that she wouldn't die. I thought there was no way that God would be so cruel, because he knew how much I loved her and he wouldn't just take her away for no reason.

"And then it was my turn to say it. She told me to move on. I remember feeling angry that she would ever think it was possible. She said I couldn't be sad forever because I had too much love to give, and she'd hate for someone else to miss out on that." Another sob escapes Meg as she covers her mouth to try and mute it. "I was so angry when she died. I laid beside her on the bed for hours, refusing to let anyone come in and take her. I wasn't ready to let her go. My brothers had to hold me back while they zipped her up in some fucking plastic bag and took her away. I lived like a zombie for months after. I hardly ate, and I'd spend hours in this park because it's the only place I felt close to her. It's where we laughed and shared secrets. It's where we cried when we first found out about the cancer.

"And then one day, I was lost in my own head and I called my solicitor to finalise the details of my will, so that I could end it all after work that night. I wanted to be wherever Liz was, and I just needed the pain to stop."

Meg's eyes are wide at my confession. "You wanted to kill yourself?"

I nod. "But I bumped into you. I spilled your coffee, and everything just stopped. It was like we were the only two people in the park. And when I looked into your eyes, I saw so much pain that I felt at home. I felt like you'd understand my sadness and wouldn't judge me or order me to move on, because you knew pain too. You were grieving like me."

"You didn't kill yourself," she murmurs. "Why?"

"I wanted to. I went home and laid the pills out, and then you popped into my head, and I thought, maybe I should just wait a while longer. I felt like I'd see you again and maybe you needed someone who understood how it felt to be abandoned. So, the next day, when you turned up, it was like a sign to keep going. Before I knew it, I was healing too. My head was full of you, wondering if I'd see you again, and something inside told me I would."

I take her hand. "I fell in love with you, Meg. I didn't mean to. In fact, the list started because I was trying to find reasons to walk away. I was terrified to fall in love again and have it ripped away. I realise I hurt you, but I never meant to. These last few weeks without you have been torture."

"You haven't thought about . . ." She trails off.

I shake my head. "No. I want to be in this world for as long as you are. I'd like it better if we were in it together. I didn't tell you all that to make you feel bad, and I'm okay if you want to walk away. I'm not going to kill myself because I'm in a much better place now. If anything, you've shown me that there's life after Liz. If you're happier without me, I'll leave you alone, but I couldn't just walk away without telling you exactly how I feel."

It's risky, but I pull out a piece of paper and open it. "Pros to loving you," I read out loud, glancing up to make sure she isn't annoyed. She gives a small smile, so I continue. "You saved me. You didn't know it, but you saved my life. You made me see there's a future ahead. You're independent. You love Izzy so fiercely, it makes me want to have kids with you just so I get to watch you love them too. You got through one of the worst times in your life with grace and dignity, and I wish I had even half your strength.

"You light up a room whenever you walk in and you don't even know it. You're kind and considerate, and you always worry about everyone you love. You even refused to take Dan to the cleaners because you worried about his newborn. The list is endless," I say, passing it to her. "I can't promise I'll never fuck up again—I probably will—but I'll never intentionally hurt you. I hate myself for putting that sad look in your eyes. I want us to try again. I miss you, Meg, and I miss Izzy."

She goes to answer, but I shake my head and she clamps her lips closed. "It's a lot to process. You need to think about it and know it's what you want before you answer, because if you tell me you can forgive me and we can try again, I'm never letting you go. I felt like I wasted time with Liz, and I won't make that mistake again. If we're doing this, we're going all in."

She'll be hungry later, so I begin to cover the uneaten containers and bag them up. She watches me in silence, and when I hold out my hand, she takes it, and we slowly walk back home.

We stop at her door, and I lean in. She closes her eyes, and when I kiss her on the cheek, she almost looks disappointed. "Thank you for hearing me out. Let me know when you're ready to talk." I kiss her on the forehead. "I love you," I whisper, placing my finger over her lips, so she can't reply. "Goodnight."

Thirty-Two

MEG

I lie awake for most of the night, tossing and turning. My heart breaks for Hugo and everything he went through. His heartbreak was evident in his voice, but somehow, through all that pain, he recognised my pain. He saw me. And when I really think about what I need from him, it's exactly that—to be seen. Because I never felt that way with Dan, not really. We got so wrapped up in life, we forgot about each other. That's why his head was so easily turned.

With Hugo, there's so much more intensity there. His love and passion for me and for Izzy is obvious in all the little things he does. And the fact he hasn't given up on us, even though I told him to, shows his dedication to getting this right.

It's three in the morning when I finally give up on sleep and head next door. I knock lightly in case he's asleep, but when he opens the door, he looks as relieved as me.

"I couldn't sleep," I whisper.

He opens the door wider, and I go inside. "My heart hurts so badly for you and Liz," I tell him. "You didn't get a fair shot at life together and that's shit, but I think you were right about us meeting like we did. Being with Dan gave me Izzy, but I think maybe we were just filling time until we could meet one another. And I'd like to think that maybe Liz was looking out for you. She didn't want you to take your own life." He smiles, nodding in agreement.

"I want to be the one to make you smile again. I want to spend my nights watching you with Izzy, reading her bedtimes stories and sneaking her sweets after I've said no. I've missed you so much these last couple weeks, and I said I needed space to figure out who I was, but I know who I am when I'm with you, because you make me feel so alive and loved and wanted. I love you too, Hugo. I really do."

He releases a long, relieved breath. "You don't know what it means to hear you say that," he murmurs. "I was lying here thinking you'd run a mile."

I smile, taking his hands in mine. "I'm not going anywhere."

"I take that kind of promise very seriously," he says, pulling me into his arms. "We're not wasting any more time." He kisses me, stealing my breath. "I'm sorry I made you sad."

Epilogue

MEG

Hugo is easy to love. He doesn't demand anything from me, and we just fit together so well.

Months have passed since we made up, and we're so sickeningly happy, we annoy everyone around us. Izzy adores him to the point she often requests he read her a story over me because he does the best voices.

Hugo leans against the wall, watching as I comfort a fifteen-year-old student who'd recently been dumped by her boyfriend. You'd think my role as teaching assistant would be something to do with teaching, but a lot of the time, it's being a counsellor to young, hormonal teens.

Once she's gone, I turn to him. "Am I in trouble?" I ask, smiling.

"I thought I'd come with you to collect Izzy from nursery and then I'd take the rest of the afternoon off so we could go out for a few drinks with my brothers."

The school bell sounds indicating the end of the day, and the corridor fills with students. I fall into step beside Hugo. "I'd like that."

Izzy is delighted when she spots Hugo beside me in the playground. Her teacher opens the door, and she rushes over, throwing herself into his arms and squealing in delight as he swings her around. She hands him yet another picture, and he holds it up to get a better look. "That's me," he says, "and Mummy." He asks, "Is that Daddy?" She nods, smiling wide that he guessed correctly. "And Ashley?" She nods again. "And who is that?"

"The baby, silly." She giggles, and I take the picture and fold it neatly. "Will the baby come this weekend?" she asks me.

I groan. She's been asking the same question every day for the last week. "I told you, Iz, I don't know. Nobody knows the exact day the baby will arrive, but Ashley still has a week before the baby is due."

Hugo drives us to Dan and Ashley's new house. Since our sale went through, they've upgraded to a three-bedroom place so both kids have a room each. I notice Dan's car isn't there yet and groan. Things are still awkward between me and Ashley, although we're both trying harder to get along for Izzy's sake.

"You want me to take her?" asks Hugo. I shake my head, and he gives my hand a squeeze. "Be nice."

I knock on the door, but she doesn't immediately answer. I turn back to look at Hugo in the car and roll my eyes. He grins. "Coming," I hear her mutter from inside.

"Be really good for Ashley," I whisper to Izzy. "Look after her until Daddy gets home from work."

The door swings open and Ashley clings to the wall. Her face is bright red, and she looks hot. I frown. "Hey, are you okay?"

She shakes her head, and I crouch down to Izzy. "Go inside and put the television on." Once she's gone, I turn back to Ashley. "What's wrong?"

"I'm in labour," she whispers, rubbing her stomach.

"Oh shit, where's Dan?"

She shrugs. "I have no idea and I can't get hold of him. I've tried."

She suddenly gasps, gripping her stomach and squeezing her eyes shut tightly. I glance back at Hugo and wave him to come over. "We need to get you to the hospital," I tell her as Hugo joins us. "She's in labour," I say.

"Where's Dan?"

"She's not sure. I'll try and call him. Get her inside."

I try Dan's phone, but it's turned off, so I leave a message. When I go inside, Ashley is on all fours in the kitchen, panting. I glare at Hugo, whose eyes are as wide as saucers. "I think the baby might be coming," he whisper-hisses. "What do we do?"

"Call an ambulance," I suggest, and he pulls his phone out.

I kneel beside Ashley. "Do you need anything?"

"I need Dan. Where the hell is he?" she hisses.

I shrug helplessly. "Isn't he at work?"

"No. I called there already, and he phoned in sick today." I glance up at Hugo, who raises his eyebrows. "I know what you're thinking," she adds. "Trust me, I am too."

"I'm not thinking anything," I say innocently, though it's clear I feel like history is repeating itself.

"He wouldn't do that to me," she whispers, tears filling her eyes, and then she turns to look at me. "Would he?"

I shake my head, rubbing her back. "Of course not, Ashley, he loves you."

The call handler begins to ask Ashley questions, and then another contraction hits and she cries out that she needs to push. "Megan," the call handler says.

"I'm here," I mutter, though I really don't want to be.

"You'll need to make sure Ashley has nothing on her bottom half."

I stare at Hugo, and he shrugs helplessly. "I can't help with that," he whispers.

"Great," I mutter, moving behind Ashley and lifting her

nightshirt. "She's all ready to go," I say, noting she's already removed her underwear.

"Ashley, on your next contraction, if you feel like pushing, push," she tells her.

Ashley reaches for my hand, and I reluctantly give it her. "Listen," she whispers, staring me in the eye, "I know you hate me, and you have every right. I'm a total bitch. But please, please help me through this."

I give a quick nod, guilt consuming me for being so cold. She's a woman in labour and she needs our help. Any personal feelings need to be put aside right now. "Okay. We've got this," I tell her.

She begins to pant and squeezes my hand. "I need to push," she hisses.

"Mummy?" Izzy appears in the doorway and frowns.

Hugo passes me the mobile phone, looking relieved he's got a reason to escape. He scoops Izzy up and carries her back into the living room. "He's so good with her," Ashley pants.

"You need to push," I tell her. "Listen to your body."

"Call him again," she orders, and I lay my phone on the floor beside Hugo's and call Dan. Again, it goes to voicemail.

"He'll only get in the way," I tell her. "Just concentrate on yourself right now."

"I won't let him leave me," she promises, crying out as the pain takes over.

"I know," I say, patting her hand. *I used to think the same.*

"He loves me," she sobs, sweat beading on her forehead. "It's just been difficult."

"Ashley, stop stressing and concentrate on getting the baby out."

She screams, pushing her chin to her chest and growling as she pushes hard. "Megan, can you see anything?" the call handler asks.

I inwardly groan before peering around the back end of Ashley. I gasp. "Holy shit, I can see the head."

"The entire head or just the top?" she asks.

"The top . . . I can see the top."

"Okay, Ashley, your baby is crowning. On the next push, you might have the head. Megan, stay around the back. Once the shoulders appear, you may need to be ready to catch."

"Oh god," I mutter, moving around and crouching behind her. I snatch a towel from beside Ashley, ready to wrap the baby. "Where is the ambulance?"

"We have a medic en route," she reassures me.

Ashley growls again. This time, it's ferocious, and the baby's head slides out farther. "Wow, keep going, Ashley, the baby is almost here," I encourage as my heart slams wildly in my chest. It's the first time I've ever been present at a birth and it's making me feel emotions I wasn't prepared for. She pushes again, and this time, the baby's head is fully out. "It's got loads of hair," I tell her in excitement.

"On the next push, you'll get the shoulders," the call handler instructs. "You need to hold the baby for support, but do not pull. The hardest bit's done, so it should just slip right out."

Ashley screams, and as if by magic, the shoulders appear and then it slips right into the waiting towel. I stare wide-eyed. "Holy shit, you did it," I whisper.

I wrap the baby in the towel, and Ashley slowly turns to lie on the floor. She's panting and sweating, and I can't help but stare in awe. "You did it without pain relief," I say, passing the baby to her.

She begins to sob. "Is it a girl or a boy?"

I frown. "I didn't even look," I say, and we both laugh as she lifts the towel. "A boy," I whisper as tears run down my cheeks. "Well done, Ash, that was amazing." She smiles at me, and it's the first time I've felt any kind of connection to this woman who barged into my life over a year ago and tipped my world upside down.

The kitchen door opens and a medic rushes in, pausing

when she sees the baby. "Seems I'm a little late," she says, laughing.

My mobile rings, and I see Dan's name on the display. "Is that him?" asks Ashley eagerly.

"I'll find out where he is," I tell her, standing and leaving the room. I answer as I step outside. "Where the fuck are you?" I spit.

"Jesus, easy, Meg. It's like we're still married."

"Thankfully, we're not. I'm at your house, and you're not here."

"Just leave Izzy with Ashley. She won't mind."

"She's been trying to call too."

He sighs. "Yeah, I know, I'll call her next."

"She's had the baby, Dan."

"Oh fuck," he growls. "I'm on my way. I'll be five minutes."

I decide to wait outside. I need to see his face when I ask him where the hell he's been, and when he pulls up minutes later and rushes along the path, I block him. "Is she okay? Is the baby okay?"

"Where were you?" I ask. He swallows nervously, and I groan. "Tell me you're not fucking about."

"Is Ash okay?" he repeats.

"Jesus, Dan, what the hell is wrong with you?" I hiss.

"It's none of your business," he mutters.

"You're right, it's not, but Izzy is just settling with our split, and now, you're doing the same thing to Ashley?"

He shifts uncomfortably. "I'm not leaving her or anything."

My eyes widen. "Oh, and she's okay with you fucking around, is she?"

"It's not got that far . . . yet."

"You're an idiot. She's just given birth to your baby," I whisper, sadness lacing my words. "And she isn't stupid,

Dan. She knows you're up to something. I'm begging you, don't hurt her like you did me."

"This is Ashley you're begging for," he snaps. "You hate her."

"It's in the past," I say firmly, and I realise I mean those words. The hate I felt towards her doesn't feel like it used to. "I don't know what's going on with you, Dan, but I do know you've got someone in there who wanted you so badly that she broke up your marriage. Don't let that be for nothing."

He gives a slight nod, and for once, he looks ashamed. "Girl or boy?" he asks.

"Boy," I say with a smile.

His head shoots up to look at me. "A boy?" he repeats. I nod, and he races past me to get to her.

When I walk back into the house, Dan is cradling his new son, crouching down so Izzy can see him. Ashley has the biggest smile on her face as she sips a cup of tea. I lean against the door frame and watch the interaction. I thought it would hurt, but it doesn't. Instead, my emotions are mixed.

Hugo comes up behind me and wraps his arms around my waist, resting his chin on my shoulder. "Are you okay?" I nod. "You did amazing back there. Most women wouldn't have done what you did."

I brush his strong arms with my fingers. "I feel bad for her," I whisper sadly. "He's about to ruin her life like he did mine, and there's nothing I can do to stop it. But I'll make the extra effort to be here for her and the baby."

"Really?" he asks.

"That baby is Izzy's sibling, no matter what. I have to make sure they stay in contact, and I have to be there to show Ashley that there's a life after Dan."

"You're amazing," he whispers, kissing my cheek. "What did I do to deserve you?"

"You realise we can't go drinking with your brothers now. We'll have to take Izzy home and give these some space."

"Nonsense. Izzy loves the pub, and I already promised her a bag of crisps and a Coke."

I smile. She does love the attention from Hugo's brothers. They treat her like a princess. "You spoil her."

"She's my little girl, she deserves it."

Dan comes over, and I peer into the towel and smile at the tiny baby boy as he wriggles around. "You have a good one there," Hugo tells him, nodding at Ashley, who's currently cuddling Izzy. "Don't be a fool a second time."

"Thanks for sticking around and helping Ash," he says. "I'm gonna sort my shit out, I swear."

Izzy comes over, and Hugo picks her up. "Ready to see the boys?" he asks her, and she nods enthusiastically. He carries her out, and I turn back to Dan.

"If I could give you any advice right now, it would be talk to her. Tell her what's going on in your head. I would've loved to have had that chance before you cheated on me, so I could tell you all the things you were about to give up." He nods, lowering his head in what I think is shame. "You told me once you didn't stop to think about the damage you were about to do. This time, you know what that damage looks like. This baby boy needs his daddy, and Izzy needs to see you happy and settled. Whether we like it or not, we have ourselves a blended family, all held together by Izzy."

"You're right," he mutters. "I'll sort it with Ashley."

"Good, because otherwise, this was all for nothing."

I kiss him on the cheek before saying goodbye to Ashley. She thanks me, embracing me tightly, and I feel the anxiety pouring from her. "You're not alone," I whisper. "Call me anytime. I know it's been difficult between us, but you're now the mother of Izzy's half-brother, so I'm in your life whether you like it or not. We'll spend some time getting to know one another and make a real effort for Iz."

She nods, pulling away. "I don't deserve your kindness, but I appreciate it."

"Things will be okay with you and Dan. Take it one day at a time and talk things through."

She looks past me to Dan. "I deserve it, right? If he's cheating."

I stroke her hair away from her face. "No one deserves that, Ashley. But relationships take work, and Dan is hard work," I say, adding a smile. "But you've got this."

When I step outside, Hugo is leaning against the car, waiting for me. Izzy is already strapped in the back seat. His eyes run over my body as I move towards him, and when I'm close enough, he grabs my hand and pulls me in for a kiss. "I love you," he whispers against my lips. "You're incredible."

"I love you millions more."

"How fucking lucky am I?" he asks, running his fingers through my hair and staring into my eyes. "I'm going to marry you."

I grin. He says those words at least five times a day. "Once we're married, what promises will you make every day then?"

"That we'll have a baby. Lots of babies."

I laugh. "Well, I might just have to hold you to that."

My future with Hugo will be forever. I feel it in the way he watches me, in the way he takes care of me, and in the way he uses his words to make me feel like the safest, most secure woman in the world. Hugo is my forever, and I know without a doubt that I'll never let him go.

He is my home. He is my forever. He is my after.

SOCIAL MEDIA

I love to hear from my readers and if you'd like to get in touch, you can find me here . . .

Facebook:
https://www.facebook.com/nicolajaneAuthor

Facebook reader group:
https://www.facebook.com/groups/287821672130708

Bookbub:
https://www.bookbub.com/authors/nicola-jane-43035143-7f71-4d27-920b-9b497aa58397

Instagram:
https://www.instagram.com/nicolajaneauthor/

Goodreads:
https://www.goodreads.com/author/show/18374765.Nicola_Jane

<u>TikTok:</u>

https://www.tiktok.com/@nicolajaneauthor?